Laura Marney is a nice person who tries to do a good deed every day. Occasionally bad deeds do slip in but there you go, nobody's perfect. Many of her short stories have been published in magazines and anthologies or broadcast on radio. She is the author of two previous novels, *No Wonder I Take a Drink* and *Nobody Loves a Ginger Baby*. She lives and works between Glasgow and Barcelona.

D0522499

www.booksattransworld.co.uk

Also by Laura Marney

NO WONDER I TAKE A DRINK
NOBODY LOVES A GINGER BABY

and published by Black Swan

ONLY STRANGE PEOPLE GO TO CHURCH

Laura Marney

BLACK SWAN

ONLY STRANGE PEOPLE GO TO CHURCH
A BLACK SWAN BOOK : 0552773131
9780552773133

First publication in Great Britain

PRINTING HISTORY
Black Swan edition published 2006

3 5 7 9 10 8 6 4 2

Set in 11/13pt Melior by
Falcon Oast Graphic Art Ltd.

Black Swan Books are published by Transworld Publishers,
61–63 Uxbridge Road, London W5 5SA,
a division of The Random House Group Ltd,
in Australia by Random House Australia (Pty) Ltd,
20 Alfred Street, Milsons Point, Sydney, NSW 2061, Australia,
in New Zealand by Random House New Zealand Ltd,
18 Poland Road, Glenfield, Auckland 10, New Zealand
in South Africa by Random House (Pty) Ltd,
Isle of Houghton, Corner of Boundary Road & Carse O'Gowrie,
Houghton 2198, South Africa
and in India by Random House Publishers India Private Limited,
301 World Trade Tower, Hotel Intercontinental Grand Complex,
Barakhamba Lane, New Delhi 110 001, India.

Printed and bound in Great Britain by
Cox & Wyman Ltd, Reading, Berkshire.

Papers used by Transworld Publishers are natural, recyclable
products made from wood grown in sustainable forests. The
manufacturing processes conform to the environmental
regulations of the country of origin.

As every time, for Holly, Max and Ellen.
But this time also for Dave.

Acknowledgements

As always, a huge thanks to my agent Jenny Brown, my editor Francesca Liversidge and Nicky Jeanes, Sam Jones, Claire Ward and Judith Welsh at Transworld. June Bone, Phyllis McGowan and Lynda Perkins also gave invaluable help as early readers. The usual thanks are also due to my Barcelona mates. Thanks to Stuart McDonald for the room with the best view in the world. Newly arrived in Barcelona ready to spend the next three months finishing the book, I had a bizarre accident involving a skateboard and a giant television. This resulted in me cradling a broken wrist for several months. I owe a huge debt of gratitude to my nurse, my scribe, my minder and my wing man. These were all the same person: my best pal David Ramos Fernandes.

Chapter 1

'Look!' says Fiona, pointing, 'that man's got his thing out!' Although Maria would rather they didn't, everyone stares. Martin, Jane and Brian follow Fiona's lead and gawk at the man. Unfortunately she's right. The man has got his thing out.

Thing is too grand a word for it. At this distance it's a slimy wee snail in the palm of his hand, that's all. Hardly worth making a fuss over but they're all squinting at it, giving him exactly what he wants: attention. The real obscenity is his face, or what they can see of it. He is of the shy bashful school of exhibitionists: his nose and chin are demurely hidden behind a thick scarf. He's looking at them but his eyes are slits, jaw tilted up, his face curling in on itself. That's the shocking thing. Really it's quite pathetic, a man exposing himself on a public street to a group of mentally disabled people.

He's a sad case and his nether regions are pitiful to behold: fly undone, pants a thousand-wash grey, underbelly slack and wanton, pubic hair like an ounce of Golden Virginia. His heavy leather belt is unbuckled. The ends of it writhe and flap like a peacock's display as he jerks, pulling at his poor flaccid dick, tugging out his resentment, exposing his contempt, his desperation.

His cock is the least of it.

'Just ignore him,' Maria says, walking smartly, forcing Brian to speed up in his electric wheelchair. But, as usual, Fiona refuses to do as she's told. She continues to stare and point at the man, giggling like a teenager.

Maria shakes her head. It's obvious to anyone that Fiona and the rest of them have learning difficulties or disabilities, that they're mentally handicapped, mentally disabled, vulnerable, special. She has lost track of what the proper term is this week. Spazzies, nungies, loonies are some of the more colourful names the kids shout at them.

The man seems to be taking Fiona's laughter as encouragement and with his free hand beckons her. He tugs and waves, moving towards her, calling her on, his body language insinuating: Come and get it baby, oh yeah. Perhaps Fiona's lack of understanding is adding to the thrill for him.

With this thought a surge of rage passes through Maria, reddening her thin bony chest. The idea that someone would abuse Fiona's innocence makes her want to vomit. She'd like to rip this pervert's dick off and throw it to a passing dog, but her first priority is to get Blue Group away from here.

'Come on, Fiona, pet,' she says, gentle but insistent. 'Let's get back to the centre and we'll get our juice and crisps.'

Maybe it was a mistake to take this quiet back street. At one time this was the busiest street in Hexton. Four times a day it was a slow-flowing river of men in working boots and overalls, men with woolly hats and newspapers rolled into batons who brought home a small brown pay packet along with the sharp smell of hot metal and Swarfega. But the factory is closed now, despite every government inducement it has lain empty for years, the deserted street an opportunity not for heavy industry but for a sad pervert.

There is no immediate danger. The man is at a safe distance, skulking on the opposite side of the road from Maria and her clients. Clients, service users, key group, Blue Group, whatever the phrase of the moment is. She would never let them see that his behaviour is in any way threatening, it would only frighten them and she's far too professional for that. But the man is keeping up with them and he's getting closer.

'Right, that's it,' she shouts across at him, pulling her bag to her and rummaging, digging for her mobile phone, 'I'm calling the police.'

At this the man stops. He laughs but it's a nervous laugh, and it doesn't stop him mauling his penis. If anything the tempo increases. He persists with his frantic wanking, turning his attention now to Maria, staring at her with shark eyes.

Until a few minutes ago he might have been the average man in the street: unobtrusive, of modest comportment, a plumber or a photocopier salesman, probably married with a couple of kids. Then he claps eyes on Blue Group and boof! He's a raging sex maniac. Obviously he can't help himself. He sees Maria's skirt clinging to her pert bottom, her gorgeous Titian hair curling behind her sexy little ears, her moist bee-stung lips. That'll be it. The effect on him is such that he must get his knob out here in the street.

11

But his eyes are red-rimmed and bloodshot, clogged with lust. He's unable to see her as everyone else sees her, as she sees herself, as she really is: a tall thin dreepy girl, a flat-chested spinster; long-nosed, long-limbed, long-skirted. A Keyhole Kate. An unsexy key worker out with her unsexy clients.

Not even the threat of her phoning the police has frightened him off. It is only a threat, an empty threat it turns out, because she now discovers that she's forgotten her phone. While it lies impotently in the staffroom back at the centre Maria is forced to watch this pervert waving his bits at adults who are as innocent as children. He won't do them any physical harm, he'd have crossed the road by now if he was planning to and he'd have to get past Maria first, but still and all. What he's doing isn't harmless. This could be the first step, the beginning of an apprenticeship in sexual deviancy that could end in rape or murder. But at last he backs off – he's leaving them alone.

'He's going away!' cries Fiona, sounding disappointed.

The man slowly turns and begins casually walking into a side street.

'Good,' says Maria, 'he's not a nice man.'

Fiona bolts across the road.

'Fiona! Come back here right now!'

Luckily there is no traffic on the road and when she reaches the other side Fiona follows the man into the side street. What is Maria to do? She can't let a client disappear up an alleyway with a sexual deviant but she can't desert the rest of them.

Martin, a small, rosy-faced, sleepy-eyed young man, finds this turn of events exciting and is jumping on the spot. Jane begins to cry. Jane is small and mousy with a runny nose and a metal plate in her head – everything scares her. Brian, the boy in the wheelchair, the nineteen-year-old baby of Blue Group, the most physically disabled, storms into action.

'Get. Her. Back,' says Brian's Dynavox machine. The words come out slow and calm but his electric wheelchair zooms out onto the road, bouncing Brian almost out of his seat as it crashes down off the kerb. Forgetting everything Maria has taught him about the Green Cross Code, Martin is right behind him.

Maria has no alternative. She grabs Jane's arm and hauls her across the road, barking a command as she runs.

'Stick together!'

She tries never to raise her voice to clients, but these are extreme circumstances.

'Jane, hold onto the chair. Martin, you round this side, now hold on. We can run together. Come on now!'

Ahead of them in the alley Fiona is following the man. His head is down, his hands busy now with trying to stuff away the offending articles. Unfortunately, due to his masturbatory zeal, he seems to have burst his zip. He is no longer strolling. He seems to be experimenting with a range of walking speeds. His strolling has become striding, then yomping, trotting, eventually settling into a light jog. So far he has resisted actual running.

For a flasher, running away from the people you are attempting to frighten might represent a loss of face, an admission of failure. Besides, running with your tackle dangling must be extremely undignified, not to say painful and potentially dangerous. Running away is probably an occupational hazard for sexual exhibitionists, but run he now must. Although Fiona hasn't yet managed to catch up with him, the gap between them is narrowing.

Fifty yards ahead of the others, Fiona is now chasing the man full tilt down the alley.

'We're coming Fiona, wait for us!' Maria shouts. She pulls Jane and Martin in close. They group defensively behind Brian's chair and run in step, one two, one two, one two, their feet beating out the rhythm on the tarmac. As if about to storm a medieval castle, Brian and his wheelchair have become both defence and weapon, a battering ram. This formation is effective in keeping them together, but as they are almost falling over each other it's impeding their progress. The gap between Blue Group and Fiona is widening. Suddenly, the man dodges to the left and out of sight. A second later they have lost visual contact with Fiona too. Again it is Brian who suggests a plan.

'Maria,' says the Dynavox in its languorous voice. 'Run. Fast.'

She breaks free of the group and instantly doubles her speed. She is surprised by how fast she can run. Fear and rage make her body light and her long legs powerful. Within seconds she reaches the left turn into which Fiona and the man have disappeared. She has lost sight of the rest of Blue Group but this is a matter of priorities.

Maria is a positive thinker. Through daily meditations, creative visualizations, spirit-guide con- sultations, mantras and incantations, every kind of educational, motivational, inspirational book and CD, she tries to stay positive. But still the black thoughts come. She can only picture Fiona lying murdered in the alley, her belly ripped wide, her innards spilled, a look of hurt confusion on her dead white face.

The left turn leads to a street on a steep hill. The gradient is so sharp that instead of pavement there are multiple flights of steps with a metal handrail running up the side to assist pedestrians. The man has not yet cleaved Fiona's belly, thank God. Fiona is still chasing him, and he shows no signs of tiring. He bounds up the stairs two at a time. A morbidly obese forty-one-year-old asthmatic, Fiona is no match for him, but she will not give up. She's made the sixth step, hauling her large frame up, hand over hand, along the railing. Her cheeks are flushed almost purple and she is wheezing noisily.

'Stop!' Maria shouts.

Maria once again rifles in her voluminous handbag. Please God don't let Fiona's inhaler be in the staffroom along with the phone. She has commanded Fiona to stop for fear that she'll give herself an asthma or heart attack, but so authoritative was Maria's order that Fiona is not the only one to obey. From the relative safety of two flights of steps above, the man stops. He leans forward, chest heaving, hands on thighs.

Maria holds the back of Fiona's head and inserts the inhaler into her panting mouth. Underneath her long tousled hair Fiona is hot and damp. Heat steams from her.

'Take a deep breath, hold it. Hold it.'

Maria shakes her head in frustration, three years in the job and still unable to keep her clients under control. Fiona is by far the worst, as untameable as a stampeding buffalo. As if to demonstrate this she exhales with a snort and tries to speak. No you don't. Maria pops the inhaler back in her mouth.

'And again, in. Hold it.'

Fiona complies but her eyes are popping, and Maria prays that this is the excitement of the chase rather than a myocardial infarction.

'You're OK, everything's OK pet. I just need you to calm down. Can you do that Fiona, can you calm down for me?'

Fiona nods, she can do that for Maria but her eyes never leave the gasping man. Maria knows that he'll probably bolt as soon as he gets his breath back and, that if she doesn't stop her, Fiona will too.

The infantry arrive. Martin and Jane, still holding onto Brian's wheelchair, form the rearguard. They run steadily, not slowing until they reach the bottom of the stairway.

With their positions on the steps, Fiona, Maria and the man have formed the outline of a triangle. Maria has her arm about Fiona, Fiona has her eyes raised to the man, the man is clearly suffering. Something about the shape of this formation reminds Maria of a religious print which hung in her old flat. But instead of the man being an angel of the Lord with spiky golden rays around his head he is a pervert with his willy hanging out. The man does not share this aesthetic perspective because, when the others turn up, he legs it pronto.

Martin and Jane begin to yell.

'He's getting away!'

'Quick, get him!'

What began as a rescue mission to bring Fiona back has become a manhunt.

'Fiona, no!'

Maria restrains her. She will not be able to hold Fiona for long; she weighs twice what Maria does or more.

16

'Leave it. Let him go. Just calm down.'

Fiona strains against Maria, reluctant to give up the chase. But the man is now almost three flights of steps away, he cannot be caught. As he disappears over the brow of the hill Maria feels the fight go out of Fiona. She begins to cry as Maria leads her back down the steps.

'He's unlucky,' Fiona sobs.

'No,' Maria corrects her, 'he was lucky. He got away.'

Maria should know better than to contradict Fiona, especially when she's this upset. She could get angry. Instead she gets surreal.

'He's got a strawberry. But you can't eat it. It's unlucky.'

Surreal and affectionate. Fiona now throws her arms around Martin in a fierce hug. This is better than trying to hit him, something she sometimes does when she's overexcited.

'Did you see his strawberry?' she asks Martin.

Martin is unable to reply as his whole head has been engulfed in Fiona's bosom. Jane receives a similarly passionate embrace and rubs Fiona's back in a comforting gesture, patting her to signal when she's had enough.

'He's a bad man,' says Fiona.

'Yes,' says Jane. 'He's a bad man.'

Brian has been sick, a common occurrence and, with all the banging around in his chair, hardly surprising, but this does not put Fiona off. She vigorously pulls him to her. Brian's thin arms are bent across his chest and Maria often worries that Fiona will break his delicate sparrow frame with her rough handling, but he never seems to mind. Fiona now moves towards Maria for the last and final cuddle. Maria tries not to look at the splodges of Brian's vomit Fiona carries on her chest. With a heavy sigh and the acid smell of Brian's bile sharp in her nostrils, she opens her arms and lets Fiona mush the sick into her pale blue blouson jacket.

A van pulls into the side street and draws to a stop beside them. What the hell is it now? The driver leans across and opens the passenger door, or tries to, but he can't seem to reach. Before Maria has a chance to stop him, Martin jumps onto the footplate and opens the door. He is about to climb into the cab when Maria's piercing scream of 'Martin!' stops him and he returns to the safety of the group. Having just avoided the clutches of a back-street pervert the last thing Blue Group needs is to be abducted by an anonymous White Van Man. She might be overreacting but you can't be too careful so she quickly commits to memory the registration: X909 JSU.

Maria has a foolproof method for remembering things. It's a skill she picked up years ago from a book called *Improve Your Memory* or something like that. The trick is to make each number or letter mean something. X is easy, that's sex, 909 is like the emergency number except that there's a zero in it. Yes, that would work: it's an emergency to have sex, the zero in the middle could represent lack of sex or the actual sex orifice, but no, that's too graphic. Unfortunately Maria's mind locks into this and immediately she has a three-dimensional image of the nines on either side of the zero as a pair of animated legs. Legs that are open and willing. Oh dear. It must be the sight of the flasher's meat and two veg which has her off on this train of thought, and she hasn't even sorted out the other letters yet. JSU suggests the word Jesus.

Someone told her once that, like hanged men, men who have been crucified have erections. This changed Christian iconography for her for ever and she's never been able to look at a crucifixion scene in quite the same way since. So, emergency sex with Jesus? It's blasphemous but it'll have to do. Along the side of the van it says *Bespoke Carpentry* and a mobile phone number. Wasn't Jesus a carpenter? That fits nicely. The mobile number is 07781 434 . . .

White Van Man speaks.

'Excuse me,' he smiles as he shouts over the noise of his diesel engine, 'I'm looking for Hexton church.' He addresses this to the whole group.

People in Hexton never speak to Blue Group. Apart from the odd verse of 'Spot the Loony' from hooligans, the populace largely shuns them. Hextors seem to believe that mental disability is contagious, keeping their distance and averting their eyes when Maria and her clients pass by. Shopkeepers speak only to Maria, and even then reluctantly.

Blue Group are momentarily speechless, stunned by the stranger's bonhomie, and then they all want to tell him at once.

'It's not in this street; you have to take a left at the top.' 'Left. At. The.' 'That church is haunted.' 'Top. Second. Right.' 'No, go back the way you came.' 'He has to carry on and keep turning right and then he'll be back to . . .' 'Second. Right. Again.' 'I know where it is. I've passed it loads of times.' 'If you go as far as Black Street then you've passed it.'

White Van Man turns his engine off and scoots across the passenger seat closer to them.

'Sorry, I can't hear you properly.'

Maria knows exactly where the church is, but with

everybody jabbering at the same time she can't think off the top of her head the best way to get to it from here.

'Left. At. The. Top. Second. Right. Second. Right. Again,' says Brian's voice machine.

'Left at the top, then second right and second right again?' says the driver, this time directly to Brian.

Brian lets his head fall forward and pulls it up again in a slow nod.

'Cheers mate.'

White Van Man wrinkles his nose. He has a concerned look on his face. It's a nice face, intelligent and inoffensive. He's quite good-looking in that generic square-jawed, broad-shouldered kind of way, and perhaps it's this observation that reminds Maria of the sick stains down the front of her jacket. And Brian and Fiona's jackets. Fiona's face is still red and blotchy from the running and the crying. Collectively they must look a right shambles.

'Is everything all right?' says the driver.

Fiona and Martin begin to speak in an excited rush. 'There was a man.' 'We chased him.' 'I was going to catch him.' 'He was scared of us.' 'He had his . . .'

'Yes,' says Maria, taking charge. 'OK Fiona, and you too Martin,' she says, chastising them with a look. It's embarrassing enough without going into it with a van driver.

'We've had a slight upset, but we're fine now, thanks.'

The van driver says nothing and smiles. All of Blue Group beam back at him.

'I'm Ray by the way, pleased to meet you.'

Maria commits this to memory: Ray, ray of light.

'I'm Fiona, pleased to meet you.'

20

'Martin,' says Martin, pointing to himself.

'I'm Jane, how d'you do.'

Maria waits for Brian's voice machine to finish.

'Brian. Charmed. I'm. Sure.'

'And I'm Maria, nice to meet you.'

'OK,' Ray says, 'thanks for the directions.' He slides back across to the driver's seat and starts the engine.

'Take care. Bye now.'

'Bye Ray!' 'See. Yah.' 'Bye bye!' 'Cheerio Ray!' 'Wouldn't. Want. To. Be. Yah.'

Fiona and Martin wave until the van is out of sight. All of them seem to be as invigorated by this encounter as by the last one. All except Maria.

With the adrenaline receding, she's absolutely knackered, and disheartened and embarrassed. It's a cruel irony that the only half-decent-looking man in Hexton who has ever spoken to her did so while she was sporting a vomit-encrusted blouson. With a sigh she rounds everyone up and heads back to the centre.

Her first priority will be to find fresh clothes for herself, Fiona and Brian as soon as they get back. That's assuming of course that, with the excitement of it all, no-one has peed themselves.

Chapter 2

Bert, the centre manager, insists on the police being called, which, as far as Maria is concerned, is a big palaver for nothing. The two constables, although they are nice – overly nice in fact – struggle to hide their smirks as they interview Maria and her clients. Blue Group are scared by the policemen, intimidated by their uniforms and confused by their official yet *übernice* manner. They may have mental disabilities but they know when they're being patronized and rather than become indignant, as Maria regularly does on their behalf, they meekly hang their heads. Even Fiona is reluctant to tell them what she knows. She volunteers nothing, only nodding and shaking her head in response to their questions.

'I'm sorry miss,' says one of them, 'it's not much to go on: man of average height and weight, skin and hair colour unknown.'

'And you're certain this was a man?' says the other, apparently sincerely.

'Yes officer,' says Maria. 'You may be surprised to discover we are cognisant of basic human anatomy.'

'Of course you are miss, just checking.'

'And his hair colour is known,' Maria corrects him, 'at least his pubic hair is. I told you: a kind of tobacco colour. Maybe the hair on his head is the same colour.'

'Tobacco,' he confirms.

'Yes, you know, golden.'

'Right. Golden pubes.'

The cop bangs his pencil down hard in his little notebook and closes it. Both men smile and thank Blue Group for their help, a little too profusely for Maria's liking. They can't doff their hats and get out of the centre quick enough, and Maria knows that they're probably sitting in their squad car right now sniggering over Goldenpubes and the five dafties.

Bert also insists that Maria informs the carers. She knows this is going to mean trouble, and it does. Jane's brother, Vince, phones the next morning demanding assurances that his sister will never again be forced to endure sexual intimidation. He makes no actual accusation but his tone of voice implies that Maria is somehow guilty, that she has low moral standards. It is as much as she can do to remain civil to Vince.

Martin's parents are much more relaxed, chuffed to bits with Martin's own account of how he single-handedly rescued Fiona from the Bad Man. They are pleased and proud, but quite unsurprised by their son's heroism. Weirdly, there is no call from Fiona's mum, usually the first person on the phone to complain. But Brian's dad's reaction more than makes up for it.

Brian's dad, Phil, is furious. But this is quite normal. Phil has a constant background level of rage. He's angry at losing his job when the factory closed down, angry that he no longer has the means to buy Brian

23

gadgetry that might alleviate his disability, angry at manufacturers who hold him to ransom for the exorbitant price of adapted equipment, exploiting Brian's needs, getting rich off his back, angry at the centre bus which picks Brian up and is a daily reminder to all the neighbours of Phil's complete failure to produce a normal healthy son, angry with strangers' sympathy or embarrassment, angry at his own sperm for being sub-standard.

And so it's quite refreshing for Phil to be angry at the flasher. Maria can see how invigorated he is with this novel channel for his fury. He arrives at the centre wanting to know where and when the flasher flashed. Maria would tell him, were it not for the baseball bat he is wielding. His twin brother Billy waits outside, similarly tooled up. They have taken the day off from Job Club to 'sort this out'.

Maria can't tell him – what if they set upon some golden-pubed innocent? She'd be complicit in murder. Even if they got the right guy: death by baseball bat? It seems unduly harsh.

Brian is also refusing to tell his father in what street the flashing occurred. They have argued, Phil tells Maria, Brian laughing and repeatedly punching 'Goldenpubes' into his voice simulator until his dad 'wanted to smash the fucking thing to smithereens'. Brian, like any teenager, despises his father.

The brothers Billy and Phil spend an ecstatically rage-filled day patrolling the streets of Hexton, but meet with no obvious sexual deviants. It must be too cold, or perhaps the sight of two heavily armed vigilantes is enough for the flasher to keep his willy in his pants.

* * *

24

Fiona knows where men keep their thing. They keep it in their pants. Mum says that's fine by her so long as it stays there, in their pants. The man is a bad man. He got his thing out and then ran away. But it's not fair because Fiona wanted to see it. She saw Martin's thing when they were at swimming lesson. The man's was pink and small, the same as Martin's. Fiona saw Martin's thing when she climbed on the seat in her cubicle and looked over into his cubicle. She didn't tell Maria that she saw Martin's thing.

Mum said Fiona was a bad girl. She said Fiona made Jenny cry about the baby's strawberry. Mum says the strawberry is unlucky but it isn't the end of the world. The strawberry is right beside the baby's nose but it can't eat it. No-one can. Mum says she is sick of all the weeping and wailing about a tiny wee strawberry birthmark and she doesn't want to hear another word about it. Mum says Sienna is a normal healthy child. She says Jenny should be grateful it's only a birthmark and not a congenital mental defect. Jenny said Fiona can hold the baby but she's not to squeeze it.

Maria is taking Fiona to the pictures. Fiona loves Maria. The packets of crisps at the pictures are bigger than the packets at the centre. Fiona is worried that Mum won't let her go to the pictures. She is worried Maria will tell Mum about the man's strawberry. Mum will get mad. But Maria didn't see the man's strawberry. The man's scarf fell down and Fiona saw it on his cheek but he pulled his scarf back up and Maria didn't see it. The man is unlucky. Fiona is a good girl. She's not going to tell about the man's strawberry. She is going to the pictures with Maria and she'll get a big packet of crisps. Fiona loves Maria.

* * *

Maria is going to be late. She's still to get the bus out to Hexton and she's not even dressed yet. She has her appraisal meeting with Mike today. Due to the importance of this meeting it's crucial that she arrive in plenty of time, but equally, due to the importance of this meeting, she had an extra-long meditation this morning.

The popular expression 'her head is full of wee beasties' has been used by her less spiritually in-touch friends to describe Maria. It's a fascinating idea. She imagines cockroaches and beetles nibbling at her brain, blindly clambering over each other in the darkness under her skull, maggots sucking and sliding, bobsleighing the grooves in her cortex. But it isn't true. Maria's head is full of much higher forms of life.

Her usual routine is to enter meditation by lying on her bedroom carpet. The carpet has an unfashionably thick woolly pile, ideal for meditative purposes. Not for Maria the prickliness of trendy woven-seagrass matting. She hates trendy things, especially uncomfortable trendy things.

Her flat in a less expensive area of the city is east-facing, which, in the morning, is a good thing. Between the bed and the chest of drawers there's enough space, just, for her to lay out her long thin body and catch the early morning light on her face.

She breathes through her legs, a technique she's read about in more than one book, and it really does work. She breathes in through her right leg, imagining the breath as light, feeding and calming her body, and then out through her left leg, expelling built-up stress and toxins. Often she relaxes enough to expel built-up toxins from her bumhole as well, which is a good thing.

26

As the relaxed feeling arrives at her brain, if she concentrates hard enough, Maria experiences bliss. Although she's never actually tried any illegal drugs, she has attended enough drug-awareness workshops to understand that this sensation must be similar to that induced by Ecstasy and other class As. She's no need of synthetic drugs; the pharmacy in her brain makes all the chemical cocktails she wants.

From this happy place, beside a shimmering river designed in her imagination, Maria progresses to planning her day, conferring and taking advice from her spiritual advisors, programming her personal development and her long-term goals. Spiritual advisors come and go depending on how they inspire her. Toni Morrison, the American author, has recently been replaced by a Portuguese woman who, having survived a plane crash in Peru, was forced to gnaw her foot off and hop out of the jungle. Before her it had been Lance Armstrong. A few remain constant. Madonna and Nelson Mandela are Maria's chief advisors; she can't imagine ever replacing them. They've been with her, by her side every day, ever since she got spiritual.

She got spiritual as a way of life after she'd done political, which was prior to promiscuous and long after religious. She's tried everything. Nothing else ever lasted long but this spirituality thing has been a grower. Maria is a seeker, she has been for years, ever since she left uni. She was a seeker then too, but what she sought in those days was easy to find: good exam results and good times. The problem is now she's not sure what it is she's seeking.

True, she is unencumbered by a relationship at the moment, but she's not so shallow as to base her happiness on whether or not she happens to have a boyf. She's a big girl. Or perhaps it's that she's not brave enough to admit, even to herself, that what she really wants, even more than career progression, is a boyf.

Time's getting on. The girls she shared a flat with at uni, the Kelvin Street Kids, they've all got nice partners now, what's wrong with her? The boyfs she's had up to now have never worked out; they've always been flawed one way or another. She's always ended up with the nerds, the geeks, the lame ducks her girlfriends wouldn't entertain. Her last boyf, the exotically named Dirk, was quite literally lame.

Maria began to believe that it was her. One deadbeat boyfriend after another can really affect a girl's self-esteem. When Dirk chucked her she knew she had to stop the rot, and the next Saturday morning she headed straight for the Mind/Body/Spirit section of the bookshop in town.

It wasn't *all* hippy-dippy shite, some of it made sense and made her feel better, better than politics, or promiscuity or religion. And there was so much to read and take in, she could seek away to her heart's content, sitting in the bookshop café lapping up frothy coffee and self-help. It whiled away Saturday afternoons.

That's what got her started on meditation and spiritual advisors. It's a harmless enough little foible, a creative and amusing diversion that helps get her through the day, but she feels it's probably best to keep this interesting interior life to herself. If she told anyone in work she'd probably be sacked or at least sent off home on the sick. This is grossly unfair, considering Bert's fascination for St Bernadette and his annual trip to Lourdes ever since his eczema miraculously cleared up. Even when the eczema came back worse than before Bert kept up his devotions, telling everyone in the staffroom faith wasn't about results.

She's going to be late, again, giving Mike another golden opportunity to spike her promotion prospects. Another year will go by with Maria at the bottom of the ladder, another year of unfulfilled potential. She feels panic creep up her spine.

Ironically, Nelson kept her back this morning with a long debate on the nature of patience.

'The most important thing,' he kept saying, 'is not that you are promoted, young lady.'

He only calls her young lady when he's annoyed with her.

'The most important thing is that you learn patience.'

Of all her advisors, Maria is reluctantly forced to concede, Nelson is far and away the most qualified on the subject.

'For what is patience but love?'

Madonna has a different take on Maria's ambitions. 'You go girl!'

She intends to go. She takes three deep centring breaths and begins visualizing a successful outcome to the meeting. When she thinks of Mike she has to check her mind leaping to its usual impression of him: a prissy, snobbish, insensitive knob end. For the purposes of the visualization she must rejig that notion and picture Mike as a smiling caring boss who values his staff.

She visualizes him coming out of his office to greet her, taking one of her long hands in both of his, leading her inside. Like a TV advert for a credit company, she pictures him nodding agreement as he ticks the boxes on her appraisal form. She envisions them sharing a joke, an affectionate chuckle at some of the antics of Blue Group. She imagines his bashful admiration of her tolerance. She sees him writing a fulsome report recommending her for promotion to Senior Key Worker, both of them smiling as they shake positively and confidently over the deal.

And, sure enough, when she arrives for the meeting, Mike does indeed come out to greet her.

Chapter 3

'Maria, you're twenty-five minutes late.'

'Sorry, I . . .'

'Look, never mind, you're here now. We'll have to get on.'

On leaving school Maria hadn't the grades for medicine, which was just as well. Even if she had been qualified, she knew she couldn't deal with blood and guts and death, eyeballs and innards. This squeamishness similarly ruled out nursing. She wanted, needed even, to do *something* therapeutic, therapeutic but unbloody. After university and years in career wastelands, she's now a low-status key worker in an Adult Learning Centre.

But despite the long hours, the tedious staffroom politics, the boring meetings, the frustrating disagreements with clients who regularly throw tantrums and scream at her or pee themselves in the supermarket, she loves her job. Sometimes she sees herself as a kind of secular nun devoting her life to this work.

Mike will find no room to criticize Maria's work when it comes to client care. Unlike colleagues who clock off at five, Maria spends evenings and weekends with her clients, taking them shopping, to the park or to the movies. None are cared for more assiduously than Blue Group. The one thing about which Mike could carp, and no doubt will, is the Inclusion Initiative.

Maria has lead responsibility for an initiative which is tasked to integrate the centre into the wider community. Her remit is to liaise with groups and ensure that centre clients play an active role in the life of the neighbourhood. Unfortunately it isn't something that she has, so far, proven to be very good at.

No-one can say she hasn't tried. She has postered everywhere, approached every voluntary group in the Hexton area. She attends every meeting hoping that an opportunity might present itself for integration with the ALC. It never does. The initiative has so far produced no integration, no centre volunteers, not one.

Others, embarrassed by their lack of success, might be reluctant to ask for promotion, but not Maria. She has the full backing of her spiritual advisors. She understands it's not logical when you're apparently failing in your job to look for career advancement but, in this case, she has rejected logic in favour of instinct. Nevertheless, she knows this meeting is not going to be easy.

She has a good idea of what's going to happen: Mike will start to bang on, as he always does, about the Inclusion Initiative and how, after three years, she still hasn't got anything off the ground. But this time instead of cowering and nodding her head, yes sir, no sir, three bags full, she's going to be ready for him.

'Right. Let's start with the plus points,' Mike says as he sits behind his desk, carefully holding his tie to stop it falling onto the file.

'As usual, an impressive hundred per cent attendance.'

Maria has never had a day's absence. Even when she's ill she makes it in, they need her.

'Again you've scored consistently high in all of this year's staff training, ninety-three per cent for the homemaker's course.'

Maria smiles, she loves staff training.

'Eighty-five per cent pass rate in your crafts class.'

Maria's smile tightens slightly on being reminded of this. It would have been one hundred per cent if it hadn't been for Martin insisting on doing his own knitting. Of course in a childish fury he ripped out the few rows of plain and purl he had managed and refused even to try again. Maria had considered quickly knitting a simple scarf in his name, it would only have taken a few hours, but she knew Martin would make a fuss. It had been selfish and disappointing of him to let the rest of Blue Group down.

'Ah, this is interesting. You're usually so hands-on with the clients, Maria. I've a note here from Bert to say that although you take your group swimming, you don't enter the pool with them.'

'There's a lifeguard on duty at all times.'

'Yes, of course, but you know the policy, clients should be assisted in the water, it helps their confidence.'

'I'm allergic. The chlorine in the water, it nips my eyes.'

'Well keep your eyes out of the water then.'

'But they thrash about and splash me, it's like a jacuzzi in there.'

'Client confidence and personal development take priority over nippy eyes. Ask Alison for petty cash and buy goggles.'

Maria's face is red. It's pointless arguing with him.

'Now to more serious matters, I've had a complaint from Fiona's mother. Fiona has been crying a lot at night again. She says she has nightmares that you are hitting her.'

'I've never laid a hand on Fiona!'

'No.'

'Or anyone, ever. Never in my life!'

'No, I know that, or, let me assure you, you wouldn't be sitting here now, but we have to look at the underlying reasons why Fiona is frightened. Her mother feels that you pick on her.'

'She picks on me; she's always trying to slap me! You know that, you've seen her.'

'I know that Fiona is one of our more challenging clients. Perhaps we need to look more closely at her specific needs.'

'I do, Mike. I spend more time with Fiona than with anyone else.'

'Of course I'm aware of the extra hours that you put in but I wonder if you're not a bit too involved with the clients? At the end of the day they need respite from us as much as we need it from them. I can't tell you how to spend your free time, but perhaps you should cultivate friendships outside the centre. Have a normal social life with normal people.'

'You're right, Mike,' says Maria, face burning. And she's off. This is going to be just the kind of outburst she has specifically meditated not to have.

'You *can't* tell me how to spend my time. Blue Group are normal people. They're our clients but they're also my friends and I won't let you speak about them like that.'

'Calm down, Maria. Emotional scenes like this aren't helpful.'

Mike rifles around in the file, giving them both a moment to compose themselves.

'OK, let's move on. Now, where are we with the Inclusion Initiative?'

'Nowhere.'

Mike lets his head collapse forward dramatically. This is all part of Maria's plan.

'I requested work placements for clients at the Breakfast Club at St Peter's school but they say they're too crowded as it is. There isn't enough space for all the kids to sit down. Rather than turn them away, they're operating a buffet.'

'A buffet? How can kids eat hot porridge while standing? St Peter's will end up getting their arses sued.'

'I attended a meeting with the Elderly Forum where it was announced that they had applied for a sports grant.'

'Typical, the most proactive group in Hexton is the Elderly.'

'They got the full amount. Enough for a fitness instructor two days a week and all the equipment.'

'Wow! That is good news. We could bus a few of our groups down there. In fact we could walk them down and that would be their warm-up. That'll kick the clients' arses into gear. And,' says Mike, pointing at Maria excitedly, 'this fits the Health Initiative remit like a glove.'

But Maria is only building his hopes to bring them crashing down again.

'Except that the Elderly Forum won't let anyone, not just us, use their equipment. A unanimous decision.'

'What? They can't do that; it's community equipment.'

'They don't want to share.'

'Selfish old gits, they want their arses kicked.'

'It stems from a complaint they raised last July about another user group, WAVAW, Women Against Violence Against Women, you know, the battered wives.'

'Right, irate husband running amok trying to chop up the missus, was it?'

'No, not this time. The problem was caused by the Elderly Forum's premises being closed for two weeks after the meeting. If it hadn't been for that everything would have been fine.'

'Eh? I'm not following.'

'WAVAW held their meeting without incident, locked up and handed back the keys. The problem was that they forgot to empty the bin. One woman had changed her baby's nappy and it was left there in the bin. You remember how hot it was last July. Two weeks later when the Elderly Forum reopened they discovered an infestation of maggots.'

'Jesus Christ.'

'And a really bad smell.'

'I'm not surprised the Elderly won't have them back. They've ruined it for everyone with their shitty nappies. Those battered wives need their arses kicked.'

A silence falls.

'That was a joke, Maria.'

Another silence.

'Yes!' she blurts. Maria's hand flies to her chest and presses hard. She pushes against her stony breastbone, trying to contain her embarrassment. She never gets his jokes.

'I'll tell you who really need their arses kicked,' says Mike.

Who, Maria wonders, is to feel the force of Mike's jackboot now? Cancer victims, holocaust survivors, disabled kiddies?

'The scrotebags that torched the community centre, that's who. I don't know how I'm supposed to run a community without a community hall.'

'Any word on when we'll get the new one?'

'Oh I wouldn't hold your breath. The planning meeting has been put off twice already and we've not even gone to consultation yet. I blame the Christians. That Pastor McKenzie keeps blocking it. He's a slippery one. How the hell did he manage to get on the Community Council?'

'He was the only candidate. His church group voted for him. Perfectly constitutional, they're entitled to support whoever they like. The Victory Mission is part of the community.'

'Oh wise up, Maria! You don't think any of these Christians actually come from Hexton, do you? They're missionaries, for Christ's sake. They're parachuted in here every Saturday night with coffee and biscuits trying to bribe people to join their weirdo Jesus sect.'

'Pizza. They're offering pizza now.'

'They're giving out free pizza now, are they? Dirty bastards! It wouldn't surprise me if it was the bloody Christians that burned the centre down. Divide and conquer, that's their game,' Mike declares.

'Although they didn't bring any pizza when they came to the centre.'

'They came here?'

'Pastor McKenzie and a few of his followers came offering pastoral care.'

Mike is outraged.

'Trying to recruit the mentally disabled, that's low.' He looks set for a bout of apoplexy.

'Unfortunately their visit clashed with "Celebrity Boob Job Challenge" on telly so they didn't actually get any takers.'

'Well thank the Lord for that.'

'I asked the Stoma Club to come in and give us a demonstration of changing their colostomy bags,' says Maria, counting off on her fingers.

'Euw!'

'It said on their publicity that they did, but they politely declined. I asked the Mother and Toddler group if we could help out but they also declined, and none too politely. Liz Marshall said they couldn't have loonies near the kids. That's what we're up against. I started a Slimming Club at the centre, WUFACS, primarily for clients but open to anyone from Hexton.'

'WUFACS?'

'Women Using Food As a Coping Strategy. Non-judgemental, so's not to make them feel bad about being fat.'

'Good title. Any luck?'

'Fiona came for a few weeks when I was trying to wean her off crisps, but no, nobody else.'

'It might have been more successful if you'd called it Women Using Food As a Stuffing Their Face Strategy.'

Maria has kept the best to last, a terrific example of the pains she has taken to fulfil the criteria for the Inclusion Initiative.

'We joined the Stop The Motorway Campaign, went to the demo, banged our pots and pans. Obviously our involvement was limited once the police turned up and the protesters took to the trees. There was talk of rigging a block and tackle to hoist Brian's chair up next time, he was pretty keen.'

If there's one thing that is sure to wind Mike up it's the idea of Brian, the youngest client at the centre, swinging from the trees like Tarzan, except in a wheelchair.

'There won't be a next time.'

'Sorry?'

'Are you kidding? We have a duty of care to our clients not to get them arrested or have them fall out of trees. No more demos. That's final.'

Mike closes Maria's appraisal file. The air that has been between the pages of the substantial dossier is forced out and smacks her face like a rebuke.

'Anyway, good effort. I can see you've put a lot of work in.'

'You don't expect me to achieve anything, do you, Mike?'

'You're a valued member of the team, Maria; don't think for a minute that you're not.'

He reaches across and pats her. He delivers his standard one, two, three pats and then a soft up-and-down reassuring rub on a generally agreed non-threatening part of the body, her elbow. She stares into Mike's eyes. She wants to see beyond his eyes, into his soul if he has one.

'Believe me Mike, it's impossible. The community councillors don't give a toss about our clients. Why should they? It's just a bunch of subnormal mentalists.'

'I don't think it's wise to call the councillors "mentalists", Maria.'

'Not the . . .'

'Joke,' says Mike, holding up his hands.

'I'm tired of begging snooty community groups to be kind, it just doesn't work. I'm sick of kissing community arses. I'm up to here with the sausage-roll circuit. I've had enough. It's time to change tactics, time to get tough.'

'Mmm,' says Mike, scratching his chin. 'An aggressively negative approach to building community networks. That's novel.'

Maria barely registers his sarcasm. It's time to deliver her master plan. The plan that came to her at the shimmering river of her meditation, the beautiful simple sweet plan that is going to solve the inclusion issue and get Maria promoted. Before she speaks she swallows the saliva that has pooled in her mouth. It tastes like bleach.

'A show,' she whispers. 'I'm going to put on a show.'

It's Mike's turn to stare into Maria's eyes now.

'Mike, it's perfect. Everyone in Hexton fancies themselves as a singer. Instead of us chasing them, pleading to be involved in their little schemes, they'll come to us. They'll be queuing up to get involved. We can host it in our assembly hall. There's room for two hundred people in there. A community show, with a theme, you know, like those tributes they have on telly on a Saturday night. I was thinking Madonna.'

Maria becomes aware of how heavily her hand is squashing her chest, constricting her breathing. She releases it and instantly feels giddy and reckless.

'A concert party; a musical extravaganza!' she blurts. 'The school choir. The Elderly Forum Glee Club, these groups are always looking for somewhere to sing.'

'Yeah,' says Mike with a tired cynicism, 'Hexton's pensioners' very own cover version of "Get Erotic".'

But Maria is too busy eyeing Mike's office curtains to be offended, she's fighting the desire to pull them off the windows and cut them up for costumes right now.

'Stop The Motorway have jugglers and guitarists. Oh, and I've just realized, Victory Mission has an organist!'

'I don't know if we'd want those church weirdos.'

'We can't exclude them, Mike, we can't exclude any of the groups. And the beauty of us hosting it is that they can't exclude us. We're in charge. My drama workshops have been going well. The clients could perform something around a framework of other acts.'

'Well, I suppose if nothing else it'll look good on the annual report,' says Mike. 'Nobody will be able to say we haven't explored every avenue.'

So far so good, he's not hostile to the idea.

'So, a show would fill the Inclusion Initiative criteria, wouldn't it?'

'Mmm, yup, mad as it is, a community show ticks all the boxes.'

'And I'd be eligible for promotion?'

'Maria, if you manage to get Hextors to set foot inside the centre you'll get my job. It'll be your ticket out of Hexton.'

She shakes her head. Mike will never understand. She doesn't want a ticket out of Hexton, her clients need her.

'Let me have a preliminary report in two weeks and diary a meeting in, say, a month from now?'

As she leaves Mike's office Maria allows herself a private smile. In the words of one of her previous spiritual advisors, Freddy Mercury, the show must go on.

Chapter 4

Next morning Maria is meditating. The sky is bright blue, the shimmering river glints in the fresh morning sunshine, the forest is piney fragrant and Maria's friends, the weightless songbird who perches on her finger, the downy squirrel who snuggles her shoulder, shyly greet her before she meets her spiritual advisors.

'Good on you!' says Madonna.

'Well done, hen!' Nelson nods.

In her meditations, Nelson and Madonna often use the local vernacular. Maria is smiling so hard her jaws hurt.

'Well, it's all thanks to you guys.'

She throws her arms around the tiny figure of Madonna, then she kisses Nelson's hand.

It's not that Nelson expects this deference, but Maria thinks it's more fitting. And she's heard he has an eye for the ladies. She doesn't want to give him any ideas. He's an old guy but still and all, there are all sorts of things he can get up to inside her head. It wouldn't be right.

'If it wasn't for you two I'd never have had the nerve,' she tells them.

Nelson shakes his head in disagreement.

'Don't give us that shite. The concert was your idea. It was you who brazened it out to ask for the promotion.'

'Nelson's right, credit where credit's due. You're smarter than you think, Maria. The concert idea: pure genius. But talking of credit, you haven't even noticed my new dress!'

It's true. Maria has been so caught up in her victory that she has failed to clock Madonna's outfit. It's an expensive-looking peach and cream 1950s-style dress with a plunging neckline perfectly displaying her enviable cleavage. She wears a matching cream-coloured straw hat and shoes, and delicate little lace gloves.

'Oh, it's gorgeous, Madonna!'

'Cheers. You really think so?'

'Definitely, peach is so your colour!'

'Well I thought your bouquet should have some of those pale orange roses that you like and that would set off my dress.'

'Do I really have to wear this tie?'

For the first time Maria notices that Nelson is wearing a cream-coloured shirt and a tie in the peach shade.

'I'm not liking it,' he says in his regal Thembu growl, 'it's too girly.'

'Oh for God's sake Nelson, how many times?' says Madonna. 'You're going to spoil the whole effect if you insist on wearing one of your African numbers.'

Madonna and Nelson are trying to marry Maria off. She's not entirely unenthusiastic. Ever since she brought them in as advisors they've been preparing for her wedding. Madonna is to be maid of honour and

Nelson will give her away. Almost every day Madonna comes up with new designs for her own and Maria's dresses. There seems to be no limit to her imagination. Until recently there were no contenders for the role of groom, but that has never put Madonna off.

Although her spirit guides are planning a white dress with a wee tartan trim, Maria is no virgin. There has been, of course, her promiscuous, or 'blue' period.

But it was all a long time ago now, years ago, not long after graduation, after the Kelvin Street Kids split up. Anna and Colette went down south chasing careers and Bethan, who swore she'd never go back, ended up returning to Inverness where her boyfriend Colin had managed to get work. Maria kept on the lease but things were never the same. The new flatmates weren't so keen on pyjama parties and girls' nights.

One of the new girls, Janice, started bringing guys back at the weekend, different guys. Maria would be in the kitchen making cocoa and a half-naked lad would stroll in, open the fridge and swig milk straight from the carton without asking. Maria started going out with Janice and before long she too was bringing lads back.

In the past Maria had been nervous of copping off with boys she didn't know and trust. Not from any moral standpoint but simply because they must inevitably discover the foam domes in her bra. Countless times she had panicked during the preliminaries when the boy was trying to feel her up. She circumvented this problem by keeping the lights out, pulling her bra off along with her jumper and swiftly moving them on to second base. If they did notice the disparity between cup size and breasts, nobody mentioned it. Maria became a practised seductress.

One night she and Janice brought one guy back between them and took turns snogging him until he got scared and left. That felt good, powerful. Another night Maria found herself slapping the naked backside of a boy whose name she couldn't remember and requesting that he give her it *hot and hard*. That felt fake and embarrassing.

In time she began to question the efficacy of this strategy. Maria had a new boyfriend virtually every week; enough ex-boyfriends to fill a playing field. If she'd put her exes end to end they would have reached to the moon and back. If she'd put the ones who'd loved her end to end they wouldn't have made it to the bedroom door.

Casual sex was exciting but ultimately fruitless. The relationships never lasted long. And so she went back to waiting and hoping that someone who might be potential husband material would find her.

Dirk found her. They met in the bicycle-repair shop. Dirk wasn't a cyclist; he was buying a tricycle for his nephew. He asked Maria for her number and he called and she went out with him. It was that simple.

She didn't sleep with him for weeks. She didn't sleep with him until he had stopped arranging a specific time to call and began just calling when he felt like it. He was calling every day.

Despite the obvious comic potential of his name, Dirk was a serious person. He was a lawyer. He was four inches smaller than Maria and had a prosthetic right foot. Sex with Dirk was good and, once they got over her initial chastity, they did it a lot. They did it any time, any place, anywhere, even, once, on a train, which wasn't easy given Dirk's limitations.

Dirk was bad-tempered and dominating. He didn't believe in Valentine's or birthday cards. He never took Maria on holiday or introduced her to his family. And then he dumped her.

'Good riddance to bad rubbish,' says Madonna. 'You were way too good for that Dirkhead.'

Madonna says not to sell herself short. When Maria notices a boy Madonna is always quick to point out his shortcomings: crooked teeth, a gammy eye or an out-size nose. But Maria is more comfortable fancying men who, like her, are not physically perfect.

'Well what about Dezzie then?' Madonna suggests for the umpteenth time.

Desmond Thompson she means, the new key worker at the centre. Maria fancies Dezzie, how could she not? He is perfect boyfriend/husband material as he's decent, caring, tall and available. He also has a generously proportioned nose.

But on so many levels Dezzie is different from her. At twenty-six he's two years younger than Maria, but he has knowledge and experience way beyond hers. Three years in the Royal Navy took him all around the world while Maria's only been to Spain a few times.

'But,' says Nelson, reading her thoughts, 'like all human beings, you and Dezzie have more similarities than differences.'

This is the great thing about her spiritual advisors: because they're already inside her head she never has to explain anything to them. And it's certainly true what Nelson says; she and Dezzie have many similarities.

Like her, Dezzie has a bike, but while Maria's is an

old pedal-powered Raleigh tourer, Dezzie's is a souped-up Suzuki: bright blue, so big it takes up a whole parking space. Maria's handlebars are high and ladylike; she pedals around in a stately Mary Poppins style, while Dezzie's riding position is that of a Grand National winner. She's scared of motorbikes, especially big powerful ones, but she occasionally fantasizes about Dezzie taking her for a spin along a country road with her hair flying behind her.

'Maria, get real,' says Madonna, 'isn't riding without a helmet illegal in this country? A girl's got to be practical.'

Maria doesn't want to be practical; she has to do it all day every day. Every day she has to apply practicality not only for herself but for all of Blue Group, the most impractical people on the planet. She wants to run away, to flee screaming from practicality, that's why she comes here. Here, down by the shimmering river, she can do what she wants. She can turn Dezzie's image round in her head, put him in whatever poses she fancies, a virtual Action Man figure.

'I know where you're going with this, you dirty girl,' says Madonna.

Having them inside her head can be a disadvantage too.

'You can get the sex carnival out of your mind right now.'

'Yes,' agrees Nelson, 'this kind of objectification is de-humanizing.'

She can understand this from Nelson but it's a bit rich coming from Madonna. She has become very moralistic since she found religion. For the moment Maria will have to suppress any raunchy Dezzie thoughts.

'Let's just focus on Dezzie's husbandly qualities, Maria,' says Madonna. 'Now, he's not the brightest but he has the look of a man who would be handy with a screwdriver and a B&Q flat-pack.'

'Oh, don't be such a snob,' Maria says. 'OK, so he's not a graduate. It's only a piece of paper. A degree's no guarantee of being smart. Look at Mike, for instance. Dezzie's smart in other ways, he's people smart, and that's what matters. He understands things about people and situations that it's taken me years to learn.'

The other thing that's different about Dezzie, and the thing that makes him most attractive, is that he is so stupendously, unrelentingly kind. The kind of guy who wouldn't hurt a fly, who'd go to hell and back to do you a favour.

'He'd give you the shirt off his back,' says Nelson, to general agreement.

Dezzie used to wear a T-shirt to work that proclaimed *live fast die young*. It was the tour T-shirt of the 80s heavy metal band Daughter Slaughter. Both Dezzie and Bert, the centre manager, are massive fans of them. Last week, on Bert's fortieth birthday, Dezzie made him a gift of it. No-one else seemed to think this was exceptional, after all it was just a beat-up old T-shirt, some of the staff even thought the new guy was trying to toady to the boss, but Maria knows the real story. Maria knows how Dezzie treasured that T-shirt, given to him by Orny, the iconic singer of Daughter Slaughter, at a concert just days before Orny was killed in a drug-crazed motorbike accident. Maria knows she could never be that generous.

Madonna is fussing around Nelson, trying him this time in a pale green top hat and tails.

'Generosity – an excellent husbandly quality,' says

Nelson. 'And the sooner we get you married off the sooner we can stop this fashion parade.'

To Maria, Dezzie is a god. If she was a Christian she could believe that Dezzie was a new Messiah, the Second Coming. That's how much she fancies him. More importantly, he also appears to fancy her.

'Madonna, I've told you, Dezzie's a colleague,' says Maria, playing the coquette.

'Oh come off it Maria, he fancies you.'

'D'you think?'

'Duh!' says Madonna, 'does a one-legged pope shit in the woods?'

'Yuhuh!' says Nelson the lawyer. 'The evidence is quite compelling. If he doesn't fancy you, why was he licking you in the coffee room?'

The other day Maria sat with Dezzie in the staffroom enjoying a cappuccino from the machine. He made her laugh while she was mid-sip, Dezzie always makes her laugh, and she spray-snorted milk foam all over the place. A dribble of creamy spume ran down the hollow between her thumb and forefinger and while they were laughing Dezzie traced his finger along her thumb, snowploughing the white foam towards her wrist. When he had gathered the froth onto his finger he sucked it into his mouth.

'Apart from the sexual athletics of your monofooted friend Dirk, this is the most erotic thing that's ever happened to you, isn't it?' asks Madonna.

Maria has to agree.

'But if he fancies me why isn't he asking me out?'

'Patience,' says Nelson, twiddling his pale green tie impatiently, 'you must learn patience.'

* * *

49

Because of her meditation, after getting off the bus and while walking to the centre, Maria smiles at everyone she sees. She loves them. Waves of her love engulf passers-by without them ever knowing it. They don't know it because, apart from her bright smile, the waves are invisible. If they were visible, bright love fumes would be seen in a pinkish vapour trail as she passed.

As she walks she feels a violent tenderness for the people she passes. She sees how they hurry around, engaged in unstinting service to their families, working hard to please them, yearning to give and receive love. She sees that even with their hacking coughs or bandy legs or roseate noses they are loving, loved, lovely.

When she reaches the centre, still buoyed up and feeling brave, she phones round the community groups. She explains that she's organizing a community show. It will be a Madonna tribute and she's calling to invite them to take part. Some of them, assuming it's a hoax call, put the phone down, some laugh, others simply tell her to piss off.

Piss-offs don't bother Maria. Over the last three years she's had plenty, had them all her life in fact. Since Social Dancing at secondary school, where the boys were forced to choose a girl, Maria has become familiar, comfortable even, with rejection.

There were good reasons why she was the only girl never to get picked. While other girls were straining in B- and even C-cup bras, Maria wore a vest. More problematic was the undisguisable fact that she was a head taller than all the boys. Fair enough, nobody's fault, no big deal. She could understand their reticence to dance eye level with her breastless nipples.

Every week, while the boys and girls giggled and Gay Gordoned their way around the gym hall, Maria sat alone. Alone and still. Silently fighting the irresistible rhythm of the country-dance music, she controlled her instincts. Her pride would not let her yield to pathetic toe-tapping.

'Early rejection has been the making of you,' Nelson frequently tells her. Probably it has, how else could she have continued for three years with the farce of the Inclusion Initiative? And so when community groups tell her to piss off and slam the phone down she stoically redials and explains that no, it's not a hoax call, and yes, they are welcome to come and sing at the auditions.

They are all interested, some more than others. The Elderly Forum Events Co-ordinator is polite but snooty. Alice O'Connor, one of the few who didn't request that Maria piss off, tries to throw her weight around. She tells her that the Glee Club members are unable to travel to Hexton High for the auditions.

'It's not safe for senior citizens around that school. Too much neddery.'

It is a few seconds before Maria realizes that Alice is talking about neds: hooligans, yobs, local young people.

'You'll have to come to us.'

So that's it. The Elderly Forum won't audition amongst hoi polloi.

'I'm afraid that's not going to be possible, Alice. I've already arranged it with the headmistress, Miss Bowman. All the other groups are coming to the high school.'

'Look pet, we might be old but we're not stupid.'

Maria laughs. Alice doesn't.

'How d'you mean, Alice?'

'You're trying to get this Inclusion Initiative scheme that you've been banging on about for years going again, aren't you?'

'Well, yes, that is part of it.'

'And you need to have all sections of the community represented, don't you?'

Maria can see where Alice is going with this. The Elderly Forum have the political savvy to know that to meet the criteria they must be included. They know that when it comes to auditions they can call the tune.

'So you'll have to have at least a few coffin-dodgers in your show then, won't you?'

Reluctantly, Maria agrees to schlep round to the Elderly Forum Centre, euphemistically named Autumn House, and hold their very own and – Alice has made quite clear – preferential audition.

As if she hasn't got enough to do. But at least she's got them on board. Maria has hit on the one thing all the groups have in common. Everyone, even the coffin-dodgers, wants to be in show business.

Hexton is a breeding ground for two British archetypes: army recruits and *Stars in Their Eyes* contestants. There are rich pickings, in quantity if not quality. Hextors are foot soldiers, cannon fodder for TV talent shows, falling usually in the first wave of elimination rounds. Their ambitions do not extend to stardom in their own right, they only aspire to imitate. Naïve enough to dream, they make great television with the disparity between their nervous shivering voices and flamboyant yet brittle self-confidence. People watching at home never hear the true music of these voices. They would need to come to Hexton for that. Maria has made it her business to research local talent thoroughly.

All of Hexton loves to sing. The Hexton Arms is full of it, for example: the Saturday Singalong from 2 p.m. to 4.30 p.m. with Bobby McCann and his Mighty Hammond.

This is mostly an over-fifties event – Bobby himself is fifty plus. Still with a full head of hair he smokes unfiltered fags, dropping ash as he tinkles the nicotine-yellowed keyboard of the Mighty Hammond.

There is a lively atmosphere and the regular crowd are comfortable with each other. Bobby is extremely versatile and can play anything pre-1989, including 'Too Drunk to Fuck' by The Dead Kennedys and 'Girlfriend in a Coma' by The Smiths. Sadly, music stopped for Bobby in 1989 when his partner, Marjory, a non-smoker, entered a coma after a protracted battle with lung cancer.

Despite Bobby's enormous repertoire, each singer has three or four favourite songs they have made their own. Singalong etiquette is such that no singer is allowed to appropriate another's song. Bobby will not countenance it, refusing to provide accompaniment. Lifelong rifts have apparently been caused by just this kind of wrongheadedness. Songs only become available when the singer reluctantly relinquishes them through long-term ill health or death.

Bobby's crowd don't drink much by Hexton standards, perhaps five or six shorts, but the combination of skipping lunch and the adrenaline buzz of performing gives the oldsters a heady Saturday night out on a Saturday afternoon. They roll home pished at half five to sleep it off in front of *Stars in Their Eyes*. Old people drunk in daylight is the norm for Hexton.

The generations use the pub in sittings, the pensioners giving way to the Saturday night karaoke for the younger ones. Rab, the karaoke singer, is a local celebrity. He's handsome and trendy and powerful in that he chooses who gets to sing next, if at all. He always keeps the last twenty minutes, and all the best contemporary hits, for himself. Invariably he finishes the evening dressed as an American Navy officer singing 'I've Had the Time of My Life' before ripping his kit off to Tom Jones's 'You Can Leave Your Hat on'. The pristine white jacket is first to come off, slowly, teasingly, exposing an orange sunbed tan on an under-developed smoker's chest. With a prodigious tug the trousers come off in one piece. For decency Rab retains his black leather thong as well as his hat.

When the Stop The Motorway campaign first began they had a rally. Feral-looking dreadlocked environ-mentalists came to tell the locals about the new motorway. Most of the protestors were arrested and were forced, as they were being dragged away by the police, to leave their amplifier and microphone with an obliging local family. When the campaigners were released and went to find their equipment they told Maria that they heard it before they saw it.

From three streets away a rich baritone crooned 'Love Me Tender' in a passable Elvis impersonation. Bewitched, they followed the haunting voice, like shepherds following a star, until it brought them to a humble tenement flat. The family who had offered to look after their sound system were now holding their own top-volume karaoke party. Not wishing to upset anyone, the tree-huggers, as the locals had begun to call them, agreed to come back the next morning.

Between songs the family told jokes through the

microphone loud enough to be heard in back courts and lanes and middens throughout Hexton, the comedy amplified by the jokers' sudden celebrity. Later, as the drink took hold, there were scuffles for control of the mic. Later still, police arrived and politely requested that the music cease.

When the tree-huggers returned the next morning they were told that their equipment had been impounded by the police on a second visit.

But there are plenty of opportunities for showboating talent other than at the pub or impromptu shebeens. There's the school choir, the Elderly Forum Glee Club, the tree-huggers' circus skills and the Victory Mission, not to mention the various talents of the clients at the centre. In Blue Group alone Maria has the drama work-shop and Fiona might make a good actor if she could ever be persuaded to stop munching crisps.

Maria has managed to escape Blue Group for half an hour to prepare audition flyers. Fiona wasn't keen on her leaving the group. Although Fiona gives Maria such a hard time, she hates to be left with any other key worker. She threatened a crying fit but Maria settled her down with a packet of cheese and onion.

Brian's also in a bit of a mood but that's nothing new. He's a typical huffy teenager: he hates the centre, hates his parents, sometimes he even hates Maria. Brian shouldn't be here. He was Dux at school, top grades in everything but despite this there isn't a place for him at university this year. There isn't the budget for him to have a carer accompany him to lectures, so in the meantime he's just been parked here at the centre. It's the wrong place for him – his mental faculties are excellent, it's his body that lets him down.

Brian has cerebral palsy. He's programmed a short cut into his Dynavox which pronounces it as *terrible* palsy and he laughs when the other clients innocently repeat it. His rebellious teenage mind is as bitter and twisted as his poor wee body. Terrible palsy, it is terrible. Brian reads all the time or plays computer chess with Bert when Bert has time, but otherwise he's bored stiff and this makes him grumpy and difficult.

Brian and Fiona are always the difficult ones but they'll be fine, they're in good hands. Dezzie, who doesn't have his own allocated group yet, operates as relief key worker, and she has left them with him. They don't know Dezzie very well yet as he's fairly new, but they'll get to know him. Dezzie's so sweet, nothing is ever too much trouble for him, he's the most obliging guy Maria's ever met.

In the computer room she Googles Madonna. There are loads of sites, mostly selling stuff: Madonna CDs, films and books. She's looking for anything she can use, photos or logos she can't get from celebrity magazines, which she never buys.

Despite the fact that Fiona can't read very well, her mother buys her the cheap gossip magazines which she pores over endlessly. She knows all the celebrities. When Maria takes her to the movies Fiona talks all the way through, telling her who the actors are, who they're divorcing and what they're in rehab for. Maria tells her that worshipping celebrities is not healthy but she can't resist seeing what Madonna is up to. The Madonna of the magazines does not always match the Madonna of the meditations. Occasionally her hair changes colour or length and Maria has to adjust the visualization to accommodate the new version.

She sighs loudly when she hears the door to the

computer room opening. She had hoped to have some time to herself to get this sorted out but, typically, someone needs her.

'We're not disturbing you, are we? D'you mind if we go on this other computer?'

It's Dezzie. Maria feels unworthy. He's tall, three inches taller than her, optimum kissing height. His hair is blond, as soft as a baby's. Although she has never actually touched it, she can see how soft it is by the way it falls over his lightly freckled brow. His eyes are turquoise, clear and innocent. He does have a large nose, but it suits him, and perhaps it puts other girls off. She likes his nose all the more for this.

But despite the wedding plans Madonna insists on making, Dezzie is out of Maria's league. He's too gorgeous for her. A boy as gorgeous as Dezzie can get a real woman with bosoms. He's A list, why would he fancy an A-cup girl?

He smells gorgeous too. Any chance she gets she stands close to him to fill her head with the scent of him. She's even had a surreptitious sniff of his discarded jumper in the staffroom. It isn't strong but it's a lovely fresh smell, like clean laundry.

'Sure, come in.'

Dezzie has brought Brian with him, who is not quite so fragrant. Maria can smell the familiar sour smell from Brian's breath.

'Eeuw, have you been sick Brian?'

Brian gives a laboured nod, his head apparently too heavy for his thin neck. His arms are coiled, awaiting the next impromptu spasm, his wrists bent at impossible angles.

'Yeah but it was only a wee bit sick, wasn't it?' says Dezzie. 'We got a wash and a funky clean shirt. Sorted.

He's now officially Hexton's coolest dude, aren't you?'

'Snappy. Dresser.'

Dezzie laughs. 'Indeed you are, mate. The snappiest.'

Brian nods again and smiles one of his irresistibly cute slow smiles. Maria knows why he's smiling. He's delighted with Dezzie's flattering banter and the fact that he's calling him 'mate'. Dezzie manages to make the tiresome chore of cleaning up vomit sound like a fun adventure. The twang of jealousy Maria feels passes almost instantaneously. And then she has a moment's distress.

'Where are the rest of them?'

'It's OK, don't worry, I haven't deserted them. They wanted to go to Bert's Health and Hygiene class.'

'I'm nearly finished here if you want this computer.'

'No, no, you carry on; you're fine. I know you're engaged in vitally important work. Bert was telling me you're organizing a concert?'

Maria nods and smiles, word travels fast.

'Me and Brian are only in to fiddle about. We'll go on this one.'

Maria would have liked to hand over her keyboard to Dezzie. She'd like to have him sit close to her and perhaps graze his lovely long fingers across hers, but he's already booting up the other computer. She turns back to her Madonna search but she can't concentrate. He obviously doesn't want to disturb her, because he is whispering in Brian's ear.

Sometimes, in order not to be heard by clients, Dezzie whispers to Maria, up close, his lips touching the brim of her ear, as close as a kiss. It makes the hairs on the back of her neck stand up. Even watching him lean in to whisper to Brian gives her a vicarious shiver.

Brian is laughing. They're up to something. She glances towards their monitor but she can't see a thing. Dezzie has pulled it round, making it easier for Brian to see and impossible for Maria.

'What are you looking up?' she tries conversationally. Both Brian and Dezzie seem to find this question funny.

'None. Of. Your. Beeswax,' says Brian's voice machine.

For someone who doesn't actually speak, Brian loves a bit of wordplay.

'Check out the headlamps on that!' says Dezzie, pointing at the screen.

'A. Fine. Pair.'

'C'mon guys, what's going on?' says Maria, feeling increasingly uncomfortable to be left out of the joke.

'Definitely a classy chassis,' says Dezzie.

'For. A. Lassie.'

Brian is laughing before the Dynavox has even finished speaking.

'Are you looking up porn, Brian McEndrick?'

Maria's voice is so high it's off the scale. Her screech startles Brian and his arms jerk like Kermit the Frog. This is all the answer she needs. She leans across and pulls the monitor round.

On screen there's a website with photos of the latest Suzuki motorbike. Maria is confused. Dezzie and Brian are helpless with laughter.

'Ha! You did it! Got her a beauty!'

Dezzie unfolds Brian's arm, holds it above his head and delivers a high five. They giggle for ages, each setting the other off again, until eventually they begin to sober up.

'Sorry Maria, he's only winding you up,' says Dezzie.

Maria presses her hand to her chest, relieved not to have looked upon other women's vaginal lips in the presence of Dezzie. Marriage would be out of the question after that.

'Nice one Brian! She totally fell for it, didn't she?'

'Brian. One. Maria. Nil.'

Maria feels herself blush. There are two ways of looking at this:

1. Dezzie has, albeit unconventionally, empowered Brian, helping him express his mischievous personality in a prank, or

2. He's broken ranks by siding with a client against a member of staff (the most heinous centre crime possible) and purposely made her look foolish.

But seeing as it's Dezzie, this time she'll make an exception and plump for the former. She belatedly joins in their giggling, glad to be included, even if it's in laughing at her.

'Listen, we've interrupted you, we'd better let you get back to your work.'

Dezzie stands behind Brian's chair and makes to wheel him out of the room.

'No, it's OK, honestly. I wasn't making much progress anyway.'

'Oh? Anything I can help with?'

'No, I don't think so. I'm just doing a bit of research for my show.'

'Well, good luck with that,' Dezzie says.

'It's for the Inclusion Initiative.'

Dezzie makes a sympathetic face.

'Say no more.'

'I'm trying to organize a community show. But the most important ingredient has to be community, obviously.'

'Obviously,' says Brian

'Obviously,' agrees Dezzie, nodding and smiling towards Brian.

Maria momentarily wonders if they are taking the piss.

'If I get the community together in a show then I've absolutely satisfied the criteria for the Inclusion Initiative.'

'Absolutely,' says Brian.

Luckily Dezzie doesn't say it too but he can't help but smile when Brian says it. They are taking the piss. Is she being really boring? No, that's paranoid. It's harmless boyish fun. She should be pleased Dezzie and Brian have hit it off so well.

'Well, anything I can do to help.'

'Really, Dezzie?'

'Yeah, sure. Don't put me down for singing or dancing or anything like that, I'm rubbish, but other than that I'll help any way I can. I think it's a brilliant idea, just what we need around here, a bit of showbiz.'

As Dezzie swings Brian's wheelchair round and out of the room he leans in close and whispers in Maria's ear, his lips almost caressing her yielding earlobe.

'We make a great team, don't you think?'

She nods shyly as the boys leave. A grubby hotness spreads up her chest and neck. The tips of her over-heated ears are likely to burst into flames. In one of her lonely unvisited places, Maria feels a moistening.

Chapter 5

Outside, on what had been the church notice board, there's a home-made notice. Written in blue felt-tip pen, on a piece of A4, inside a clear plastic cover to keep the rain out, it says:

> *why not come in for a nice sit down, a cup of tea and a blether?*
> *come as you please,*
> *come one, come all,*
> *come away in!*

Alice sticks her head round the door. She knows this church. Used to come here when they first moved to Hexton, all the wives did, it was expected. Many moons ago.

The new guy has decimated the place. He's shoved all the pews to either side and has made his workshop right in the middle of the floor. Like the way the butcher's shop used to be, there's sawdust everywhere, on the floor, settled on the rail to the altarpiece, flying in the air; she can see it floating in the beams of orange and yellow and purple light that stream through the stained glass. Thin parings and planings of wood, pale yellow curls, lie on the floor like a baby's first haircut.

'Hello!'

He's small for a man, the same height as her. He has a manly broad-shouldered walk, but light-footed, careful, like an animal. He must be strong; he's carrying planks of wood as lightly as if he were carrying a snooker cue. A young fella, maybe forty, not handsome but good teeth, clean brown hair, nice arse. But married, big wedding ring on his finger. You don't see that so much nowadays. Nice that, old-fashioned.

'Nice to see you.'

Forward, cheeky, fancies himself as a charmer. She's never seen him before in her life.

'Do I know you?'

That stops him in his tracks but he's still smiling.

'Don't think so, but you're welcome to come in.'

'You've decimated this place.'

'Sorry?'

'I used to come here.'

'They told me it was unused for the last six years.'

'Did you get it from the council?'

'Yes.'

'Are you a joiner?'

'Yes.'

'My kitchen cupboard door is hanging off.'

'Sorry love, not that kind of joiner, I don't do homers.' He turns back to his planks of wood. He's making a dresser, big old-fashioned thing, lovely piece of wood.

'So, where's the tea?'

'Sorry?'

'Nice cup of tea it says outside.'

'Oh right, I'll just put the kettle on. Sorry but I've no

63

biscuits, I only stuck the sign up ten minutes ago. I wasn't expecting anyone as quick as this but that's great, come away in. What's your name?'

'Alice.'

'Ray. Pleased to meet you.'

He goes off through the vestry into the kitchen and leaves Alice alone in the dismantled church.

Underneath the sawdust, it still feels like a church. Except for the pews being moved everything is still here, all present and correct. The oak pulpit is intact, all its carving preserved, the windows still in one piece. It's amazing, in the hellhole that Hexton has become, that the church hasn't been stripped or set on fire.

He comes back with the tea.

'I don't know what you take.'

'Milk and two.'

'Same as me.'

He smiles again. Does he fancy her? There's more than twenty years between them. Maybe he has a thing for older women. He offers a cigarette. How does he know she smokes?

'Is it OK to smoke in here?'

'It's not a church any more. They de-blessed it, or whatever it is that they do, six years ago. Don't worry, we're not desecrating it.'

She had said decimated when she first spoke to him. Alice is embarrassed at getting the word wrong, but he doesn't show any signs of remembering.

'So if it's not a church you could have a snooker table in here.'

'Could do.'

With the cigarette in his mouth he pulls out a pack of cards and shuffles them. He spreads them out in his hands and offers her one.

'Pick a card, any card.'

Alice is reluctant but he thrusts them at her until she takes one.

'Don't look at it. Just hold it.'

He touches her hand, restrains her from looking at it.

'Now, think of a card, just picture it in your mind.'

The Jack of Clubs is the first card she thinks of. That's what he's expecting her to say.

'Now, what's the card you're thinking of?'

She has to try to think of another one quickly.

'The Queen of Hearts.'

He takes her hand and turns the card over. It's the Queen of Hearts.

'Good trick.'

Alice doesn't know what else to say. She says nothing and he shuffles his cards. Time passes. They both finish their tea.

'So, what're you selling?'

'Nothing. This is my workshop.'

'Are you trying to save souls?'

Ray smiles.

'Nope.'

'Then why did you put the notice up? Why do you want people to come in?'

'I'm going to be in here myself all day, working away. I'll get lonely.'

'Will you?'

People, even people her age, don't admit to lone-liness. They'd rather admit to being a thief than to being lonely. Maybe she's been too hard on him. Now he looks embarrassed.

'Och, yeah, a wee bit, sometimes.'

He's a young guy, what's he got to be lonely about?

Alice, astonished, hears herself say, 'Yeah, I know what you mean.'

'Next!' Maria calls, trying hard not to sound like a jaded 1930s Broadway producer. But jaded she is. It isn't that there's no talent in Hexton; the problem is that there's too much and it isn't self-selecting. Those who possessed ability are often shy and reluctant to perform, while those who are spectacularly untalented are blissfully oblivious and line up to make fools of themselves. Sifting through the dross is time-consuming, exhausting and has already used up Maria's limited reserve of tact.

'Yeah, thanks, eh . . .' Maria consults her list. 'Thanks Gerry, we'll let you know.'

'Does that mean I'm in?'

'Eh, not sure yet, we'll get back to you.'

'Well, when's the rehearsals? I'll need to know. I'm a bus driver; I'll have to sort out my shifts.'

'To be honest I'm not sure we've got space for another rapper, we've already seen quite a few today.'

'Aye, but have you seen anybody else who can do this?' Gerry gets down on the floor and prepares to spin on his head, except that he can't. He tries four times, the last time falling forward and squashing his nose on his square of linoleum.

'True, we haven't seen anybody do that.'

'You tryin' to be funny?' says Gerry, somewhat nasally. 'Get it up you,' he mutters as he leaves with his rolled lino under his arm.

'Charming!' Maria tuts.

Marianne agrees.

Marianne Bowman is the headmistress of Hexton High and has volunteered to help with today's open auditions. A career woman, Marianne is conventional in that she is of traditional headmistress age: an immaculately conserved forty-something, she has her glasses dangling from a string of pink pearls. She wears knee-length tweed skirts and chunky heels. Judging from the smell, she appears to steep herself in a tub of Giorgio every morning. Before addressing a remark to Marianne, Maria turns aside to breathe, trying not to fill her lungs and nose with the heavy perfume.

It was this headmistressy tweediness that initially distanced Maria from Marianne, but in fact Marianne has been terrific. As soon as Maria put the idea to her of a community concert on a Madonna theme, she was immediately behind it. Within a week she had organized the school choir into an Eighties, Nineties and Noughties Queen of Pop tribute. Marianne also had her schoolkids go out and poster the neighbourhood to advertise the auditions which she is generously hosting in the school assembly hall.

'You could have the place for rehearsals as well if we weren't about to get our major refurb. And not before time, we've waited years. This place is falling apart.'

The question of rehearsal space is not one that until now Maria has considered. Bert won't let her have the assembly hall; she knows that without asking. The evening concert is one thing, but daytime use is going to be pretty much out of the question. Apart from it being the clients' gym and dining hall, classes are scheduled in there all day every day. This is a problem that Maria will have to solve, but not now, her head is bursting with it all. Audition day has been exhausting but it certainly hasn't been fruitless.

There are good singers aplenty. This in itself is a problem: who to choose and who to reject? Marianne, who is, from the outset, more organized than Maria, has devised a system: after they have performed the hopefuls are filed in one of two boxes, Accept or Reject. The difficulty is that the Accept box is brimming over.

'Maria, we can't have them all, there just isn't time. If we take everyone you've put in the Accept box the show'll run till four in the morning. We'll have to throw buckets of water over the audience to keep them awake.'

'Well OK, which of them are we going to reject? You tell me.'

'God knows. Anyway, we've still loads to get through. Who's next?'

Maria consults the list.

'The Victory Singers.'

'The hunky minister?'

'Pastor McKenzie, yes.'

'Oh goody.'

Maria rolls her eyes, 'OK, wheel them in. Next!'

Pastor McKenzie and four of his flock enter.

'Sorry, we weren't sure if we were next.'

Maria doesn't trust him: he's too handsome to be a cleric, and he's always smiling.

Pastor McKenzie is as slim and tall as a male model in a catalogue. His suit looks neat on his broad shoulders. As he enters he undoes the three buttons on his jacket, which now falls open informally to display his trim waist and slim hips. His legs are long, his feet are big and his backside is extremely tidy for a middle-aged man. He probably works out, and his blue-black hair has got to be dyed. His dark eyebrows and slick sideburns seem indecent on a reverend. All he needs is a thin moustache and a watch chain and he'd be a riverboat card sharp.

Despite being kept waiting almost three hours, McKenzie's smile lights up the room. Always in a good mood, he is never less than radiant. The man seems to emanate joy.

'Thank you for your patience, Pastor McKenzie,' says a coyly smiling Marianne. 'Please, in your own time, begin.'

So far the headmistress has been hard-nosed and no nonsense, but now she's way too gushy for Maria's liking.

They begin, the pastor tapping his foot and snapping his fingers to keep the beat.

'A one, two, a one two three four:

> *Give me oil in my lamp keep it burning,*
> *Give me oil in my lamp I pray*
> *Give me oil in my lamp keep it burning,*
> *Keep it burning till the break of day!'*

It has to be conceded that the pastor has a more than passable voice. As he conducts his choristers they seem to become charged with his burning exuberance. They smile and click their fingers too. Soon, the rhythm has infected their hips; they're nodding their heads and clicking their fingers and shaking their booties in fervour. Filled with confidence, they sing with gusto.

> *'Sing Hosanna,*
> *Sing Hosanna,*
> *Sing Hosanna to the King of Kings!'*

Unfortunately the King of Kings has not seen fit to bless the pastor's followers with the gift of music. They're tone-deaf, an enthusiastic rabble.

When they finish, they are laughing and triumphantly swapping high fives. It takes Pastor McKenzie to put his finger to his lips to restore their former modest demeanour.

'Well,' says Marianne, not quite speechless, 'that was certainly something!'

'Thank you, Miss Bowman,' the pastor nods diffidently, 'Christ be with you.'

'Yeah, we'll let you know, Pastor,' Maria says in a voice that should leave him in no doubt as to what it is that they'll let him know. His immaculate eyebrows are momentarily snagged, but the beaming smile quickly makes a comeback.

'Oh, I don't think we should be too hasty,' says Marianne as soon as they've left the hall.

'But they were terrible!'

'Yes, I know, but . . . Actually, I find myself unable to dispute that,' says Marianne, smirking.

'They were God-awful!'

'Maria: Inclusion Initiative? Surely it's your duty to encompass all sections of community life, including the religious.'

'You only want him in because you fancy him.'

'Again,' says Marianne, this time openly chuckling, 'I am unable to dispute that. But the fact is that the Victory Mission is the only religious group left in Hexton, you *have* to include them.'

Maria lets out a huffy sigh. She knows she's beat. Standards are crashing and they haven't even finished the auditions yet.

'Or no promotion for yoohoo!' Marianne sings

gleefully as she files the paperwork in the overflowing Accept box.

The next time Alice sticks her head round the door of the church it's a different matter. He's not the poor lonely soul he's made himself out to be. He's whittling away at his sideboard while three young neds sit on a pew, smoking and carrying on. He, the Ray fella, is telling jokes.

'Here, I've got one for you: why do women wear white wedding dresses? To match the other kitchen appliances.'

The neds are snorting their approval.

'No bad eh?' says Ray, laughing along with them until he spots her.

'Alice, come away in!'

He makes out he's pleased to see her, but the Young Ones squirm the way Young Ones do when confronted with a senior citizen.

She comes in, but hesitantly, she's had trouble with the Young Ones before, at the post office, if not these actual Ones then similar Ones. She used to know all the Young Ones in the area, she knew their parents, but she hardly recognizes a soul in the street now.

Ray is as friendly as ever which is a bit embarrassing in front of these hooligans.

'A wee cup of tea, hen? The kettle's just boiled; I was giving the lads a cuppa.'

Alice thinks about it a minute. She should stick around and make sure they're not going to steal from him.

'Aye, go on then, if I'm not keeping you off your work.'

As she says this she stares pointedly at the Young

71

Ones. They *are* keeping him off his work. They should be out looking for jobs.

'I'll get it myself, Ray; I can see you're busy there.'

'Cheers hen!'

The neds seems to find this exchange funny. They're sniggering. With a screwed-up face and a nod in their direction Alice silently questions Ray: what's going on? Why are they sniggering, in fact, why are these neds here? A look quickly flits across Ray's face and, thank God, he seems to realize now. He'll ruin his wee business if he encourages these neds to come into his place. But this is apparently not the realization he has reached.

'Sorry, Alice. Lads, can I introduce you to my friend Alice? This is Bob, Aldo, and, Gerry is it?'

The ned nods.

'Aye, Gerry, right. The lads have been keeping me going, telling me jokes. Mind you, I don't think they're the kind of jokes you'd like, Alice, a nice lady like yourself.'

She sees what he's doing. He knows that they'll try to take the piss out of a pensioner; it's what Young Ones nowadays do. He's trying to tell them not to, but it won't work. She doesn't like it; these Young Ones are taking advantage of his good nature, he'll come a cropper. Ray's loneliness puts him at risk. It doesn't do to let them know you're weak.

'I'll take another cup if you're making one, milk and three,' says the one called Gerry but he doesn't look at her, he's more interested in making his pals laugh. He's showing off, ripping the pish out of an OAP. Without looking at him directly she takes the mug from his hand.

'Never heard of the word "please"?'

They all snigger, including Ray.

'Aye OK, please.'

One nil to Alice. As she's walking away she hears him add, 'Nan.'

He wasn't quick enough to think of it at the time. Or maybe not brave enough. Everyone laughs again, Ray as much as the rest of them, and Alice feels her face burn.

'I'm not your nan and I'm not here to run about after you. Get your own tea.'

This time Ray doesn't join in the laughter – *now* does he understand what they're playing at?

'Gerry's only kidding you on, Alice,' Ray says, and she hears the reproach in his voice.

He's taking sides with the Young Ones; he's actually ganging up with them against a senior citizen.

Alice is preparing to leave, she won't put up with this, when she hears another of them, the tall stupid-looking one, Aldo, openly abuse her.

'I don't know what that is but it needs a right good ironing.'

This is intolerable; this is what comes of bringing neds in off the street.

Nobody laughs this time. Big Stupid Aldo looks to his cronies for support for his witticism, who in turn look to Ray. Ray puts his tools down. He moves to the pew, sits beside Aldo and puts an arm around him.

'Hey, bit a respect, eh?' says Ray gently.

'Aye, man. You've taken that too far,' agrees Gerry.

Bob nods.

Aldo either pretends not to know what he means or is too thick to understand, so Ray elucidates.

'The thing is, Aldo, Alice is one of my mates. I've known her longer than I've known you, so if I have to choose I'd choose her. Don't make me do that, Aldo.'

'I'm no making you do anything!' says Aldo in a thin scared voice.

'Well, see, if you give Alice, or any of my pals, any bother? See that two by two?'

Still with his arm lightly around Aldo's shoulders, Ray indicates a long narrow piece of wood propped against the wall.

'I'll have to shove that so far up your arse you'll be using the splinters as a toothpick. D'you get me, Aldo? See where I'm coming from, man?'

Aldo doesn't speak, he seems unable to, but he nods his head.

'Well, that's us sorted then,' says Ray with a satisfied smile. He gives Aldo a gentle pat on the back.

'Right Alice, you sit down hen and give us your patter, Aldo here'll stick the kettle on. Milk and two for me please Aldo, and Alice as well, she's the same as me.'

Chapter 6

So far the show is turning out to be top-heavy with singers. They're good, but too much of the same thing will be boring. For the last four weeks, Blue Group has been role-playing a familiar scenario in their Wednesday afternoon drama workshop. This has potential as a sketch sandwiched between other acts. If they can get it right it'll give Maria's clients a prominent profile in the show. But this is going to require stamina and Zen-inspired patience of everyone. She is confident they can do it, much more confident than they are.

Clients at the centre are aware that they're different, that other people are smarter, but although there is often frustration, this isn't generally a cause for sadness or feeling inferior. Maria has learned a lot about dignity and humility from her clients.

When she first got this job she called her girlfriends and told them how proud she was of the work she was doing now. At last she had found her vocation. At the time they were all supportive, but last year in Inverness Anna said things, horrible things, that have haunted Maria ever since.

They'd got together for Bethan's hen night. Colette and Anna were already married by then, Colette to a merchant banker and Anna to a television executive producer. Bethan's wedding, to the modest forestry worker Colin, was to be a milestone. There was already a long list of such events: their housewarming party in the Kelvin Street flat where Bethan met Colin, Anna's engagement party, Colette's wedding, Anna's wedding, Colette's baby's christening. But for Maria, Bethan getting married would be the most significant milestone so far. She'd be the only one left of the Kelvin Street Kids who could be described with so many 'un' words: unaccompanied, unattached, unwed.

She tried to stay positive, enthusiastically telling the girls about a new art class she had initiated at the centre. Colette was pregnant again at the time and therefore off the sauce, but Anna was hammering it and it was beginning to show.

'My cousin George goes to one of those places you work in,' said Anna. 'It's a shame.'

'Is it? Why's that then, Anna?' Maria let a reproving tone creep into her voice.

'What I *mean* is it's a shame that those places are all the provision there is. Short classes and long tea breaks, it's hardly a stimulating or meaningful way for anyone to spend their lives, is it?'

Anna has changed since Kelvin Street. Now she's a big-shot publicity guru in London. She's used to speaking her mind and getting her own way.

'Leave it, Anna,' said Colette.

'No, Colette,' said Maria, quite capable of holding her ground. 'I'm interested in Anna's perspective. I'm keen to find out what Anna actually knows about caring for people.'

'Oh excuse me, I know, and *you* know, that my cousin George gets parked there during the day to take the strain off his mum and dad and prevent him going into care. I know you're doing a great job providing a cheap babysitting service. You're saving the taxpayer a fortune: Saint Maria of the Blessed Finger-Painting.'

Colette and Bethan were quick to jump to Maria's defence. The next morning Anna apologized tearfully, profusely and repeatedly. Of course Maria accepted her apology, but the damage was done. It was clear that Anna had no respect for Maria's vocation, and if anyone felt pity for anyone else it was the rest of the Kelvin Street Kids for Maria.

But Maria is convinced her work is relevant. Clients might not be undertaking PhDs but they enjoy their day at the centre. It *is* stimulating. It *is* meaningful. To a hotshot London-based publicity guru it might only be setting a table or writing a poem, but these tasks are challenging and therefore rewarding to someone with fewer abilities. So, with Anna's sneering words still ringing in her ears, Maria does everything she can to stretch her clients.

'OK, from the top. Jane, you're the customer, and Martin, you're the shopkeeper.'

Maria claps her hands directorially; if she had a riding crop she'd whip her thigh with it.

'Everybody ready? And, action!'

Martin takes the floor. He immediately begins miming carrying a heavy box and filling shelves from it. Some of the shelves are taller than he is, forcing him to reach up on his tiptoes. When he empties the box he stores it carefully away and begins ticking off items from an invisible clipboard. His face is creased in a frown; he looks worried, perhaps about discrepancies in his shop stock.

Martin enjoys drama workshop much more than any of the other Blue Group clients. He takes his role seriously and tries hard to bring his character to life by getting inside the skin of the shopkeeper. It is a joy to have a client like Martin. He's tremendously sociable and throws himself wholeheartedly into every activity. When he loves something he loves it passionately – music, sport, swimming, drama group, breasts – and he embraces life with an enviable lack of inhibition. Every opportunity he gets, Martin will look at and attempt to feel breasts.

Maria thinks that Martin is different from other men, not because his fascination for mammaries is excessive, but because he doesn't attempt to conceal it. Maria also suspects, no, actually, she's sure, that Martin was moved to Blue Group because of her A-cup status. Her lack of rack might be less of a distraction for him.

Having concluded his stocktaking, Martin commences checking the contents of the till, playing his part with conviction and confidence. Martin's elderly parents, who appear to be almost unaware that Martin has a disability, hero-worship him. They find him endlessly fascinating, funny and charming, which, for the most part, he is. Although he's a small tubby lad, his self-image is of a movie star whose rightful place is in the limelight. It is for Martin's sake that Maria has kept the Wednesday afternoon drama workshop going, always hoping that his enthusiasm might infect the others. So far it hasn't worked.

Jane, supposed to be playing the customer, dithers on the sidelines.

'Jane, what is it?' says Maria, frustrated.

It has been going so well.

'What am I supposed to say?'

'Just say what you say when you go into a shop.'

Jane thinks about this while everyone waits and then she says, 'I'm not allowed to go into a shop by myself.'

'I'm not allowed to go into a shop,' concurs Fiona, casually leafing through a magazine. 'Mum says I've not to, that bastard at the end of the street steals my money, Mum says.'

Fiona licks her fingers every time she turns a page so that the corners become damp and dog-eared, curled at the edges like an ancient manuscript.

'Yes, thanks for that Fiona,' says Maria briskly. 'Anyway, Jane, let's pretend that you are allowed. Improvise, just make it up, OK?'

They begin again. Martin goes through his elaborate mime with the heavy box. As Jane enters the performance space Martin puts down his clipboard with studied calm and greets his customer.

'Good morning madam, can I help you?'

Jane hesitates. She seems to be searching the invisible shelves and Martin, following her gaze, turns and scrutinizes them too.

'Can I get a shot now?' says Fiona, bored already.

'Hold on a minute Fiona, let Jane get her turn.'

Jane stops looking at the shelves and stares at her feet.

'See anything you fancy, madam?' says Martin.

Jane shakes her head.

'Jane, what is it you want to buy?' asks the director.

'Don't know.'

'Well think something up, what about a Mars bar?'

'Not fair!' cries Fiona, 'I'm going to buy a Mars bar!'

'I don't like Mars bars,' says Jane quietly.

There are few things that Jane likes, and even those she does like probably scare her.

She was not always like this. Jane was once an intrepid adventurer in her spare time. She and her husband spent their holidays crossing deserts, canoeing rivers and climbing mountains. That was until she fell off a mountain. Without the recent improvements in medical technology she would have died, but a thin sheet of titanium has been patched over the part of her brain that got pulped.

'Well what do you like?'

'Don't know.'

'She's rubbish Maria, it's my turn now.'

'Not yet Fiona, Jane can you . . .'

Jane turns back towards Martin.

'Mars bar.'

'Certainly madam,' says Martin, making an elaborate mime of putting a Mars bar in a paper bag. He holds the corners of the invisible bag between the pincers of his thumb and forefinger, twisting it, tossing it up and over, around itself, several times.

'Anything else I can help you with today madam?'

Jane grabs at the imaginary bag and turns to leave.

'That'll be fifty-two pence, thank you madam,' Martin says, holding out his hand.

'That's it Jane, give him the money.'

Martin takes the mime money and rings it up on his till before returning to his stocktaking.

'Good. Well done!' Maria says.

Jane scurries back to her seat. Before she fell off the mountain, when Jane was not being an intrepid adventurer, she was a nurse.

'It's my shot now.'

'In a minute, Fiona. Now, everyone, what do we think of that?'

'Crap,' says Fiona.

'Compelling. Drama,' says Brian.

It would be wrong to say that Brian has a sarcastic tongue. He has an ineffectual lolling mouth muscle that only frustrates him because it refuses to work properly. He does, however, have a ruthlessly incisive left-hand middle finger. This he uses, when the spasms allow him, to poke at the Dynavox touch screen mounted on his chair. The regulated monotone voice of his machine sometimes makes it difficult to know when Brian is taking the piss but in this case there can be little doubt.

Maria chooses to ignore their negativity.

'Now, let's take it on a bit further. Remember last week when we said there could be some conflict?'

All except Fiona nod their heads.

'Well, let's think of ways we can expand the plot by bringing in a bit of conflict. Now when I say conflict I mean trouble, something exciting that makes it more interesting. Successfully negotiating the purchase of a Mars bar is hardly high drama, is it? OK, never mind. Martin, you're always good at thinking up ideas and you're pretty good at making trouble. Can you think of a way we can make it more exciting?'

'She could be a robber!'

'Good.'

'She could steal the Mars bar and I could shoot her!'

Martin mimes aiming a rifle and firing it at Jane.

'Doof! Doof!'

Jane is alarmed; the familiar expression of panic crosses her face.

'I'm not a thief!'

'No, Jane,' say Maria gently, 'we're not talking about you. We mean the character you're playing. What did we call the customer last week? Mrs Jones, was it?'

'I'm not married.'

'I know that but . . .'

'Divorced.'

This is a painful subject for Jane and one that frequently makes her cry. When the consultant said she might never walk or talk again Jane's husband left the hospital that afternoon. Despite the tremendous progress she has made, she has never seen him since.

'Now Jane, please let's not start that. We're having a nice time this afternoon.'

Jane does not cry although some saliva escapes from the side of her mouth.

'I'm Mrs Jones, not her,' says Fiona.

'Now, be fair Fiona. You played Mrs Jones last week. It's Jane's turn today.'

'So who's my husband? Is it still Brian?'

'No, Brian was the shopkeeper.'

'He's my husband and he's to kiss me!'

'Fiona I don't think . . .'

But Fiona has taken the bull by the horns, the boy by the lips, and planted a ferocious kiss on Brian's mouth. Brian is taken by surprise. The rest of them giggle or gasp. Martin jumps up and down.

'Me! Me!' he cries, 'I'll be her husband!'

'Fiona, leave Brian alone! Fiona!'

Maria tries gently to disengage the kissing couple but Fiona wriggles away from her while maintaining a fierce clamp on Brian's lips.

'Fiona stop it! For goodness sake, Brian's half your age, leave him alone!'

Fiona, insulted, comes up for air.

'He likes it!'

'Do you, Brian?'

All eyes are on Brian. The middle finger of his left hand hovers provocatively over his keyboard. He begins to lift his head in preparation for a nod or a shake, it's hard to tell, but instead he throws up.

'See what you've done now, Fiona?'

'He's my husband!'

'You don't have a husband,' says Maria.

'*You* don't have a husband. And neither does she!' shouts Fiona, pointing an accusing finger at Jane.

'Behave. You're upsetting everyone with your carry-on. Look at what you've done to poor Jane.'

Jane is quietly crying now.

'*You* behave!' screams Fiona.

She launches a punch at Maria that glances off her shoulder. Maria dodges out of range of Fiona's fists but she comes after her.

This is not a problem. Maria has been trained to deal with this situation. The thing to do is not to retaliate, that's illegal. The thing to do is direct Fiona's attention away from the subject of her anger, i.e. Maria, and towards a pleasant and peaceful activity.

'Fiona, do you want a packet of crisps?'

Fiona stops.

'Yes.'

'What do we say?'

'Yes please.'

The soothing effect of the crisps is immediate. To calm things down a bit and because everyone has been so good this afternoon, Maria rewards them all with a bag. Once they have sorted out who wants salt and vinegar and who wants cheese and onion, everyone sits contentedly munching while Maria wipes the vomit from Brian's clothes. These kinds of outbursts are commonplace, easily managed and quickly forgotten. But Fiona, possibly feeling some remorse, wants to make amends.

'I don't want to be Mrs Jones,' she says, tongue-sweeping her mouth for crisp crumbs. 'Jane can be Mrs Jones, I can sing a song. I'll sing "Donal Og".'

'That's very kind of you Fiona, I'm sure Jane appreciates the gesture but . . .'

Even while Maria is still talking Fiona begins to sing. A love song, soppy and sentimental, the tune is unfamiliar to Maria but she remembers the words well enough from studying the poem at school.

'It is late last night the dog was speaking of you;
the snipe was speaking of you in her deep marsh.
It is you are the lonely bird through the woods;
and that you may be without a mate until you
*   find me.'*

Fiona sits amongst Blue Group with her head tilted back and her eyes closed. Her hair, black and messy, curly and beautiful, flows to her waist. At key points in the song her eyeballs roll behind squeezed-shut lids, her chubby cheeks jiggling slightly on the high notes, her full lips stretching wide to accommodate the beautiful sound.

This is not commonplace. Maria and the other members of Blue Group have never heard Fiona sing before, and are so stunned by the beauty of her voice that they forget to eat their crisps. Or perhaps they don't want to make any rustling sound. Maria sees that Jane is crying again, tears plopping into her crisp bag.

Maria pulls Jane to her and wraps her arms around her. She rubs her back, her palm working up and down Jane's spine.

> 'When I go by myself to the Well of Loneliness,
> I sit down and I go through my trouble;
> when I see the world and do not see my boy,
> he that has an amber shade in his hair.'

She continues to do this throughout Fiona's mesmerizing rendition of 'Donal Og'. She can already feel her jumper soaked with Jane's tears and saliva.

Chapter 7

Ray has wired up the speakers and placed them facing out the way at either side of the church altar. This is where he'll get the best acoustic effect. Now to choose what to play. It's important that he christens the place with something appropriate. Sacred would be best, seeing as it is, or was, a church. And yet he wants it to be cheery and celebratory. Ah yes, he thinks as he rifles through his extensive Mozart collection, the very dab: 'Exultate, Jubilate': Exult! Rejoice! In Hexton terms: cheer up and straighten your miserable face.

And indeed within the opening bars his miserable face does miraculously straighten. Despite the nightmare of the last years, he feels exultant. Mozart is working his usual genius. Ray raises his awl like a conductor's baton as he anticipates the singer's entrance. Repeatedly she advises him to cheer up, but it is not so much what she sings as the way she sings it that he finds so irresistibly uplifting. Mozart has given her a brilliantly fun and inspired vocal workout, her beautiful voice trilling up and down, filling the church space like an orchestra of birdsong. He can't help but smile, and here in Hexton it's OK to smile.

No-one in Hexton knows him; they don't care that he feels good. They won't think he's insensitive if he rejoices in life. That's why he moved here, that and the fact that he neglected the business so much that this is all he can now get.

Hexton is a designated Initiative Area, an Area of Priority Treatment and a recipient of the European Social Fund. Bedecked with every badge of deprivation and poverty, it wears them like a blinged-up chav.

No-one wants to live here or even nearby. Hexton is isolated from the city, hidden away from foreign visitors, and becoming more so. This is one of the few places left in Britain where the green belt is actually widening; where factory yards are being reclaimed by weeds, turning from rust and muck to green again. Flat-capped granddads point to the emerging meadowlands and say wistfully, 'Once this was all factory land.'

So that local people might be offered credit or employment in the city, local government has tried to eradicate the stigma of the area by the revisionist tactic of simply changing the name. Hexton has been broken down into smaller areas, grouping four or five streets together and calling them something cute and rural like Pine Walk or Pheasant's Close. But no-one has ever heard of Pheasant's Close, and eventually locals have to make the shameful admission that it is actually the housing scheme formerly known as Hexton.

The council does try. Embarrassed by the shocking health statistics, it throws money at well-intentioned high-target, low-expectation projects. These at least look good on paper.

When the factory shut down the butchers, the dairy

and the ironmongers went with it. The minimarts were not far behind. Within a radius of four miles, excluding the all-night garage that sells milk, fresh produce is no longer available in Hexton. The council has set up, as part of the Hexton Healthy Heart Campaign, a mobile shop: a van which goes round the streets selling fruit and vegetables at subsidized prices. Business has always been slow although there is no shortage of customers. Twice the drivers have been sacked, caught selling contraband sausages and duty-free fags. There are unsubstantiated rumours that, like the countless ice-cream vans that ply their trade around the neglected streets, the Healthy Heart mobile shop also sells hash, eckies and whiz.

To Ray, or any business willing to operate from Hexton, the Government offers sweeteners: start-up grants, employment grants, interest-free loans, preferential rates for business equipment, free rent of premises, rates rebates, tax breaks. Yet, apart from Ray and a few corner shops, there are no businesses.

The disused church is a long way from the smart custom-built carpentry workshop he used to have. This place is far too big. Along with the church there's a kitchen, a meeting hall, an office and various committee rooms. There's even a bell tower he hasn't explored yet, with bells and everything. On the pews he's pushed back to make space for his workbench lie red leatherette hymnals inlaid with a flaking golden cross. They're piled on top of each other, ready and waiting for the congregation to return. The sad little books have been softened by time and dampness, the page edges faded to a dirty grey from all the fingers and thumbs that have leafed through them, searching. Searching for what?

The foosty smell pervades all the rooms. There are curtains limp with dirt, broken-backed chairs. There are shelves of dusty books, old Penguin novels as well as religious ones. On the walls, the green paint bubbling with rot, there are small tapestry samplers with quotations, *Love thy Neighbour*, *God is Love*. And a longer one, *Yea though I walk through the Valley of the Shadow of Death I shall fear no Evil*. The whole place has a musty deadness to it that comforts and spooks him in equal measure.

Ray understands death.

But his favourite aphorism is in the kitchen. Beside the yellowing painted cupboards with the brown-stained mugs and the tea towels with printed recipes for scones, there is a postcard which reads,

> *I only work here because:*
> *I'm too old for a paper round,*
> *Too young for a pension and*
> *Too tired for an affair.*

This makes him smile; perhaps those are his reasons too. He's rattling around in this scary old church all on his own. He had to let the four other carpenters, the two apprentices and the part-time administrator go when he ran out of money and customers.

After the liquidators came in he was lucky to get out with his tool bag. Hexton council gave him this place for free. He can make furniture here and sell it; it's the only way he can keep himself in work. He has to go on working just to keep his brain active, to stop the horrible memories coming back, and carpentry is all he knows.

He doesn't have a plan other than to keep going. He

stopped making plans when he realized the futility of planning, of dreaming, of hoping and wishing. He'll make furniture, what else can he do?

Maria has arrived to hold auditions at Autumn House, run by the Elderly Forum. She curses herself for having forgotten her diary and with it the name of the woman she is to meet, Jean is it? She's met her before several times and can picture exactly what she looks like: a slim woman with white hair she wears in a ponytail. But she cannot remember her bloody name. Jean, or was it Betty?

'Good afternoon,' she says confidently to the aged yet fully made-up receptionist. 'I represent the Hexton Community Madonna Extravaganza. I have an appointment with Jean.'

All women in Hexton over the age of sixty are called Jean. There is the occasional Margaret or Betty but for the most part you can't go wrong with Jean.

'And you are?' asks the receptionist somewhat imperiously.

'Maria Whyte, Community Development.'

The snooty old bag is examining the appointments book, probably too vain to wear glasses, her nose almost touching the page. Maria tries to get a look at it upside down to see the name but the old dear is hogging it.

'I'm afraid I don't have a Jean.'

'You're joking! This place is heaving with Jeans, surely.'

The receptionist smiles and shakes her head. 'Not on this list.'

'Margaret? Betty?'

Another gleeful smirk.

'I'm sorry, no.'

'D'you have my name in your book?'

'Eh . . .'

The receptionist goes back to studying the appointments diary.

'Oh yes, we have you down, don't worry.'

'And is there a name beside mine?'

Again she studies.

'Yes.'

'And that name is?'

'Alice. Alice O'Connor. Alice is the centre's Events Co-ordinator.'

How could she have forgotten that? Alice. Gallus Alice. Gallus is a word more often used to describe a cheeky sassy teenager. This is obviously where her memory device has let her down. As gallus as Alice undoubtedly is, she's no teenager.

'In that case may I speak with Gall . . . with Alice O'Connor please?'

'Certainly miss, just one moment.'

'You're new, aren't you?' asks Maria, intent on reporting such incompetence up the line to management.

'Yes, I am!' says the delighted receptionist. 'Jean's away, Jean McGowan that is, to her sister's funeral. I'm filling in.'

'I see, and what's your name?'

'It's Jean, Jean Scott, pleased to meet you.'

Alice O'Connor, in full Moulin Rouge costume, is a strikingly glamorous figure. It turns out that not only is she the centre's Events Co-ordinator but she's also the founder and leading light of the Golden Belles, an all-singing all-dancing entertainment troupe who tour elderly day centres.

'The audiences aren't great,' Alice tells Maria. 'God

91

love them, most of them don't know their own name.'

Alice has to be in her sixties, maybe older, yet she wears bright red lipstick and smokes menthol fags. Her white hair is scraped back into a high ponytail which is surprisingly long and thick. She's a bit skinny but she has fantastic legs and despite the damage years of smoking have obviously done to her skin, her wide cheekbones support a strikingly chiselled nose and jawline.

The Golden Belles are first to try out. They are, unfortunately, brimming with talent, as are most of the other acts. The Glee Club ensemble and a rather charming magician with rabbits are the ones that stand out. Maria wonders how the hell she's going to fit them all in.

'The big problem is rehearsal space,' she tells Alice when the auditions are over. Autumn House has loads of underused space, but Alice doesn't take the bait.

'Forget it. I can't offer you space here. The committee won't wear it.'

Maria's used to knock-backs, she's not giving up that easily.

'It's frustrating. There's so much talent in Hexton, loads of good singers and of course, the Golden Belles. Your act is bound to steal the show. It'll probably be the headline act.'

Alice is apparently not susceptible to flattery or the veiled bribe of top billing.

'We have our own space here,' she says. 'We can rehearse till the cows come home; it's your other acts that need it. We can't have them here, not after the business with the shitey nappy.'

Maria can't argue with the shitey nappy and would prefer not to dwell on it, so now she tries pleading.

'It's so sad that we have all this talent without the available resources to nurture it.'

The Golden Belle remains unmoved.

Mention the kiddies. All old ladies love kiddies.

'It's the kiddies I feel for,' says Maria, 'the wee souls, singing their hearts out.'

Alice doesn't flinch. The woman must have a heart of stone.

Time to apply a little more leverage. Alice made a tactical error earlier when she admitted her dissatisfaction with the elderly day centres circuit. She's hungry for larger, more appreciative audiences. Maria's only hope now is to exploit this.

'I just don't know what we're going to do,' she says disingenuously.

Now that they have retired, the Elderly Forum members no longer practise their crafts as plumbers and teachers and bakers. They no longer command respect for their knowledge, wisdom and experience. They shuffle to and from the post office invisible to all except themselves, gradually fading in the community memory and consciousness as their bodies fade towards death. They have lost the attention of everyone younger than themselves.

Maria can't look Alice in the face with what she's about to say, but for the good of the community, the whole community, she must say it.

'If I can't find anywhere I'll have to cancel the show.'

'So cancel,' says Alice, shrugging her shoulders.

This afternoon pensioners have queued patiently for hours in the corridor in full make-up and costume, waiting to audition. They want this show to happen, they want it bad, Alice and the Golden Belles want it most of all.

'You don't really want that to happen, do you Alice?'

'No, and neither do you, so don't start the amateur dramatics and the blackmail with me, my dear. It won't work.'

Maria is stuck for a comeback. There doesn't seem to be anything left to say, she's tried everything: brought out her big guns, threatened to cancel and still Alice won't relent.

'You'll find somewhere else,' says Alice, softer now. 'Have you tried the church?'

'You mean the Victory Mission?'

'No, I mean the church, the old church.'

'But it's closed. It's been closed for years.'

'Well it's open now, not as a church mind you. A joiner has taken it over; he's making furniture in it. He might let you use it for your rehearsals, he's a nice guy, and he could maybe do with the company. Ray, his name is. You should pop yourself round there and see him.'

Chapter 8

Maria feels a bit self-conscious standing here. It seems a strange thing to do, knock on the door of a church. But then again, if what Alice says is true, it's not a church any more. It must be the same person, the guy in the van asking directions to the church, his name was Ray. He was rather tasty she seems to remember.

Even from the outside this place is depressing. The perimeter fence has all but disappeared; all that remain are stumps of wall and a few rotting fence posts. The gravestones have either fallen or sunk. Those left standing lurch at odd angles, too tired and beaten to remain erect, too worn out to fight the neglect and moss that is slowly burying them. Clearly nobody looks after the graves. There are no urns or vases for fresh flowers. The only vessels are discarded Buckfast bottles and empty Coke cans, faded to pink.

She's chapping pretty loudly, leaving intervals between each insistent knock, but no-one is answering. Perhaps she should just go in. There is a piece of paper stuck on the notice board but the rain has got to it and the ink has run. She can just make out the bottom line: *come away in!*

I now find an excellent rehearsal space, Maria incants, I now find an excellent rehearsal space, I now find an excellent rehearsal space. She's meditated on it several times now and each time, despite her knowledge of Hexton's very limited resources, she becomes clearer in her mind of what she needs and more confident that she's going to find it.

The heavy church door creaks open easily, invitingly, like the creaky old door in a horror movie. And there is something else like a horror movie: music. There appears, by the sounds of it, to be a full choir and orchestra performing in the church. The music is beautiful but it's frightening. She can't make out what they are singing but it's heavy-hearted, sombre, funereal. Maria stops in her tracks. Has she got it wrong?

Is there a funeral on in here? How can that be? This place has lain empty for years. Has she somehow got caught in a time warp? Preparing to be met by a dance macabre at a phantom funeral, she puts her hand to her chest and creeps in.

The place is empty. There is no choir, no orchestra, there are no dancing skeletons or ghosts. There is a lot of wood strewn around the place and two massive stereo speakers. It's a record. But who's playing it? There's no-one here. A door in the back corridor of the church is open and from there, above the sounds of the bone-shaking music, a voice is calling.

'Hello!'

'Hello?' Maria replies.

It's a narrow stairway and so she shouts up the way, reasoning that the voice must have come from there.

'Up here!'

She quickly scoots up the stairs away from the

ghostly dirge, towards the live human voice. It must be the joiner. The music doesn't get further away, if anything it gets louder and clearer as it's funnelled up the tapering space. Thick dusty ropes run up the centre of the stairwell and as she reaches the top she sees that the ropes are attached to large metal bells. At the top there is a small open door and Maria has to duck to pass through it. A one-eyed hunchbacked midget meets her.

'The bells made me deaf you know!' the midget slavers in her face.

Maria screams.

She staggers back towards the open door. The midget suddenly transforms himself into a normal-looking guy, Ray, the man who asked for directions.

'Sorry, I didn't mean to scare you.'

Ray's laughing.

'I was only joking, the hunchback of Notre Dame, d'you get it?'

By way of demonstration he leans forward and hunches his back, closes one eye and screws his face up.

Maria's heart is pounding, she is confused and the sudden reappearance of the gargoyle frightens her all over again. Instinctively she backs away from him but as she does so he lunges towards her. Now he's Ray again but he has a look of intensity on his face that is worrying.

'Careful!'

He quickly grabs both her arms and pulls her towards him. Maria is about to be raped by a split-personality hunchback/normal guy on top of a church bell tower for all of Hexton to see. Fleetingly she wonders at the chances of a woman who has had no male attention for so long being sexually harassed in two separate incidents, first a flasher then a hunchback, in the same month. As she considers this she becomes aware that her left foot is no longer making contact with solid ground. She turns to see that on this side of the tower there is no guardrail or barrier, nothing to stop her falling, and she is close, too close, to the edge.

Ray's not trying to assault her; he's trying to save her.

Her initial reluctance to be taken into his arms has turned into enthusiasm. She throws herself towards him and clings on for dear life.

'I've got you, you're OK,' he says. He has stopped being the hunchback.

'Let's get you down out of here.'

He leads her to the doorway to the stairs but she is fearful of letting go of him.

'OK, we'll go together,' he says softly. 'That's it, take it slow, you're fine.'

When they reach the bottom and re-enter the church the music is still booming. He gently lowers Maria onto a pew and then goes to turn the stereo down. He doesn't turn it off.

He returns to squat low beside her, his face close to hers. She can smell tobacco off him. He's chuckling again.

'I'm really sorry, I shouldn't have called you up there. I thought it was the lads. I was just going to show them the view. And the hunchback thing, it was really stupid, I'm sorry,' he says.

But he's still laughing.

Maria would like to slap him. The hand that she has clasped to her chest is itching to smack the stupid grin off his face.

'It's Maria, isn't it? We met the other day when you and your friends gave me directions, do you remember?'

'Yes, of course.'

'And I'm Ray.'

Ray holds out his hand and smiles. Maria hesitates, a formal handshake seems strange now after she's wrapped her body so tightly around him two minutes ago on the bell tower, but she puts her hand out warily. It strikes her that perhaps he thinks she's mentally disabled too; it wouldn't be the first time it's happened. She makes a point of never correcting people.

'Can I get you some tea? What do you take in it?'

'Black and weak, please.'

By the time he returns with two steaming mugs Maria has gathered her thoughts and got her breath back. The guy's an arse, no doubt about it, but he does have a church.

For the sake of the show, and the community, she'll put her feelings to one side. Nelson approves, he's all for personal sacrifice, she can feel him with her on this. She'll be the bigger person; she'll be calm and polite.

'Thank you,' she says. 'And don't worry about it, really, it's OK.'

'Thanks,' he says.

He's obviously relieved, and so he should be.

'I'm from Community Development. I'm organizing a community show.'

Ray stands up, excited. He hits his forehead with a noisy slap, the fright from which almost makes Maria spill her tea. Her nerves are in tatters.

'Right! Maria, Community Development! Sorry, I've got it now. Alice said you might come round.'

'Really?'

'She says I've to give you the church hall for your show, your rehearsals and that. I've looked out a set of keys for you.' Ray goes to a toolbox beside a workbench and returns with a set of keys.

'There you go,' he says, handing them to Maria.

This isn't right. It's too easy.

'I'm afraid we don't have any budget so we wouldn't be able to pay for the hire of the hall.'

'Don't be daft, it's free.'

There must be a catch.

'Are you sure?'

'No bother. I'm getting the whole place free off the council, it's not costing me anything.'

'I'm not sure exactly when we would need it, rehearsals might be at awkward times.'

'Well, you've got your keys, come any time you like. I'm here most of the time anyway.'

'But the rehearsals will be noisy, we wouldn't want to disrupt your work; maybe we should organize a rehearsal rota?'

'I like it noisy; it's good to have a bit of life about the place. If it gets too bad I'll just drown you out with my Mozart.'

He's smiling. Maria reciprocates but she's confused. Her instinct is to smile, he doesn't seem such a bad guy really. But why would he give her the free run of the place? He doesn't even know her. People don't just do things like this. Unless they're up to something.

'I'm afraid as we'll be working with children there are certain forms you'll have to fill in. Sorry about this, but they just need to know that you . . .'

'That I'm not a criminal or a paedophile. Aye, fair enough, absolutely.'

100

Ray's turning out to be actually quite a nice person. And not bad-looking too.

'OK I'll come clean,' he says with a big grin.

Maria smiles.

'I'm an axe-murderer.'

Her smile is fading when he follows this up.

'But I've given up murdering axes. It's just no fun any more.'

Ray hangs his head, smirking, a naughty-boy expression on his face. She can't decide whether to laugh or smash his nose. An involuntary snort breaks from her throat and she gives herself up to laughter.

As their mirth subsides Ray produces a tobacco tin from his back pocket and offers her a roll-up.

'No thank you.'

He knows that she's a non-smoker but still he lights his cigarette in front of her. Not only that, but as he proffered the cigarette she noticed that he has a big gold band on his finger. A smoker and married. To disguise her disappointment Maria brings up the subject of his musical taste. He doesn't seem the type of person who likes Mozart.

'So, Mozart, eh?'

Maria knows next to nothing about classical music.

'Sorry, want me to change the CD? It is a bit heavy going, isn't it? It's the Requiem, not his cheeriest. Would you like me to put something else on?'

'Actually, do you have any Madonna?'

During her morning meditation Maria has a brilliant idea. She's just at the part where she's down by the shimmering river at the edge of the forest. Often, when she's at the river, cute forest animals approach her. They seem instinctively to lose their shyness around

Maria. In fact they're irresistibly drawn to her. Sometimes her companion is a baby deer, sometimes a rabbit or a squirrel. Today the little yellow-breasted bird comes and sits on her shoulder, where he sings a song. What's different today is that the bird is accompanied by wonderful orchestral music.

Something has been nagging at Maria for a while now. Everyone in Hexton is a singer but nobody's a musician. There are a few accordion and flute players but they have been banned from doing so in the show on the grounds that they only know sectarian marching tunes. For lack of a band she's had to ask people to provide their own backing tapes, but these have been of varying quality. While the orchestra elegantly accompanies the yellow-breasted bird in its song, Maria remembers: Alice showed her a brochure, a directory of voluntary services.

At the Elderly Forum auditions, while a very elderly lady gave a bizarre warbling rendition of 'Like a Virgin', Maria leafed through the directory. Now it comes to her that she saw an entry for an orchestra of retired musicians based ten miles away in the city. At the time she was so focused on this being a Hexton show that it didn't register. But there's no law to say that participants *have* to come from Hexton. Surely an orchestra could only enhance the show.

Now, down by the shimmering river with the yellow bird on her shoulder, she understands that she must book this orchestra.

For a moment Maria inhabits two imaginary worlds. Whilst still by the river with her musical bird friend, she is simultaneously at the opening night of the show. The orchestra, handsome and distinguished in their dinner suits, are playing something classical, Mozart maybe. The centre is buzzing with excitement. The audience, Hextors and clients, conduct themselves with style and grace. They nod their hellos, the ladies demure behind fans, the gentlemen attentive and gallant.

Meanwhile, back at the river, the yellow bird is singing his little heart out. Maria and he nod in time to the music and occasionally exchange knowing glances. The little yellow fellow seems to be singing, Hurrah! Tally ho! Life is wonderful! And similar exuberant expressions. Whatever it is he's singing, it fills Maria with joy.

It's a brilliant meditation, the best she's had this week. She emerges from the med physically and mentally tip-top. She can feel her serotonin levels soar. As soon as she sets foot back in the real world she goes and finds the directory brochure.

Chapter 9

Maria is confused.

'Rangers?' she says. 'I thought you were a Celtic man, Brian.'

Dezzie is standing behind Brian's chair. He seems to have taken a special interest in Brian and now spends a lot of time with Blue Group, chatting to him. Maria wonders if it is a strategy to get close to her. If it is then it's working, she no longer simply fancies Dezzie, she might be falling in love with him.

With a huge effort Brian shrugs his shoulders. His left hand is bent out of shape, as is his mood. Without a physio session it will probably remain this way for the rest of the day. His fingers are curled so tight he won't be able to access his keyboard, he is effectively mute and this usually makes him angry and difficult.

Brian can speak: years invested with a very patient therapist trying to train his unruly tongue have given him blurry words that only his parents, and sometimes Maria, can properly understand. Maria wants him to speak, use it or lose it she says, but he refuses. He says his own voice makes him sound like a spastic. Maria discourages him thinking in such negative and un-PC terms, but she secretly agrees. When he uses his natural voice rather than his electronic one, strangers speak slowly, moronically simply, repeating themselves, louder and louder. Luckily Dezzie doesn't speak to him like this.

'Aye, he used to be Celtic but he's seen the light, haven't you my man?' says Dezzie.

Another demanding shrug, a slow smile. Brian is obviously chuffed to be called 'my man'. It's a guy thing, of course. For lots of reasons Maria calling Brian 'my man' would not be appropriate, but she wishes she had such an easy rapport with him. Although it's sweet of Dezzie to take an interest in Brian, she is after all his key worker.

'But you've always been a Celtic supporter. Don't tell me you've switched teams?'

Tired out from the shrugging Brian is non-committal.

'C'mon, Brian: Rangers,' Dezzie teases. 'You know it makes sense.'

Brian's face displays the quandary he is in and Maria knows exactly what's going on in his head: he doesn't wish to be seen as a turncoat but neither does he want to lose alliance with his new friend. Maria and Dezzie both watch Brian for the slightest flicker.

'It's just that if you were a Rangers supporter we could go to the home game next Wednesday night. They're playing Aberdeen.'

Maria is worried about these underhand tactics. She tries to speak to Dezzie discreetly.

'Dezzie, don't. You'll disappoint him. He doesn't realize you're kidding.'

'I'm not kidding!'

Dezzie addresses Brian directly. The teasing finished, his voice and face are serious.

'If you want to come to the match I'll take you.'

Brian lifts his head and lets it fall in an emphatic nod. With supreme effort he unfurls his middle finger to the knuckle and raps at the keyboard.

'The. Choice. Is. Clear. Rangers.'

Maria shakes her head in mock sorrow. Dezzie laughs.

'Yes! Front row disabled area here we come!'

Dezzie lifts Brian's arm and gives him a victorious high five, but it is all too much for Brian and he vomits.

'Oh, you've got him too excited. He'll need changing now.'

'It's OK, I'm on it.'

'Really?'

This is one of the other things Maria likes about Dezzie. He's never afraid to get his hands dirty. The cleaning and changing of any client in Blue Group is her responsibility. Dezzie has already changed Brian once today, but he doesn't seem to mind at all. Brian, usually so shy, even with Maria, seems OK with it.

'Yeah, no bother. We'll see if we can find you a Rangers top, eh Brian?'

The two lads are giggling.

'Hello. Hello. We. Are. The. Billy. Boys,' says Brian's suave electronic voice as Dezzie wheels him up the corridor.

She shouldn't be encouraging unruly behaviour, but Maria can't help but smile. Dezzie really gets the best out of people, he'd make a wonderful father. She must have another word with Madonna about this.

*   *   *

'Hello, Mr Spencer?'

'Yes.'

'Oh hello Mr Spencer, I'm so glad to finally get a hold of you. You're not an easy man to track down, I've been trying to get you all week.'

'Yes, I've been a bit busy. My wife was very ill.'

'Oh I'm sorry, but anyway, I've got you now.'

'I'm sorry miss but I don't have time at the moment, I'm actually on my way out the door.'

'Mr Spencer I'll just be a second, I'll tell you what it is. My name is Maria Whyte. I'm a Community Development Worker and I'm organizing a community show.'

'Could you call me later? I'm actually on my way out to bury my wife.'

'Oh my God! I'm so sorry. I'm sorry to hear that.'

'Thank you. She was very brave.'

'Oh Mr Spencer, I'm so sorry, that's terrible.'

'Yes, terrible.'

'Of course I'll call back but, to save me wasting your time, is the orchestra available six weeks today?'

'Well, I haven't got the diary to hand . . .'

'It's a Madonna Extravaganza.'

'A what?'

'You know, Madonna?'

'Never heard of them.'

'It's for Hexton Comm . . .'

'Hexton? Sorry miss, we don't play Hexton, too dodgy. Sorry.'

'But it says in the brochure that you come and play in communities. The centre are hosting it, we . . .'

'What centre? Autumn House, is it?'

'Eh, no actually it's the Adult Learning Centre for . . .'

'For mongols?'

Not wanting to contradict him, Maria is stuck for words, but before she can think up a tactful reply Mr Spencer has continued.

'She had a cousin who went to the spastic training centre. Andy his name was, he was a mongol. She loved Andy. She used to bring him to our performances.'

'That's nice.'

Normally Maria would be the first person to correct such pejorative old-fashioned terminology as spastic and mongol, but she doesn't want to spoil her chances with him. Silence descends, and Mr Spencer appears to be lost in a reverie about his wife and her spastic mongoloid cousin Andy.

'You should have told me it was for the spastics. We'll do it.'

'Sorry?'

'We'll do your show. The members won't like travelling to Hexton but they'll do it. It's what she would have wanted.'

'Oh that's fantastic! Thanks a lot, Mr Spencer. Now, I'll give you the address and we have to talk about rehearsals and . . .'

'Can you call back? I'm going to be late for the funeral.'

'But the orchestra will definitely do it?'

'Yes. I'll explain to them. They'll do it for her.'

As per Maria's plans and creative visualizations, things are progressing nicely. As per usual, this is not for long.

*   *   *

Maria has been looking forward to this meeting. She's relishing Mike's face becoming infused with the light of Inclusion Initiative fervour when she tells him how many groups she has on board. He's got to admit that she's struck Community Development gold with this show.

She's already decided that her response should be a qualified smile and a gracious nod. She'll be smart enough to avoid crowing; or rather she has been strenuously warned against it this morning by old Mr Soberpants Mandela.

'Nobody loves a smart-arse, Maria,' Nelson said.

She sometimes wishes Nelson would just lighten up a bit, but, as he never tires of telling her, 'the struggle is my life.'

Mike has no idea of Maria's rich spiritual life and relationship with Nelson. This is just as well, as he would certainly pooh-pooh it. She knows she would not be able to stop herself punching his smug face to a bloody pulp if he dared pooh-pooh Nelson.

'Come in, come in Maria! Don't hang about out there in the corridor.'

It's less that he's keen to be in her presence, and more that he's in a hurry, as he always is, to get the meeting done and dusted. It must stick in his craw to praise me, she thinks with some satisfaction.

'Maria, first things first, have you bought yourself goggles yet?'

Goggles? What the hell is he talking about?

'Eh, no, I . . .'

'Well, get a pair. Bert says you still haven't got in the pool with the clients. It's your job. Do it.'

Maria is too stunned to make a reply and Mike carries on as though nothing had happened.

'So how's it all coming along?' he says lightly, not looking at her, flicking through her file at lightning speed. 'I'm hearing great things. Bert tells me you've got all the community groups involved.'

So not only has he dubbed her in for not swimming, Bert's also stolen her thunder. What did she ever do to him? Maria is winded by the double whammy but she'll have to take it on the chin.

'Yeah, the concert's shaping up nicely.'

'Yeah? So what have you got?'

Impress me, he seems to be challenging her. Well, he's going to be impressed.

'Them all, the full set: school choir and various schoolkid acts, Elderly Forum Glee Club and Golden Belles . . .'

'Golden Belles?'

'Old-lady cabaret group.'

Mike nods and takes notes, ticking boxes.

'Our own Blue Group, obviously, with a drama presentation. Mothers and Toddlers . . .'

'Any non-affiliated? Like, just random members of the community?'

Oh puhlease, does he imagine she won't have this covered?

'Tons of them, up to our stumps in Randoms. Mostly singers and break dancers.'

'Religious groups?'

'Yep, Pastor McKenzie's Victory Singers.'

'Good.'

'No, actually, they're shit, but they're in.'

It's fun to sit here and contradict the boss, and there isn't a damn thing he can do about it.

'Even better,' says Mike. 'I love to see Christians making an arse of themselves.'

She had forgotten his Christians phobia.

'Oh yeah, and I've got an orchestra.' She drops this one in casually.

Mike looks surprised. Bert obviously hasn't briefed him on the orchestra.

'What, from the school? Kids playing kazoos?'

'No Mike, not kazoos,' she says in the superior tone she can now afford. 'An orchestra. Retired professional musicians with proper instruments: Orchestre Octogéne, they're called, it's French, it means orchestra of eighty-year-olds.'

'I'd kind of gathered that.'

'Although they don't actually have any in their eighties any more.'

'What, you mean they're ninety now?'

'No, the eighty-year-olds died. The rest of them are younger.'

'Oh good, that's what we need, the lifeblood of septuagenarians coursing through the community,' Mike says, happier now that he's found something wrong with them, something to moan about.

'They've agreed to back a few of the more professional singers, those with their own sheet music, as well as perform a few of their own classical numbers.'

'Classical numbers? That's going to go down like a cup of cold sick in Hexton.'

Maria's jaw clenches as her hand presses her sternum. Why does he have to reduce everything to ugliness?

'How many of these frisky seventy-year-olds have you got then, four?'

'Actually Mike, four would only be a quartet,' she says sweetly. 'Mr Spencer said the full complement is thirty-four but not all of them have transport, so it might be a few less.'

111

'I don't think you've thought this through, Maria. You won't get thirty-four musicians and their instruments on that stage.'

'I'm not putting them on the stage; I'm putting them on the floor in front of the audience.'

'Well you're not leaving much space for audience, that's going to cut down your seating capacity quite a bit.'

'We'll manage.'

'And how are you going to rehearse these people? We can't have thirty-four doddering musos wandering round the centre.'

'I have rehearsal space, in the church.'

'What church?'

Mike's lip is twisted into a disbelieving scoff now, or perhaps it's the mention of a church that so freaks him out. Maria is beginning to wonder, with his aversion to all things Christ-related, if Mike isn't some sort of devil-worshipper.

'*The* church, the only church in Hexton.'

'No, you're wrong there Maria, it's empty, boarded up, it has been for years.'

'No, I'm afraid *you're* wrong, Mike. There's a joinery company in there now, or at least a joiner. He's offered us his main hall, which is twice the size of the centre's.'

'Oh,' he says, obviously stumped, 'right.'

Maria shifts triumphantly in her chair. Nobody likes a smart-arse, Nelson whispers in her ear, but it's too late. She leans back and slowly uncrosses and then crosses her legs in a Sharon Stone stylee. This would be much more impertinent if she had chosen this morning to go commando instead of the big sensible pants she's wearing. Perhaps he'll catch a glimpse of her gusset. An evil smile spreads across her face.

'Well done. Good job,' Mike says, his head down in the records.

Maria waits, but that's all she's getting. He closes the file; the interview is at an end. Maria stands up to leave.

'Oh and Maria?'

Her hand is on the door handle.

'Yes Mike?' she asks breezily.

'Seeing as it's so much bigger and better, I think we should hold the performance in the church hall.'

'What? But we want people to come to the centre, to get an understanding of what we do here. What about integration? I thought that was the idea in the first place.'

'Yes but you said it yourself, the church hall is twice the size, ergo: twice the audience; twice the community. And anyway, Bert doesn't want to be left having to clear up the mess. The clients'll get excited; some of them are bound to be sick. It'll be a bacchanalian orgy. It's Bert's budget the cleaner's over-time will have to come out of.'

Mike's negativity is taking the shine off her triumphal moment. It's melting away like snow on her hair, becoming a cold drip down her back.

'And so long as our clients are involved with all the other groups it still fits the requirements for the Inclusion Initiative.'

'And that's the most important thing, is it Mike? Ticking the fucking boxes!'

Maria's getting shrill. Mike takes the high ground by dropping his voice to a whisper.

'It doesn't matter where the show's held.'

'But Mike, rehearsal space is one thing, but I might

not get the church hall for the show, I don't know if the joiner will give me it.'

'Oh I'm sure he'll give you it, Maria,' he says with a sleazy grin, 'just flash your pants.'

Often on her way home, tired out after a day of Fiona's antics and Brian's sulks, Maria pulls up the hood on her high-vis jacket and avoids eye contact with anyone on the bus. It is at these times, while heading towards her cold expensive flat to put a sausage under the grill for her tea, that life becomes unbearably real.

Chapter 10

Maria's nipps stick out like knobs on a cheap chest of drawers. They are long and thick, looking as though they could support the weight of a damp trench coat. They couldn't, in fact they are vulnerable and extremely sensitive. She sighs as she takes her navy blue Lycra swimming costume out of her bag. It still fits, unfortunately, but she has not worn this costume since she was fifteen, with good reason.

When Maria's little breast buds first appeared her mum celebrated by buying her a grown-up swimming suit, comprising cotton-reinforced gusset and foam-cupped trainer bra with adjustable straps. This was something of a false dawn as, nearly thirteen years later, the buds have not yet blossomed. But, apart from wisdom teeth, the tender breast sprouts are the newest part of Maria's body. Thirteen years younger than the rest of her, she meditates every day that they will eventually catch up.

The costume looks OK when it's dry, quite flattering actually, giving her at least the appearance of the bosom she dreams of. Although the foam constructions are size A, they are more than big enough.

Maria knows that unless she moves carefully in the water the cups, almost empty of breast tissue, will create tremendous drag, dredging the pool, netting corn plasters and bits of hair, pulling her down – worst of all, pulling the front of her costume down.

In third year at secondary school, she was selected for the water-polo team. She played well, confident in her fashionable and figure-enhancing new cossie. As she jumped and lunged in the water she was blissfully unaware, and no-one told her, that the entire school could see what they had long suspected. What had been the subject of gossip and conjecture was now the cause of girlish tittering and boyish guffawing: there was considerable disparity between the size of Maria's foam domes and her actual chest. She was that most despised of creatures: a bra stuffer. She never bathed publicly again.

Until now. She is resentful of Mike's diktat that she must enter the pool with the clients, but what can she do? Until now she has always enjoyed the swimming-pool outings, where, warm and fully clothed at the side of the pool, she was able to shout encouragement to Blue Group who mostly just stood there, red-eyed, shivering and gormless, waist-deep in the chlorinated water.

As she has a physically disabled member in her group, now that she has to get changed, she requires another key worker to assist with Brian. Dezzie has been helping out with Brian recently, and co-incidentally is always available when Blue Group's swimming trips are scheduled. Maria smiles at this; he must be checking the rotas in the staffroom and making himself available so he can hang out with her.

The pool has recently been revamped. It now has a

changing village: the same rows of cubicles it always had but now with a fancy name. The old segregation of men and women has gone, and Blue Group grab available cubicles where they can. Maria chooses one as far as possible away from the rest of them, who call to each other loudly, arguing about who is the best swimmer. Martin is the only member of the group who appears to enjoy and learn anything from the swimming lessons.

Fiona as usual complains about having to undress. Her mum dresses her at home and, although she is perfectly capable of removing her own clothes, she's reluctant to do so. Maria often has to stand with her head poked round the door of Fiona's cubicle, nagging and persuading her to remove her greyish-white bra and pants.

It is not modesty that makes Fiona unwilling, but laziness. Once undressed, she often has to be persuaded that it's not a good idea to leave the cubicle whilst naked. The other embarrassing thing about Fiona is that she has the thickest mat of pubic hair Maria has ever seen. Wide clumps of black fuzz stick out the sides of her costume and down her legs. It's probably not even correct to call it pubic hair as it extends at least three inches down her thighs, stopping at the same point as her head hair, giving her a troll-like appearance. Maria did once mention it to Mrs Simpson, requesting much-needed depilation on Fiona's behalf, but Fiona's mother seemed to think the idea was obscene.

If today Fiona takes it upon herself to stroll along the poolside without her costume, her luxuriant pubes catching the breeze, then there's nothing Maria can do about it. She can't be in two places at once. If Mike wants her to swim he'll have to take the consequences. She half expects and, if she's honest, rather hopes, that Fiona *will* emerge naked and she'll hear the terrified screams of witnesses as they run from the building.

Maria wonders if Dezzie is keen to see her in a swimsuit and simultaneously worries that he might catch a glimpse of her shamefully underdeveloped bust. There would be no chance of marriage then.

She's folding her clothes but her mind is elsewhere, making a list of things she has to organize before the big rehearsal tomorrow. She's still angry at Mike for pushing the show out of the centre. It's just as well that Ray's prepared to let them stage it in the church.

When she went to ask him about it yesterday and give him the Disclosure forms, he had a crowd of young neds, girls and lads, around him. She'd hoped to have more of a chat, get to know him a bit, but he was busy holding them spellbound with lame jokes.

'Why do women have smaller feet?' he asked. 'So that they can get that wee bit closer to the sink.'

And him a married man, pathetic. Isn't it hen-pecked men who talk like that? The neds brayed and whinnied at everything he said, of course. Ray spent ages with them, showing them card tricks. But, Maria supposes, while they're with him they're off the streets and out of trouble.

And he seems to be taking his *come one come all* thing quite literally. Someone had pushed two pews together and there were blankets strewn around the place. It looks like he's letting homeless people sleep there now.

Maria steps gingerly into her old costume. Her bare feet are cold on the tiled floor but a sudden change of temperature, a warm pleasant humidity spreading across the tops of her toes, causes her to look down. She discovers the reason for this: the balmy breeze is Martin's breath. Martin is spreadeagled on the tiles outside with his head poking in under her cubicle door. He's smiling, a friendly interested smile. Maria, in shock and fright, kicks out at him. She does this instinctively and instantly curses herself. It is another shock to make skin-to-skin contact, her toes crumpling painfully against his cheekbone, her toenails scraping his soft downy face. Martin stares up at her, seemingly confused. He doesn't move but she can't bring herself to kick him again.

The first rule of being a good key worker is to avoid beating the clients at all costs. Apart from the fact that she has no desire to inflict actual bodily harm on sweet guileless Martin, she'd be instantly dismissed if Mike got wind of her kicking his face in.

'Martin! What the hell d'you think you are playing at?'

'I only wanted to see your titties,' he says, beginning to cry, 'you didn't have to kick me! I'm telling on you!'

A trickle of blood runs down his cheek. Martin has a phobia about blood, especially his own. Maria must come out of the cubicle and wipe it away before he realizes, or he could become hysterical. Last month he cut his hand in art class and had to be sedated.

Such is her rush to exit the cubicle that Maria almost forgets to cover herself. As she hurriedly pulls up her costume the tight elasticated material snares on her breasts. This causes eyewateringly painful nipple fold. She has to pull the Lycra wide of her bony chest until her nipples are safe inside the cavernous cups.

As she emerges she sees Dezzie pushing Brian's

chair towards her. Both of them are in swimming trunks. Dezzie looks lovely. His legs and arms are long and thin and lovely. Thank God she remembered to pull up her cossie.

'Everything OK?' asks Dezzie, obviously concerned to see Martin lying on the floor with his head under her cubicle.

'Yes, fine,' says Maria, 'can you give me a hand with Martin?'

'Sure.'

Maria bends carefully. Not that Dezzie's that kind of guy, but he is a guy. She notices his eyes sweep across her almost naked body and wishes she had a better view to offer him.

'Martin, come out of there for goodness sake.'

They each take one of Martin's legs and haul him out. As he turns to face them it's obvious that he's in a state of excitement.

Pretending to be mopping his sweat, Maria wipes Martin's cheek and dabs at the rest of his face. Luckily it's no more than a light graze and he's already stopped bleeding. She stands up holding a hand out to Martin, to help him to his feet, but she has come up too fast. The shock, the poolside heat and humidity, make her feel faint and she stumbles. She almost falls but Dezzie catches her. For the first time in her life, Maria swoons. Dezzie has his arms around her; his bare arms are touching hers. His bare legs rub against hers.

'Maria, are you OK?' he asks, his beautiful big nose less than an inch from her face.

Later, in the swimming-pool café, after their lesson when Blue Group have got their clothes back on and are having their snacks and juice, Maria and Dezzie take their coffee at the next table.

'I just got a fright when I saw him staring up at me, that's all,' says Maria. 'I'm not angry with him, he can't help his impulses.'

'That's very understanding of you,' says Dezzie, obviously impressed with her enlightened views.

'Well, I won't pretend that Martin's sexuality isn't a challenge. For him and everyone else. I actually had a word with him about this last week. We discussed, and he agreed, that other people's breasts are out of bounds.'

Maria licks her cappuccino foam in what she hopes is a seductive manner. 'He agreed, he always does, but he'll forget and then he'll take what he can get.'

'I know, I had to counsel Robert for hours . . .'

'Robert?'

'You know, Robert. Big fat guy from Yellow Group.'

'Oh yeah.'

'He wanted to make a formal complaint about Martin groping him.'

'Martin groped Robert! Why didn't you tell me?'

'Oh, it wasn't anything I couldn't handle, he dropped the complaint anyway.'

Maria is slightly perturbed by this. *She* is Martin's key worker, she should have been told.

'Anyway, I can understand Martin's interest,' says Dezzie with a wink, 'Robert does have spectacularly abundant jubblies.'

'I've never actually seen them but I've heard about his . . . man breasts,' says Maria sniggering.

'Bitch tits.'

'Oh that's gross!' she squeals, but she's laughing. 'Poor old Martin, reduced to fondling Robert, he needs a girlfriend.'

'Well, at least one for the night.'

'He's a twenty-eight-year-old man with a tremendous sex drive and nowhere to take it.'

'Absolutely. Down's syndrome is the least of his problems.'

'He'd just be a lot happier if he could get sex once in a while, a lot calmer.'

'Wouldn't we all?'

This throwaway remark is music to Maria's ears. He's telling her that he doesn't have a girlfriend. And that he wants one. What should she do about this? She doesn't want to seem frivolous or desperate. Best to let it go for the moment. She'll carry on expounding her radical theory.

'Best practice is that we facilitate clients leading a normal life,' she says rationally.

Whenever Maria wants to appear thoughtful and academic she finds that posing a series of difficult questions usually does the trick.

'But what's normal? Isn't having a sex life normal? Why couldn't Martin visit a prostitute once in a while? Don't lots of other "normal" men do that?'

So as not to appear fixated on normality, she makes inverted commas in the air around the word 'normal'.

'Yeah, but prostitutes? They're mostly junkies, they're dangerous one way or another.'

'Well, I don't know. I mean, why don't the NHS provide some kind of sex therapy? All legal and above board, certified and disease-free.'

'I had no idea you were such a hopeless romantic, Maria.'

Maria is embarrassed. She puts her head down to hide the flush she can feel creeping up her face. She's taken the argument too far. She wanted to show him she's a caring non-judgemental person. Now he's got her down as some kind of sleazy procurer.

'I'm sorry, I didn't mean to be vulgar.'

Dezzie reaches across the table, takes her hand and squeezes it.

'I don't think you're vulgar,' he says laughing, 'I think you're lovely.'

Chapter 11

As she hurries towards the church-hall entrance, Maria's heart sinks. This is the first rehearsal she's called and she's already twenty minutes late. Not for the first time, the bus into Hexton broke down. The front tyre blew out, burst on the shards of a smashed bottle of Buckfast.

Luckily she was able to phone the centre and ask Dezzie to bring Blue Group down here to meet her, but she's still really late and there are only a few people standing outside.

All the auditions she held, all the phone calls she made, and there's only a handful prepared to turn up. And where's Dezzie with Blue Group? Oh well, for the sake of these few hardy souls she'll have to put on a happy face and make the best of it. She'll make a success of this show; she has to. Madonna and Nelson have backed her all the way, she can't let them down.

But the people standing outside are not even here for the rehearsal, these are the Unemployed that Ray allows to roam around the church building. The young people sit or stand on the church steps smoking, looking disgruntled that they have to share the space with proper members of the community. Maria finds this vaguely satisfying.

As she pulls open the door to the church hall she sees that the place is full. There must be a hundred people here; the orchestra is thirty strong at least. Marianne Bowman, the all-too-fragrant headmistress, is here with the school choir. As well as the many individual acts there's the Hexton Hot Steppers Dance School, the full Glee Club complement, the seven Golden Belles and Pastor McKenzie and his Victory Singers. Despite the number of people here, there is no more than a low background hum of sound. Perhaps because it once was a church, each group keeps noise down to a whisper amongst themselves.

As Maria enters the church, almost as if it were cued to her arrival, orchestral music starts up. Not loud but audible. But it's not coming from the orchestra members. The musicians turn their heads towards the source of it, as surprised as everyone else. Ray is playing records again. Something classical, Mozart probably.

Blue Group are here safe, thank God. Dezzie has brought them but he isn't with them now. They sit in silence huddled together in a corner, obviously uncomfortable, intimidated by the crowd. Brian is sulking as he always does in public, embarrassed by his wheelchair and his body, pretending to be invisible around other young people. The group look so innocent and vulnerable. Maria's heart rushes out of her body, reaching and embracing them sooner than she can get to them across the hall. She quickly makes physical contact with everyone, firmly patting an elbow here, a shoulder there and then in reverse order spends time with each of them hugging and making eye contact, bringing them out of their own heads, leading them gently into this scary environment of the rehearsal. Fiona got the first pat and so is last for a cuddle. Fiona doesn't want a cuddle, she wants to go back to the centre and is threatening to cry.

'Come on Fiona, you want to sing "Donal Og", don't you?'

She can't argue with that.

To make things worse, Brian is pissed off because his dad, Phil, has turned up. Phil and Brian's uncle are sweeping slowly and methodically through the crowd. Phil is not here, as Brian suspects, to embarrass his son. Neither does he, as Maria imagines, want to audition in a twin novelty act with his brother. He and Billy are here to see if they can catch the flasher.

'This is a magnet for perverts: people getting changed, wearing fancy costumes, showing off . . .'

Phil's voice trails away in disgust. The idea of someone showing off seems to him comparable to them exposing themselves.

'Well Phil, I appreciate your concern,' says Maria, 'but I'm afraid I'll have to ask you to leave. It's performers only today, this is a rehearsal.'

'You just give me a shout if you get any trouble, eh?'

'Oh yes, I'll be sure to.'

Luckily Phil doesn't catch the sarcasm in Maria's voice.

She scans the room looking for Dezzie, and her eyes light on a strange sight. Alice has led Ray to another of the Golden Belles, a small grey woman sitting on a chair. Then something very odd happens. Ray puts his hand on the old lady's shoulder and she closes her eyes. He whispers in her ear and her body goes limp. What the hell is he whispering?

Just then Dezzie crosses in front of Ray and the woman, obscuring her view. He's spotted Maria and waves. Although she's delighted to see him, she's surprised and a little let down that he didn't stay with Blue Group when they were so obviously miserable.

A few minutes later Ray approaches, all big smiles.

'Hi Maria, and . . .' Ray is obviously racking his brains to remember everyone's names. She'll be amazed if he does, it's been a few weeks.

'Eh, Jane?'

Jane nods yes and smiles. He turns and looks at each person intently and hesitates for a few seconds before saying their name. 'Brian. Fiona.'

'Hello Ray,' says Fiona.

Fiona has remembered his name, but that's not so surprising. It is rare that anyone new comes into Blue Group's social circle. Ray stares hard at Martin. Martin starts to speak but Ray holds up his hand to stop him.

'Wait, let me get it. Marty, is it? Martin?'

'Yes. Hello Ray.'

'One hundred per cent recall,' says Maria, amazed. 'How the hell did you do that?'

'Oh,' says Ray, batting the air with his hand, 'it's just a memory technique I learned.'

Now Maria is even more amazed. She's never met anyone else who uses memory tools. She thinks back to how she stored and filed Blue Group when she first met them. Brian is Brainiac (the Maniac), a moniker which suits him so well she has to restrain herself from saying it aloud. Jane is GI Jane because of her short hair and military neatness. Martin is Martin the Martian, but she has long since stopped imagining him with little antennae coming out of his head. Due to her man-eating tendencies, Fiona is Fee Fi Fo Fum. Maria wonders what aides-memoires Ray has used and, more interestingly, what he used to remember *her* name. She'd love to ask but now is not the time.

'This is going to be some rehearsal!' says Ray, excited. 'All these people turning up, eh? Well done, Maria.'

'Thank you, Ray.'

Maria reflects for a moment. He's right; getting all these people here is an achievement in itself.

'I should be thanking you for the use of the hall.'

'It's nothing. I told you, it's free!'

'Well,' Maria is momentarily stuck for something to thank him for. 'Well, thanks for nothing.'

Ray is the first to laugh, and then all of Blue Group join in. Maria is particularly pleased with her little off-the-cuff joke.

'Not at all. An absolute pleasure. It's exciting having real live performers and musicians about the place.'

'Are you playing your Mozart again?' she asks, referring to the music wafting from the speaker system.

'It's an Ave Maria,' says Ray. 'I put it on to honour you for having set up the concert.'

Maria has to lower her eyes to hide her delight at having music played in her honour.

'And to honour the orchestra. And to let people know that, although it used to be a church . . .'

Now, for Blue Group's entertainment, Ray changes to an exaggerated stage whisper. *'They don't have to be so quiet!'*

'I think you're right. It's beginning to work.'

In just a few minutes, conversation throughout the hall has got louder and more relaxed. To be heard above the amplified music, people have given up whispering and now speak at normal volume. A hundred voices increase the noise significantly, creating more space, widening the boundaries of what is acceptable noise. The new levels afford anonymity within the general hubbub; people have lost their shyness and started to warm their voices, tune their instruments and practise their routines. It's quickly become a madhouse.

'Do you like the music?' Ray asks everyone else.

They do.

'Well, I'd better crack on,' says Ray, slapping both thighs energetically. 'I'll get the tea sorted out.'

He heads off towards the kitchen. Maria looks for Dezzie in the crowd but can't see him anywhere. People are growing restive, milling around apparently aimlessly. She needs to get this show on the road. She spots Marianne at the other side of the hall organizing people, and takes Blue Group over to her.

Marianne is trying to establish some kind of order but she pleads with Maria to make an announcement. 'We'll never get anything done otherwise,' she says as she bangs a radiator with her baton.

As the crowd quieten Maria clears her throat to speak.

'First of all, ladies and gentlemen, let me apologize for being late but the bus broke down.'

They whistle and tut dramatically, a collective expression of disapproval, but it's good-natured.

'Secondly, I'd like to thank you all for coming. I must say I'm overwhelmed by the turnout. There is a tremendous amount of talent in this room and I know we are going to have a show that Hexton will be proud of.'

Everyone cheers and claps. Maria feels quite emotional but she must keep her business head on.

'Miss Bowman, the lady here at the desk, will register you all and if you give us a few minutes, we'll organize a running order of rehearsal.'

As the crowd surges towards Marianne's desk another voice is heard.

'Anyone fancy a cuppa?' shouts Ray above the noise. 'I've made a big pot and left out milk and sugar, just help yourselves.'

The crowd cheer enthusiastically.

'There's no biscuits,' Ray adds.

'Aww!' they say with one voice.

'Bring your own biscuits!' Ray shouts to general laughter.

Community spirit is tangible. It is rowdy and warm, exciting and fun, but it is not all-inclusive. Blue Group still sits outside the throng.

She sees Dezzie again. He's chatting to an older man and he gestures for her to come over. She shakes her head, she can't desert Blue Group and she waves him to her. He doesn't understand her gesture and turns back to continue chatting with the older man.

'Right,' says Maria to her clients, 'we'll have to go and register as well, everybody ready?'

No-one answers, they look scared again.

'I don't want to. They'll laugh at us,' whines Fiona.

The rest of the group, in tacit agreement, say nothing. Maria gives them an encouraging smile but they refuse to meet her eye.

'They're not going to laugh, I promise you. They're just the same as us.'

'No they're not. Look at them!' Fiona gesticulates aggressively. 'They're like celebrities.'

Maria sighs and hunkers down beside Brian's chair,

speaking quietly so that only Blue Group can hear. Everyone crouches or leans in to listen.

'Those old men there with the violins, do they look like celebrities?'

All of Blue Group take sneaky looks at the violinists, then discreetly shake their heads.

'And those girls there, what about that one with the spots on her face, is she a celeb? I don't think so.'

Despite her Machiavellian scheming they are still hesitant, all except Martin, but they do want to be in the show and, with a mixture of rumour-mongering, cajoling and nagging, Maria finally gets them up to the desk.

Chapter 12

While they tell Marianne their names and what their act is Dezzie rejoins them.

'All right, guys?'

All of Blue Group smile broadly, they think Dezzie is great.

'All right, my man?' he says to Brian, mock-punching him on the shoulder.

The clients might think Dezzie is great, as does Maria, but he still has a lot to learn about life at the centre. She doesn't believe in singling anyone out for too much attention, it encourages jealousy and paranoia. In her experience clients should all be treated equally or it leads to trouble.

'Hey Maria, I've just been talking to Spencer, you know, the orchestra leader?'

'Oh yeah? I talked to him on the phone but I haven't met him yet.'

'He was pretty excited when he saw the church has bells. Says they've been working on some overture or other. They want to use the bells in the performance. He's asked me to ring them for him. Cool, eh? I'm in showbiz!'

He makes an exaggeratedly overjoyed face and everyone laughs.

Maria knows from past experience that not everybody always gets Dezzie's jokes. She knows because they sometimes shyly ask her later what he meant. They want to understand him. But his face is so expressive and they are so flattered that he includes them in his jokes that they always laugh.

She wonders if Dezzie realizes they're laughing to please him. Probably not. But his, and Blue Group's, intentions are good and everyone's happy. There's nothing wrong with a bit of harmless hero worship, and after all, church is traditionally the place for it.

Meanwhile, at the other side of the hall, devotion to hero is rife. Ray is performing card tricks for Alice and the other Golden Belles. The women crowd around him, laughing and pushing in close. They're obviously enjoying this girlish fun, having the nice young joiner all to themselves. Although none of them are quite as glamorous as Alice, they are all trim, well-dressed women: Jean Stevenson, Margaret Cameron, Margaret Wallace, Nancy Smith, Betty McAuslan, Jean Anderson, Margaret Kennedy.

They refer to themselves as *the girls*, girls who were married in the 1950s, and led the secret double life of the full-time housewife. A life of rollers and hairnets, of unhitched suspenders and stockings rolled down to doughnuts around their ankles while hubby was at work. Girls who exercised discretion with sanitary products and fiddled the housekeeping, who washed the flour off their faces, applied lipstick and threw their aprons under the sink before their men came home.

These are the lucky ones, the generation whose

husbands had jobs and left them well provided for, probably the most affluent people in Hexton.

Although elderly, these ladies still maintain high standards: leather shoes and matching handbags which will be carefully returned to tissue-paper-filled boxes at the back of the wardrobe when they get home.

'Pick a card, any card,' Ray says as though it were a brand new expression. 'Are you girls here with your mums?'

Margaret Wallace and Jean Stevenson give his shoulders playful slaps. They push at his side, warm and affectionate, like cows hoping for barncake.

'I need a few good-looking volunteers to help with the tea things. But, be honest with me, are you strong enough for these big tea trays? You look like awful delicate wee things to me.'

Rolling up her floral sleeve Alice flexes a taut bicep, but despite workouts with the new equipment at Autumn House she has not entirely banished bingo wings. Her loose underarm flesh dances before Ray but he doesn't seem to notice. He concentrates on giving the girls a magic show. Suddenly he reaches inside Alice's rolled sleeve and produces the Queen of Hearts.

'Is this your card?'

No-one is wearing their reading glasses and so they have to squint but, yes, they verify that this indeed is the card. Holding onto each other for support against the onslaught of his dazzling magic, the girls laugh and hoot like teenagers.

Just behind them, the clock whizzes back half a century. The teenage choir of Hexton High are dressing each other's hair, swapping bows and clips, talking about boys and giggling. Today, because they are representing the school and required to wear full uniform, they design hairdos that are individual and radical. Miss Bowman, otherwise engaged with registration, allows the girls a bit of leeway as long as they keep it quiet and don't let the school down.

Other singers, the Hexton veterans of TV shows and karaoke competitions, take a much more professional approach. They sip at honey in warm water from flasks and practise vocal exercises: me me me, ma ma ma. Their professionalism allows them to zone out the amateurs: the Victory Singers murdering their Sunday school songs and the Hexton Hot Steppers clumping out a number on the wooden floor.

Gerry, Bob and Aldo had arrived an hour ago, not for the rehearsal but because the church has become their regular hang-out. They walked out, silent and sullen, outnumbered by the freaks and weirdos who invaded the space. Now, nosey to find out what all the noise is about, they've moved back inside.

None of them is aware who took the decision to go outside or move back in, it just kind of happened. Hypersensitive to the delicate balance of power within the trio, they anticipate and pre-empt each other's every action. They move and react like one organism.

But this is not to say that they are perfectly in tune. For a bit of sport Gerry and Aldo will sometimes gang up on Bob. Or Aldo and Bob will have a go at Gerry. They will call the victim's mother a cow or, mock-riding him from behind, they'll call him a homo or take his mobile phone and play games on it until the battery dies. The victim must accept his fate and take it on the chin, that's the rules.

It's rare that the other two will join forces against Aldo. He's more than a match for them. Although

Gerry is good-looking and smart and Bob's parents still live together, what gives Aldo the edge is that he simply does not give a fuck. With little self-esteem and nothing to lose, he will often do and say admirably mental things that Bob and Gerry just don't have the balls for.

Although they're too cool to show it, even to each other, they are quite excited by this event. This is the biggest thing in Hexton since the Tree-Huggers' Demo. They sit on the sidelines, crouching low in their seats, attempting invisibility. They silently observe people, mostly old cunts who should be dead by now, cavorting around in a stupid and embarrassing way. After a sniggering and whispered consultation, they appoint top candidates for ridicule and list the girls they would shag.

Elsewhere in the hall the musicians take their instruments out of black plastic cases. They begin, unhurriedly, to tune up. There's no rush. Orchestral musicians are used to sitting around waiting. Once they've tuned they'll sit with their instruments on their knees or by their sides, awaiting further instruction. They've not yet been allocated a seating position in the orchestra because their conductor, Mr Spencer, hasn't yet been able to ascertain where and when they'll rehearse. So they sit in groups, in random twos and threes, sprinkled throughout the hall amidst the young and old, the amateur and professional, the ridiculous and the shaggable.

The music on the sound system has changed. Despite the noise in the hall, Graham Thornton, lead violin since Angus McKay died last year, recognizes something from their repertoire. It is the overture from *The Marriage of Figaro*, and he begins to play along with the CD. He plays from memory, knowing it, as most of his colleagues do, from playing it a million times throughout his long and faintly distinguished career. This church hall in Hexton is a long way from the opera houses he used to play in Europe. Perhaps it is the enthusiasm of these people or the refreshing exposure to so many young women, but he plays as loudly and as vigorously as his worn fingers are able.

During the opening bars Graham energetically saws his violin, as though he's furious with it. It responds by singing back at him like an angry bee. At first he is simply playing, across the miles and the years, along with the musicians who recorded the CD, some of them no doubt known to him, most of them dead probably. But, as loud as it is, his violin is inviting a response from the other instruments that sit redundant between their owners' knees. Then Graham hears a reply from across the hall, a clarinet and then another violin somewhere behind him. Being removed from the other performers is an unusual experience for him, but as the overture proceeds he hears more musicians take up their instruments. Momentum builds.

People gather around him. This too is an unusual experience. He has never before performed so close to an audience, never been without the buffer of his colleagues. He cannot see any of the other musicians; he can only send musical smoke signals and hope they are picked up. Fortunately the replies are getting louder and stronger. The entire orchestra must be playing by now. They're no longer playing along with the CD, Graham can't hear it any more, they're drowning it out with real live music.

Everyone seems to have caught the buzz of the music. All through the hall people are standing amongst the musicians, listening hard, eyes shining, cheeks flushed. The sound is all-inclusive, wrapping everyone together in the posh, complicated exhilaration of the busy violins.

Martin, always an uninhibited music lover, stands waving an imaginary baton, conducting two violinists and a man playing a bassoon. A few kids follow suit. Fiona hops from side to side, a way she has of expressing joy, while Jane stands behind her preparing to catch her if she falls. Brian smiles. Dezzie has apparently disappeared again.

The members of the orchestra, for no other reason than the pleasure it gives, practise their long-practised art. Liver-spotted hands caress wood and metal, knobbly fingers fly across fretboards and keys. Sweat breaches foreheads wrinkled with time and concentration. Off-the-peg jackets, practical and uniform, take the strain of the idiosyncratic activity inside them. Hair falls dramatically across wizened faces as the music climaxes in a whirling rush of violins.

The crowd's appreciation is warm and sincere. Each musician gets applause from his own audience, who clap and whistle long and hard. Musicians' thin bony backs are subject to patting. Long thin loops of damp comb-over hair are replaced on balding scalps.

The orchestra's performance has a galvanizing effect on everyone.

'Right,' says Marianne to Maria, 'that's everybody registered, only three no-shows.'

Marianne's face and neck are slightly pink, a very becoming girlish flush is upon her.

'I've organized a rehearsal rota, the hall's going to be in almost constant use but for now I've sorted out a running order for this afternoon. I think it'll be better if we get the young ones done and dusted first, the others won't mind waiting on the kids. So, first up are my choir, then the Hot Steppers . . .'

'Oh Marianne, you're brilliant! What would I do without you?'

Behind her bifocals, Marianne's eyes are shining as she gives Maria a sardonic stare.

'You'd get lynched. Now, let's get this show on the road.'

After the last singer sings and Marianne has stopped her stopwatch, everyone drifts away. Maria and Marianne gather cups and mugs and take them into the kitchen.

'Oh, leave those cups Marianne,' says Maria. 'I'll pop back tomorrow and wash them.'

'I'm sure you've better things to do with your weekend.'

'Sadly I haven't. But I'll have to get my lot back to the centre now or they'll miss their buses. I'll come back tomorrow.'

Marianne pulls on her coat and now Maria notices Dezzie is here too, standing right behind her. How long has he been here? She hopes he hasn't heard the conversation, especially the bit about her having nothing to do on the weekend. There's nothing less attractive to a man than a woman no-one else wants.

'Hear that, Dezzie?' says Marianne chirpily as she exits. 'Can you believe this young lady doesn't have a date this weekend?'

Maria presses her chest and concentrates on sorting the blue mugs from the yellow ones.

'You could come out with me,' says Dezzie quietly.

'Well I've got to . . .'

Maria is pointing at the mugs. For God's sake woman, get a grip. Try to come out of this humiliation with at least a little dignity.

'I've . . .'

She's pointing again. She doesn't know what she's trying to say but it seems to be along the lines of: she can't go on a date with him because she has to wash a load of old mugs.

'Would you come out with me?'

He's been put in this embarrassing position by that big mouth Marianne. Under these circumstances Dezzie would feel obliged to ask anyone out, whether he fancied them or not, he's that kind of guy. But what if he really does fancy her and Marianne has just provided him with the perfect opportunity?

She has deliberated too long.

'OK,' he says, 'fair enough,' as he turns to leave.

And she's blown it.

'Dezzie!' she calls, rather too stridently. 'Yes. Thank you. I'd like to go out. That would be nice.'

Chapter 13

Maria is on the phone to Colette, her best friend among the Kelvin Street Kids. They've only been on for ten minutes and already the conversation has dried up. Colette doesn't talk much about herself. She has two babies. She and her husband are very happy and quite well off. Maria is happy for her but Colette probably thinks talking about the good things in her life will make Maria feel bad in some way. She's also long since stopped asking Maria, probably for the same reasons, what she's up to at the weekend. This often makes for awkward silences between them.

For once Maria has something to report on that front, but she doesn't want to blurt it out like a school-girl. She wants to drop it in casually, and so she must take a rather circuitous route. She does this by giving Colette a blow-by-blow account of the rehearsal.

'The Hot Steppers are pretty good but the Golden Belles are amazing. Every one of them can kick their height and they're all over sixty.'

'God,' says Colette, 'I can't kick my own arse. I've just no energy with running after the kids all day. And not just physically, my brain's turning to mush.'

This is one subject Colette can talk about for hours, how the kids are draining her, but it's not on Maria's agenda today.

'Ray, the guy who gave us the hall, made tea for everyone and of course nobody thought to wash their cups . . .'

'Ray? What's he like, tasty?'

'Not bad. So there were all the dirty cups lying . . .'

'Boyf material?'

'No.'

'Why not?'

'Married. Smoker.'

'Right.'

'I told Marianne I'd come back and . . .'

'You're lucky, working with tasty men, even if they are married. My libido's packed in. I've shut up shop; Gerry hasn't got near me for months, he's stopped trying.'

Colette has everything and yet she moans. Maria knows why: to make her underachieving best friend feel better. Ever since Anna said what she said, all of the Kelvin Street Kids have been doing this: patronizing her, overcompensating for the fact that they have husbands and kids and money and cleavages.

'I'm sorry Colette, I'll have to go. I'm off out tonight; some bloke in my work has asked me out on a date.'

Maria has plumped for her best bra, a pale blue seamless underwired one with matching pants. The material is unpatterned and silky smooth. She experiments with cupping her breast through her dress, the sensation Dezzie would get were he to get lucky, which he won't. It feels nice. She should stop worrying about it. After all, he must be aware by now she's not buxom. He sees her every day with her workaday unwired bra under her jumper and he still asked her out. The manner of his asking could have been better, though.

The dress is also blue: short but not too short, button-through for ease of access, and when she walks the skirt swings nicely, accenting her best feature, her high tight bum. She has on wee boxy heels, feminine without being slutty. They are by no means *fuck me* shoes. Rather they are *take me for a nice meal and then ask nicely* shoes.

'Wow! Miss Maria, what a stunner!' Dezzie says enthusiastically when they meet outside the restaurant. 'You look terrific. Your dress is lovely, is it new? It really suits you.'

'Thanks,' she says. 'I like your tie.'

She's not just being polite, she really does like it. It makes him look older and more responsible. As far as she can remember, Dezzie has never worn a tie to work.

The restaurant is in the trendier part of the city. Maria has never been to Il Trattoria before, but it looks very nice. It's old-fashioned Italian with posh pink damask table covers and heavy napkins. There are bottles of wine in wicker baskets and paintings of old Napoli on a high shelf around the wall. As the waiter shows them to their table by the window Dezzie puts his hand gently on the small of her back, protectively guiding her to the table, although it's only four yards away and there seem to be no dangerous hazards en route. This is what boyfriends do.

The menu is on huge unwieldy laminated cards. There are no surprises, just all the usual Italian-type dishes.

'So what do you fancy?'

'Oh I don't know, I'm easy,' says Maria.

She knows what she doesn't want. She'd already ruled out spaghetti before she saw the menu. It would be embarrassing to get sauce on her face or spill it on her dress, and to avoid that she'd have to wear her napkin like a bib.

'Yeah I know you're easy, but what do you fancy to eat?'

Dezzie snickers at his own joke and it is a few seconds before Maria can join him. She's never heard him use this suggestive kind of banter before, but then again she's never met him before in a situation unrelated to work. She'll have to readjust her impression of him to accommodate this, but it's fine, it's fine.

'So what's it to be?' he says.

The waiter is hovering.

'I'll have the veal, thank you Dezzie.'

'No starter?'

'Eh . . .'

She breaks into a mild panic as her eyes rove across the menu. Maria's hand is pressing down on her chest, restricting her breathing. Relax, relax. She hasn't thought about a starter, hasn't even looked at them.

'No thanks, just the veal will be fine.'

Veal in a cream sauce, this seems like a safe knife-and-fork option. She likes cream and has never tried veal before.

'Fair enough. No starter for me either, thanks. I'll have mushroom risotto. And a bottle of Soave, cheers.'

He's a veggie, she'd forgotten that. She should have remembered. Once, in the staffroom, someone put a sausage on his plate by accident. Quietly, without anyone else noticing, Dezzie had washed his plate before eating from it. The meat must have disgusted him. And now she's chosen the most unvegetarian thing possible – baby cow, taken from its mother's womb for the express purpose of being slaughtered for her dining pleasure. He must be offended but he doesn't show it.

'I would've had the spaghetti but I didn't want to end up with sauce all over my face. You might not fancy me then.'

Maria laughs in recognition of that dilemma. It's little things like this that convince her that she and Dezzie are made for each other. Won't it be fun to have spaghetti for their first anniversary dinner? For every anniversary, for that matter; it could become their tradition. They can eat and kiss and mush tomato sauce into each other's faces, even when they're over forty.

Really she should turn veggie too, and sooner rather than later. She might as well, when they're married she'll have to, it's too much hassle cooking separate meals. She should change her order and join him in the vegetarian option, but she's thought about it too long; the chef will have started cooking the veal by now. She doesn't want the baby cow to have died in vain; she shouldn't waste the nutritional value in it.

Dezzie is pouring big ones from the bottle of Soave, but the second time Maria puts her hand demurely over her glass.

'That's enough for me, thanks.'

She sips at this glassful until the end of the meal. She wouldn't mind getting a bit squiffy, it is a special occasion, but she doesn't want Dezzie to think that anything she might do, she might do because of drunkenness. The fact is that anything she might do she might do because she wants to. She *really* wants to. And she might do anything.

'I managed to scrounge the car off my sister tonight, so I can give you a lift up the road if you like,' he says.

Of course, she hadn't noticed, he doesn't have his motorbike helmet with him.

'That would be great.'

'By the looks of it, it's going to pour down any minute now.'

A few moments later drops of water hit the window beside them. Dezzie gently takes her hand and, smiling, says, 'Look.'

He was right, it's raining now. It's raining and he's holding her hand as they sit warm and cosy in the restaurant looking out on the dark rainy night. He's even borrowed a car to take her home. They'll soon be sitting in the car listening to the windscreen wipers and Dezzie will kiss her. Really this date couldn't be any more perfect.

When the bill comes they tussle over it and Maria eventually lets him win. But this will have to stop. She has accepted his generosity graciously this time, but if they're to be going out on regular dates she'll have to pay her way.

It's still raining when they leave the restaurant.

'You wait here and I'll bring the car across. We don't want your pretty blue dress getting ruined, now do we?'

He heads across the road while Maria shelters under the restaurant canopy.

Dezzie goes towards a car and then stops and speaks to a man who, despite the downpour, is standing in the street. It's hard to see what's going on through the thick curtain of rain, but after a few minutes it looks as if

Dezzie has put his arm around the man. They are engrossed in conversation, both nodding their heads. Amazingly, Dezzie unlocks the passenger door and appears to invite the man into the car. Maria wants to call out and remind him that she's here; he seems to have forgotten her. Surely he's not going to drive off and leave her?

'Maria!' Dezzie calls.

He waves his arm, beckoning her to come across the road. He isn't going to bring the car to her after all. What about her pretty blue dress?

She has to dodge puddles and passing cars to get to them. As she approaches she sees that Dezzie's friend is an old man. He's as tall and thin as she is, stooped with the weight of his wet clothes.

'Maria, this is Peter,' Dezzie says.

'Hello Peter.'

Maria speaks as she does when meeting a new client at the centre: in a warm, accepting manner. Peter grunts a reply but doesn't look at her. He seems unaware of how wet he is and stares straight ahead, even when replying to Dezzie's questions. His hands are basketed together in front of him, collecting rain, until Dezzie gently unclasps them.

'You're freezing, Peter. How long have you been here?'

Peter reminds Maria of a faithful old hound that's been given the command *stay* by his master and then been abandoned. The rain has found paths through his wispy white hair, which lies in clumps. It drips off his brow and the end of his nose. He shivers convulsively from the toes up, spraying fine droplets that fly out horizontally. Peter isn't wearing socks and the rain bubbles through some of the eyelets of his old shoes, which lack laces.

'Have you had something to eat?' asks Dezzie.

Peter mumbles. Maria can tell that Dezzie hasn't understood the reply but he doesn't repeat the question. She and Dezzie are now almost as wet as Peter is. Rain drips down the back of her neck and inside her dress.

'Hang on a minute,' says Dezzie to Peter, and Peter nods.

He takes Maria aside and whispers.

'Do you mind if we give the old fella a lift? He'll never make it home on his own.'

Dezzie's so nice. The downside with nice guys is they're undiscerning in their niceness; they're equally nice to everyone. But it's a small price to pay for such a lovely boyf and so she tries, and succeeds, in pushing uncharitable thoughts out of her head.

'No, of course not.'

Dezzie doesn't ask her twice. He returns immediately to Peter for another huddled conversation. After some convincing he helps Peter into the front passenger seat, pushing the seat back and carefully folding the old man's thin legs into the tiny space. He crosses to the driver's side and signals for Maria to get in behind. Dezzie has jumped in and closed his door before Maria can push herself into the confined space of the back seat. She squashes in, her legs wetting her chest, and feels the damp spread out across her back.

It's warm and dry in here, at least. Being inside the car is better than being outside, except that there's a bad smell. It's one that Maria is well acquainted with: the sharp fizzy smell of fresh urine. Less familiar, but nonetheless unmistakable, there is also a top note of stale alcohol. When Dezzie starts the engine the rank potpourri of urine and alcohol intensifies to noxious levels. The windows quickly mist and the air in the small car becomes fuggy. She would open a window, lashing rain is preferable to this, but it's not her car. It's not even Dezzie's. Maria wonders what Dezzie's sister will have to say about her little car being doused in wino piss.

As he drives, Dezzie keeps up a cheery one-sided conversation with Peter. Maria would like to take part but leaning forward fills her nostrils with Peter's stench, and she fears she may chuck up her veal dinner. Then the baby cow really will have died in vain, and Dezzie's sister will have the smell of vomit to contend with as well.

She notices that they are travelling in the opposite direction, away from where she lives. They ride for about fifteen minutes, by which time Maria has stopped noticing the smell and is now worrying that it has permeated her good blue dress. Finally Dezzie slows the car.

'OK Peter, Wilson Street. Where do you want me to drop you?' Peter continues staring ahead.

'I'm saying we're here, Peter,' Dezzie says, this time much louder. 'Where d'you want dropped?'

With great effort, Peter shakes himself to attention. He points towards a block of flats they have just cruised past.

'No problem, mate. I'll turn and go back.'

It is a good five minutes before the traffic allows Dezzie to turn the car.

They pull up outside a dilapidated block of flats on the main road, next door to a late-night Spar shop.

'Here?'

Peter nods.

'Here,' says Dezzie again, this time with relief in his

voice. But Peter has returned to his catatonic state.

'Hang on a second, Peter,' says Dezzie, although it's obvious that Peter isn't trying to get out. From the back seat Maria can't see what's causing the delay. She feels the weight of the car shift slightly as Dezzie lifts a bum cheek and checks his back pocket. It shifts again as he tries the other one.

'Actually Maria,' he says, 'you couldn't lend us a couple of quid, could you?'

Embarrassed by her slowness of understanding, she rushes at her bag. She frantically scrambles for her purse and pulls out a five-pound note. There then follows a fast cash transfer where Maria, somewhat rashly, she later considers, hands the money to Dezzie who immediately hands it on to Peter.

Almost resignedly, Peter discreetly palms it with the dignity and practised ease of a regular recipient of kind deeds and small change. It's only then that he fumbles for the door handle. He weakly claws at the door while Dezzie springs from his seat to help him. When he gets him upright the old fellow is a little unsteady on his feet. He begins to totter off in the wrong direction until Dezzie corrects his trajectory back on to the path towards the flats.

'Now, mind what I said Peter, a nice hot bath and you'll be right as rain tomorrow,' Dezzie calls as he climbs back in. To Maria's relief, he doesn't ask if she wants to sit in the front. There probably a residual pool of piss on the seat and her dress is ruined as it is.

The road is quieter now, so Dezzie begins to negotiate a three-point turn.

'How do you know Peter then, Dezzie?' she asks innocently.

Perhaps he's a friend; she hopes he's not a relative.

'I don't,' Dezzie says, laughing, 'I just met him.'

Maria chastises herself, humbled by his compassion for a poor old soul. She doesn't deserve a man as good as Dezzie. Thank God he's not party to her snooty internal monologue. He thinks she's a nice person.

As Dezzie turns the car Maria sees Peter taking another wrong turning.

'Dezzie, look! He's not going into the flats.'

The old man has wandered back towards the Spar shop. Dezzie stops the car and they watch Peter, with surprising energy, pull open the door. It bangs closed below a neon sign advertising Tennant's lager, which flickers intermittently in the rain.

Dezzie is open-mouthed. He lifts both hands from the steering wheel and leaves them in the air.

'Ack,' he says.

His hands come back down onto the wheel and then he lifts and bangs them down hard.

'He promised me he'd go straight home.'

Maria looks down.

'D'you think maybe Peter is an alcoholic?' she offers.

'Yeah obviously he is, but he promised me he'd go straight home.'

They sit in silence for a few moments while Dezzie leans back and lets a breath escape slowly from closed lips. He doesn't start the car. Maria's keen to get moving; she wants to be gone from this street before Peter emerges with a bottle of cheap wine and a couple of cans paid for with her fiver.

'Ack,' he says again, this time more philosophically. 'What are you gonna do?'

Dezzie catches Maria's eye in the rear-view mirror and gives her a sheepish smile. She eagerly returns it.

She doesn't want Peter to completely ruin their evening. Then she reaches forward and squeezes his hand.

'Let's go home.'

Dezzie looks back at the shop but Peter still hasn't come out.

'Yeah,' he says as he returns her squeeze and starts the engine.

At the front door to Maria's flat there is confused hesitation. It looks like Dezzie isn't going to kiss her. She gives him every opportunity. After thanking him for a lovely night she leans towards him and looks into his eyes. He doesn't say he's had a lovely night or we must do this again sometime or do you have plans for next weekend, all the things she had creatively visualized him doing. He just stands there. Not smiling, but not frowning either. She's done everything but close her eyes and pucker up. Why did he walk her to her door if he isn't going to kiss her? So, with a sigh, she turns to put her key in the lock.

Dezzie takes a step towards her. She can feel his breath on her neck. He gently touches her arm and this is all the encouragement she needs. She turns swiftly and clamps her mouth to his. For one horrible millisecond it occurs to her, what if he wasn't about to kiss her? What if he only wanted to say *cheerio; mind how you go*? But he responds, he's a good kisser. Maria feels an immediate moistening.

Sometimes, alone, under the duvet, she likens her excitable body to a fruit. She used to think of herself as a peach, to imagine a man pushing at her, opening her like a ripe peach. Sometimes, when she's had an ugly day, when a character on TV has made some cruel remark about a female character being unattractive, she can only think of herself as a pear. Obviously this is to do with her shape, which she accepts; even the humblest of pears is juicy, comparing favourably with the peach. But recently she has begun to think of a pear that, left for very much longer, will turn to a dry grainy mush. She throws her arms around Dezzie's neck and kisses him hard.

Dezzie puts his hands on either side of her waist, elbows bent, holding her as though he's about to hoist her up in a romantic ballet move. They stay in this position for several minutes until Maria breaks, looks into his face, smiles, and then hugs him tight. Dezzie returns the hug, tenderly rubbing his arms across her back. They are cheek to cheek and Maria kisses him, closer and closer to his mouth until they are snogging again. This time Dezzie's hand slides down and across Maria's bum. Instinctively she pushes in towards him.

She has decided, after a long consultation with Madonna and Nelson earlier, that she will not be sleeping with Dezzie tonight.

'Whoa! You're getting a bit ahead of yourself, missy,' said Madonna. 'Who says he'll want to move things on to a physical level?'

But she was teasing. 'Who am I kidding; he's a guy, isn't he?' she laughed.

Although Madonna and Nelson enjoyed a bit of sport at Maria's expense, their advice was unequivocal.

'Always leave them gasping for more,' said Madonna, 'it'll raise your stock.'

Madonna and Nelson often gave conflicting points of view, that was after all why she'd hired them, to get both sides of every story, but for once Nelson concurred.

'Relationships between men and women should be about mutual respect. People should not be in such a hurry to drop their drawers,' he said.

Madonna had laughed.

'That's rich coming from you, you old goat!'

Nelson laughed too. They were both having a great time tormenting her. Meditation was supposed to be relaxing.

'But he's right, Maria. Men don't want a wife who's a slut.'

'Hen,' said Nelson gently, 'you keep your hand on your ha'penny.'

Maria fully intends to do so. It would be unseemly for her to jump straight into bed with Dezzie, he's a colleague and, more importantly, the man she hopes to marry. She doesn't want their first date to be marred by memories of how she behaved like a common slapper.

Still and all, the kissing is so delicious that she can't bear that it should end just yet. But, if she was to invite him in, would he understand that it didn't mean sex? Surely he knows her well enough by now to know that she's not like that. She tilts her pelvis up, getting closer to his, and he answers by fondling her buttocks. Dezzie's a gentleman, she's sure of it.

'Do you want to come up for . . .'

Kissing has caused all the blood to run to her groin, she has forgotten the word. What's she trying to say? And then she remembers.

'For a coffee?'

She has taken too long to find the word and now they're both embarrassed. Dezzie probably thinks she means it as code.

'Just a quick one,' she adds.

Dezzie looks alarmed.

'I mean a quick coffee!'

He looks away.

'I better get back,' he mumbles. 'I'll need to give the car a bit of a sluice out, get rid of the smell.'

This is the first time either of them has mentioned Peter's rich aroma.

'Jan'll go mad, she'll never lend me it again.'

Maria struggles to disguise her bafflement. He was squeezing her butt cheeks a second ago.

'Yeah, the car, of course.'

'But next time, eh?'

So there's going to be a next time. She breathes a sigh of relief.

'OK,' she says softly, 'that'll be nice. I'll look forward to it.'

Maria closes the door and listens for his footsteps walking briskly down the hall. What was all that about? Does he not fancy her? He said there was going to be a next time, so presumably he does. Maybe he, like her, felt it was too soon. Maybe he's thinking about the long term too. He's a sensitive guy, and probably not one to let his prick dictate. They have so much in common. As she's brushing her teeth she makes another decision. She won't do anything about the moistening. Out of respect for Dezzie, her hand won't stray to her ha'penny tonight.

As she's pulling her nightie on over her head, a loud insistent banging starts at her door.

Chapter 14

Maria puts the chain on and opens the door a crack. It's Dezzie. She quickly closes the door again, takes the chain off and opens the door properly. He rushes into her arms and kisses her passionately there in the doorway. It's a matter of half a minute before they're on the bed and he's pulling her nightie over her head. In the hurried fumblings she hasn't had a chance to unbutton it and gets snagged, her head bagged inside, breathless, until she can undo it.

Despite this initial clumsiness, Dezzie is a great lover. When she's naked he kisses all over her body, light butterfly kisses that drive her crazy.

He touches her breasts, her back arching with the delicious coolness of his fingers. He lightly strokes the sides, the slopes, the undersides of her breasts, teasingly avoiding her nipples, though she writhes and sighs.

She opens her eyes to find his mouth and kiss him but as soon as she does, she becomes embarrassed. Dezzie is staring at her pathetically underdeveloped breasts.

She rolls onto her side away from him and pulls up her legs.

'I don't have much. I'm sorry, they're too small.'

She puts up little resistance when he slowly pulls her onto her back and looks into her face.

'Too small for what?' he says, smiling.

Then, faint as a breath, he kisses her nipple.

'You're beautiful, Maria.'

These are magic words. They transport Maria to a place where breast size is of no significance. In this place there are no pimples or bad smells or squelchy noises, there exists only pleasure.

Maria wants to touch Dezzie, to let him feel something of the ecstasy she feels, but every time she puts a hand on him he gently removes it. He's concentrating only on her satisfaction.

'What do you want me to do? What do you like?' he whispers.

And he continues to whisper until Maria, shyly, tells him.

'There, down there,' she murmurs.

This seems to excite him and he moans with pleasure as he explores her.

Dezzie's so different from other men she's slept with, never mind the proper boyfriends she's had. He's a hundred times better than her last boyf, Dirk. Apart from the fact that Dezzie has the added bonus of having two feet, Dirk was too controlling. He hated it if she tried to tell him what to do. Once when she asked him to touch her a little more gently he shouted, 'Don't tell me how to touch a woman's tits, I know what I'm doing!'

This was embarrassing enough, but there were other people in the train carriage and they must have heard him.

Maria has reached the point where she has to have

Dezzie inside her or she'll explode. She pulls at his trouser pockets, feeling his slim hips underneath. For the first time it strikes her that he's still fully dressed.

'Take your clothes off,' she says, pulling at his belt.

He resists at first.

'Please,' she begs.

Dezzie has nothing to be shy about. His penis is beautiful, not as big as Dirk's was but much nicer-looking. His foreskin is pale and creamy, like the skin of a baby.

'Please Dezzie, please put it in me.'

He lies on top of her and puts his penis inside her. His fingers are splayed on the sheet, his elbows locked as he supports his weight, something Dirk never did. He rocks to and fro, in and out. His breath is fast and shallow. She wraps her arms and legs around him and feels his body clench. Waves of euphoria wash over her.

'Oh my God,' she says.

She keeps on saying it. 'Oh my God, oh my God,' she says over and over again until the waves recede. And then she cries.

Dezzie holds her tight, wiping and kissing her tears.

'Are you OK?' he whispers.

'Yeah,' Maria gulps, 'I'm fine.'

'Was it OK?'

'It was fantastic, Dezzie. Was it good for you?'

Dezzie smiles.

'Fantastic.'

'Thank you. Thank you, Dezzie, that was amazing.'

Maria is beginning to nod off. She has been faintly aware of him moving on the bed but now she realizes that he's putting his clothes on.

'Dezzie?'

The significance of this hits her. He's not staying the night, he's not going to fall asleep cuddling into her and wake up beside her tomorrow. He got what he wanted and now he's leaving. He probably feels dirty: he's made a mistake, had a one-night stand with a workmate and can't bear to face her. He doesn't want to set eyes on her ever again.

Dezzie leans over and kisses Maria, an automatic, see you later, kiss.

'Aren't you going to stay?'

'I have to get Jan's car sorted out.'

'You don't have to go now,' she says, trying to keep the desperation out of her voice. 'We could clean it in the morning. We can get up early and give it a good scrub . . .'

'I've got to go Maria, I'm sorry.'

'OK.'

'Bye bye.'

Maria sees him to the door and then pulls her nightie back on. She's too relaxed and sleepy to let the grief begin now. Plenty of time for grief and humiliation tomorrow.

Three hours later she's opening the door again. She hasn't put the chain on this time.

'I got it valeted. All-night car wash in Westwood,' Dezzie explains, 'cost a bloody fortune.'

Maria takes his hand and leads him back to bed. He's more careful with the nightie this time.

Ray has finished the sideboard. It's taken three times longer to make than it should have, but it's a job well done and gives him pleasure. Working at this rate he's unlikely to make any real money, he'll hardly turn a profit but it'll be enough. The buyer was pretty pleased with it and has commissioned two more, that'll keep him going for the foreseeable. Ray doesn't think beyond that. He's bought the wood and will make a start on the next sideboard once they get the snooker table in. He decides to play his guitar while he waits for it to arrive.

Inspired by the orchestra's performance at the rehearsal, Ray has dug out his guitar and dusted it down. He runs through his repertoire of old tunes while the metal strings bite his soft fingertips. He thought he'd never lift this guitar again. A few months ago he poured his soul into these familiar melodies, playing until his fingers cracked and bled. Now he just plays, without hope or despair, he just plays.

Alice from the OAP centre offered him the snooker table. It seemed strange, when she mentioned it the first time, that an old lady should be interested in snooker, but she must have been thinking of this place as a home for it. A full-size proper slate table with balls and cues and all the gubbins, it must be worth a packet. It was a bequest to Autumn House but there's no room for it there and they can't sell it.

Getting it here was going to be a problem. Ray's had to give up his works van. He couldn't afford to keep up the lease so, once he unloaded his tools into the church, back it went. He was sorry to see it go, it was a smart van and he always liked the company name on it in the professional livery, but what the hell. Young Bob has volunteered his dad's van to bring the snooker table.

'You didn't tell me it was a fish van,' says Alice through gritted teeth when it arrives, 'the table'll be stinking.'

'Not necessarily,' Ray says, but there's an overpowering whiff of fish when Bob's dad opens the back door.

The blankets thrown around the table to protect the woodwork have come off one corner and Alice is making a fuss. She is barking instructions at the volunteer driver and the crowd of youngsters who have rallied round to help bring it in. Alice doesn't seem to like the young people who come around the church, but she knows Ray's policy.

A dozen lads are lifting and pulling and heaving at the table to bring it out of the van. When they get it out Bob, Gerry and Aldo each grab a corner. As if lifting this elephantine weight were a great honour, they fight off the others for the corner spots and keep the last corner for Ray. The others bunch together along the sides, shoving in to make a space for themselves. After a count of three they lift together, but their forward progress is ragged and dangerously wobbly. The lads are rushing at it, trying to get it inside before they humiliate themselves. From experience, Ray knows what's required. They need a beat, a slow beat.

'Wait!' he calls.

He's surprised by how quickly they obey.

'Right, let's get it up on our shoulders, OK? One two three!'

They get it up on their shoulders.

'OK, wait. Everybody happy?'

Everybody's happy.

'Now, let's move together, slow and steady as she goes, OK? Starting on the right leg, one two three!'

> *'I went down to St James's Infirmary*
> *To see my baby there.'*

161

Their entrance into the church is slow and metrical.

> *'She was stretched out on a long white table,*
> *So pale*
> *So cold,*
> *So fair.'*

With processional solemnity, they bring the table through the church doors. Once they have safely put it down Aldo asks Ray, 'What was that song you were singing?'

Ray is shocked by this. He's unaware that he had been singing. He thought it was only in his head. He has to get away from this question and goes to stand outside again.

Bob's dad is shutting up the van while Alice waves a ten-pound note at him.

'Don't be silly; put your money away hen!'

'No, come on now, it must have cost you something in petrol,' she argues.

'Listen, I'm only pleased to lend a hand. Good on you for starting it up,' Bob's dad says as he climbs into the driver's seat.

Alice turns to Ray, a quizzical expression making deep grooves in her face.

'Starting what up?' she asks him.

Ray shrugs, as bemused as she is.

'Give me a shout if you need any more equipment moved. Any time. Best of luck with your wee youth club. Good on you.'

Bob's dad gives Alice and Ray an American-style salute as he drives off. They stand and watch him pull away. Neither of them returns the salute.

When they go back into the church the young people

have wasted no time. They are unpacking cues and setting the balls on the table.

'Oh no you don't!' says Alice, moving quickly to the table and sweeping the balls together.

'Ho! Wait a wee minute!' says Aldo. 'We humphed the fucker in here, we're getting the first game!'

'The *first* game?' says Alice. 'Who says you're getting a game at all?'

Pandemonium breaks out at this, but Alice stands with her hand on her hip. Ray decides he's going to take a back seat on this one.

'This table is the property of Autumn House and I'm responsible for it. I'm not having you lot wreck it.'

The youngsters surge towards her with aggressive displays of chest jutting and noisy remonstration, but Alice stays put.

'Fuck's sake!' says Bob. 'My dad brought it here. We're not going to wreck it!'

Encouraged by Bob's swearing at the old woman and perhaps Ray's non-intervention, the rest of them take up the 'fuck's sake' theme.

'Well, what guarantee have I got?' says Alice, looking to Ray to back her up.

Ray says nothing. If they're all going to come in here then they'll have to find a way of getting along. She's a feisty old bird, but she's a troublemaker as well as a chancer. Maybe the *come one come all* idea isn't going to work out after all. If it can't be resolved he has the ultimate sanction of having the snooker table removed – it's not worth all this hassle.

'I'm keeping the stuff. If you want to use the balls and cues you pay a deposit. End of story.'

Alice turns away and then back again as another thought appears to strike her.

'Ten pounds.'

The shouting begins again, accompanied by disbelieving laughter at the effrontery of the old dear.

'Ten pound? We don't have ten pound between us. Where are we gonna get a tenner?' says Gerry without rancour.

'Well here's a wee idea for you,' says Alice with mock patience, before yelling, 'away and work!'

'D'you see any jobs around here?' says Bob, once the furore dies down. 'You're OK, you've got your pension every week and your own house . . .'

'Aye,' agrees Aldo. 'And your wee gumsy pensioners' club with fucking snooker tables you're too fucking decrepit and gumsy to play.' Aldo now impersonates a decrepit gumsy pensioner feebly trying to play snooker. Everyone laughs. Ray laughs and doesn't try to hide it. Why should he? Fair play, he thinks, Aldo's a moron but he's funny sometimes and anyway, she had it coming. She has shown them nothing but contempt, why should they be deferential? She's a cheeky bastard as far as Ray can see.

'Listen you!' Alice shouts. 'I don't know where you're getting gumsy from, I've got my own teeth.'

To prove this she taps a long painted fingernail on her front teeth.

'And pensioner or no, I'll hammer any one of you at snooker. Any one of you that can raise the deposit, that is.'

The kids are buzzing with the challenge she's thrown down. They go into a strategy huddle, sharing fund-raising ideas to get the money together.

'What about this Burberry shirt, would you take that?' says Bob, the most pragmatic of the group. 'I paid seventy-five quid for it.'

'Seventy-five quid! Did the shop have big windows? Because they must have seen you coming.'

'It's worth a hundred, it was in the sale!'

'Listen son, what it's worth and what you paid for it are two different things. That shirt's no use to me, it's not my colour. Ten pounds deposit or nobody plays.'

After a few minutes of grumbling and pocket-shaking the ten pounds deposit is assembled. Alice chooses Aldo as her opponent. Not surprisingly, she has no support; the rest of the assembly are firmly behind Aldo. Ray returns to playing his guitar. He should be getting on with the next sideboard but he's interested to see who wins, stopping to watch when either of them takes a shot.

Alice, it seems, is all talk. Her snooker skills are minimal. Aldo is no expert either; both of them miss shots and even occasionally pot the white ball. For this reason the game takes a long time but eventually, to the jubilant delight of his cheering audience, Aldo wins. Alice takes her defeat on the chin, stoically returning the ten pounds deposit. Aldo, magnanimous in triumph, holds out his hand. With dignity and a smile playing around her lips, Alice returns his firm handshake. Fair play. After that she secures and returns the ten pounds for every game, until they've all had a turn on the table. Later, when everyone else has gone home, she approaches Ray.

'I was thinking, with the rehearsals going on here for the community show and all these young ones hanging about, we could start a café.'

'We?'

'I don't mean you, I mean me. Me and some of the girls. We've got time on our hands. And you know, they're right. In some ways pensioners have got a better deal. I was thinking about what Bob's dad said, about a youth club. We've got everything we need in the kitchen here: the urn and cups and that. Maybe we could have a youth club.'

'I think we already have.'

'Well, about a café, what d'you think?'

'I think that would be very public-spirited of you, Alice.'

Although he doesn't say so, Ray is surprised and pleased. Outwardly Alice is a hard-boiled old roaster, but she's obviously got a kind heart in there.

'Public-spirited my arse. I only want this lot to come in so I can give them a good spanking at the snooker.'

'Are you sure about that? I don't want to hurt your feelings but you looked pretty rubbish to me.'

'Oh, don't let the old granny act fool you. I'm hiding my light under a bushel. Nobody calls me gumsy and gets away with it,' she says with grim determination. 'I'm only reeling them in, Ray, only reeling them in.'

Chapter 15

There is wonderful news. In a cold and officious memo to Maria, and copied to Dezzie, Mike reveals that Brian's application for independent living is currently being assessed. This means if successful, he'll get his own flat. He'll need help around the clock, of course, but the important thing is that he'll be free to do what he wants when he wants.

It is just after lunch, and Blue Group are assembled in the common room watching the afternoon news. The common room is busy at this time of day. Yellow Group and Green Group are also here. The two other groups sit quietly, engrossed in the programme, but Maria's lot banter and bicker between themselves. Several members of the other groups have already shot disapproving glances and a few irate 'shhhs' towards Blue Group's corner. Things are not helped with the exciting arrival of Blue Group's best pal, Dezzie.

Initially Maria had not been keen to encourage Brian's application. She was scared that it might break his heart not to get it; he stands a much better chance when he's a bit older. Brian's still only nineteen, a very young nineteen. But Dezzie has no such qualms; he's bursting to tell him the news.

Dezzie, who only recently arrived at the centre, has written a much stronger application than Maria could ever have achieved. He worked hard on the submission, doing endless Internet research and putting his heart and soul into writing it. And now it seems he may have been right to be optimistic.

Still and all, she wonders if it's wise to build Brian's hopes when he could yet be disappointed. But she knows that it's almost a foregone conclusion that, with his infectious optimism and sensual whispers in her ear, Dezzie will eventually win her over, and he does.

On hearing the news, Brian throws up as anticipated. But they are prepared: Maria has already popped the plastic lunch bib around his neck. Once the vomit has been removed Blue Group form an orderly queue to congratulate him with hugs, kisses and hair touslings.

'That's it mate: party back at yours every night! Plenty of birds, plenty of booze, we can't go wrong,' says Dezzie with a secret wink to Maria.

'Like. A. Club. I'll. Charge. An. Entry. Fee.'

'Discount rates for your mates though, eh?'

'I'll come and stay with you for my holidays,' says Martin, as excited as Brian and Dezzie.

'Brian, you realize that it's only being assessed at this stage,' warns Maria. 'Not everyone who applies actually gets a flat. There aren't enough to go around.'

'Yeah but with the professor here off to uni next year, he's in with a good chance. All those university birds Brian, eh?'

'Good. To. Get. Away. From. Philious. And. Bilious. Never. See. Those. Goons. Again.'

Everyone knows who Philious and Bilious are: Brian's dad and his brother. They're well used to the acrimony with which Brian speaks of his father and the inventively insulting names he has for him: Philibuster, Philbert, Phil the Fool.

'Come on now Brian, let's not get bitter and twisted,' says Maria gently.

'Next. Year. University. My. Own. Place. No. Phil. No. Bill.'

To the consternation of the members of Green Group and Yellow Group, Brian drives his wheelchair as fast as he can around the perimeter of the common room. Blue Group watch and giggle as he careens into the back of occupied chairs before reversing, like a dodgem car, and then carries on around the room at speed. At the request of their key workers, the other service users do their best to ignore this attention-seeking behaviour.

Brian's still smiling like a maniac as he makes Grand Prix circuits around the room, all the while ignoring Maria's requests, and then demands, that he stop it right now. He apparently feels that he's still not quite as annoying as he could be, and ramps it up a bit. The Dynavox has a remote-control facility that allows him to take over the television. As he passes the telly he flips the channel to a noisy cowboys and Indians shoot-out movie, and all hell breaks loose.

It's funny how these things work out. Never in a million years did Alice think she'd end up playing snooker.

She'd never wanted to leave the city, it was all she knew. Her mother lived above them in the same close, her sisters and aunties in the close next door.

She didn't want to take Paul away from his cousins.

They came to Hexton, the outlying village that grew into a satellite town, when George got promoted. With the opening of the factory George took up a management position, the lowest rung, but a start. He came up from the factory floor through his own hard work and determination. He never tired of telling her that: his own work and determination. Even when he could no longer properly form words, he still tried to tell her.

His rise was all the more impressive seeing as his last name, O'Connor, was so Irish-sounding. But that was in the past, a generation ago at least. George worked hard and he drove his workers into the ground, increasing productivity on his shift by 36 per cent. In Hexton's burgeoning Masonic lodge there were opportunities for an ambitious man, and his promotion through management kept pace with his ascendancy in the Masons. At George's funeral there was a big turnout of men she'd never met before.

Their new house had patio doors that gave onto the back garden, management housing, very continental and dead modern. Alice and George agreed that the room with the patio doors was the ideal choice for Paul's bedroom, it was quieter at the back, away from the noise of the road, and once Paul got a bit older he'd be able to go straight out and play in the garden. A garden to play in was a luxury neither Alice nor George had ever had, and she wanted Paul to get the full benefit of it.

George was a good man to her, a good provider; he worked hard and he wasn't a drinker. That's what people thought, what she wanted them to think. He liked a game of snooker. Him and his pal Tommy

170

Sanderson played snooker in the factory social club. What with the snooker and his commitments at the Lodge, he spent more time with Tommy Sanderson than he did with family. 'That wean doesn't know his own daddy. He never sees you,' she said to him.

Meningitis took Paul when he was four and a half. Dead in six hours. The longest six hours of her life. The doctor said it was a particularly virulent strain, that's why he went so quick.

George was in the social club playing snooker. Half a mile away and he never saw the boy before he died. He blamed her: she should have known the fever was serious; she should've got the doctor right away. She knew that herself.

After they buried Paul George stopped going to the club. He stayed in nearly every night. They tried for another baby, but it never happened. Conversations became brief, made up of her saying, 'What?' And him saying, 'Never mind.'

Before he took ill with the first stroke, George was earning good money. That was how he could afford the big slate snooker table. Hundreds of pounds it cost. It wasn't a table for a house, not an ordinary house anyway. If they hadn't had the patio doors he'd never have got it in the house. He had them deliver it when she was away at her sister's, eight men it took to bring it in. Once it was in, it wouldn't fit anywhere else. He must have known that when he bought it.

They sat it right in the middle of the room, where Paul's wee white coffin had stood on its trestles. She pleaded with him but he wouldn't listen. He said they had to move on. He tried to throw Paul's toys out, they were getting in the way of his snooker table, but she wouldn't let him. She fought him. She bit into his arm and refused to let go. The bite turned septic and took a long time to heal. He was scared of her after that and never tried to move the stuff again. For years him and Tommy Sanderson were in there most nights playing snooker, with the wean's toys all round the room and the wee choo choo trains chuffing across the wallpaper.

George was young for a stroke, only forty-one. It was only a wee one and the doctor said there was every chance of a full recovery. Then he had another one. After that he never went back to the factory, he couldn't. He was frozen all down the one side. He walked with a stick. He couldn't speak, he'd mumble something and she'd say, 'What?' And he'd shake his head, never mind. Unless she turned his plate for him he only ate half his dinner. He cried a lot. There was no more snooker, but Tommy Sanderson still came round and sat with him for hours until she told him not to. She asked Tommy if he could get rid of the snooker table, but he didn't know anyone who'd want it. And so it stayed there, a monument to their empty lives.

In sickness and in health, that was what she'd signed up for. She was never going to leave him, but they had their moments. Sometimes he was pathetically grateful and other times he'd try to lash out at her with his stick. Correspondingly, she sometimes felt a tenderness for his helplessness, a melancholy when she remembered the man he'd been. Some nights, just to cheer him up, to get him inter-ested in something, anything, she'd bring him through to Paul's room and sit him down where he could watch her. She'd play the table taking both her turn and his, and he'd watch, criticizing and getting angry at her hopelessness, and slowly teaching her how to play.

At other times she hated him. Sometimes she said terrible things. She told him Paul wasn't his; that she and Tommy had carried on that time he went on management training to London. The dates fitted. He cried and cried and she tried to take it back. She tried to tell him she'd only said it to hurt him, because she was angry with him, because she was a horrible evil bitch. But still he would bring it up again and cry for hours on end. The dates fitted.

Every time she saw him parked in front of the telly, shuffling to the toilet, mumbling about his glory days at the factory or with tears of self-pity dripping off his chin, she felt she was being buried alive. She wasn't ready for this living death, she would never be ready. That was why she started the Golden Belles.

She came back one day from performing in a show in an OAP home somewhere on the other side of the city. By the time they paid for a minibus there and back it had actually cost them, but it was a terrific show. The staff in the home were lively and fun, and they encouraged the residents to call for an encore.

When she came into the house she saw immediately that George's spirit had departed. It had left only the rubbery rind that was his body sitting on the chair. For old times' sake she kissed it on the head and cried a little. Then she had to change out of her show tights before she called the doctor.

These days, every day's a holiday. Ray can't help it, he feels good. Feeling this good makes him feel bad, or at least guilty, but he tries to ignore this. He keeps himself busy. He has his work, his sideboards to be getting on with, all the young ones coming in every day, all the performers rehearsing for the show, endless jokes and fag breaks and cups of tea. He looks forward to his day. He arrives at the church in the morning with a spring in his step, lead in his pencil, wick in his candle, sap in his stem. This makes him feel scared. Experience has taught him that this kind of feeling good will end in tragedy.

He's gone back to showering every morning and trying on different shirts in front of the mirror. He's planning a haircut. He even contemplated new aftershave. The old stuff must have gone off by now, it's lain at the back of the bathroom cabinet too long.

Because of the show she comes to the church nearly every day. He watches her while he pretends to keep his head down and get on with his work. He fancies her, plain and simple. He has no idea why. He knows he shouldn't, there's the age discrepancy for a start. She's no beauty and she's bossy and snappy but maybe that's what it is: that vitality.

Ray has long since given up asking God for any favours, he knows how pointless and humiliating that is. He's not doing anything wrong, he tries to remind himself, it's not wrong to fancy a woman. Nothing to stop you looking, so long as you don't touch. He only has to resist temptation until the show's over.

One Month Later

Chapter 16

Down by the shimmering river, at the edge of the forest, Maria's squirrel friend puts his tiny paw in her hand. She brushes her face against his soft fur and giggles as his little bushy tail tickles her nose. In the bright morning sunshine she looks into the quiet river pool and sees her reflection, fresh and beautiful. These days every meditation is filled with this spiritual ecstasy.

She has already had her consultation with Madonna and Nelson, and outlined, with their help, how wonderful her busy day is going to be.

'I can't wait to get to work,' she'd told them, partly hinting that they should get a move on. These days Nelson's ponderous wisdom is beginning to get on her nerves.

'Fulfilling work is not only our goal but also our reward,' he'd preached.

Madonna had backed him up. Who would have thought that these two would make such a good team?

'Yeah,' said Madonna, 'so don't get complacent. She's fly, that Alice one.'

'Aye,' Nelson had corrected her, 'she *thinks* she's fly.'

'He's right. You heard what she was like when you asked about work experience. She doesn't want Blue Group in her kitchen; she'll try everything to put you off.'

'Do not be distracted from your purpose. Focus.'

They wouldn't let her away until she promised to focus. Now she can take a few moments to savour the bliss before returning to the external world. Often she used to linger here, milking her reverie for every bead of joy she could squeeze from it, but these days the external world is every bit as blissful.

Everything is going well. The Madonna Extravaganza has hurtled into life. This is the final week of rehearsals. Tomorrow is Saturday, the last big rehearsal before the dress. The biggest surprise of all has been Blue Group.

This is all credit to Brian's irrepressibly mischievous nature and his scriptwriting talents. Due to his rewrite of the script, which now features his sly automated comments throughout, Martin the have-a-go-hero shopkeeper and Jane the gun-wielding robber have moved from lacklustre melodrama into the realms of surreal comedy.

At first Martin was not best pleased with what he considered to be barefaced upstaging by Brian, but he's forgotten his churlishness and adapted. Now that they're getting a good reaction from other performers, Martin works hard to create maximum comedic effect.

Weeks ago, bored and embarrassed by the piss-poor script and shambling performances, Brian had re-interpreted the play and completely turned it around. He'd had a cold and was unable to go to the swimming lesson with the rest of them. Dezzie had volunteered to stay with him and by the time Blue Group came back

Brian had reworked the script. Dezzie insisted it was all Brian's work, he had merely taken dictation.

It's basically the same story: woman tries to rob shop and is disarmed by shopkeeper while disabled assistant looks on. Shopkeeper and thief fall in love. Assistant looks on. They live happily ever after.

But now all the characters are named after Brian's chess heroes: Kramnik (Jane), Kasparov (Martin) and Fischer (Brian). Now there's a *Pulp Fiction* homage in Kramnik's monologue and a *Matrix* reference in the fight scene. Now there's comedy, rather than awkwardness and embarrassment, in the pauses between the words Fischer says with his computerized voice. Brian parodies his voice machine's complete lack of intonation and spontaneity. The laughs are all in the silences, which they milk for all they can.

FISCHER   How. Long. Is. It.
Pause while Kasparov waits for question to be completed.
KASPAROV   How long is what?
He reacts – shocked at such a personal question. He checks his fly and covers himself protectively as though fearful that Fischer can see the dimensions of his manhood.
FISCHER   Since. The. Shop. Was. Last. Robbed.
KASPAROV   (*Relieved*) Oh! Since the shop was last robbed? (*Looks at his watch.*) Two years, three months, four days, six hours and twenty minutes ago. Approximately.
FISCHER   She. Got. To. You. Huh.
KASPAROV   Yes, I don't think I'll ever forget that thieving she-devil Kramnik. *Romantic music plays as Kasparov gets a faraway*

179

look in his eyes. That wonderful hunny bunny crazy no-good thieving beautiful lady. But if I ever see her again I'll be ready for her.

FISCHER   Is. It. Hard.

Long pause.

KASPAROV   Is what hard?

Kasparov turns away from the audience as he covers himself again.

FISCHER   To. Forget. Her.

KASPAROV   Oh! (*Relieved*) Yes, yes it is hard. To forget her, I mean! But it's impossible. They put her in jail and threw away the key. I'll never see my hunny bunny ever again. (*He is bereft.*)

Kramnik enters shop unnoticed by Kasparov and Fischer. She stands on top of the counter, pulls out a gun and screams hysterically.

KRAMNIK   Any of you move and I'll execute every motherflippin' last one of ya!

FISCHER   Look. Out. She's. Got. A.

Extremely long silence while Kramnik and Kasparov remain in freeze frame.

FISCHER   Gun.

Kasparov reacts. In slow motion he runs towards Kramnik.

KASPAROV   Noooooo!

They fight slow-motion kung fu as though they are in The Matrix.

Kasparov addresses the audience.

KASPAROV   (*Staring at his hands, baffled*) I know kung fu!

Eventually Kasparov wrestles the gun from Kramnik and has her in a romantic clinch.

FISCHER   Are. You. Going. To. Take. Her.
Long pause. Both Kasparov and Kramnik look at Fischer.
FISCHER   To. The. Police.
KASPAROV   No. I'm going to do what I should have done two years, three months, four days, six hours and (*he looks at his watch*) twenty-four minutes ago. I'm going to make her my wife!
Kasparov leans forward and pulls Kramnik into a passionate embrace while the romantic music reaches a climax.
FISCHER   And. So. They. Lived.
Long pause.
Music fizzles out. Kasparov and Kramnik are forced to stop canoodling and let Fischer have the last word.
FISCHER   In. Hexton. Kasparov. Worked. Hard. Business. Was. Good. And. Before. Long. Kramnik. Had. Two. Little.
Long pause.
Kramnik nurses her tummy.
FISCHER   Kalashnikovs.
She pulls out two rifles and waves them murderously while Kasparov smiles proudly.
FISCHER   And. They. Were. Never. Robbed. Again. The.
Short pause.
FISCHER   End.

So long as the audience understand that it's intended as comedy, it's going to be the smash hit of the show. And a welcome relief from all these singers. Except for Fiona, of course.

181

Her voice is a rare gift, a one-in-a-million talent. The thing that Hextors rate most highly, the ability to sing well, is the thing that a mentally disabled woman can do better than any of them. Hopefully, they're going to love her for it.

Chapter 17

The time has flown in; every minute of the last month has been filled with drama and excitement. A month in a wonderful blur of auditions, talent, costumes, songs, sets, backstage nerves, strops, magicians and rabbits. The church is busy every day with groups rehearsing and the Golden Belles have set up a café.

In Hexton this in itself is a community triumph. Fair enough, Ray has provided the space and the ladies of Autumn House are serving the teas, but Maria feels justified in taking at least some of the credit. That's why it's only fair that Blue Group get a piece of the action.

When she spoke to Alice and Margaret about it yesterday they were less than enthusiastic, trotting out the usual excuses about the dangers of work in a kitchen. Luckily Ray was there to intercede on Blue Group's behalf.

'You know how it is, girls, come one, come all,' he said simply.

When they tried to argue he shrugged and said, 'No work experience, no café. No café, no snooker.'

Weirdly, this seemed to do the trick and suddenly

Alice was fixing times and dates for Blue Group to come in and wait tables. She's only allowing two-hour shifts once a week but this is a tremendous breakthrough, something no other key worker has ever managed, and one which Maria can't wait to wave under Mike's nose.

But even if the show wasn't going as well as it is, nothing can get her down. Maria is in love. Every day with Dezzie gets better and better. She's staggered in a love-struck swoon from midweek to weekend date, each one more successful and more romantic than the last. The last date, two nights ago, was the best so far. Not because the film was so good, because it wasn't, and not because he bought her popcorn and then held her hand all the way through the film so she couldn't eat it. What was so good was that as they were leaving the cinema Dezzie bumped into a friend of his and introduced Maria.

'This is Maria, my girlfriend,' he said.

And the sex. It's just sex, sex, sex, sex, sex. Maria never gets tired of it, or sore the way she used to with Dirk. Dezzie's gentle. Constantly he asks her: what d'you want? Is this OK? But she's no slouch either in the bedroom department.

Every time they do it she goes down there, sucking him with the instinct and hunger of a newborn. Dezzie never asks but she knows he likes it. She wants to do it. She needs to. She has to bury her head in his smell, in his softest, most vulnerable places. He's new bread, a succulent roast, spiced rum. She has to consume him, to have her senses overwhelmed by him.

Going down has become her new religion; like her meditations, it is an important touchstone in her life. She knows that so long as she does it everything will be all right. Down there she practises her devotions. When they're married she'll do this every morning. She'll wake his brain and his cock with as much pleasure as she can give him, in gratitude and reverence for what it is he gives her. He gives her everything.

But it's his nature to be generous. The cinema date was the first time she had managed to pay for anything, and even then it was only her own ticket. He earns the same money as she does, he hasn't the means to pay for everything but he keeps wanting to. He's as free with his time as he is with his money. At the centre he is always on hand to help her with Blue Group. He should be floating between the various groups, but he does what's asked of him elsewhere and then comes and helps Maria. He's always funny and sweet with everyone – Blue Group are as much in love with him as she is.

Really she doesn't deserve a boyf as good as Dezzie but nevertheless, it's official. He said so to his friend outside the cinema. 'This is Maria,' he said, 'my girlfriend.'

At the centre they are discreet. They have to be. Sauce for the goose, Mike always says. If they see us doing it, what's to stop the clients? Staff openly fraternizing is a sackable offence, regarded in the same light as if a staff member were to conduct a physical relationship with a client. So at the centre they restrict themselves to smiles and winks.

Dezzie's on swimming-pool duty with Green Group so she doesn't see him until nearly lunch, and when she does she has to smile. Since he gave his prized T-shirt to Bert he's worn nothing of note, but today he's wearing a new red one with a slogan on it

that perfectly encapsulates his charming insouciance:
Ride Bikes
Drink Beer
Talk Bollocks
No-one else could get away with this. He's proudly showing it off around the groups and everyone is admiring it.

'Where did you get it Dezzie?' Martin asks.

'D'you like it?'

'Yeah, I'm getting one.'

Dezzie laughs.

'You trying to copy my style, wee man?'

'I can buy stuff like that if I want, you know,' says Martin briskly. 'I can get anything I want.'

Maria rolls her eyes, slightly embarrassed at Martin's rudeness. Dezzie wasn't patronizing him, he was only joking.

'No, sorry mate. No offence,' says Dezzie quickly, putting an arm around Martin. 'I got it in Hexton, in that wee shop beside the pub. I'm just worried that it'll look better on you than it does on me.'

'Yeah, well,' says Martin, only slightly mollified, 'I'm getting my mum to get me one.'

'I'm taking my group to the church after lunch,' says Maria, changing the subject. 'We've got work experience.'

This she says in an understated throwaway manner, but she hopes Dezzie will appreciate the magnitude of the news. He does not disappoint.

'Way to go, Miss Maria!' he cries.

As though declaring the winner in a boxing contest he lifts her arm and shakes it, and then goes round Blue Group dispensing high fives.

'I could do with a hand getting everyone down there, d'you want to come with us?'

'Do I want to? Just try and stop me!'

To maximize the time spent together and also for the exercise the clients will get from the walk, Maria chooses the long route through the park.

'Look!' says Fiona, excited, 'wee squirrels!'

'Where?' says Maria, frantic to catch sight of them.

To be with Dezzie and see a squirrel must be an omen. Fiona points to a tree and everyone gasps when they see a little squirrel scamper along a branch. Alarmed by its fast movement, Jane runs for cover behind Maria.

'It's OK pet,' Maria laughs, 'it won't touch you.'

But Jane is not convinced and cowers.

'It's only a wee creature. It can't do you any harm. It's more scared of you than you are of it.'

But Jane's fright has spooked Martin and now he looks worried too.

'I don't like squirrels,' he says.

'I'm with you, mate,' says Dezzie. 'Bloody tree rats, that's what those things are, hoaching with fleas and God knows what else. In fact, they're worse than rats. The other week I saw a squirrel kill a rat down at the embankment. Ripped it to pieces. Vicious buggers. In a fight a squirrel will take a rat out every time.'

'Please, Dezzie,' Maria says softly, 'Jane's frightened.'

'Sorry, Jane,' he says.

But the damage is done. No-one wants to look at the squirrels any more and they hurry past. So vivid is his description of the killer squirrels that everyone is quiet for a while.

Maria understands why Dezzie said this. He's angry with himself for offending Martin earlier and now he's trying to make it up to him, agreeing with him, trying to bond. But he's trying too hard. This is something she is beginning to notice about Dezzie. He works so hard to keep everyone happy that sometimes he inadvertently upsets them.

It's a very human weakness and one that makes him all the more lovable, but she hopes he doesn't really feel like this about squirrels. All this talk of them being flea-ridden savagers of rats, she'll never be able to think of her little friend by the shimmering river in quite the same way again.

Chapter 18

When they arrive at the church Ray is painting a rural idyll on a canvas framed by old strips of MDF. By way of a greeting he calls to Blue Group in an Australian accent and rotten impersonation of Rolf Harris.

'Can you see what it is yet, kids?'

At his direction some of the unemployed young people who hang around here are moving bits of scenery and/or joinery, it's hard to tell. The other spaces are no less hectic.

The main hall is a factory of creativity, with multiple simultaneous rehearsals taking place amidst the busy bustle of the café. This is going to be terrific experience for Blue Group. A primary class is practising a puppet show where the older kids use smaller ones, with thick cords tied to their wrists, as live puppets. Amidst the mayhem the teacher is untying one of the small ones. He's crying from the rough treatment he's receiving from the excitable girl yanking his strings.

The school choir are using the stage to rehearse their Madonna tribute. It's strange to see them in rows, identical in their smart school uniforms, singing 'Papa

Don't Preach' with such regimented formality. A month ago who would have thought it? This show is positive evidence that dreams can come true. The way everything has taken off, the café, the work experience and her relationship with Dezzie, especially her relationship with Dezzie: these things are all compelling evidence of the power of positive thinking.

In the kitchen the ladies from Autumn House, about eight of them, are busy getting in each other's way, banging pots and producing steam from urns. The café is mostly patronized by mums waiting to pick up children, although Maria recognizes and waves to a group from the motorway demonstration. They are busily folding leaflets and have recruited a table of mums to help stuff envelopes.

There is a table of Pastor McKenzie's Victory Singers, sitting with cups of tea before them. They are a peculiar-looking bunch of oddballs and misfits; the only thing they have in common is a dreamy religious haze that hangs over them.

Maria smiles when she thinks of what Mike would make of this. He'd have a good rant about how he knows very well what the Victory Singers' agenda is, she can hear his voice in her head right now. Don't kid yourself Maria, he'd say, McKenzie's mob aren't here for the soup. They're feeding off the misery of the redundant, the suicidal, the recently bereaved. They're scavenging souls, sniffing out anyone experiencing a life crisis. They'll catch them at a low ebb and ensnare them. Chalk it up, another soul saved, another notch on their crucifix. They probably have league tables, he'd say.

Mike's a cynic but he's not alone. She knows plenty of people who have an open animosity to organized religion. She suspects there are others who don't mention the lack of community and the spiritual void they feel in their lives. To do so would be an admission of weakness, of failure. Maria knows this because it's the way she felt.

Her experimentation with Christianity began after she woke up one morning with her tights dangling from one leg and an unknown boy from the other. There had to be more to Sundays than self-revulsion and killer hangovers.

The Kelvin Street Kids' tight foursome (all four one and one four all!) was no more. Those days were gone. The rest of them were hooked up, going steady. Over time this new larger crowd diffused to become bigger, less focused, subsets of girlfriends and boyfriends, wives and husbands, mothers and fathers, parents and children.

Maria still saw them, but it wasn't the same. Even Colette, now that she'd returned from London to marry Gerry and settle down, faded her out. Nights at the pub became dinner at Colette's with Colette's husband and not long after that, Colette's kids. A new social scene had been established, a scene which Maria was unable to penetrate: the mother and toddler group. She missed the girls, especially Colette, she missed the laughs and the mad nights out. They were all baby bores now. 'Ooh,' they'd cry, 'Katie's on solids!' or 'Oliver did a poo in the potty all by himself!'

Maria knew nothing about breast pumps or sterilizing solution. Without a baby she couldn't be in that club. So she began, on the q.t., going to church. Or rather she began the process of selecting a church, one that could provide her with a club membership but also anonymity.

She wasn't ready to tell her friends. Although she didn't know Mike at the time, she knew plenty of people like him. In the social circles she moved in it was deeply uncool to hold faith in God. Anyone ingenuous enough to come out as a *Christian* was regarded with suspicion. The word itself was almost a dirty word, a word with judgemental or hypocritical overtones. Going to church was perceived as questionable behaviour.

So it couldn't be anywhere too close to Kelvin Street or where she worked. It couldn't be anywhere too nosey, where the minister invited you to stay for tea and a half-hour interrogation. It couldn't be anywhere too sad. With her usual optimism she had begun with high hopes of finding a nice man, but most churches she tried had only a pitifully small congregation of old or strange people. Eventually she found one which met her rigorous standards.

This one, St David's, had a sign outside which said *Those who choose to worship in private will not be disturbed*. It was good marketing.

The minister wasn't young or trendy, but he seemed nice and he did have his finger on the pulse. The church was equipped with PowerPoint. The words of the hymns were projected onto a large screen, animated, sometimes dancing or in flames, under a bouncing ball which kept the beat. The hymns had sweet sad tunes or lively rousing ones. There was a wee choir but the minister encouraged everyone to sing out. Maria, hiding amongst their unsteady voices, joined in. Towards the end of the service there was karaoke. Anyone could choose a hymn from a list of about forty and step up to the altar with the microphone.

Every week there was the Sign of Peace. She shook hands with everyone seated around her and was touched and surprised by their warmth and generous fellowship. These people didn't know her or want anything from her.

When the minister said, 'Now let us pray,' Maria put her head down and closed her eyes.

Except for family weddings and funerals, her parents never took her to church. At school there was the odd service at the end of term, but really the only pupils who practised religious devotions were the Muslim kids. Maria didn't know how to pray. The first time she did it she felt self-conscious, panicky even, but she bowed her head, screwed her eyes closed and concentrated.

She became aware of the smells of incense and damp. The opulent fustiness of the church comforted her; it was the smell of serenity. She started to get a light-headed feeling. A current of something – contentment, grace – buzzed through her, becoming stronger every time. Was this a spiritual high? It seemed like everyone in the church was getting it, she could feel it in the atmosphere.

Before now she'd never understood communal prayer. Just for a few minutes, while she had her eyes closed, while there was silence and they all prayed together, Maria felt an outpouring of love for everyone in the room. It was a great feeling; she only wished the church was full. Now she realized why churches were built to accommodate so many people, and why Christians spent so much effort proselytizing. These few minutes of enlightenment would sustain her for days. But just as she was beginning to enjoy it, it all went wrong. She got caught.

She'd been attending St David's for about four weeks when she ran into Colette. She'd just come out and bumped into Colette pushing Oliver's buggy, on her way to a baby-swimming class.

'I've got to do something,' said Colette, 'I'm getting cabin fever sitting in the house all day staring at four walls.'

Maria could pray for a miracle to get out of this and she would have, but she felt it was hypocritical to ask God's assistance in denying him.

'I didn't know you'd gone happy clappy.'

Colette said it enthusiastically, but Maria saw the pity in her eyes. God forgive her, Maria could only think of denial.

'Me go to church? Don't be ridiculous!'

Colette sniggered at the misunderstanding.

'I thought you'd finally *let Jesus come into your life*.'

This was a reference to an incident from years ago.

Maria and Colette had been in a club with the other KSKs. They were finding it difficult to shake off two boring but tenacious boys. With a straight face Colette told the boys that she and Maria had *let Jesus come into their lives*. Maria joined her in pretending to try to convert them, bowing her head every time she said the word *Jesus*. The boys soon made their excuses.

'Well, what the hell were you doing coming out of a church on a Sunday morning, then?' asked Colette, still hooting with laughter at her own joke. She obviously did need to get out of the house more often. It wasn't that funny.

Maria couldn't tell her. Not now, not after the *let Jesus come into your life* remembrance.

'I went in to ask about a yoga class that runs there.'

Maria knew it was blasphemy. But although she had covered her tracks, the game was up.

It turned out that with the baby-swimming class Colette would be passing the church at this time every Sunday. Unless St David's had a back exit Maria would no longer be able to come. She didn't have the stamina to start again at another church. But more importantly – and it was an ugly revelation – she hadn't the moral rectitude to make it as a Christian. She'd much rather deny Christ than suffer a friend's pity.

But that was a long time ago. She doesn't beat herself up about it any more. Since then she has accepted and forgiven herself for her moral failings. Now she has honed and perfected that spiritual high in the privacy of her own home. She respects all religious groups but she knows it's not for her.

Good luck to Pastor McKenzie and the Victory Mission; whatever floats their boat. It can't be easy standing every Saturday night outside the Hexton Arms singing off-key whilst being pelted with kebab containers. They must go home dripping in chilli sauce, but that's the price they pay. And if they can comfort a few people and help them to make some kind of sense of their personal tragedies, then why not? They're not doing any harm.

Pastor McKenzie, with his good looks and easy charm, must be a super-smooth salesman of Christianity. If they do have league tables he must be premier division.

The pastor is playing snooker with one of the men from the orchestra. The orchestra are not due to rehearse today, but perhaps the musician has come for the soup or the snooker or the vibrant atmosphere that now fills the church. Maria overhears what sounds like a philosophical debate between the two of them as she herds her group past.

'But you know, Arnold, it's not possible to achieve permanent happiness,' says Pastor McKenzie, 'the best we can aim for is to be good.'

'Life is hard,' says the musician, 'I accept that. And once you do, it makes things a bit easier, but I really miss her. Brown in the top left pocket.'

Chapter 19

At the far end of the café there is an electric sewing machine on a table festooned with pieces of bright yellow, red, blue and green shiny material. These must be the cancan costumes for the Golden Belles that Alice was talking about yesterday. There is a casting of coloured threads littering the floor all around. Some have been carried by through traffic to different parts of the café floor and a few remain stuck in the grooves of customers' shoes.

The face of the woman operating the machine is not visible as her head is down, her eyes following the line of thread and the fast pneumatic action of the needle as she feeds the material through. She's concentrating on what she's doing. Maria can only see the crown of her head, her thin hair neatly sectioned into tight uniform curls. When she lifts her head she looks very professional. She's wearing an overall, buttoned all the way up, and a pair of glasses on a chain.

Alice O'Connor does not look happy to see Blue Group shuffling nervously around the noisy café. They've not yet got used to this social interaction with strangers but, although it may be uncomfortable for them, Maria is committed to pushing her clients out of their comfort zones. These experiences will be a positive step in their development.

'Here we are then Alice, I think you know everybody by now: Fiona, Jane, Brian, Martin, and my colleague Dezzie.'

'You're very welcome,' Alice says.

Dezzie nods but stays in the background behind Brian's chair, for which Maria is grateful. This is her team, her work experience triumph. But although Dezzie's quiet, his T-shirt is a conversation piece.

'I hope you don't do them all at the same time,' says Alice.

'Sorry?'

'Drink and ride and talk, I mean, you'd spill it all over the place!'

It takes a second before Dezzie and Maria catch up with her but when they do, they laugh enthusiastically. This naturally radiates out to Blue Group.

'I like your T-shirt, but there's someone here who can top that. Would you like to see the slogan the Seniors are wearing this season?'

Dezzie looks to Maria for approval. Maria isn't sure what Alice means and begins to worry that Alice is using Dezzie's T-shirt to foil her work experience plans. They're not here for a social visit. Alice doesn't wait for a reply but calls to one of her kitchen assistants.

'Jean? Could you ask Jean Stevenson to pop out for a minute, I want to show off her jumper.'

One Jean calls another and Jean Stevenson emerges from the kitchen, preceded by her big, pointy, rather low-slung boobs. It always depresses Maria to see old women with such impressive racks. What good are they to them? It's such a waste. Jean Stevenson employs hers to buttress a lilac appliquéd sweatshirt. She's laughing, mock-embarrassed to be summoned in this way.

Jean, though elderly, is a smart-looking woman, pink-lipped and fully made up. Her shoulder-length hair is thick and shiny, a shade of auburn that begins dark and rich on her shoulders and gets lighter towards her head. At the roots it's a light pink colour. Her turquoise eyeshadow has been smudged by the wrinkles at the corner of her eyes, but the overall effect is bright and cheery.

'Go on then Jean, give us a twirl,' says Alice.

Jean obliges, smiling and turning with the careful deliberation of a schoolgirl with a stack of books on her head. In this elaborate fashion, she models her sweatshirt.

Around appliquéd butterflies, flowers, teddy bears and rocking horses, in a feminine and florid script are the words:

Old Ladies are just Antique Little Girls

'I got it on holiday in Florida,' Jean explains. 'It's a nice way of looking at it, isn't it?'

She vigorously nods her head, eliciting baffled nods from Blue Group.

'Thanks Jean,' says Alice dismissively.

As Jean sashays off to the kitchen Alice turns back to Maria and Dezzie.

'Creepy, isn't it?'

Maria and Dezzie quickly agree.

'Jean's single at the moment, she's looking for an antique paedophile boyfriend.'

Alice cackles at her own joke and Dezzie hesitantly joins her, causing another wave of tittering from

Martin, Jane, Fiona and Brian. Maria is unable to laugh, she's getting anxious. This is all very well, but she's not here to laugh at deluded pensioners. She wants to crack on with the work placements, but yet another Jean approaches the table. Alice is in big demand here today and Maria can see she's loving it. It's the seamstress, Maria recognizes her now as the ditzy receptionist at Autumn House.

'Alice, did you manage to get the broderie anglaise?'

'Yes, I got a big roll of it. It's in the back kitchen, I've left it on top of the fridge.'

Arnold, the musician who was playing snooker earlier, passes and softly puts his hand on Jean's back.

'Thanks Jean, very much appreciated,' he says.

'He needed all his trousers taken in,' Jean whispers loudly in explanation once he has safely passed. 'Och it wasn't any bother, two minutes through the machine. He's lost a lot of weight since she's gone. A shadow of his former self so he is, a shadow.'

Jean and Alice share a pained and pensive look, but after a few moments they both recommence as if Arnold had never interrupted.

'There should be plenty of lace there for you, Jean, but let me know and I'll pick up more on my way home tonight if you need it.'

'Right you are.'

As soon as she moves off Alice shifts back into a gossip huddle and Maria and Dezzie are obliged to lean in and listen.

'I've got them all working here now. That's Jean Scott, the relief receptionist at Autumn House. She's good-hearted. She's never done sewing buttons on for the men, anything they ask her. She's just a girl who can't say no. One of they homeless fellas that Ray lets doss in the back room came up to her with a button and said, "Hey missus, could you sew a shirt on that for me, hen?" '

Alice is slapping the table and laughing.

'The worst receptionist we've ever had but a great wee seamstress. Worked at it full-time all her days she did, never married, the wee soul, God love her. Worked there until the place shut down. Stuart's the Kiltmaker. They moved the business abroad, Far East somewhere I think. She's done a smashing job on our outfits, and for next to nothing. I got white pyjama bottoms and she's putting a wee bit lace on them, there you go: authentic Parisian cancan bloomers. The pyjammy trousers were cheap made right enough; you could spit peas through the cotton but guess how much I paid for them at that Firstbrand?'

It is a few seconds before Maria realizes that Alice is looking for an answer. She has absolutely no idea how much pyjama bottoms cost. Since she took out her mortgage she has become out of touch with retail prices.

'Eh, five pounds?'

'Nope.'

Maria's hand presses hard against her breastbone. Really she could do without the guessing games. Blue Group are here, ready and waiting to work. Normally she enjoys the buzz in the church, but today she's picking up their nerves and amplifying them. She's probably more nervous than they are now.

'Fifty pence. Fifty pence a pair. You wouldn't credit it, would you? You wonder that they can make a profit on them at that price, and all the way from Indonesia, that's where they're made, you know. Probably in a wee sweatshop owned by Stuarts.'

Alice is at it. No doubt, because they work in a centre for people with mental disabilities, she has taken Maria and Dezzie for activist socialists. She's deliberately time-wasting, trying to lure them into what would no doubt be a stimulating debate on the decline of British manufacturing and rising consumerism.

'Aye, and the people that made them are probably on starvation wages,' says Dezzie, walking right into the trap.

'Talking of starvation,' says Maria chirpily, jumping up from her chair, 'these customers won't serve themselves. Right then, we'd better get on with our work experience, eh? Now, where do you want us?'

Chapter 20

To set a good example, Maria begins by rolling up her sleeves enthusiastically.

Alice has stopped cackling.

'It's just that I'm not sure where I can put you all,' she says. 'As you can see, we've plenty of help at the moment.'

'There must be something we can do.'

'I'm sorry Maria; I don't see how this is going to work. It's dangerous with the hot plates and everything. Why don't you all sit down and we can get you some soup. Anyone fancy a nice plate of soup?'

Fiona, Jane, and Martin agree they would like a nice plate of soup, even though they had lunch only an hour ago. They are nervous of working in the café but eating is something they are quite confident about.

'Or there's lovely jam roly-poly, made with Margaret's own home-made jam, fresh out of the oven.'

'Alice, stop,' says Maria. 'It's hardly work experience, is it?'

'Well,' Alice says, hastily assembling more chairs round a table in a quiet corner, 'let's take this slow.

One step at a time. Maybe to begin with the girls can serve the rest of you and then . . .'

Alice looks at the boys, her eyes trailing slowly across Brian, her expression a mixture of sympathy and exasperation.

'And then we'll see how we get on from there. I'm sorry Maria, that's the best I can do at the moment.'

Maria sighs.

'OK.'

What else can she do?

'Now Fiona and Jane, is it? Yes. Do you want to come with me into the kitchen and you can pick up your customers' orders?'

'I want crisps,' says Fiona petulantly.

Maria knows that if any of them are going to let her down, it'll be Fiona. Usually, to encourage her to do anything, Maria has to bribe Fiona with a packet of crisps. She has a few emergency packets of cheese and onion in her bag just in case, but Fiona will have to learn that a normal working environment does not include regular crisp breaks.

'No Fiona, you're not getting crisps. If you're hungry you can have soup in a minute,' Maria says in a quiet controlled voice. 'But first you do your work experience.'

'No,' says Fiona, mimicking her tone, 'first I take the orders.'

'Quite right, Fiona,' says Alice, 'd'you want to ask the customers what they want?'

Maria drums her fingers on the Formica table and tries to focus on this being a first step towards valid work experience, rather than a hopeless charade.

'Come on then Fiona, ask us.'

'What d'you want,' Fiona moans.

Martin takes his role as customer seriously.

'Mmm,' he says thoughtfully, 'what flavour of jam is the roly-poly?'

'Strawberry,' says Alice.

'Strawberry,' repeats Fiona.

'I see. And the soup?'

'Oh for God's sake Martin,' says Maria, 'will you hurry up and order something?'

'It's lentil and tomato,' says Alice, 'delicious, I can recommend it.'

'Hmmm, lentil and tomato you say?'

Martin considers this for a minute.

'Yes, well I'll have the soup then please. And the roly-poly.'

'Good choice,' says Dezzie. 'I'll go with the soup.'

'Soup for me too, thank you,' says Maria. 'Brian, what would you like?'

'Lobster.'

Maria sighs.

'The lobster's off. Do you want something or not?'

Even as she's saying it Maria remembers how self-conscious Brian is about eating in public. She's annoyed him and he'll probably sulk all day now.

'Not,' says his Dynavox pleasantly, but Brian's face is dark with teenage fury.

'Right, so that's three lentil and tomato soups and one roly-poly please, Fiona.'

Fiona and Jane stand waiting for further instruction. With the noise and the steam and all the grief Fiona is giving her, Maria's head is starting to pound.

'Go on, off you go. Jane, you and Fiona go with Alice, she'll give you the soup. Bring one plate each and be careful. Take your time, there's no rush.'

'Don't want to,' says Fiona.

Maria tugs Fiona's sleeve.

'D'you want to sing in the show, Fiona?'

Fiona pulls away aggressively but doesn't reply.

'Well then, can you bring us our order please.'

Alice shepherds the two women away and Maria lets her breath out. Her hand has been clamped hard on her chest. When she takes it away she knows Dezzie will see the unattractive red mark it will leave.

She's annoyed with Fiona for trying to embarrass her in front of Alice and especially in front of Dezzie. Ever since she and Dezzie started dating Fiona has been playing up, almost as if she knows there's something between them and is deliberately trying to make Maria look bad in front of him.

While they are waiting Maria spots Ray coming into the café, flanked by Aldo. He's rolling a cigarette while he walks, but he lifts his head and smiles and nods as people greet him. Everyone here seems to know him. Even the weirdos from the Victory Mission are apparently his friends. As he walks into the kitchen Maria can hear appreciative giggles from the old ladies. Everybody loves Ray.

'Look,' says Dezzie, nodding towards Ray and Aldo, 'even the gangsters come here. Are you not taking this social inclusion a bit too far, Maria?'

'Gangsters? Ray's a gangster?'

'I don't know about that. His wee pal Aldo is anyway, or he thinks he is. I saw him in the Hexton Arms, in the Gents.'

'What was he doing?'

'Dealing I think, but he was up to something. He was talking to some guy, heavy atmosphere, I walked in on something.'

'What did you do?'

'Nothing. Walked straight back out again.'

Maria takes a closer look at Aldo. He's standing with Ray, laughing at something Alice has said. Alice slaps at him with her tea towel and Aldo steps back, pretending to be wounded. Then, apparently on Alice's orders, he lifts a tray and begins to clear dirty plates from a table. With his tall thin frame and glaikit expression he's an unlikely-looking gangster. But then, being nice to old ladies is a perfect cover for a drug dealer.

'Are you sure?'

'Well I wouldn't testify, if that's what you're asking. All I know is I've seen him in the toilets before; he uses those toilets as his office.'

This conversation is abruptly interrupted by the arrival at the table of Marianne Bowman, in a cloud of her pungent perfume. Marianne politely says hello to everyone, pulls up a chair and engages Maria in an exclusive conference. The lads pretend not to notice and talk amongst themselves.

'Alice said you were coming in today. The timing's perfect.'

'Sorry?'

'Listen, we've had a late entry. One of Pastor McKenzie's crowd. Now I know what you're thinking . . .'

Maria has no clue as to what Marianne is talking about.

'But wait till you hear him. He's going on stage once the primary class finishes. I asked him to come in and let you see him.'

'Marianne, are you talking about someone auditioning?'

'Well, I've kind of already offered him a spot. I hope you don't mind.'

'Are you serious? The auditions were a month ago. The show is set; it's been set for weeks, running order and times agreed. We only have two more full rehearsals. We can't change things now, it'll cause chaos. And anyway, never mind all that: another singer? Marianne, you were the one who said we already have too many singers.'

'I know, but none of them are as good as this guy. Look, here he is now.'

A woman in a long spangly silver dress comes out on stage. There is something very familiar about her, about the way she walks, but Maria can't quite put her finger on it. She is slim and blonde, with a big black beauty spot exactly where Madonna used to wear one. In fact, she looks a lot like Madonna.

'He looks amazing, doesn't he?'

'This is the guy? That's a *guy*?'

'Oh yeah.'

The woman, or rather the guy, the female impersonator, puts his CD on and Maria instantly recognizes it as Madonna's 'Express Yourself'.

It is uncanny. He looks and sounds exactly like Madonna. Not only has he got her voice to a T, his dance moves incorporate many Madonna stylings, including a wee bit of vogueing, although this is obviously anachronistic as she recorded 'Express Yourself' years before getting into the vogue. He has tremendous confidence and stage presence, head and shoulders above all their other acts. The people in the café are responding well, and Maria could imagine him doing a great job. But still and all . . .

Changing the show at this stage could throw the other acts into a panic, especially Blue Group, she can't risk that. If she lets Marianne away with this, others will want to change things. Alice has been agitating for more time for her Golden Belles routine. It's got to stop.

'So what do you think, he's brilliant isn't he?'

'Yes, he's good, but I'm afraid we can't have him.'

'What, are you kidding? Apart from the orchestra he's the best thing we've got!'

'I'm sorry, but we've no space for any more acts.'

'But I've already told him he's in.'

'Well you shouldn't have.'

'Oh for God's sake Maria . . .'

'I'm sorry, but I'm busy with my clients on work experience at the moment, so if you'll excuse me.'

Maria turns away as Marianne walks off. She's shaking. Effectively she's just pulled rank on the head teacher of Hexton High and dismissed her. She has barely had time to get her head round this when another irritating distraction occurs. Ray emerges from the kitchen and comes over to their table.

'Hello Maria,' he says.

Before a conversation has a chance to develop, a tiny little woman taps Ray's shoulder. He turns, delighted to see her, and immediately introduces her to everyone sitting at the table by pointing at them.

'Maggie – Maria, Martin, Brian and Dezzie.'

Everyone nods politely as their name is called, and Maggie beams a smile at each of them individually.

'You're looking well,' Ray says to Maggie, 'how's the hip?'

'Och, you know. In saying that, the pain-control thing you showed me, that's great. It means I can get about a bit more. But it's just like you said, Ray, it's all about attitude isn't it?'

'Absolutely, and you've got a great attitude, love, you're a wee star.'

Ray puts his arm around the tiny woman and squeezes her shoulders.

'Well, I've perked up a lot since you zapped me! I'll be tap-dancing with the Golden Belles before you know it.'

Maggie moves off, still laughing at her own joke, and Ray turns his attention back to the table. None of this has meant anything to them but they have sat, crane-necked, listening and smiling politely at the cryptic exchanges between Ray and his strange little friend Maggie.

Ray addresses Maria now.

'How's the work experience going?'

'Em, OK so far.'

Maria cannot really concentrate on what she's being asked; her attention is taken up with watching Marianne speak to the Madonna guy at the side of the stage. If Marianne is telling him he's out of the show he seems to be taking it rather well.

'Here she comes!' says Ray.

And now Jane is slowly walking out of the kitchen with a bowl of soup. Alice is three steps behind her all the way. Jane carries her own lunch every day at the centre canteen, but she's making a big production of this. She holds the bowl out in front of her as if it's a holy chalice. Maria knows from Jane's records, and from what she's told her, that she was once a staff nurse in an intensive care unit, saving patients' lives on a daily basis.

When she finally sets the soup down in front of Martin she's beaming with pride. This is a rare experience for Jane – she almost never smiles. The deep bowl only has half an inch of soup swilling around the bottom but even so, Martin leads off a modest round of applause.

'So is this one of the new starts we have in the café?' says Ray to Alice. 'I think you'll need to watch your back, Alice, if Jane carries on like this she'll be after your job.'

Fiona's progress from the kitchen is faster and much less careful. She slaps the plate down in front of Maria and says, 'It's rotten, I've tasted it. Too much salt.'

She has no sooner put it down than she goes to snatch it back up again.

'I'm going to take it back.'

'No, Fiona, thank you, it'll be fine,' says Maria tightly.

She knows very well what game Fiona is playing. She's annoyed because she didn't get crisps on demand and she's making sure everyone knows it. This is so typical of her selfishness.

'I'm the waitress, give me it. I'm taking it back,' says Fiona. She is pulling at the rim on one side of the plate but Maria is firmly holding onto the other side.

'It's fine Fiona, leave the plate alone.'

The plate is an old white shallow soup dish, its only decoration a ring of sombre blue. Its cracked glaze is covered in fine grey jigsaw lines, any one of which could burst like a dam spilling hot soup all over them both, but Fiona will not let go.

'Stinkin' soup's going . . .'

'Leave it!' Maria hisses.

The rest of the people in the café continue making noise and steam and clatter, unaware of the grim battle that is being fought at the corner table. But this makes it no less humiliating for Maria. Ray is watching, Dezzie is watching. The rest of Blue Group do nothing to help her and stand or sit impassively, watching Fiona try to wrench the plate away. Fiona is standing over her, so close she can smell her armpits and greasy hair. Her knuckles are white, her face is red and her cheeks wobble with the effort of gripping the plate.

As a professional health-care worker it's beneath Maria's dignity to tussle with a client over a plate of soup, but this is no longer about soup. It's about whether the group will stay here and benefit from work experience, or do as Fiona wants and return to the centre to munch bags of crisps.

The soup quivers in the plate, like the contents of an angry volcano. Lentils jump and roll like hot lava rocks across the shifting livid red. Maria can't let go now even if she wanted to. The plate is under so much pressure it'll go flying, probably all over her. But she's losing the battle. Positive visualization cannot help her now. Fiona has the double advantage of her wilful determination and hulking weight. Maria feels her grip on the plate slip away and then the hot sting of soup on her skin. She jumps up in fright.

'Oh for God's sake, Fiona, you stupid . . . !'

Though it hasn't burned her it has spilled all down the front of her jumper and jeans, making her look like the victim of a road traffic accident.

'Aoow!' wails Fiona.

A small amount of soup has spilled on her hand. She holds it in the air and stares at it with a pitiful tenderness.

'Right, you've done it; you've spilled it all over me. Are you happy now?'

Maria only knows that she's lost, that she's covered in soup, that Fiona has foiled her best efforts once again. She doesn't know that she is almost screaming and that the rest of the café has fallen silent.

'Oh my sore hand, it's nipping,' cries Fiona.

'Aww, is Fiona hurt, is poor Fiona crying? Does she want a bag of crisps?'

Maria dives under the table to find her handbag. She pulls out several packets of cheese and onion and begins hurling them, one by one, at Fiona. The first bag hits her shoulder. Fiona doesn't move out of range but closes her eyes and flinches when she's hit. The second bag gets the side of her head. Her attention-seeking wail changes to an all-out distress cry. The third bag is right on target and hits Fiona a bullseye in the face.

'That's enough,' says Ray, placing himself between Fiona and Maria.

Maria, only now aware of what she has done, and who has witnessed it, runs from the café and locks herself in the vestry toilet. She half expects Dezzie to come chapping the door, asking if she's OK, but no-one comes. As the soup turns cold and gluey on her clothes she takes a few big deep breaths, low into her stomach, breathing in through her left leg, and out through her right. She would sit on the pan and perform a full meditation, but that would take twenty minutes and she can't leave her group that long.

Dezzie will now be looking after Fiona and the rest of Blue Group in her absence.

She's so ashamed.

Not only has she publicly abused and assaulted Fiona, she has deserted the rest of her team. Dezzie must think she's a monster. He'll never want to see her again as long as she lives. It's so unfair. God gives other girls beauty, breasts, brains or even wealth as a means of attracting a mate. What has she got? In the personality stakes Maria knows she's not particularly witty or charming. The only attractive thing about her is that she's kind. It's her only allure, the only currency she holds.

It's so unfair. She's never done anything like this before. Until this minute her reputation at the centre has been irreproachable. She's always maintained a spotless record of being big-hearted, self-sacrificing, compassionate, kindly. So she threw a few bags of crisps, it's not the end of the world. But even as she's trying to convince herself of this she knows it's not true.

Something must have snapped. Obviously she was aware that Fiona was annoying her, but she had no idea she was harbouring such resentment towards a client. It scares her to be so out of touch with her own feelings. The really scary thing is that if Mike hears of this it'll mean instant dismissal. Fiona's mother is sure to complain.

Instant dismissal. To be dismissed, instantly, from the work you put your heart and soul into, from trust, respect, relationships. One minute you have a position, a career, people who look up to you, a community, a life, and the next: nothing. Dismissed; shooed away like a fly.

But she deserves it, she's assaulted a client. And not just any client, but Fiona: big, daft, innocent, infuriating Fiona. She can hardly believe it's happened. Poor Fiona is upset and Maria has run out on her. She should have stayed and comforted Fiona, told her how sorry she is, told her it isn't her fault. She has to explain that she was stressed out. She has to hope that Fiona's mum won't demand Maria's instant dismissal.

Chapter 21

When Maria emerges from the toilet the café has returned to normal. No-one bats an eye as she passes. Her heart leaps to her throat when she realizes the table they had occupied is now empty. There's no sign of Dezzie or Blue Group. Fiona must have insisted that they go back to the centre immediately to report the assault. Assault. It's an ugly word. Assault with a dangerous weapon: a three-ounce bag of air and grease.

'They're in his office,' says Alice.

They're still here, thank God. She turns and follows the path indicated by Alice's flicking finger. She doesn't speak to Alice or meet her eye but, surprisingly, Alice's tone doesn't sound recriminatory.

On her way to Ray's office Maria has a moment's hesitation. Fiona will probably still be hysterical. If she is, she might try to attack Maria and have to be restrained. Maybe it's better to give her a chance to cool down. Then, when she's calm and able to listen, Maria can tell her how sorry she is. For the moment she's safe enough here and in good hands with Dezzie. While she's still thinking about it Pastor McKenzie stops her.

'Hello Maria, I was wondering if I could have a quick word?'

'Eh, yes. I do have a few minutes, Pastor.'

In case Dezzie decides to take Blue Group back to the centre, Maria chooses a table where she can keep an eye on the door of Ray's office while the pastor buys her a coffee.

'It's about our new member Ronald, I was hoping I could petition on his behalf.'

'D'you mean the drag queen?'

'I think he prefers the term female impersonator.'

'I'm afraid I've already spoken to Miss Bowman.'

'Yes, Marianne told me what you said and I do understand that there's a limit to how many acts you can put on.'

At the audition he referred to her as Miss Bowman, now it's Marianne. When did that change? Everyone's getting helluva friendly all of a sudden: orchestra and Christians, tree-huggers and mums, pensioners and drug pushers, Marianne and McKenzie. And of course Ray, he's at the centre of everything.

'Ronald's a new member. Before joining the Victory Mission he had problems fitting in. He's been very isolated since his mum died, and, I think, lonely.'

'And that's why it's so great that you've taken him into the Victory Mission.'

'We don't pick and choose who comes. It is our task only to open the path towards Our Lord Jesus Christ. So long as sinners are prepared to give their heart to Jesus and sin no more He offers them redemption. They can be saved. I know, I've seen it, I've seen men change through God's grace.'

This is all getting a bit deep and Maria has other things to worry about. How did she get caught up in this? It was a mistake to accept the coffee. He must sense her unease because the pastor instantly changes tack.

'I hope I can speak off the record.'

'Feel free.'

'I'm not trying to be unkind but you might have felt that Ronald's a strange bloke, he doesn't find it easy to be accepted in social situations. I know that you of all people, Maria, can understand that.'

She looks at him. What the hell does that mean?

'You work with people who face social exclusion every day. I've seen how hard you're working to make a success of the show. I've seen the way you are with your clients and I have nothing but admiration. You're working all hours, far beyond what you're being paid for I'm sure, doing this community show, aren't you?'

'Yes.'

Can't argue with that.

'And you're doing it, not for money, not for the glory, but for your clients, aren't you?'

Maria nods.

'So that your clients aren't left on the outside; so that they can have their place in the community.'

'Yes.'

He's good, very good. He's wasted here in Hexton, he should have his own show on American evangelical telly and be raking it in. She'll have to be careful here. He's got her nodding her head and agreeing with everything.

'Well, Ronald's in the same situation. Like your clients, he has a valuable contribution to make to the community and the show. God has given him a talent that cries out to be expressed.'

'Is that why he sang "Express Yourself"?'

217

'Yes, I think he took our little chat quite literally in his choice of song.'

Pastor McKenzie is chuckling and Maria has to admit, it is amusing. The sort of thing her clients would do. He's putting up a sound case for Ronald's inclusion but Maria's already said no. She doesn't want to back down; she doesn't want Marianne to imagine for one minute that she can be manipulated by a smooth-talking evangelist.

'I'm sorry, Pastor. It's nothing personal, it's certainly not because he's a bit different. I personally love Madonna and would love to have him but we simply don't have room in the programme.'

'Is this the reason you can't have him in the show?'

'Yes. That's it exactly, there's only so much we can cram into a two-hour show.'

'In that case I have a suggestion. I've spoken to the Victory Singers and, although we were excited about praising Our Lord in front of a big audience, we're prepared to stand down.'

Oh shit. This is serious. Maria has obviously under-estimated McKenzie. If he pulls out of the show she's lost her only religious group, a vital component in the Inclusion Initiative criteria. He wouldn't know this himself, Marianne must have told him, and they've cooked it up between them. It's not fair; they're trying to hold her to ransom.

'Our set is seven and a half minutes long, Ronald's is four. If we substitute Ronald for us you'll gain three minutes. And I think a pop song excellently sung will go down a lot better with the audience than "Sing Hosanna".'

'You mean, you're stepping down to give him your spot, you're not pulling out?'

'Oh no we're not pulling out, please don't think that. We want to be involved in some way. It's our mission to work within the community, in whatever role is required.'

Perhaps she has misjudged him. Really it's quite sweet that his singing group would sacrifice their chance in the limelight. She can understand why: he's so handsome and charming and humble and passionate, the type of inspirational leader that his flock would follow on to the battlefield and certain death. Onward Christian soldiers, marching as to war. And it's kind of him to give up his chance of more converts for the sake of including this new member.

Maria thinks about this.

'Well, I will need people on the door to take the ticket money.' There have been no volunteers so far.

'We can do that, no problem.'

Well, if you can't trust a Christian, who can you trust? Plus there's the added bonus of this really pissing Mike off.

'So if I take, what's his name? Ronald? If I take Ronald into the show the Victory Singers will man the door and remain involved with the show?'

'Absolutely.'

'OK then. When is the Victory Singers' next rehearsal?'

'Tomorrow. Marianne has asked us to rehearse after the Golden Belles.'

'OK, tell him to come in tomorrow.'

'Praise the Lord!'

A win-win situation all round. Pastor McKenzie holds out his hand to shake on the deal.

'The show's going to be fantastic, you're making Hexton history, Maria.'

If only she can hold onto her job long enough to enjoy it.

Chapter 22

Maria enters Ray's office unnoticed and is immediately wary. Something is wrong; it's too quiet, too calm. Fiona and Jane are facing her, seated side by side opposite a large leather wing-back chair. They have not seen her because they have their heads bowed low, the way they are when they've been naughty and Maria's had to give them a telling-off. Her protective hackles rise. Ray better not have given her clients any telling off.

She asks, 'What's going on?'

'Oh there you are, Maria.'

The big chair swivels and Ray appears, like some Bond villain, from inside it. He smiles, not fazed by her aggressive enquiry. The girls lift their heads and smile too.

'I was telling the girls a story, just to help them relax. Feeling better now, Fiona?'

Fiona nods at Ray and smiles bashfully. She does not acknowledge Maria's presence in the room. Maria doesn't blame her. Hitting a disabled person, she's despicable. She wants to rush across the room and throw herself at Fiona's feet and beg her forgiveness, but Ray's chair is in her way and Fiona won't even look at her.

'I feel better too,' says Jane, also to Ray; she's punishing Maria too.

Despite having had weekly committee meetings since rehearsals began, this is the first time Maria has actually seen inside Ray's office. Apart from his 1970s Evil Genius-style chair, everything is old and gloomy. There is an antique mahogany desk with matching glass cabinets and bookshelves: old-fashioned and depressing, probably the original furniture from when the church was built and probably worth a fortune.

What is surprising is the selection of books that line the bookshelf. These certainly didn't belong to the minister, they're mostly paperbacks, new, or relatively new, a few years old at most. Their spines are cracked and they look well thumbed.

Many of them are old friends, the very same books Maria has at home. There are books on healing your life, on positive thinking, creative visualization, herbs for health, self-love, self-hypnosis. She's amazed. As her eyes travel around the room she sees that lying open on his desk is a copy of her favourite book of all time, *The Road Less Travelled*. Ray follows Maria's eyes and smiles.

'Would you like to borrow it? It's a good book you know, really helpful.'

'Oh yes, I know,' Maria replies.

'Funny title, isn't it? It's from a poem apparently, Robert Frost.'

'Yes, I know.'

Little does Ray know that Maria carries that book around in her head and her heart.

'There's a load of other books there on the top shelf you might be interested in.'

'No thanks, Ray.'

She'd love to get into this with him, but right now she only wants to patch things up with the girls. She needs to be back in their good books. They can't just ignore her; the three of them need to sort things out.

'No, I know what you mean,' says Ray. 'They're not my kind of thing either. I can't take any of that "smell to get well" stuff seriously.'

Jane becomes engrossed in checking the Band-Aid on Fiona's thumb. Fiona's other hand is cramming a large piece of roly-poly pudding into her mouth. She is, as usual, enjoying the attention and moaning softly.

'Not only an excellent waitress but a nurse into the bargain?' says Ray. 'Is there no end to your talents, Nurse Jane?'

Jane is beaming again, the most she's ever smiled in one day. Unfortunately Maria is excluded from the warmth of Jane's beam. Both Jane and Fiona are directing their intensive smiles at Ray. He bounces this goodwill to Maria. She had expected some kind of reproach from him. It was, after all, Ray who intervened and put himself in the firing line of Maria's lethal weapons, but he seems, like Alice, to have forgotten the incident.

But the girls freezing her out like this cannot go on.

'Fiona, I'm so sorry,' Maria says, but Fiona will not acknowledge her.

'Please Fiona; at least tell me you're all right.'

Maria is close to tears but still Fiona will not speak.

Ray steps in. 'She's got a burn on her finger but she's a brave wee soldier, she's not said a word, not a peep, have you Fiona?'

He's trying to make Maria feel better, but it won't work. Fiona goes to speak, bits of strawberry jam roly-poly visible behind her teeth, then remembers the legend of her stoicism and keeps her mouth shut.

It's at this point Maria notices the absence of the others, and panics.

'Where are Brian and Martin?'

'Don't worry. Dezzie took the lads back to the centre. Too many cooks, and all that. The kitchen's no place for men; we leave that to you ladies. You're so much better at all that stuff.'

Maria can't work Ray out. He often makes these outrageously chauvinistic statements, accompanying them with a naughty smile. Is he doing the contemporary thing: telling women what men think they want to hear, rolling on his belly apologizing for his inferior status as a man? Or is he doing just the opposite as a way of sabotaging political correctness? Is this new-man postmodern irony or is he simply taking the piss?

'Too many cooks spoil the broth,' says Jane.

'Absolutely,' says Ray and then lowers his voice to a conspiratorial whisper. 'Typical women. Everybody thinks they're in charge of the soup. Three of those daft old bats in there salting it, no wonder it was ruined.'

Well, this is pretty bald. Jane and Fiona are in no doubt as to what he means and this makes them giggle. Maria briskly hands them their anoraks.

'Well, anyway, thanks for looking after the girls. We'd better be getting back to the centre.'

'Aye, any time.'

'Sorry.'

Maria looks at Ray and by way of explanation nods in the direction of the café.

'Nothing to be sorry about,' he says.

'Well, I'm sorry the work experience didn't work out.'

'Eh? Oh no. That's not the way it works around here. If you sign up for a shift, you do your shift. We don't tolerate malingering. These two are made of sterner stuff; I've seen them in action. Fiona's not going to let a wee burned finger put her off, are you Fiona?'

'No way,' she says emphatically.

'Right, well, same time next week?'

This he addresses to the girls, who giggle and nod and beam.

Ray accompanies them through the hall to the front porch of the church. Like a minister after Sunday service, he stands on the doorstep and shakes each of them by the hand, covering their hand with both of his.

'Now make sure you're here on time,' he jokes, wagging a finger at both girls.

'No, we will be, Ray, don't worry,' says Jane seriously. 'Maria'll get us here in plenty of time.'

The girls, filled with a new-found work ethic, have started to walk off. Unusually pally, the comrades link arms. Maria has already moved past Ray when she feels his hand on her shoulder. She hears his voice in her ear, quiet, conspiring.

'Don't be so hard on yourself, they love you to bits.'

Before he's finished speaking she has pulled away. She doesn't look back. His sympathy and understanding get in under her protective glaze and three long strides later Maria is crying.

She could never hurt any of her clients and she

would kill anyone, yes, kill is not too strong a word, she'd kill anyone who tried to hurt them. Tears are running down her cheeks.

When they are well clear of the church she dries off her tears by vigorously rubbing her jacket sleeve across her face. This is painful, the rough material scratching at the sensitive skin around her eyes, but she welcomes the stimulation. She swallows a mouthful of phlegm and takes a few deep breaths.

'I'm sorry I threw the crisps at you, Fiona,' she blurts. 'I'm so sorry I hurt you. I have a lot on my mind and I was angry with you but I shouldn't have done it. It was very wrong of me to throw the crisps. I'm very sorry. I hope you can forgive me.'

Fiona stops and looks at Maria. She looks into her eyes and smiles.

'I forgive you,' she says quietly.

Fiona never does anything quietly but on this occasion she utters these words with such simple dignity that Maria, overwhelmed with relief and gratitude and love, wants to throw her arms around her, or as far around Fiona as her arms will go. She wants to hug and squeeze her and demonstrate with the full force of the squeeze how much she means to her. She wants to squash and physically imprint on Fiona's big body her strength of feeling. But she won't.

With Fiona, hugs and kisses must always be on her terms. She has to be the one to initiate physical contact or else she freaks out. So, carefully, Maria lifts Fiona's hand. Slowly and while maintaining reassuring eye contact, she brings the hand to her lips. Without any sudden movements to startle her, Maria deposits a passionate kiss of gratitude and love on the back of Fiona's hand.

Fiona tolerates this contact. She receives the fawning kiss as her due and then pulls Maria into her ample bosom and squeezes her tight.

'I'm so sorry, Fiona. I lost my temper, it was very very bad.' Not only must she apologize for her own appalling behaviour, but she must also make Fiona understand that violence of any description is unacceptable.

'Very bad,' agrees Fiona, releasing her from the violent bear hug.

Maria lets out a relieved laugh. They are in agreement; everything is back to normal.

'Yes. Very very bad,' she says.

'He's a bad man.'

'Who is?'

'The man,' says Fiona. 'The man with the strawberry.' Her tone is chatty and friendly. 'But it wasn't a strawberry today, unless you can get black strawberries.'

When she doesn't want to talk about something, or she becomes bored, Fiona has a habit of changing the subject. She almost always changes it to one of her favourite subjects, crisps or cake. Obviously she doesn't want to discuss the crisp-throwing incident any longer, and Maria is happy to drop it.

'Yes,' says Maria, trying to match Fiona's lightness of tone, 'I think it was strawberry, it was strawberry jam roly-poly. That's what Alice said anyway.'

Maria is keen to widen out the conversation to include Jane.

'Jane, you make a terrific waitress.'

'I'm a nurse. Grade G staff nurse.'

'Oh yes I know that, but you make a great waitress too. It's still a good job, still helping people.' Maria tails off unconvincingly. 'But you had a good time didn't you, you want to go back, right?'

'I am going back,' says Jane boldly. 'Same time next week. You have to take me,' she says imperiously.

'Yes, that's right. We're all going back, same time next week. It'll be great fun.'

'I don't want to go back,' says Fiona.

She says this calmly. There is no hint of acrimony; she's simply stating a fact.

'And why is that then?' says Maria, trying to laugh but only producing a soprano cackle from her throat.

'The man with the strawberry, but it wasn't a strawberry today.'

'What man?'

'Can I have crisps please Maria?'

Maria sighs. She knows it was only going to be a matter of time before the thorny question of potato-snack provision came up again.

'What, you want crisps now?'

'Yes. Now, please.'

Maria knows it's wrong. Apart from the damage the crisps are undoubtedly doing to Fiona – her blood thickened to paste thundering through her kinked and frayed blood vessels like stringy chewed offal, her arterial walls plaqued like chewing-gum-spattered pavement, her blood pressure a ticking bomb – apart from all that, she knows it's wrong to give in.

'OK then,' Maria says, reaching into her bag, 'cheese and onion all right?'

Once they get over this crisis she can refocus Fiona on healthy eating, get her off the crisps for good.

'No,' says Fiona quietly, 'I want Walker's Sensations Thai Chilli flavour,' and then she puts an affectionate hand on Jane's arm.

'Do you want crisps Jane?'

'Yes, I'll have a packet of Seasons, Sea Salt and Crushed Pepper please.'

The day that had been shaping up in Maria's meditation to be so perfect has so far turned out to be a nightmare, but if she thinks this is bad, it's about to get worse.

Chapter 23

Once he waves off Maria and the girls, Ray makes a start again on his sideboard. Stevie King, the guy that commissioned the work, phoned him yesterday. He had a laugh and a joke with him and put him off for another couple of weeks. He's hardly made any progress on the sideboards since the rehearsals started. Every day someone asks him to do something or other, paint a backdrop or build a set. It's getting out of hand.

Marianne is doing her usual thing of coming up with brilliant ideas. Her latest is to run a coffee bar during the interval in the show.

'I'll check it out, Ray, but as far as I know we don't need a licence so long as we're not selling alcohol.'

'You weren't thinking of selling alcohol, were you?'

'Good grief! Believe me, absolutely the last thing I was thinking of was selling alcohol. We've got enough on our hands with this lot, never mind a load of drunken Hextors. Mind you, it might make them enjoy the show more.'

'I think they'll enjoy the show just fine.'

'Well, thank you for your vote of confidence.'

Ray lets Marianne lead him towards the snooker table.

'This thing is a bit of a liability. It's the opportunity cost I'm thinking of.'

'Opportunity cost?' says Ray, baffled. She's obviously forgotten who she's talking to. He's just a joiner.

'Yes. It's taking up valuable seating space – on the night of the show we could have at least six more paying customers in there. It's costing us bums on seats.'

'And you can never have too many bums,' says Ray. Coincidentally, as they approach the table he can see a magnificent example of quality bum, a perfect specimen. Some of the choirgirls are playing snooker, four of them at a time. One is leaning across the table trying to make a shot and meanwhile presenting a deliciously juicy young arse.

Jailbait. It's exciting but unnerving to be around them. Ray will never understand teenage girls. It's the giggling. What the hell do they find so hysterically funny? He always thinks they're laughing at him and he doesn't know why, or how to stop them. The girls are now standing around the snooker table bickering about whose turn it is. They hassle everyone else who plays snooker, the ones who take it seriously, for their turn on the table, and then when they do get on they're less interested in playing than in who's watching them.

The rest of the choir hang together in clumps whispering with occasional noisy explosions of giggling, waiting for their turn.

'Excuse me please Chantelle,' says Marianne to one of the snooker players, 'could you let us in a minute here, please? Ray needs to measure the table. Thank you.'

All four snooker players move towards the other choirgirls who lounge around on one of the pews that have been brought from the church into the hall.

'I thought if you could make some sort of lid that fits on top,' explains Marianne.

Ray understands quickly and easily what it is she wants.

'That way we could use it to serve coffee from on the night.'

Although he's nodding his head he has tuned in to the buzz and increased volume from the choirgirls. Something's going on, but with Marianne talking at him he can't work out what it is.

An old sheet, recently pressed into service as a dust cover, is draped over the pew the girls are standing around. It's daubed here and there with the burgundy paint Ray used in the backdrop for the Hexton Hot Steppers. There seems to be something moving beneath the sheet. The girls are giggling and pushing each other towards it. One or two of them prod it and then retreat sniggering to their friends.

Marianne is deliberately tuning out the noise from the girls, and raises her voice to compensate.

'Not only that,' she almost shouts, 'but it would mean the table was protected from anyone spilling anything on it. Alice gets really antsy if any of my lot go near it with their cans of Coke.'

Ray has stopped listening. Something is about to happen. The girls are laughing and squealing, shoving each other towards the thing under the sheet. Agitation rises to fever pitch, until one girl runs forward and tugs the sheet off the pew.

The girls shriek in terror. They start crying. The burgundy paint was not paint but blood. There under the sheet, pinned to the pew by a six-inch nail through the neck, is one of the magician's rabbits.

Amidst the screaming, Ray and Marianne run to the girls. All other activity in the hall ceases as people rush forward, jostling to get a view. One girl screeches and points.

'Miss, the rabbit, the rabbit! Please miss, please!'

Marianne turns to Ray.

'Can you deal with this? I'll have to get the girls out of here.' She moves forward with her arms wide, trying to sweep her charges together.

'Girls! Come on now,' she says, 'let's move outside.'

But Ray can't deal with this. He's not good with blood. He doesn't like to get it on his hands, it scares him.

The rabbit is not dead. Though it is impaled through the neck and bleeding profusely, it is fully conscious. Just because he's handy with woodwork doesn't mean he can deal with this. If he has to touch it he might faint, here, in front of everyone.

'Come on now, Alison love,' Marianne says in a soothing sing-song voice to the most hysterical girl. 'Let's go outside and get a breath of air. It's going to be all right, we'll leave Ray to sort this out, shall we?'

'Miss, we have to help it!'

'We can't leave it like this, we have to do something! *Please*, miss!'

Despite their protests the headmistress gently puts her arm around Alison but she fights her off, howling and clinging to her friends. Then Marianne's shouting above the chaos.

'Please pay attention, girls! Now we are going to

233

leave calmly and quietly. I insist that you leave the building with me immediately!'

But this end of the hall is too congested now for them to push through the excited crowd. She's forced to give up and let them weep and cling to each other, alternately watching the rabbit and burying their heads in each other's necks.

The rabbit is lying on its side on top of the pew, but as it struggles it slides off. Everyone in the hall screams. They're all expecting him to do something, to fix it, Mr Fixit. Now the rabbit is dangling, suspended by the nail which is slowly tearing through its throat. Blood is bubbling from the hole in its neck.

Ray grits his teeth and lifts the rabbit back up onto the pew, taking the strain off its neck wound while he tries to figure out what to do. He can feel its heart beating, the throb of its pulse through his fingers, and with each throb he feels a hot quiver of nausea. He tries not to look at it, to avoid seeing its torn flesh as he takes his hammer from his tool belt. This increases the volume of the girls' screams.

He's going to be sick. The screaming is like two thin steel blades entering his head via his ears. He can't think straight, the blades of noise are fighting a bloody duel, slicing and cutting his brain to chump meat. He hates to hear a woman scream, he's heard enough screaming to last a lifetime.

'Don't hurt him!'

'Ray, help the wee fella!'

He holds the rabbit with one hand while he engages the nail between the prongs of the claw hammer. He's trying to be gentle but his hand is shaking, knocking the hammer against the nail. He's hurting it, making things worse. He pulls hard on the hammer, trying to ease the nail out of the wood and out of the rabbit's throat. The nail is deeply embedded and although it bends, it won't leave the wood. The blood flows more quickly now from the rabbit. It's sticky and hot in his hands. Ray feels dizzy.

He's bent the nail, he'll never get it out now, and still they scream at him. The rabbit is more trapped now than when he started. Even if he can get the nail out it'll only increase blood loss. Ray can't save the rabbit. He's hurting it. Its breathing is becoming more laboured, it's drowning in its own blood. The kindest thing to do would be to end this slow asphyxiation. He has to kill it. He can't deal with this.

The rabbit looks at him out of the side of its eye. It isn't angry or scared or accepting, it just watches him as though gathering evidence. It knows the way this scene plays out. It will not cower.

Ray has seen this look before.

He turns the hammer in his hands.

'Miss, please don't let him kill it! Please!'

'For God's sake put the wee thing out of its misery!' a man's voice shouts, setting off another round of screaming from the teenagers. The crowd have moved closer, crowding in on top of him, so close he hasn't the elbow room to work.

Ray turns and faces them. 'Would you just please move back!' he shouts. 'Look, what is it you want? You want me to take the nail out? Yes? No? Look, the rabbit's going to die, whatever I do. I can't work miracles, I don't know what it is you expect. What the fuck do you people want from me? Eh?'

The crowd has fallen silent. Ray is wiping the sweat from his forehead when someone pushes through. Alice emerges and takes the hammer from his slack hand.

'Give me the bliddy thing,' she says.

As if practising a putting shot, Alice puts the hammer to the rabbit's head and then with one swift tap kills it stone dead. There is a squashing sound as its skull bursts, followed by a collective gasp of shock.

'OK, show's over, get back to whatever you were doing, the lot of you.'

Transfixed by the horror of the executed rabbit and the ponytailed woman with the blood-streaked face, nobody moves.

'You heard me!' she yells.

This shout galvanizes them into action and they start to disperse. Marianne pulls her girls, still weeping and clinging but calmer, away from the scene.

What the fuck is he doing here? Why did he come to this place? These people expect too much. They don't know him, they don't know. When space has cleared Ray turns and walks out the hall. He's uncertain at this moment if he'll ever return.

Chapter 24

When Maria and the girls arrive back at the centre, there is no sign of Dezzie and the boys. Where are they? They left the church before her; they should have got here ages ago. It's not as though she can ask anyone. That would be admitting that she doesn't know where they are and, as key worker, she is responsible. Perhaps they went the long way back through the park. Half an hour later, when they have still not returned, she has to discount this theory.

She imagines the faces of Brian's mum and dad when she has to tell them she's lost their son. Despite Brian's difficult relationship with them, especially his dad Phil, they are devoted to him. He's their only child. Like other parents of disabled children they blame themselves, and ceaselessly try to make up for it by spoiling him with every indulgence they can possibly afford. Maria is scared of what Brian's dad might do with his baseball bat if Brian was ever to come to any harm.

Martin's parents are different: they're elderly and very easy-going. Too easy-going. They make light of the fact that Martin has Down's syndrome, and give him far too much freedom. This lenient attitude has led Martin to have an inflated idea of his own capabilities.

What if they've had an accident or been mugged? The streets of Hexton have, up to now, been a safe place for clients. Though the locals might not let them into their clubs, they don't generally attack them on the street. But there's a first time for everything.

If some doped-up junkie with a kitchen knife, desperate for his next fix, thought they had a few quid between them, they could get mugged. She knows exactly how Dezzie would react. He'd protect the boys, her boys, with his life if necessary.

Worst-case scenario would be trouble from Martin. Martin is affectionate and fun-loving, especially with the women clients, but he hates people taking the piss and he can be aggressive. He's young and strong and has high self-esteem. Over the years, through various disputes and tussles for dominance with the other men clients, Martin has become recognized as the alpha male. Centre staff do all they can to discourage these power struggles, but they are inevitable. Unfortunately this has led Martin to believe that he's a hard man. He's unlikely, given the reputation he has to maintain, to allow anyone, even a crazed junkie with a kitchen knife, to mug him.

His tough-guy standing is based on a few shouted arguments and a bit of pushing in the lunch queue but he's not up to armed combat. Maria prays that he wouldn't try any of the have-a-go-hero stunts he uses in the show.

She's crying again. This is all her fault. If she hadn't lost her temper with Fiona they would all be here now, warm and safe inside the centre. The buses will be here in a minute to take everybody home. And still no sign of them.

What if Dezzie does put himself between Martin and a drug-crazed knife-wielding mugger? If he sacrifices his own sweet firm, but nonetheless vulnerable, body for Martin's flabby pink one? Would she still love Dezzie if he was disabled? If he was crippled and unable to father children? Yes. Or physically intact but brain-damaged? Of course. Even if he was drooling and vacant? Her love is unconditional. If she was ever lucky enough to become Mrs Desmond Thompson, it would be for better or worse, in sickness and in health. Although making love to a drooling swivel-eyed husband doesn't seem right somehow.

Buses are pulling up outside the centre. The drivers are opening the back doors and operating the lifts, making ready for the wheelchairs.

'Time to go home,' says Jane.

Distracted with thoughts of Dezzie lying on top of her, not like he is now, but with his eyes rolling and his saliva dribbling onto her, Maria dries her eyes and gives her stock reply.

'In a minute.'

'But the bus is here!'

Jane is frightened. Every day she worries that she'll miss the bus. Some clients, Martin and sometimes Fiona for instance, don't want to go home and have to be led persuasively, if not with mild force, on to their bus, but Jane is always keen to get home.

'I want to go home,' she snivels.

'She wants to go home,' says Fiona.

'Yes OK Fiona, calm down, we'll be going in a minute.'

'Well give her her anorak then!'

239

'I want my anorak.'

'She wants her anorak,' says Fiona.

'OK, wait here. I'm getting it. And yours too, Fiona Simpson, you're going home as well.'

'Good,' says Fiona.

Maria can't put it off any longer; she'll have to tell Bert. Unusually, the door to his office is closed. She knocks.

'With you in a second!' Bert calls.

He's on the phone.

'Yes certainly, officer,' she hears him say.

This is an odd time of day for him to be on the phone. Bert always checks the clients on to their buses and waves them off. He likes doing this; since he went into management he misses the client contact.

Fear makes Maria's hand fly to her chest. He said *officer*. Why is Bert talking to a policeman?

'Maria!' she suddenly hears someone roar.

Several hours later, Ray gets off a bus which has pulled into Hexton. When he paid the bus driver he became aware, as did the driver, that his hands were covered in dried blood. He makes straight for the public toilets and scrubs the blood from his hands. It's everywhere, between his fingers, under his nails, encrusted around his wedding ring. He looks at his left hand and pulls off the thick gold band that he has worn every day for fifteen and a half years. He puts it in his shirt pocket, the breast pocket close to his heart, and smiles at his reflection in the mirror. He's changing.

When he left the church he walked out along the main road. He only wanted to be moving, he didn't want to have to think about where he was going. It would have been easier to take the long straight road to the city, but something made him choose the quieter country roads surrounding Hexton. He must have circled the town three or four times before he got hungry and tired enough to come back. But he's had a good think.

What freaked him out wasn't the blood and pain and death of the wee rabbit. Well, yes, actually, when he thinks about it, that did freak him out. He thought he'd left all that behind, blood and pain and death have dogged him, but of course that's rubbish. He'll never get away from it. What really freaked him was his own response.

Since he opened the doors of the church he's had to take more and more responsibility for the people that come around and the fucking weird things they do. Some of these bozos know not what they do. Nailing a rabbit to a pew? What the fuck was that? How the hell is he supposed to deal with it? He's only a joiner, not a fucking vet. And why is it his problem? He's spent hours tramping round the back roads of Hexton when he should have been working on his sideboard.

When he came to Hexton it was to leave all the shit behind and make a fresh start. Today, with the girls screaming at him and the rabbit bleeding on him, Ray realized that although he'd changed location, he hadn't moved on. He was still feeling the guilt, still taking the blame. What happened today was that he let the hysteria of a bunch of schoolgirls infect him. That's all. He shouldn't read anything into it. He doesn't have to do that any more, he's free to move on. It's time now. As he heads back to the church he checks his breast pocket for the ring. It's still there.

*   *   *

'It was that sick nutcase McGraw that did it,' explains Alice as she cuts the bread.

Ray had expected everyone to have gone home by now, but Alice and Marianne are still in the kitchen waiting for him when he gets back. Alice heats him a plate of soup and relates the whole story as he sups greedily.

'As a warning, apparently,' she adds.

'It's pathetic but I suppose it's Hexton's version of waking up with a horse's head in your bed,' says Marianne.

'Exactly,' agrees Alice. 'Magic Marshall owed him fifty quid and he decided to use strong-arm tactics. He said he couldn't break Magic's fingers because that would interfere with his income.'

'Does Magic make any money from magic shows?' asks Marianne.

'Not as much as he needs to.'

'But why did he ever go to a moneylender?'

'He didn't, it was his son Peter. When the factory shut down Peter left Hexton and he's never been back, but Magic had to take on the debt. He didn't want to but you don't argue with McGraw.'

Ray is loath to interrupt this fascinating discussion and he's really enjoying his soup, but he wants to be sure he's got the story right.

'So: Magic Marshall was paying off his son's debt but he didn't keep up the repayments so the money-lender mutilated his rabbit.'

'As a warning.'

Ray shakes his head, as do Alice and Marianne.

'I noticed Magic did a vanishing act when McGraw appeared.'

'Well, Magic's a senior citizen now,' says Alice. 'He's

not fit to take on that big thug, so he scooted. Who was to know McGraw would do that to the poor wee thing?'

'I can't believe there was a moneylender operating from here.'

'Ray, he's been in here every other day since the café opened.'

'Why didn't you tell me?'

'Excuse me, you're the guy that dreamed up the great *come one come all* philosophy.'

'Well, I tell you, if McGraw or any other money-lender sets foot in this church I'll fucking . . . sorry, ladies. Well, you let me know if you see any.'

'Anyway, it's sorted now. McGraw's been paid off, he'll not be back,' says Alice, ladling more soup into Ray's now empty plate.

'How come?'

'Oh,' says Marianne, smiling, 'Alice was a bit naughty.'

'No I wasn't.'

Ray and Marianne look at Alice but they don't say a word.

'I bliddy wasn't! Look, the kids wanted to make a donation. That's what people do nowadays, if there's a tragedy folk fall over themselves to give money, God knows why but they do. I organized a wee tin in the café, that's all.'

'And you laid the rabbit out in state and gave him a name,' adds Marianne.

'OK, so I gave him a name.'

'What did you call him?' asks Ray.

'Norman.'

'Norman the Rabbit?'

'Listen, there was fifty-two pounds forty-three pence

in that tin! Magic took it round and paid off McGraw.'

'Well at least the rabbit never died in vain.'

Ray and Marianne exchange smirks at this.

'Nope,' agrees Alice, swiping his plate away briskly.

He knows he's pissed Alice off now, so as she passes he tries to take her hand but she dodges away. He'll have to try something else.

'That soup was fantastic, Alice, I'm not kidding, I think that was your best yet. What was in it?'

'Och, nothing really, just a rabbit and a handful of veg,' says Alice.

Ray is not entirely sure she's joking.

Chapter 25

Maria turns to see that it is Martin who has roared her name. He's standing in the doorway, against the flow of clients making their way past him to their buses. He appears to be wearing Dezzie's T-shirt, his new red one, the one that says *Ride Bikes, Drink Beer, Talk Bollocks*. Martin's head is tilted. He plants his feet wide and holds out his arms to Maria, not in a distressed way. The gesture is magnanimous, loving, drunken.

'Maria!' he bawls again.

She rushes towards him, fighting her way through clients. She grabs both his arms and looks into his face. Martin smiles up at her benignly and then burps.

The burp is so close she can taste it: she's getting hops and barley, golden ale, smooth brown velvet below a creamy head. She's getting busty barmaid with frothing pint pots of dark sweet beer, saloon bar with darts and doms, sodden beer mats and overflowing ashtrays. She's getting Hexton Arms. With a definite aftertaste of cheese and onion crisps.

'Oh,' Martin giggles, 'sorry about that.'

'You're drunk.'

Martin seems to think hard about this and then, as if remembering his lines, he begins to declaim:

' "I, madam, may be drunk, but you are . . ." '

He looks at Maria, squinting and tilting, and then he throws his arms wide again.

'I think you're lovely!'

Martin makes a lunge for Maria's breasts but he's slow off the mark and she easily sidesteps him.

'Where are Brian and Dezzie?'

'They're here!' says Martin, pointing back towards the centre.

Maria turns and sees Brian's wheelchair emerging from the gents' toilets. It seems to be jammed in the doorway. Dezzie is pushing it from behind, none too gently, and Brian is laughing so hard he's in danger of falling out of the chair.

'I want a word with you,' says Maria to them both, but this only makes Brian laugh harder.

'I'm really sorry we're late, Maria, we just lost track,' says Dezzie.

He has his head hung and his eyes coy. He obviously thinks because he's gorgeous that Maria will let him away with this. Not bloody likely.

'I'm putting the girls on their buses. Wait for me in Arts and Crafts,' she barks.

Maria strong-arms the somewhat bewildered Fiona and Jane on to their respective buses with such urgency that they don't have time to complain.

Bert has taken up his post by the buses.

'Just the two coats today, Susan?' he says to an extremely well-wrapped-up client as he helps her aboard. He winks at Maria as she hurries past. Bert is always full of cheeky banter at this time of day, all the staff are. Relieved to be waving them off home,

246

they affectionately mock their clients' amusing little foibles. But Maria is not amused.

It is not until she walks back into the Arts and Crafts room that she notices all three boys are wearing identical bikes, beer and bollocks T-shirts. She chooses to ignore this and concentrate on more important matters, beginning with interrogating Dezzie.

'What do you think you're doing getting my clients drunk?'

'Who's drunk?'

Dezzie gives a light laugh, but as a more defensive tone creeps into his voice Maria can tell he's uncomfortable being called to account.

'We had two pints.'

'And crisps,' adds Martin helpfully.

'We could see that we weren't needed in the church so we made a sharp exit . . .'

With hand gestures and a descriptive whistle Martin demonstrates their sharp exit.

'The lads wanted a T-shirt, so we went shopping. After that we . . .'

Maria is furious. She has easily spotted a flaw in his story.

'You went shopping? How the hell did you manage that then? I know for a fact that these two don't have any money on them, I sorted out their cash this morning.'

Dezzie hangs his head, embarrassed. She's caught him out.

'Present,' says Brian, plucking with weak fingers at his T-shirt.

'You've not to tell!' Martin shouts at Brian. 'You were told, it's a secret!'

'I had money,' says Dezzie.

'*You* paid for them?'

'Boys' club secret!' shouts Martin, annoyed that the secret is no longer exclusive to the boys' club.

Dezzie shrugs.

'They weren't expensive.'

'We were feeling a bit thirsty . . .' interjects Martin.

Maria puts her hand up to stop him.

'Thanks Martin, but I'm speaking to Dezzie at the moment. It's important that I find out exactly what happened.'

'Hexton Arms,' says Dezzie, 'two pints.'

'Two pints of lager,' says Martin, counting it off on his fingers, 'two pints of beer and two pints of, what d'you call that other stuff Dezzie?'

'He's kidding,' says Dezzie, 'two pints, total.'

'Because of the soup,' says Martin.

Despite Maria's rebuke, Martin has continued to explain himself. They are both speaking at the same time and she's confused.

'Martin, what are you talking about pet?'

'The soup. Fiona was right. It was far too salty. That's why we were gasping for a drink.'

'Salt. Poisoning. We. Intend. To. Sue,' confirms Brian.

This reminder of the debacle over the soup only makes Maria angrier.

'Is that the best excuse you can come up with? The soup was salty so you took it upon yourself to take them to the pub and fill them with drink? These are my clients!'

Maria is shouting.

'Clients. Not. Pets. Adults,' says Brian.

This is the first time he has ever spoken like this, he's thrown strops but he's never been so vicious. There is no reply she can make to him.

The lads, despite their matching *Talk Bollocks* T-shirts, are strangely silent.

'You don't own us,' says Martin eventually, in a quiet but audible mumble.

Maria is shocked by this spreading insurgence. This has never happened in Blue Group before.

'Martin, just be quiet please till we sort this out.'

'We can do what we like,' Martin says in his 'no fair' huffy voice.

There is another heavy silence.

'He's right, Maria,' says Dezzie gently. 'They were thirsty, Martin suggested we go to the pub and get a drink. I didn't see the harm. I wasn't forcing anyone; I wasn't pouring it down their throats.'

Maria is thinking about this and so is Dezzie, apparently, because they both begin to speak at the same time.

'Well how did Brian manage to . . . ?'

'OK, OK, I did pour it down his throat, I mean, no, I didn't, I held it to his lips.'

Brian is nodding his heavy head as fast as he is able, fervently supporting what Dezzie is saying while angrily stabbing a crooked finger at the Dynavox. Brian is operating a double standard here. He hates eating and drinking in public but he let Dezzie hold a pint glass to his lips.

'We. Are. Service. Users. You. Provide. Service. Serve. Us.'

'Brian swallowed,' explains Dezzie somewhat needlessly, 'he wanted to. Martin and Brian are over eighteen.'

'Yes but you can't just give them pints,' Maria complains, 'they're not used to drink.'

Dezzie seems exasperated and worn out with the arguing.

'Well, how the hell are they ever going to get used to it if they're not allowed to go for a pint?'

'Not. Pets. Or. Prisoners.'

Maria rushes to put her arms around Brian.

'I'm sorry.'

She feels ashamed and tears spring to her eyes. She doesn't want them to hate her. Perhaps the reason she's so angry is that she's jealous of the loyalty Martin and Brian have shown Dezzie.

'Don't. Cry. Borrow. My. T. Shirt.'

Maria laughs. Brian doesn't hate her. Neither do Martin or Dezzie, who also laugh. And they did seem to have a good time. And they are back in time for the buses, just.

'Did you have a good time?'

Martin says yes, Brian says splendid.

'And you want to go to the pub again?'

Brian nods. Martin thinks it over.

'Yes, but not every day. There's no need to go every day.'

As the anger drains from Maria she's left with a cold unease. That was a professional dispute, wasn't it? Not personal. She was angry with Dezzie her colleague, not Dezzie her boyfriend. It was important that they resolve it, but it shouldn't creep into their personal life. She hopes Dezzie will see things the same way. She hopes she's still his girlfriend. And it was sweet of him to buy their T-shirts and all those pints; it must have cost him a fortune.

'And we've kept the best to last. This one's for you, Maria. Check this out: we got a T-shirt for Mike,' says Dezzie, pulling open a poly bag.

'For *Mike*?'

Dezzie has bought a T-shirt – not for her – but for

Mike? Maria is horrified. By his own admission, Dezzie barely knows Mike. He's only ever met him once, at his interview. When Maria moans about how unfair Mike is, Dezzie's always sympathetic. She thought he was on her side. Buying Mike a T-shirt, making him one of the boys' gang, this is the ultimate act of disloyalty.

'It's not the same as ours,' says Martin, flapping his arms, sensitive to her dismay.

As Dezzie is smoothing the T-shirt out, the three of them are giggling. It's a nice one, one that she would have appreciated herself, a pale yellow colour, very retro, very Seventies. It says in bubbly lettering,

I snogged the girl out of Hanson.

Maria doesn't understand. As far as she remembers the band Hanson was made up of three brothers.

'I didn't know there were any girls in the band.'

The giggling peaks.

'There aren't,' says Dezzie.

Now she comes to think of it, the brothers Hanson had long hair and were kind of androgynous. High fives all round in the boys' club.

'Oh, right!' she says, relieved.

Martin and Brian nod their heads and high-five her, bringing her in on the joke.

'He'll know!'

'No he won't.'

'But if he finds out. Somebody might tell him. He'll realize you're taking the piss.'

Dezzie exchanges sly glances with his co-conspirators.

'Not if Martin gives him it,' he says artlessly. 'Go on Martin, show her.'

Martin stands, clears his throat, opens his eyes wide, shuffles forward and says in a fake ingénue voice, 'Mike, I would be honoured if you would accept this gift. Hanson is my favourite band. It would mean so much to me if you would wear it at the show.'

Martin the consummate actor is playing a character they all know well: a well-meaning mentally disabled person hero-worshipping a member of staff.

'You. Are. Beautiful. Man. Who. Could. Refuse. A. Face. Like. That,' says Brian.

Martin turns to Brian, his arms open in supplication, his face as vacant as a saint's.

'It's a cracker though, eh?' says Dezzie, 'it was Brian's idea.'

'Mmm. Bop,' says Brian's machine.

Maria nods her recognition, it's the title of Hanson's one and only famous song.

'Subvert. Their. Expectations.' The Dynavox says dispassionately, but Brian is bouncing excitedly in his chair. Maria joins in with the laughter. Until now it has never occurred to her to question her clients' sincerity. Hats off to Brian, a typical chess-player's manoeuvre.

'Who. Are. The. Dafties. Now.'

'Mike's going to look a right daftie with this on at the show,' says Dezzie. 'Serves him right for being rotten to my . . . to Maria.'

Maria has a moment's fear when it seems Dezzie might say the G word in front of the boys. It's also a moment's pride. She'd like the boys to know that she's Dezzie's girlfriend; then she might be accepted as an honorary member in the boys' club. It's a relief to know that Dezzie is on her side, but she can't approve of his methods.

She is probably being old-fashioned but instinctively she feels it's not right to denigrate a member of staff, especially the most high-ranking member, however much of a tosser he is. Respect for authority has to be maintained, for the clients' sake as much as anything. It might have been Brian's idea, but Dezzie has incited him to this subtle mutiny. Dezzie's full of surprises.

Chapter 26

Maria didn't ask Fiona to go to the pictures this week. She didn't ask last week. Fiona can't remember about the week before. Maria shouted at Fiona and threw crisps at her and put soup on her and burnt her hand. Fiona doesn't know why. Fiona forgave Maria and they are friends again but still she has a scared feeling in her tummy. Something is wrong. She has been a bad girl. She wants to go to the pictures with Maria.

Fiona thinks that Maria is going to the pictures without her. She is going with someone else. This is because Fiona was bad. She tried to take the soup back to the kitchen. Jane was a good girl. She brought the soup. The soup was rotten. It had too much salt. Maria shouted at Fiona and she was crying. She was a crybaby.

Ray said Fiona was a good girl. She was a clever girl. She told everybody the soup was rotten. Ray told Fiona a nice story and she stopped crying. She wishes she could remember the story. Ray's voice is quiet. Fiona likes Ray's voice. He said she was brave when she got the plaster on her finger. She wasn't a crybaby. Fiona likes the café. She is scared of the café.

Mum doesn't love Maria. She smiles when she speaks to Maria. Maria smiles back. Mum says Maria thinks she knows everything, she says Maria is a little Hitler. Fiona doesn't know what a little Hitler is. She asked Martin but Martin doesn't know. Mum is wrong. Maria doesn't know everything. She doesn't know that Mum says she's a little Hitler. Fiona is scared to tell Maria this.

Mum doesn't know everything. She doesn't know that Maria shouted at Fiona and threw crisps at her and put soup on her and burnt her hand. She doesn't know that Fiona was a bad girl. Fiona is scared to tell Mum this.

Maria is sorry. She said she is sorry that she shouted at Fiona and threw crisps at her and put soup on her and burnt her hand. Fiona doesn't know why Maria was crying. She doesn't like it when Maria is a cry-baby. It makes her frightened. Maria loves Fiona. She gives Fiona crisps, nice ones. Fiona loves Maria. She wants to go to the pictures with her.

It's been a long week, a long week and a very long day. The church hall has started to fill up again, but not with rehearsals. There are no rehearsals tonight, the big one is planned for tomorrow. Tonight the young ones are in, Bob, Gerry and Aldo and all of them. They come almost every night to play snooker until Ray eventually throws them out. Aldo wants him to play doubles against Alice and Bob, but Pastor McKenzie has asked to speak to him privately.

'I wouldn't want anybody put at risk, there's a lot of vulnerable young people here,' says Ray, gathering up the cards.

'No, of course. With your help supervision will be a hundred per cent. You have my absolute assurance on that. There's nothing to worry about. I just felt you should know,' says Pastor McKenzie.

'But I think you're right to keep it quiet, there's no point in frightening people, or encouraging neighbourhood-watch death squads.'

'Thanks, I appreciate it,' says the pastor.

In Ray's office, due to the sensitive nature of what they have been discussing, the two men have kept their voices to a whisper. Now the conversation moves on and they speak at a more normal volume.

They have also moved on to what has become their customary evening game of cards. It's Ray's turn to be dealer. Neither of them is ever in a hurry to get home. This is becoming Ray's favourite time of day; Stuart McKenzie is a good card player and excellent company when he's not trying to recruit converts to his mission.

Before playing another hand Ray takes out his tobacco and rolls a cigarette.

'You know, you'd make an excellent pastor,' says Stuart.

Ray laughs. Here we go. Stuart is full of this kind of bullshit.

'No, really, pastoral care these days is all about charisma. And, without inflating your ego too much, Ray, you've got it in abundance. People like you. Would you not fancy it?'

Ray deals the cards, draws on his fag and thinks about this briefly.

'Eh . . . no.'

He can see the pastor is slightly miffed by such a swift dismissal, and so tries to soften the blow.

'Stuart, you don't need me. You're doing a grand job.'

'Hmmm,' says McKenzie, reaching into his pocket. He pulls out a fifty-pence piece, looks at it for a moment, and puts it on the desk. So far the stakes have been twenty pence. He must reckon he has a good hand. Ray matches the fifty-pence stake from his stack of winnings.

'Stick or twist?' he asks.

The pastor studies his cards and turns his hand swiftly, as though he is removing a light bulb from its socket or wringing a chicken's neck.

'Hit me.'

An ace. Excellent card.

'Yes!'

Stuart makes a triumphant fist and pulls it down.

'Praise the Lord!'

Ray watches as he scrapes the money over to his side of the table. Apart from his fixation with the Lord, Stuart seems such a normal bloke.

'Are you not a bit old for an imaginary friend?'

Stuart looks baffled and Ray has to explain.

'I mean your imaginary wee friend, Jesus.'

'Oh, right. He's real to me, Ray, as real as you are. So that's what puts you off, is it? Well, I suppose a belief in Our Lord Jesus Christ is a pretty central tenet of Christianity,' says the pastor ruefully, 'we even named the religion after him.'

'Oh aye, I've heard it: Jesus is the good guy and we're all sinners,' says Ray, 'How does that help anybody? You should be teaching people how to be good, to themselves and to each other, not all this guilt and blame and sinners guff.'

'So what do you believe in then, Ray?'

Ray shrugs and lets out a sigh big enough to blind himself with smoke from his roll-up. He squeezes his eyes closed and puts two fingers to their inside corners.

'Nature: science 'n' nature, death 'n' disease.'

'That seems very nihilistic.'

Ray shakes his head sadly. 'I don't even know what that word means, Stuart.'

'Well, if you don't believe in anything, why do you open the church?'

Ray looks at the cards in his hand. He looks at his fingers, conscious of the ring no longer being there. He's left the past – everything from here is the future.

Stuart continues his line of questioning.

'Why d'you do so much for the people who come in here?'

'Faith 'n' community.'

'Ah, now we're getting somewhere. So do you mean faith *and* community or faith *in* community?'

Ray shrugs again.

'My God's different from yours Stuart, my God's in me, my God *is* me, and all he wants is a bit of company. Simple as that.'

Stuart looks ready to nag him to explain further, but luckily Ray is rescued by Aldo knocking the door. There's been a snooker dispute and he's being asked to adjudicate.

'Excuse me Stuart, I'll need to leave saving the world till later.'

It's been a long week. Friday nights are not always good nights for Maria. Sometimes she is so caught up just getting through the week that by the time it gets to Friday she hasn't had a chance to make plans for the weekend. If she hasn't arranged to take Fiona out to a movie or something, the weekend can lie before her like an open grave. That's changed recently; Dezzie has asked her out every weekend. Until now, that is.

As the boys were so late back, when Dezzie offered to take Brian out to his bus she was forced to accept his help. She would rather have seen both Martin and Brian off herself as she normally does, but she couldn't keep the buses waiting any longer. She put Martin on his bus, which took much longer than usual. Martin's driver gave her a lengthy and time-consuming telling-off for keeping the bus late. Now he'd be caught in rush-hour traffic, he moaned. Ten minutes' delay at this end meant an hour's delay in him getting home tonight. By the time the bus finally pulled away Dezzie, and all the rest of the staff, had left the building.

As soon as she comes home she closes her eyes and has a quick session with Madonna and Nelson.

'Would you stop giving yourself such a hard time?' says Madonna.

'But I . . .'

'Yeah, and you shouldn't have, but it's done now.'

'We cannot change the past,' says Nelson sadly, 'but what we learn from the past makes our future.'

None of this is very satisfactory. She still feels bad about what she did to Fiona and how things were left with Dezzie.

After several hours of standing guard over a phone that doesn't ring, Maria brings it with her into the bathroom, just in case, and has a long soak in the tub. She needs it; her neck and shoulders are as tight as piano strings. Three top-ups later, with her hands wrinkled and her neck as tight as ever, she gives up on the water therapy. A meditation, she decides, a good long one, there's nothing else for it.

The wind and rain are making her loose old windows shake tonight. She closes the curtains and puts on her meditation music, and within minutes she is sitting on the banks of the shimmering river, lifting her face to the sunlight. She reviews her day, thanking herself for the positive work she did, mentally ticking off the tasks she achieved from her list. Routinely she selects five golden moments from her day.

Even on the worst days she can always find at least five golden moments. Usually it's the simple stuff like a bright morning when the bus turns up on time, or a smile from Brian as she changes his vomit-covered jumper for a clean one, chips at lunchtime, or teaching Blue Group something new, for instance the words to 'Tainted Love'. Despite everything that's gone wrong, today has had its share of golden moments: the walk in the park – like a family – with Dezzie and Blue Group, Jane's waitressing triumph, the rehearsals going so well, the Victory Mission win-win solution, making space for the Madonna drag act in the show.

After reminding herself of the nice things, Maria routinely forgives anyone who has annoyed or hurt her that day. She acknowledges the mistakes she has made, then asks for and humbly accepts forgiveness. Those she has to pardon and those from whom she must ask pardon will walk towards her out of the trees: the forgiving and the forgiven.

Sometimes she is surprised by the people who emerge from the forest. Often it is not until they come out that she even realizes there has been an issue between them. Fiona, her most regular visitor here in the golden forest, now walks towards her. This is not the Fiona she encounters at the centre, the difficult, demanding Fiona. This is a calm, loving, repentant and forgiving Fiona. Yes, Maria nods, she understands, and she lets the forgiveness flow. Both ways. She's full of love for Fiona. She puts her arm around her.

'I'm sorry for throwing the crisps.'

'I know,' says Fiona, full of grace, 'I forgive you.'

Maria begins to feel the familiar tingle.

'But we've stopped going to the pictures,' says Fiona, sadly.

'I know. I'm sorry, I've been busy.'

'The man's got a strawberry but it wasn't a strawberry today. You're not busy now.'

'I know, you're right, I'm not busy now.'

'It's a strawberry but you can't eat it.'

'I know.'

Something isn't right. She's not feeling it, the usual warm glow; the ecstasy of redemption. Something is niggling at her. It's not the fact that Fiona keeps changing the subject, she does this anyway, though she's usually more rational when she's here inside Maria's head. And it's not the strawberry obsession, that doesn't bother her, Maria accepts all of Fiona's weird fixations and loves her for them.

Perhaps it's guilt. She dumped Fiona as her weekend movie date the minute Dezzie asked her out. Fiona's probably sitting by the phone waiting for Maria the same way Maria's waiting for Dezzie to call. But she doesn't usually feel guilt. That's the whole point of the meditation, to practise good mental hygiene, to rinse guilt and anger out of her headspace.

This niggle is preventing her having a good med but Maria knows not to dismiss it, thoughts like these have given her some of her best ideas, including the show and bringing in the orchestra. It never ceases to amaze her, the insights that bubble to the surface from her unconscious mind. Things that, were it not for her meditation, might stay there buried deep in her psyche, poisoning her from the inside. The best plan is to go with the thought and see where it takes her.

'Hello Mrs Simpson, it's Maria.'

It has taken nerves of steel for Maria to make this call. If Mrs Simpson knows about the crisp assault she might rack up the guilt factor: *Why? Why? What did my poor innocent Fiona do to deserve such treatment?*

Maria has no explanation for this one.

Mrs Simpson might, of course, not say a word but wait until the centre opens on Monday morning to demand Maria's instant dismissal. Or she might not know anything about it. Fiona might never tell her. Either way, Maria needs to know where she stands. And she has to make things right with Fiona.

'Oh hello Maria love! It's so lovely to hear from you.'

This is a promising start but no guarantee that Mrs Simpson is not just keeping her powder dry.

'We've not heard from you for ages.'

She keeps the tinkle in her voice but Maria can hear the recrimination. Fiona's mum is always overnice to Maria, not because she likes her, if the truth be told Maria reckons she's jealous of her relationship with Fiona. But she pretends to be nice and to like Maria, it's her modus operandi.

'Yes, I've been a bit busy. Is Fiona there? I'd like a word.'

Mrs Simpson delivers her delightful tinkle. 'Of course she's here, sitting in front of the telly, where else would she be?'

She's going for guilt and recrimination. This is good; this must be all she's got.

'Fiona? It's me.'

'Are we going to the pictures?'

Maria feels a powerful ripple. Poor Fiona, waiting three weekends in a row for Maria to take her out.

'If you want to, that's why I'm calling.'

'Can we get crisps?'

'Well OK, but just a small packet. And diet juice.'

'Nice crisps?'

'Yes, nice ones. Tell your mum I'll be round tomorrow night at seven to get you, OK?'

'OK.'

'And Fiona, the thing about the strawberry, what is that? Why can't you eat the strawberry? Tell me again.'

'Don't want to.'

'Why not?'

'Cos he's a bad man.'

'Who is?'

'He got his thing out.'

Maria's senses are tingling, his *thing* out? The flasher? She's onto something here.

'The man who got his thing out, have you seen him again?'

'His strawberry was black, you don't get black strawberries. Martin says you don't.'

Black strawberries, what does it mean? She was talking about black strawberries today.

'Did you see the man who got his thing out today?'

'He thinks he's Madonna, he's not Madonna.'

Ronald. Ronald the drag queen. She knew there was something familiar about him. It was the way he moved, although she didn't realize it at the time. But who could have known it was the same person?

'I can sing better than him.'

'Fiona, please, why do you think the man who sang the Madonna song is the man who got his thing out?'

Fiona shouts down the phone.

'Because of his strawberry!'

'OK.'

Maria is scared to ask, but she has to.

'What's his strawberry like?'

'I told you. It was black today but I ran after him and his scarf fell down and I saw it, it was a red strawberry. It's not like Sienna's, it's not the same.'

Sienna? Fiona's baby niece? Maria now remembers the upset caused in the family when Sienna was born with a red birthmark on her face. Come to think of it, the Madonna impersonator did have a black beauty spot above his lip. Maria had assumed that it was part of his costume but perhaps it was a disguised birthmark.

'Do you mean Sienna's wee birthmark?'

Roles are reversed. Fiona, her patience with Maria apparently worn thin, lets out an exasperated sigh.

'It's a strawberry.'

Maria gets off the phone to Fiona as quickly and politely as possible. She has a lot to think about.

When she sent home the letters to the carers about the flasher, Mrs Simpson didn't respond. Maria was a bit surprised by this at the time but, up to her neck in preparations for her big meeting with Mike, she thought no more about it. It would seem from Mrs Simpson's lack of response that Fiona never gave her the letter. And she almost certainly hasn't told her about the strawberry birthmark.

Maria had no idea that Fiona kept secrets from her mother. Perhaps she's more sensitive than Maria gives her credit for. Fiona must know the fuss her mother would make and perhaps she's scared. She was, after all, the one who chased the flasher, the only witness to the incriminating strawberry birthmark.

But it's not much to go on. Maria can hardly denounce the guy on the strength of it. Not only does the perpetrator have golden pubes but also a black strawberry stuck to his face: the police would die laughing. Brian's dad and his twin brother wouldn't. They'd smash Ronald's skull to a pulp, Fiona would be permanently traumatized and they'd lose the second best act in the show. That's why she had to get off the phone quickly. She didn't want Mrs Simpson to get wind of what they were talking about and interrogate Fiona.

A few discreet enquiries will have to be made before this goes any further. A quiet word with Pastor McKenzie might also be in order. His enigmatic talk of 'sinners who sin no more' might have been a hint. The first thing to be done is to establish whether or not the guy has the birthmark. She can find that out tomorrow at the rehearsal, if necessary by walking into his dressing room accidentally. The shading of his pubic triangle might be a little more difficult to ascertain but it should prove matters definitively. She'd recognize those golden pubes anywhere.

Chapter 27

'Right. How much was it?'

Alice is hardly in the door and he's on at her. She knew this would happen. She's trying to ignore him, to get on with setting up. Saturday and so many folk in here rehearsing today, the café is going to be mobbed, never mind that she's got her main Golden Belles run-through and still not sure of the tap routine.

'How much?'

'None of your business.'

'Alice, I know how much it is, I just want to hear you say it.'

Alice stares at Ray defiantly. It's her money; she won it fair and square.

'So,' Ray begins, mock-patiently, 'you started at a fiver, double or quits, you did your wee gumsy pensioner act, played five games – of which you generously let him win three – and then closed him down for what? Eighty notes?'

'Eighty large ones,' Alice confirms, toasting Ray with her coffee cup, swigging back a big gulp.

'That's a lot of money to a boy like him.'

Now he's trying to make her feel guilty. Well, it

won't work. She wonders if he'd be doing this if it wasn't Aldo she'd stiffed. He and Aldo are damned cosy these days. Alice remembers when he used to stick up for her.

'Listen, it's a lot of money to a girl like me.'

Ray has picked up a tea towel and is drying off a cup.

'Well, you've had your fun; you've proved your point. They know now that you're not a sweet wee old wifie,' he says, wiping the inside of the cup with slow thoughtful sweeps.

'Aye, too right they do.'

'They know now that you're a fucking shark.'

This is a bit strong but Alice can see the smile Ray's trying to hide.

'Oh Aldo,' he says in a high desperate voice, a terrible impersonation of her, 'please Aldo, give me another game, double or quits again, I need that money for my electricity bill.'

Now it's Alice who's hiding her smile. This is more like it; they're having a laugh now. She can tell he's impressed; he just doesn't want to say so. She's finished her coffee and opens the fridge, pulling out all the veg to be prepared for today's soup.

'So now it's time to give it back.'

'Give it back my arse,' she says into the crisper box, 'I won that money, I'm keeping it.'

'Look, this isn't a beauty contest between you and Aldo. I like you both, equally. I'd be asking him the same if he took the money off you.'

'Huh! There's no danger of that. Your daft pal Aldo hardly knows one end of a snooker cue from the other.'

'I'm asking you, Alice, as a friend, as the decent human being that I know you are,' he says. Ray's

267

speaking a bit quieter now, the tone of his voice slightly deeper, there's a rhythm to it like waves washing a rock to smoothness. He continues, 'I'm asking you as someone who's earned the respect of these young people.'

But Alice isn't smoothed. Too much to do, too much to lose, too scared of being exploited makes her jagged and watchful.

'Are you trying to zap me?' she says, using a carrot as a pointer, wagging it from side to side like a censorious finger. 'Don't you try to work your mumbo-jumbo with me!'

'I'm not trying to zap you, for God's sake; I'm trying to reason with you!'

Ray's annoyed. He's not being fair but still and all, she's uncomfortable. There must be a way to appease him.

'I could donate the money to Autumn House.'

'Or you could give it back. Alice, you're one of the few people who know the problems Aldo's got just now. He can't afford to lose eighty quid; he'll end up in big trouble. I would have hoped you'd understand that.'

'Or I could put it towards the show.'

Alice has her head down chopping onions. She's trying to find a way back to where they were without completely caving in, but even as she's saying it she knows it won't work. Ray has thrown down his tea towel and now he's shouting.

'Or you could strap your snooker table to your back and get it the hell out of my church!'

Alice stops chopping and stares at her knife. Ray stands still too, probably as shocked as she is, probably as sad and as sorry that it's come to this.

'It was never about the money, Ray.'

'I know that.'

'Aldo was quick enough to take the bet.'

'I know.'

'Quick enough to exploit what he mistook for a foolish old woman.'

'Yes. But two wrongs don't make a right, Alice.'

'So it's my fault?'

Now Alice is the one who's shouting.

'It's not my bliddy job to teach him trust and respect and decency!'

'Isn't it?'

Alice could cry. But he might think she was abusing her position as a poor old pensioner who'd worked her arse off for this place and these kids. And he has blindsided her with this question. She doesn't want to have to strap her snooker table to her back.

'Oh, to hell with it. I'll give him the money back if it'll straighten your bliddy face.'

'Thank you. I knew you would. You're setting a wonderful example, Alice. You're not really short for your electricity bill, are you? Because I could maybe help you out . . .'

Without thinking Alice touches Ray's arm and speaks softly.

'No, you're all right son.'

And with that the crisis is over. As if it never happened.

Ray takes up his tea towel and lifts a new cup to dry. He takes even more care drying this one, wiping gently then meticulously, polishing it ceremoniously. This reminds Alice of when her brother married a Catholic, the way the priest cleaned and wiped the Communion chalice. That was the first time she'd been in a chapel, but she's been to plenty of Catholic funerals since. Priests do a lot of malarkey with that chalice. They always take at least three or four minutes cleaning it. Ray sets down the cup and begins to fold the tea towel. Alice watches him, fascinated. She half expects him to fold it, kiss it and then drape it over the cup.

'Did you ever study for the priesthood, Ray?'

Ray stops and looks at her, then smiles. She has to smile back. Having surrendered, it doesn't feel so bad. Waves over smooth rock. He puts down the tea towel.

'I was just thinking,' he says. 'We could have a tournament with a cash prize. We could charge I don't know, a pound say, and winner takes all.'

'A fiver. Those young ones spend a fiver a day on fags.'

'Well we could sort out the details later. And to make it fair this time we could have you seeded as our number one player. What d'you think?'

'Eh,' says Alice, she won't be able to work her scam any longer and she was only getting started with that. On the other hand, Ray has kind of shut her down anyway, and seeded as number one . . . She's never been number one at anything in her life.

'Aye well, it's got potential.'

'Right,' says Ray, 'I'll get a poster organized and you collect the names and entry money.'

'D'you trust me with the entry money; you don't think I'm going to run away with it?'

'I don't trust you as far as I could throw you, Alice,' Ray says, but he's laughing. 'And while we're on the subject, you'd better give me Aldo's money before you run away with that.'

She still has the money in her purse. Might as well get it over and done with. Having finished chopping the veg she digs the purse out of her overall pocket and gives him a sideways look.

'Just make sure and tell your big pal that nobody gets a rise out of me.'

She is momentarily distracted by the creak of the main door opening. Who the hell's this at this hour of the morning?

Alice is fumbling for the cash from her purse when she hears footsteps coming towards the kitchen door. She balls the notes quickly and furtively in her hand. But it is not quickly enough.

That nosey witch Maria walks into Alice's kitchen without so much as an excuse me and catches her passing the money to Ray. None of her business. Alice hopes Ray's not going to try to explain. What the hell is Maria doing here?

'Hello there Maria! Thank God you're here, she was trying to attack me again,' Ray says, pointing an accusing finger at Alice. Alice flicks her tea towel menacingly and Ray jumps back as though painfully stung. They are a double act of frighteningly powerful woman and subjugated man. Alice is annoyed by Maria's intrusion, but also pleased that someone bears witness to the intimacy of her relationship with Ray.

'Morning Alice,' says Maria.

Despite his cheery morning banter Maria only seems able to manage a cold nod for Ray. What is her problem?

'Cup of coffee, love?' Alice asks Maria.

If it was up to her she wouldn't bother her arse with Maria. She doesn't have to be this nice to her; she's only doing it for Ray. Setting a good example. He's right. It's nice to be nice. Alice is becoming a nicer person.

'Oh go on then, *love*,' says Ray, still horsing.

Maria gives another stiff nod. She's that tight-arsed, that lassie. Here's Ray giving her his church, the run of the place, filled all day from dawn to dusk with kids running about and people playing bliddy trumpets and all sorts. He gives her that out the kindness of his heart, for the sake of her show, for her mentally handicapped ones, God love them, they're nice wee souls, and she's not got the decency to be halfway grateful.

Alice stops with the spoonful of coffee hovering over the cup as realization dawns on her. The reason she was so fascinated with him drying the cup, the reason she thought of a priest, that was it: he's not wearing his wedding ring. She flicks her eyes towards him now to check, and catches sight of the white newly exposed circle of skin around his finger. Right enough, the ring's gone. Alice smiles; good, it's time.

She doesn't want him to see that she's noticed, he'll bring it up in his own good time, and she certainly doesn't want to draw Maria's attention to it, it might encourage her. A big skinny girl like her needs a boyfriend. Maria doesn't seem to have noticed anyway, she's too busy rummaging about in her bag, turning her mobile phone on and off, that's the third time since she got here.

The outside door creaks again and someone else comes in. Aye, as she suspected. Big stupid Aldo. There's no show without Punch. He's sheepish and so he should be, trying to fleece a Senior for her electric-bill money. He seems nervous as well, he's often nervy but more so this morning.

'Hiya Alice, Maria.'

He's so tight with Ray that they don't even have to speak. The briefest dip of the head, man to man, an intimacy that Alice doesn't, and probably never will, have with Ray.

Maria gives Aldo the cold shoulder. That lassie likes nobody but herself. Aldo is just the same as he always is with Alice, though. He doesn't seem to hold it against her that she played him for a fool and took all his money. These kids seem to expect to get ripped off, God love them.

Ray waits until Aldo has got himself a coffee and then without a word walks out of the kitchen and into his office. Surprise surprise, his lieutenant is not far behind him and when he gets in there the door closes behind him. Aye, it's a man's world right enough. Alice is left peeling totties, waiting for the Belles, with only the torn-faced Maria for company.

Maria had come to the church this morning to uncover the truth about Ronald and has perhaps walked in on a much bigger scandal.

There's something very fishy going on. First of all, what are Ray and Aldo doing here so early on a Saturday morning? Ray supposedly works here but he hardly ever does any joinery work these days. Every time Maria sees him he's either building sets or playing his guitar. He spends a lot of time just hanging around smoking and chatting to people. How does he actually make a living from this?

And as for Aldo, he's not even in the show, why is he here all the time? Yes, he's unemployed and OK, he's helped with scenery and stuff, but at this time in the morning? After a lot of shifty glances the two of them disappeared into Ray's office, closed the door and now it's all gone quiet. Very suspicious. But that's nothing compared to what she saw earlier.

As she walked into the kitchen she saw money change hands – in a very secretive way – from Alice to Ray. That she could swear to. Alice gave Ray money, notes; it looked like a lot, hundreds of pounds. Dezzie said he saw Aldo with a drugs dealer in the Hexton Arms – is he supplying people who come into the church? Surely Alice couldn't be mixed up in it? Maria had been planning on making a few discreet enquiries, finding out what Alice knew of Ronald and, just for interest's sake, what she might have heard on the grapevine about Aldo and Ray. That had been the plan. Now it looks as though even Alice could be involved.

Probably best for the moment just to keep her head down, her eyes open and her mouth shut until she gets to the bottom of this.

As Alice is the only one currently available, Maria makes a start on her. Slowly and gently, softly softly catchee monkey. She begins by volunteering to peel potatoes for today's chips. She asks a few innocuous questions but Alice is not very forthcoming. She only really comes to life when the rest of the Golden Belles arrive. They have a tap-dancing rehearsal this morning and although the food must be prepared now, the café will not open until their rehearsal is done.

'Right girls, Jean Anderson is our nominated Soup Dragon today so nobody else touch it, OK?' Alice says once she has her troupe assembled.

The Golden Belles take this briefing seriously and nod their agreement. As far as Maria can see they are ready to obey her every command. Alice is the Events Co-ordinator at Autumn House, Creative Director of the Golden Belles, and now she's created a post for herself as Head Chef and Chief Executive in the café kitchen. Her natural abilities as a leader are undisputed, but now Maria wonders if Alice has some more sinister hold over these women.

The old ladies work fast and rhythmically to prepare the café food. In the same way that they dance together, the Golden Belles now cook together as if performing a ballet. One moves forward to the cooker as another steps back to the sink. Onions and cabbages are lobbed and caught over synchronized ducked heads. Within half an hour they are on the stage tying on their tap shoes.

Maria is left in charge of the simmering soup pots but she can see the stage from the kitchen door, and she stands leaning against it with her arms folded. Her mobile phone isn't holding a charge though she had it plugged in overnight. She turns it on again to check for any missed calls. There are none so she turns it off again to conserve energy. As more performers arrive she now concentrates on looking for Ronald. Watching. Watching everything, every little move and gesture of everybody. Waiting for someone to say or do something that will expose what the hell is really going on in this church.

'Don't bother with costumes, we haven't got time,' says Alice. 'There'll be a chance to get the full kit on at the dress rehearsal.'

As she says this she hitches up her dress and overall and tucks them into the legs of her knickers, creating a puffball-skirt effect. Alice has a fantastic pair of legs and she can certainly move them. She taps out a complicated rhythm as she flies across the stage. From this distance, with her long white ponytail and red lipstick, she could be thirty. It's only up close that the damage the cigarettes have wreaked is visible.

Ray emerges from his office and directs a tremendously loud and exuberant wolf whistle at Alice.

'It's the Cancan Grans!' he shouts.

This sets off other whistles from the gathering performers. Alice holds her hand up to acknowledge receipt of the compliments but she's concentrating on her feet. Every so often she stops and privately instructs one of the other dancers on a particular move.

Jean Scott, the seamstress, sidles up to Maria.

'They're great, aren't they?' Maria says enthusiastically.

'Oh yeah, so they are. Mind you,' says Jean, 'it's not necessarily the best dancers that get picked for the Golden Belles. It's only those and such as those.'

'What d'you mean?'

'Och, it's just her pals she picks. I mean, that Betty McAuslan, look at her!'

'What about her?'

'She's rolling her bottom set around her mouth like a mint imperial, d'you see her?'

Now that she mentions it, Maria notices the hyper-mobility of Betty McAuslan's bottom teeth, and once she has noticed it she's unable to take her eyes off it.

'Yeah, I see what you mean. It does kind of spoil the effect.'

'It's nerves with her. She's not cut out for the stage.'

Maria forcibly drags her eyes away from Betty McAuslan and fixes her stare on Ray's office. Aldo is still in there, as far as she knows. He didn't come out with Ray. What's he doing in there?

'That's why Alice has got her at the back like that,' Jean explains.

Aldo now appears from out of the office. He's smiling. He wasn't smiling before he went in there; in fact he seemed quite nervous. He's more than smiling. He seems calm and happy, almost ecstatically happy and – of course, that's it: he's on drugs. He's actually taking drugs in the building, around children and vulnerable people.

'Oh, would you look at that,' says Jean, indicating with her eyes the blissed-out Aldo. 'That's what I call serene.'

'Serene?'

'Aye, look at him. I wouldn't mind a bit of that myself. But I can't get near him. He's got his favourites as well.'

'Aldo you mean, Jean?'

'No, not Aldo, not that big numptie. I mean Ray. I can't get an appointment; it's only his favourites he'll see.'

Well, now Maria has heard everything. This is almost unbelievable. So Ray's involved in the drugs thing as well. And not only involved, he's doing great business by the sound of it. He's so busy peddling drugs he has to operate an appointments system.

'Wee Maggie saw him last week with her back and she said he was marvellous. All the years she's been attending the doctor and paying a fortune every month for an osteopath. She's in there five minutes with Ray and comes out prancing around like a young thing. He said she was a particularly good subject, very suggestible apparently.'

Maria is confused. Can these be drug users' code words?

'Wait a minute, slow down. I don't have a clue what you're talking about.'

277

'Well, he's tried to keep it under wraps, they all want it.'

The expression on Maria's face must adequately reflect the confused state of her mind because Jean, at last, elucidates.

'It's Ray I'm talking about. He doesn't want everybody to know but he takes people – only his favourites – he takes them in there and he zaps them. He's done it for a few, he says it's only pain control but they all rave about it. He does it to some of them three or four times and some only the once. He says it depends on your frame of mind. God knows what Aldo's frame of mind is like because he gets zapped all the time. He's never out that office and every time he comes out he's like that, on cloud nine. It makes you sick. Aldo is his special project and the rest of us can't get near him.'

'What does Ray do when he zaps them?'

'Well this is the thing. None of them'll tell you. They just say that they're "under" and all they can remember is a nice wee story. Then they wake up and feel great, like they've had a great sleep.'

'A nice wee story?'

'Aye, that's what they say.'

This only makes things more confusing, but Maria hasn't time to dwell on it because something much more pressing is happening.

The hall is filling up now. Marianne Bowman has arrived with the choir, and Pastor McKenzie with his group. She scans the Victory Singers, looking for a red-headed man. There are three redheads: the youngest of them is carrying a clear plastic suit bag over his arm. Inside the suit bag is what looks like a shimmering silver dress. And that's not all. As he turns around to face Maria she can clearly see the red strawberry birth-mark on the boy's face. This zapping business will have to wait.

'Excuse me a minute would you, Jean? Oh, and could you keep an eye on the soup for me?'

As Maria crosses the floor she slows down, unsure as to how to proceed. First of all she has to establish that the Madonna impersonator, Ronald, and the man who exposed himself to Blue Group several weeks ago, are one and the same person. But short of asking him, how else can she find out for sure? She thinks back to what McKenzie said about him yesterday; some sob story about him being an outsider and very lonely since his mother died. He has an ugly purplish skin tone and the look of a boozer. Surely this is not the guy who looked so amazing dressed as Madonna yester-day? If so he must be able to work miracles with a panstick.

Ray is showing off his card tricks. He has a crowd of Marianne's choirgirls round him and he's turning ordinary-looking playing cards into cards bearing bouquets of flowers. The girls titter as, with an elaborately gallant flourish, he hands one to Marianne.

If Pastor McKenzie knows he has a pervert in his midst he's remarkably casual about it. He's chalking a pool cue and laughing with some of his followers. Maybe yesterday he was trying to hint at Ronald being a pervert without actually saying so. Perhaps, like Maria, he's sworn to client confidentiality. But he's a man of God and therefore bound to tell the truth.

'Pastor, could I have a word?'

McKenzie puts down his cue and follows her to a table in the café area. As she passes Ronald she stares him down. Ronald, who had previously been smiling, has stopped. Unable to meet her gaze, he gathers up his suit bag and scurries out the church.

'Pastor, I want you to be honest with me.'

Pastor McKenzie says nothing.

'About Ronald.'

He looks at Maria. He seems to be trying to read her, but she's set her face to neutral.

'OK,' he says after a pause.

Maria waits, but through another long pause McKenzie does not expand.

'Does he have any tendencies that you know of?'

'Ah. You know about his conviction.'

'No Pastor, I don't know about his conviction, you failed to mention it yesterday so I think you'd better tell me about it now, don't you?'

'OK. Ronald has a conviction for lewd and libidinous behaviour.'

'And you didn't . . .'

'I know what you're thinking, Maria, but it's a spent conviction, for a crime he committed two years ago. He brought me a letter from his lawyer. Legally he's not obliged to disclose anything, but he wanted to. He came to the Victory Mission seeking forgiveness from Jesus. I believe him to be sincere. He has a good heart.'

'And you just forgive him, do you?'

McKenzie opens his hands wide, palms up: a Jesus gesture.

'That's the business we're in.'

'I can't believe how irresponsible you religious maniacs are. There are young and vulnerable people here, what about them? What about the risk to them?'

'Please Maria, calm down. Above all we need to maintain confidentiality. If word gets out Ronald's life could be in danger. Certain elements in Hexton might make a very ugly mob indeed.'

Thinking back to Brian's dad and uncle, Maria would be inclined to agree if she wasn't so furious with McKenzie. She drops her voice to a whispered snarl.

'Well they might be interested to know that your boy's recently been waggling his willy again! I want him out of my show.'

'That's your prerogative, Maria.'

'If he ever sets foot in here again . . .'

'I'm afraid *that's* not.'

'What?'

'Whether he comes in here or not is Ray's call. Ray has a *come one come all* policy, there's a sign outside.'

Maria is speechless and despite what he's just said, McKenzie is trying to be placatory.

'Don't worry. I promise you no-one is at any risk. Ronald has agreed to be escorted by myself or Ray at all times throughout his involvement with the show, for his safety as well as others. I can assure you, he's quite harmless.'

'Ray knows about this?'

'Well, yes . . .'

'But you never thought to tell me?'

'It was purely a political decision, Maria. Ray's a respected figure in this community now, the most respected.'

'The Godfather,' Maria snorts.

'Well, yes, if you like. Under Ray's patronage Ronald won't come to any harm.'

'Pastor McKenzie, you're an intelligent man,' says Maria, trying to curb her sarcastic tone, 'have you ever stopped to think why that might be? Why everybody has such tremendous respect for Ray?'

'I have, actually. For my own professional reasons I've made a study of Ray. I know that, unfortunately, he seems to reject Christianity. I know, that like the rest of us, he's an ordinary sinner, but it cannot be denied that his goodness, and the goodness he fosters in others, *is divine*. I know he's an unlikely messiah but he's offered every person who's walked in the door a chance for redemption.'

Maria had hoped that Pastor McKenzie might be an ally but it looks like he's partisan. The pastor has the evangelic lust in his eye he usually has when he mentions Jesus.

The revelations have come thick and fast this morning. It's all so shocking. Maria's worried about Ray, no doubt about it. In the world of social work where transparency is so important he's now beginning to seem a dangerously opaque character. There are too many unanswered questions. Why has he, along with Pastor McKenzie, shielded a known sex offender? What exactly is his relationship with Aldo and is he involved in drugs? Why is this community held so in thrall by Ray and his 'zapping'? Maria's beginning to feel that there may be a sinister tinge to his charisma.

She likes him, just as everyone else does. It's hard *not* to like him, but she must decide what to do. Should she call in the police? McKenzie's right, Hexton parents would be up in arms: a convicted pervert, a drugs ring and God knows what else? There could be serious trouble. She has to be careful and think this through properly. She needs to speak to someone.

She waited and waited but Dezzie didn't call last night. She's trying not to worry about it but this is the first time they haven't spent Friday night together since they started dating. She'd hoped he'd call today to make arrangements for tonight, but in any case she's agreed to take Fiona to the pictures. She checks her phone again. Still no calls.

If ever she needed to speak to Dezzie it's now. Right, that's it. This is no time for pride. This is an emergency. She turns her phone on and hits the speed-dial button. Dezzie's number briefly shows on the screen before the light in the phone dies. It's turned itself off. She turns it on again and redials. The same again, the battery is completely flat. And then she has a brainwave.

She'll ask Ray if she can use his office phone. He won't refuse her and with a bit of luck she'll be un-supervised. Maybe she can gather some evidence of drugs involvement, something concrete that she can take to the police.

The café has opened now and most of the tables are occupied. It takes Maria a minute to locate Ray. He's sitting alone, apparently engrossed in playing his guitar. As she approaches him, now with everything she suspects, she's pressing her hand to her chest to contain the shaking.

'My phone's dead and I need to,' Maria says, and then swallows a mouthful of saliva, 'to make a call. Could I use your office?'

'On you go,' Ray says with a friendly smile, 'it's open.'

And it is. Maria is amazed to find it unlocked. Her first priority is to get a hold of Dezzie and ask him to come down here. She dials his number, both his house and his mobile, but there's no answer at either. She tries both numbers again. Of course, it's Saturday, he must be out at the football match.

Dezzie's number continues to ring out but she still holds the phone to her ear. On Ray's desk, beside a large white roll of toilet paper, there's a Celtic Football Club mug which has lost its handle. It's filled to overflowing with pens and pencils and she moves it out of sight behind the curtain. With her heart thumping at her ribs, Maria slides open the deep drawer of Ray's desk as quietly as she can. There are thirty choirgirls singing 'Material Girl' at the tops of their voices so it's unlikely that anyone can hear her shifty fumblings, but she's taking no chances. If anyone does happen to walk in she can pretend she's looking for a pen to write down a number.

Maria fears and/or hopes she'll find something incriminating, but all she finds is a bottle of wine, a corkscrew and some books.

There are books on professional card tricks and Spanish guitar, but also some seriously technical manuals with heavy-duty titles like *Trance-formations: Neurolinguistic Programming and the Structure of Hypnosis*, *Prometheus Rising* and *Insider's Guide to Submodality*, whatever the hell that might mean.

This stuff is disturbing and compelling evidence that Ray's using mind control. He's the Derren Brown of Hexton. Why would he want to hypnotize anyone? Maria can just imagine trying to explain her suspicions to the police. *I have reason to believe that the current proprietor of Hexton church is operating a drugs ring using a network of mesmerized pensioners as drug mules.* It's ridiculous. The police will never believe it; she's having trouble getting her head round it herself. *No, but think about it, Detective Inspector: why do drug pushers come to the attention of the police? Because of the dodgy company they keep!*

Unreliable and unwashed addicts as runners are a huge signpost that leads back to Mr Big. D'you see? This is flawless! He's got spellbound OAPs making drug drops! Their Rainmates and erstwhile respectability are their disguise, a cloak of invisibility. And, even better, in the unlikely event that they get caught, in their zombified state what can they tell the police? They've been pre-programmed never to squeal. It's the perfect crime.

The police would lock *her* up if she went to them with a story like that. And yet . . . She needs to speak to Dezzie about this, and more than anything she wants to hear his voice. If only he would answer his phone.

A bolt of panic strikes her: what if he's deliberately not answering? What if Dezzie knows she's trying to call and just doesn't want to speak to her? She has to speak to him, to know that things are OK between them. She can't split up with him, she can't. She's not prepared to lose her boyfriend, her future husband, because of a tiff about Brian drinking two pints.

She thought it had been resolved yesterday before they went for the buses, but maybe he was only being professional in front of the clients. Maybe he was angry with her because she criticized him. She's never seen Dezzie angry; no-one has, it might be impossible to tell. Why does she always have to criticize him? In her heart of hearts she knows why. It's because she's jealous of him, because she's scared Blue Group will love him more than they love her. She has to stop being such a control freak, it's so unattractive. Is this why she's checking up on Ray? Is she creating a drama just to have a good excuse to call Dezzie? Is she losing her professional judgement?

She reviews the evidence: the money changing hands, the known sex offender, the zapping, the technical hypnosis books. It stinks to high heaven, but realistically there just isn't enough to justify calling in the police. She's going to have to rely on her instinct. It breaks her heart to think of all the hard work, the hours of rehearsal and set-building and costume-making that so many people have put in, only for it to be soured by organized crime and perverts. But even without definitive proof she has a duty of care to provide a safe environment for the young and vulnerable people who come here. She has a responsibility to their parents to ensure they don't get brainwashed, drugged or molested.

Maria knows, from the endless meetings she has attended, the strength of feeling among parents. People here feel politically powerless and dread sex offenders being dumped amidst them. Really, she has no other option. For the safety of all the community she has to cancel the show.

Chapter 28

There's no point in causing a scene. Better to tell the various group leaders and let them quietly disseminate the bad news, preferably later on, once everyone has gone home. If the groups make a fuss they can say there's a problem with the church building.

Luckily Ray is still absorbed with his guitar; he doesn't even look up when she comes out of the office. The first person she finds is Marianne Bowman, who has just finished conducting the choir through their interpretation of Madonna's 'Hung Up'. Marianne's leading the girls off the stage.

'That's great that you've managed to squeeze Ronald in,' she says. 'I don't think you'll regret it.'

Maria allows herself a little ironic laugh.

'I need to talk to you, Marianne.'

'Up to my eyes at the minute . . .'

'No, seriously, this takes priority over everything else. I'm going to round up a few others, meet me in Ray's office and please, keep it quiet.'

Marianne seems gobsmacked but puts up no further argument. Maria makes a mental list of those she'll need to tell: Mr Spencer the orchestra leader, Pastor McKenzie for the Victory Singers and Alice of course for Autumn House. Unfortunately these last two are in Ray's camp but there's nothing she can do about that. They'll have to be told.

They crowd into the office, the air in the small room being quickly overwhelmed by Marianne's perfume.

'I'm really sorry to have to do this,' Maria tells them, 'but I'm afraid I'm cancelling the show.'

As expected this is not well received.

'You're what?'

'I'm cancelling the show.'

'No you're bliddy not!' shouts Alice. 'On what grounds?'

'I'd really rather not go into that at the moment, but if you need to tell your group something tell them the building is hazardous.'

'There's nothing wrong with the church, it was here before you came along and it'll be here after you're gone,' says Alice.

'Nevertheless . . .'

'On what authority are you cancelling?' Marianne asks.

'On the authority of the Hexton Adult Learning Centre, under whose auspices the show was set up.'

'Has Ray cancelled the show?'

'No. Ray hasn't been involved in my decision and I'd prefer it if . . .'

'Well unless Ray says the show is cancelled then it goes ahead,' says Alice. 'We don't need your centre. Autumn House has spent time and money on this and we're not cancelling. If you want to pull out that's one thing, but you can't cancel the whole show and not even give us a reason.'

'Alice has a point, Maria,' says Marianne as the others nod their agreement. 'Why, if the building is sound, do we have to cancel?'

'Certain irregularities have come to light, which for security reasons I'm not at liberty to discuss.'

'Who do you think you are?' spits Alice. 'MI5? Sorry Pastor for swearing, but this is a bliddy joke.'

At this Pastor McKenzie comes to life and moves to stand between Maria and the rest of them who are lined defiantly against her. He opens his arms wide either to protect Maria from Alice or in an all-encompassing gesture.

'Shouldn't we all sit down and discuss this calmly?' he suggests.

Maria, grateful for his intervention, is the first to take a seat. The rest follow except the pastor himself, who has his own announcement to make.

'I think I know what this is about, and it may not be as big a problem as it might seem. This is something we can sort out if we work together. Maria is quite right to say there's a need for confidentiality, but we must be able to trust each other and our colleagues deserve an explanation. So, please, can I rely upon you to keep this discussion confidential?'

They all agree immediately.

'Praise the Lord.'

Maria is relieved; they'll understand her reticence once they know and this will take the heat off her.

'There's no need to name names but suffice it to say that there is amongst us, not amongst us here I hasten to add, but amongst the company of performers, a person whose past deeds are, understandably, causing concern to our organizer Maria. But I can assure you all that any risk, while it can never be completely eliminated, is absolutely minimal.'

Maria would love to tell them, especially Marianne, about the lovely Ronald and his most recent exploits, but she fears that if it got out his life would be in danger.

'I and Ray have undertaken to supervise this individual at all times,' says the pastor.

'Well, if the pastor and Ray have got it under control that's good enough for me,' says Alice.

Mr Spencer speaks for the first time.

'Not a problem for me,' he says with a shrug.

Marianne nods.

Maria set this show up but it seems she's no longer in charge. It has grown legs and run away from her. The lunatics have taken over the asylum. If they want to carry on with the show, and it seems they do, there's absolutely nothing she can do about it.

'Well, if that's it,' says Alice, standing up and pushing back her chair, 'I can't hang about gossiping. I need to get back to my kitchen.'

'Hold on,' says Maria, jumping to her feet. 'I'm afraid there's more to it than that. I also have concerns about the very man who is supposedly supervising.'

'Me?' says the pastor, aghast.

'No, sorry Pastor, not you.'

'Ray?' says Alice with her mouth open.

A heartbeat later Ray walks in the door.

'Oh sorry, didn't mean to disturb you. I'm just in to put my guitar to bed,' he says with a self-effacing smile as he squeezes past them in the cramped space to put his guitar back in its case.

There is a shocked silence – he must be aware of it. As soon as he has put away his guitar he turns to creep unobtrusively out of the office, and as he makes it to the door Alice calls him back.

'Ray?'

He sticks his head round the door again.

'Yeah?'

'Can you come back in please?' Alice says, all the while staring hard at Maria.

Maria feels the blood drain from her face.

'You're all very serious, what's wrong, financial crisis?' says Ray chirpily as he finds a seat.

No-one answers or even looks at him, but once again the pastor takes the floor.

'Alice is right. In the spirit of openness and with the promise of confidentiality, I think we should continue to speak plainly. Maria, you were saying?'

'Yeah,' says Alice, daring her, 'you were saying?'

Maria inadvertently makes a loud noise in her throat as she gulps a mouthful of acid saliva.

'I was saying that . . . Of course I can't prove anything, but this morning I witnessed Alice hand over to Ray a large amount of money. This appeared to me to be under duress. Aldo, Ray's constant companion, is known to have links to local drug dealers. Make of that what you will, but another thing is this "zapping" business. You may or may not be aware that Ray is hypnotizing people. He has a selection of books on professional hypnosis in that drawer there. Look if you don't believe me. I'm afraid these suspicious circumstances give me no confidence in Ray. I can't guarantee the personal safety of anyone entering this building, and for this reason I am forced to cancel the show.'

No-one says a word but all eyes are on Ray, who sits with an expression of bemusement on his face.

'Ray,' says Pastor McKenzie gently, 'these are rather serious allegations, is there anything you want to say?'

'It's none of her bliddy business making allegations about him and me!' shouts Alice.

Ray smiles.

'Alice, Alice. Calm down,' he says dismissively. 'Business conducted between Alice and myself is nobody else's concern.'

'We're all friends here, Ray,' says the pastor. 'We've already promised that what is said at this meeting will not go beyond this room.'

Ray smiles again but remains silent.

'He's a gentleman, that's why he won't say,' declares Alice. 'I took eighty quid off Aldo in a snooker game, gambling. Ray convinced me to give it back. There, happy now?' she fires at Maria. 'Oh and I might as well tell you because Ray won't: Aldo's off the junk, he has been for weeks. And the only reason he's off it is because that man there,' she says, pointing at Ray, 'helped Aldo untangle hisself from the drug dealers. Ray's helped a lot of folk around here one way or another and this is the gratitude he gets: to be accused of being a drug dealer.' Again she looks directly at Maria.

'You make me sick.'

Nobody speaks for a few minutes.

'Is what Alice says true, Ray?' asks the pastor.

Ray shrugs and continues to look at the floor.

'It seems to be an admirable thing to do and nothing to hide,' McKenzie pronounces.

'Listen,' says Ray in a slow disappointed voice, directly addressing Maria. 'I don't know what you were doing going through my drawer, but you've got the wrong idea. And as for zapping, as you call it, it's assisted self-hypnosis. It's good for pain management and relaxation. I just showed a few people how to do it, Harry McCabe and wee Maggie for instance. They can do it themselves whenever they need it.'

'And Aldo,' says Alice.

'Yeah, and Aldo.'

With long exhalations, the release of tension from the group is audible.

'Right,' says the pastor. 'I'm satisfied with Ray's explanation. What does everyone else think?'

Everyone else is nodding, plainly embarrassed, all except Alice who is plainly furious with Maria. She stands and addresses the top of Maria's bowed head.

'Your problem, young lady, is that you're a snob. You think everybody's a criminal. Well, we might all live in Hexton but we're not all the same. Believe it or not there are good people here. *And* bad people, good and bad, smart and stupid, sick and well, but that's a community. That's what you wanted, isn't it?'

'Alice,' says Ray, 'leave it. Your soup'll be ruined.'

Marianne stands and leaves with Alice, followed by Mr Spencer and the pastor.

Maria is left alone, shamefaced, in the office with Ray.

Chapter 29

Maria and Ray both sit in silence with their eyes cast down.

'I don't know what to say,' Maria whispers. 'I feel awful.'

Ray laughs.

'Well, don't ask me to zap you. Zapping's off the menu. I've already got a reputation as some kind of evil mesmerist.'

'I'm sorry, this is all my fault,' she says and starts to cry. 'I feel such an idiot.'

'Oh no,' says Ray when he sees her tears, 'now *I'm* sorry. I didn't mean to make you cry.'

'You didn't. It's just . . . everything.'

Worse than falsely accusing a well-meaning man and suffering the humiliation of being proved wrong, on top of all this Maria's had to swallow the fact that, quite literally, she's no longer running the show.

'Need a hanky?'

She nods. Ray takes the white toilet paper from his desk, unrolls a wodge and hands it to her.

'Got to keep the bog roll in the office now,' he says

by way of explanation, 'some bastard keeps stealing it out of the Gents.'

Maria blows her nose and smiles. She echoes Alice's words, but without rancour.

'Well, that's a community for you.'

'I suppose so,' he agrees, but he smiles too.

Ray settles himself in his chair and opens the desk drawer. He pulls out the bottle of wine and plants it on the desk.

'Want one?' he asks.

Maria nods.

He pulls out two glasses and the corkscrew.

'Hypnotism's good for all sorts of things, you know.'

'Ray, please, you don't have to explain . . .'

'Surgery: amputations, tooth extractions,' he continues, ignoring her. 'Much better than opiates. Pain, relentless acute pain, that's the cruellest thing in the world, and what everybody fears the most. I was married. I mean, I still am married.'

This is a swift change of subject, but Ray keeps his pitch light and so it takes a while before the full impact of what he's saying hits Maria.

'Her name's Suzanne, Suzy. She had cancer of the cervix. The stupid cow wouldn't go for the smear tests. She said she wouldn't let anyone stick a cold metal duck bill up her box, said she'd rather have cancer. It was hard. A lot of pain. We were in and out of hospital for a year and a half. We never knew how long it was going to be.'

Ray peels the soft metal from the neck of the bottle and slowly works the screw into the yielding cork.

'At first we didn't know how long it would be before they could get rid of it. And then, after all the shit: all the chemo and the sickness and hair loss and pain when they couldn't get rid of it, we didn't know how long it would be.'

He pours two large glasses and hands one to Maria. She's keen to get to the end of the story. This is pretty grim stuff, but going by his tone it must have a happy ending.

'That's when I got into hypnotism. The palliatives knocked her off her head, like bloody horse tranquillizers so they are. They made her la la, saying crazy things that neither of us wanted to hear but, without them ... The worst thing about the pain was how much it embarrassed her. She cried and moaned, she couldn't hold it in and she hated herself for it. She thought she was letting me down.'

All of this Ray says as though he's telling a joke. Maria throws the glassful of wine down her throat, anesthetizing herself against what she's hearing. She wouldn't normally touch alcohol during the day, but this is different. It's not every day you accuse someone of being a brainwashing drug peddler and then they casually tell you the agonies their wife has suffered.

'The hypnotherapy, once I got a handle on it, was brilliant for relaxing her. We used to have a great laugh sometimes. The doctors couldn't believe that someone whose insides were being eaten away was able to sit up and play cards or sing along with the guitar. But that's the power of the mind for you. Suzy was a great subject, the best.'

Ray smiles and leans over and pours them both another glass of wine. Maria swigs this one in relief and pictures Ray and his wife laughing and singing. It is a happy ending after all, thank God.

'And when it was time, it was easy. She went out like a dimming lantern. That's what she was: a warm glowing lantern whose light went out. It was soft, she wasn't sad or scared. And I was happy for her. A bit jealous, but happy too.'

Ray has a broad smile on his face, although he seems to be saying that his beloved wife is dead.

'We'd wanted kids but in the end I suppose it was for the best that we couldn't. It was a while ago now. I promised her there'd be no grief but I think that's a bit unrealistic. Coming here has certainly helped. I'm not saying it's perfect, I mean, the place is full of weirdos, not to mention the bog-roll thief, but it's been a great experience for me. It's helped me to take responsibility. I have to keep moving forward, we all have to. As for the pain, well, Suzy's been a great help and I've got all the books. I've seen a few wee souls around here struggling with it, physical or emotional, and I've tried to show them a way of coping. I hope it's helped. I didn't mention Suzy. Alice knows, she's been fantastic, but I haven't told anyone else because . . .'

Ray tails off and sits quietly.

'Because it's nobody else's business,' says Maria with her head dipped in shame. 'I'm so sorry, Ray.'

'Don't be. This has been good. I'm glad I told you, it's time now. Thanks for listening.'

Maria nods. They simultaneously sip their wine. They glance and smile and fall into a silence which last several minutes. Maria can't think of anything to say, but, and perhaps it's the effect of the wine, she doesn't feel she needs to say anything.

'You've done a fantastic job getting this show together,' Ray says finally. 'I've never said it and it needs to be said, you've really pulled it off. I don't think anyone else in Hexton could have done it.'

'I don't think anyone else is stupid or desperate enough to try,' says Maria.

'True,' Ray concedes, and raises his glass.

Maria lifts her drink and clinks glasses and they both laugh. It's easy to see why everybody loves Ray. In a short space of time he's forgiven her for trying to blacken his name, and for the sake of clarification he's shared his most intimate and painful memories. And he's getting her drunk. All with a lovely smile. She likes Ray.

'Bob's dad was in yesterday asking about setting up five-a-side football. I wondered if Martin was any good?' Ray asks.

'Martin's great! He'd love to get a game with you. Blue Group is mixed physical ability but some of our other groups are pretty good at football.'

'Well bring them down here then.'

Maria and Ray discuss five-a-side football, and the show, and Alice's legs, and Pastor McKenzie's obsession with Ray.

'I think he thinks you're a modern messiah,' Maria tells him.

'He will not let it go, will he? The only miracle I can perform is turning wine into water.'

'Turning wine into . . . ?'

'Aye, off for a pee. I'll be back in a minute.'

Maria is left alone. She and Ray have been having a good chat; he's such a lovely bloke. Thinking of lovely blokes, the squiffy smile fades from her face when her thoughts turn to Dezzie. She still hasn't heard from him. She turns her phone on again – no missed calls. She calls his mobile again from the office phone. This time Dezzie picks up and Maria laughs with joy and relief.

'It's me.'

'Hello Miss Maria!'

He sounds pleased to hear from her.

'I've tried you a few times.'

She tries to keep it light, not like an accusation.

'I thought maybe you were at a game and couldn't hear your phone.'

'No, no, it's an away game this week. I'm sitting here watching it on telly at Brian's. We've got a few cans in. It gives his mum and dad a chance to get out on their own. They're away up to the Hexton Arms for Bobby McCann's Saturday Singalong.'

This might ordinarily cause Maria to struggle with her own jealousy: Dezzie bonding like this, not only with Brian but with his family. But she's just happy for them, happy that Dezzie and Brian enjoy each other's company and that his parents can get out. Most of all she's happy that Dezzie isn't angry with her. Things seem to be back to normal, thank God.

'Hold on a tick Maria, I'll take this out in the hall.'

Maria hears Dezzie moving out of the room away from the noisy television.

'So, I'm glad we're talking again,' Dezzie says in a semi-whisper, quiet enough that Brian won't hear. 'I've missed you.'

Dezzie's the one who didn't phone but maybe he thought she wasn't speaking to him, and anyway it doesn't matter any more. The warmth Maria feels in her cheeks and her belly is not just from the wine.

'I've missed you too.'

'So when am I going to see you? Tonight?'

'Oh Dezzie, I'm sorry. When I didn't hear from you last night I arranged to take Fiona out tonight.'

'But I've hardly seen you all week!' says Dezzie, sounding like a disappointed child.

'You see me every day.'

'Yeah, but you know what I mean. I haven't seen you naked. I miss your body.'

'Oh Dezzie,' says Maria, smiling, 'is that all you're after?'

'You know that's not all I'm after, Maria.'

Dezzie sounds offended and Maria moves quickly to reassure him.

'I know, sorry, I'm being flippant, too much wine.'

'Wine?'

'It's a long story which I'll tell you when I see you.'

'What are you doing tomorrow?'

'I was planning on coming down to rehearsals; see if anyone needs a hand with last-minute stuff. We're getting close to showtime.'

'You can't be there every day. You need some time off. All work and no play makes Maria a dull girlfriend.'

Maria smiles, there it is again, her favourite word. She laughs with delight: he wants to see her, he needs her.

'Why don't I take you down to the seaside, give you a bit of a break? We can go on the bike, I've got a spare helmet.'

'Oh I don't know, I'm a bit scared of motorbikes.'

'Maria, don't worry. I'll drive slow, d'you think I'd let anything happen to my most precious cargo? Look, forget the bike. I'll see if Jan will lend me the car.'

'I thought she said "never again" after Peter's little accident.'

'Yeah, but I'll work my boyish charm on her.'

Maria laughs. As Ray walks back into the office she

lifts her eyes and acknowledges him and leans forward. Ray makes a 'take your time' gesture, but not only is she on the phone to Dezzie, her secret boyfriend, she's calling an expensive mobile from Ray's line.

'I'll have to go,' she says, careful not to say his name.

'OK, I'll come round in the morning, early. Don't bother getting up and dressed, I'll just climb in beside you.'

'OK.'

'I love you,' he whispers.

'Yes,' says Maria, stunned, 'I'm with people just now.' But she wants to scream: I love you, Dezzie!

'OK. Tomorrow then, yeah?'

'OK, bye.'

Maria puts down the phone and mentally prepares to leave. She'll have to wait a few minutes with Ray just to be polite, especially after using his phone. But thankfully it's Ray who calls their meeting to a close.

'Sorry, I've got to finish this bloody sideboard off,' he says, getting to his feet.

Maria stands and as she is about to leave he calls her back.

'Mind if I ask your advice, Maria?'

He has sat down again and pulled out his tobacco tin.

'Fire away.'

'D'you think I'm ready?'

'Ready?'

Maria is delighted to do anything she can to help Ray, but she doesn't know what he means.

'I mean, to meet someone else? I don't know,' says Ray, and then lights his roll-up.

'I've met so many nice people here, one woman in particular, d'you think I should ask her out?'

301

'Do *you* think you're ready, Ray?'

'Well, kind of. I've taken my ring off,' he says, indicating his ringless hand. 'I think that must be why I told you about Suzy. I don't want to miss my moment with this woman, she's really nice.'

Naturally Maria is dying to know who the woman is: Marianne, or maybe one of the young mums? Really, Ray could have his pick of the women who come around the church, they probably all fancy him, but she's not going to ask. She's been privileged to be let in to a little of Ray's life today; he'll tell her if and when he wants to, when he's ready. But whoever it is, she's a lucky dog. Except for his smoking, Ray is a fantastic catch.

'Ray, why do you smoke? You know it'll kill you.'

'Well, that was the general idea,' he smiles.

'It sounds to me like you're not quite ready.'

His smile fades as she says this. Perhaps she's been a bit hasty.

'But you're getting there.'

Chapter 30

Maria bought Fiona a dress. It's a smasher, Mum says. It's for the show and Fiona is not allowed to wear it. She's to keep it good. Maria says thank God it fits because she wasn't sure and she can't take it back. It's green. Maria saw it in the window. Mum says that was a helluva price to pay for a dress out of Oxfam even if it is velvet. Mum says she hopes to Christ Maria's not expecting her to pay for it, a posh frock to wear for just one night. She says that lassie must have money to burn.

Fiona was crying because she wanted to wear it to the pictures but Maria and Mum said she has to keep it good. Maria said they were a bit early for the pictures so they could go to the pub if Fiona wanted. Maria was very happy. She winked at Fiona and said, 'Come on girl, live a little, we're both over twenty-one.' Fiona said yes. They sell crisps in the pub. Fiona's dad used to bring her crisps from the pub before he went away. They went in but Fiona is scared of the pub. It is noisy and too smoky and Maria said OK let's get out of here.

Maria took Fiona to a posh coffee shop. They had

coffee in big cups. The cups were bigger than the soup bowls in the centre. Fiona wanted a cake but Maria said she won't fit into her dress if she keeps eating crisps and cakes. She wants to fit into her dress. Maria said if she has too much sugar in her blood she'll get diet beetles. Fiona has got sugar in her blood. She's tasted it. Fiona is scared of diet beetles but she didn't tell Maria.

The film was very funny. Maria and Fiona were laughing all the time. It was a rom com. At the end, Juliet, the screwball girl who walked dogs, was a beautiful bride. Fiona knew Juliet was going to be beautiful. She tried to tell Maria. But Maria said shh!

They got the bus home and Maria was very happy. She smiled and squeezed Fiona's arm. This made Fiona feel happy too. Fiona told Maria she wants to be beautiful. Maria said Fiona is beautiful, she just needs to lose a few pounds. Maria said that when the show is over they can start running in the morning. She says it is great exercise and they'll soon have Fiona in shape. Fiona wants to be in shape. She doesn't want to have diet beetles. She wants to look nice in her dress. She wants Martin to see her in her dress. Fiona did not tell Maria this. Fiona took Maria's arm. Maria said Fiona is her best gal pal and always will be. She said even if either of them gets married they will still be best pals. Fiona wants to get married. She wants Maria to get married too. It was the best night out at the pictures ever. And they didn't even get crisps.

Maria sets the alarm ten minutes early, just in case. When she lets Dezzie in she pretends she's just woken but she's already brushed her teeth, had a quick shower and slipped into a clean sexy nightie.

Dezzie brings the cold morning air in with him and his body is cool against hers. His fingers are freezing. Maria squeals and giggles and makes him rub them under the duvet for a few minutes before she'll let him touch her. It is two hours of play and tea and toast and naughtiness and then Dezzie is gently shaking Maria's shoulder. She must have dozed off.

'C'mon. Shake a leg, we're burning daylight.'

He's up and pulling on his jeans.

'Do we have to go?'

'Yep.'

'Can we not just stay in bed for the day?'

'Nope.'

'Ooohh!' says Maria, pulling the duvet around her and pretending to cry like a baby.

Dezzie changes tack. He comes over to the bed and kisses her ear.

'C'mon babes. It's a lovely day. I'm taking you down to Culzean. It's the most beautiful place in the world. I want to show it to you. And when we get there I've got a surprise.'

Dezzie takes his opportunity and grabs the duvet but Maria holds on so tight that she's dragged, screaming and giggling, out the bed onto the floor.

Maria has heard of it of course, a National Trust stately home on the Ayrshire coast. They drive down from Ayr along a rugged coastline of dramatic sea cliffs and ruined castles. As they turn a corner, Culzean Castle, perched on the very edge of a cliff, is spread in front of them. It has a huge round tower with long windows facing out to sea. Gulls swoop and turn on the cliffs below, and boats with white triangular sails bob in the water like bath toys. It's a fairy-tale castle, the kind of place where a full-sized living Ken and Barbie might raise a family.

Dezzie stops the car halfway down a steep hill at a signpost which reads *Electric Brae*.

'Watch this,' he says mysteriously.

He takes off the handbrake and studies Maria for a reaction. Her face registers surprise; despite the absence of brakes, the car has not started to roll down the hill. Her expression progresses to disbelief and fear when she realizes that the car is slowly beginning to roll *up* the hill. This cannot be happening. This defies the laws of physics.

'What is it?' she cries in panic, 'why is it doing this?'

'It's magic,' says Dezzie, clearly delighted with her response.

Maria badgers him and he reluctantly explains. When vehicles were first discovered to be rolling uphill it was the subject of much scientific debate and exploration. The first theory was that it was caused by strong electricity or other, as yet undiscovered, natural forces; forces strong enough to haul a car and passengers up a hill. Eventually, after exhaustive research, it was discovered that the Electric Brae phenomenon was related to the angle of the hill and the hills beyond. It was merely an impression on the senses caused by the lie of the land.

'Some smart-arse clever clogs worked out that it's just an optical illusion.'

'You mean it's not magic?' cries Maria, deflated.

'It is if you want it to be, darling,' says Dezzie.

'It's magic!' Maria shouts out of the open window at the car behind them, which is loaded with awestruck children and now rolling up the magical, electrical brae.

They park Dezzie's sister's car in the village of Maidens and buy cans of juice from the local shop. He has brought sandwiches in his rucksack. They wander slowly along the beach hand in hand, without speaking, without needing to. They explore the rock pools and caves at the foot of the cliff, finding crabs and shells and a long slimy seaweed stem with thick fronds like tagliatelle. It reminds Maria of a whip, a cat-o'-nine-tails. She affects a pirate accent and chases Dezzie along the deserted beach, thrashing out at him with the whip but never quite catching him.

'Shiver me timbers Jim lad, I'll see the colour of your innards!'

Dezzie climbs up onto the slippery black rocks and holds his jacket open and his arms out wide, impersonating the black cormorants who stand drying their wings in the stiff sea breeze.

The sky is a bright wide blue, entirely clear except for the fluffy clouds that hang over the mountains of Arran across the water. The sea is blue and then grey and then green and then blue again, shifting and changing with every wave. The waves smash the rocks, fizzling and sizzling in the pebbles at their feet, as if to say, 'I'll be back.' And they do come back seconds later, angrier and more fizzy than the last time. Dezzie and Maria dare each other to stand closer and wait longer, toying with the wave, jumping and laughing when it catches them off guard.

When their feet are wet and they tire of the game, they go up through the woods into the Culzean estate. The trees are tall and widely spaced, letting in sunlight that dapples their faces as they move through. Dezzie knows the place well and shows her everything, the swans, the deer, the vinery, the peach house, the formal gardens, the secret gardens, the sweeping lawns and the overgrown paths. They look at the castle from outside but they do not go in.

'I'll pay to see inside other people's houses when they start paying to see mine,' says Dezzie, and Maria laughingly agrees.

'I've saved the best bit,' he says as he drags her down a path which leads to the cliff top. They follow it until Dezzie gently guides Maria by the hand onto a lower grassy outcrop. They are surrounded on three sides by the sea. This is a secret place, cut off from the estate but with views to Ireland and Arran, which is now swathed in evening mist. The sun is beginning to go down behind the Ailsa Craig, known as Paddy's Milestone. Dezzie explains that this large lump of rock halfway between Scotland and Ireland was supposedly used as a stepping stone by Paddy.

'And other local giants.' He smiles. 'This is my favourite place in the whole world.'

'Mine too,' says Maria, backing against him for security and warmth.

They stand for some time, Dezzie's arms locked around her and his head on her shoulder. They watch the sun slide behind the big rock, splaying out rays that filter gold through the clouds and bounce on the water like diamonds.

Dezzie pulls Maria to face him and holds both her hands in his.

'I said I had a surprise.'

She's confused; she thought Electric Brae was the surprise. Dezzie is breathing heavily and his hands are as cold and damp as a fish. He fumbles in his pocket for something and then produces a red velvet box.

Before Maria really has a chance to process this information or worry about it, Dezzie has made his intentions clear. He has dropped down onto one knee.

Chapter 31

What a bliddy laugh! That was the first time Alice had ever been in one of those places. She'd made out to the other Belles that she was used to clubs but she was dead nervous when they got to the door. They had free tickets so there was no problem getting in, and the bouncer was flirting with them like nobody's business. Handsome big boy he was, made Alice feel like a young thing again. Even if he probably was a poof, it's still nice to get a bit of attention.

She'd been expecting it to be dirty and sleazy but actually it was quite classy. Classy prices too, despite the fact that they'd got free tickets the drinks were a fortune, and the show went on so late they had to get taxis back to Hexton.

The whole thing had been Alice's idea, and even Ray said it was brilliant.

After that moaning-faced cow Maria left, half pished, Alice noted, she'd gone in and pestered Ray until he confirmed what it was all about – that weird fella Ronald. Alice knew right away it was him, it was that obvious. A man that dresses up as a woman, it's not right. A boy like that's guaranteed to be a homosexualist.

She was pleased that Ray trusted her enough to tell her – and she'll obviously keep it under her hat – but at the same time she was a bit worried. Although she didn't say so, she agreed with Maria that it was dodgy having him around the place.

'Don't get me wrong Ray, he's definitely got talent. Apart from the Belles he's the best thing in the show,' she said.

Ray agreed and said there was also his *come one come all* policy thing that he's always banging on about.

'It's just a shame the boy can't do something a bit more constructive than parading his bits and flashing them at innocent bystanders,' she told Ray.

Alice's view of young people has changed radically in the last few weeks. Ray's noticed. When she suggested Bob and Gerry for stagehands, 'give them something useful to do rather than hanging about here like a bad smell all day,' Ray said that was a great idea. He said Alice was turning into a 'solutions person'. Alice didn't have a clue what that meant but she knew it was something good. Since then she's been thinking up loads of great ideas.

'Plenty of them, homosexualists I mean, earn a living at it,' she told Ray, 'strip shows and that kind of thing. I've seen them on the telly. With Ronald's talent he should be getting paid for it instead of getting arrested.'

He laughed and said something about 'context', but then he went serious and said he had a contact. A guy he'd done a lot of joinery work for owned strip clubs in the city. He phoned the guy, who apparently couldn't do enough to help. Everybody loves Ray.

A couple of days later – did Ronald not come in and

offer them all free tickets! He said he wasn't 'a name' yet so the club weren't expecting a big crowd, and would some of them want to come along? Bums on seats, he said.

Ray and McKenzie weren't interested, they seemed embarrassed to be asked but that's typical men. Alice and the Belles jumped at it, and what a night!

All the turns were good, but Ronald was far and away the best. He sang while he took his clothes off. And he didn't just strip, what a showman! He never laid a hand on anybody and yet he made love to every woman at that table. Some of them were helluva grateful. Some of the girls had forgotten what it looked like. They only thing was, not everybody liked the colour of his downstairs hair. Nancy Smith said she liked fiery pubes. Years ago, before he went grey, her man had fiery pubes. But the rest of them, Alice included, found the gingerness a wee bit off-putting. Still and all, they never let it spoil their night. They still had a bliddy laugh.

Maria almost said no. She can laugh about it now as she watches her solitaire sparkle on her finger, but then, on the cliff top, she was scared.

Her first thought was that it was a prank, that the whole time they had been dating was a big set-up for this elaborate joke on her. How could this be? That, in such an unbelievably romantic setting, a bona fide proposal of marriage would be made to a flat-chested girl like her. It couldn't be true.

She panicked, she even tried to run away, but on that promontory, that cliff-top eyrie, there was nowhere else to run but straight back into Dezzie's arms. He later joked that he'd planned it that way, saying that if she'd refused he was going to throw her off the cliff.

They agreed to keep it quiet for the meantime, at least until after the show, when Dezzie has had a chance to speak to Mike and Bert. Neither of them is very sure what the position is with engaged couples working together at the centre. Dezzie said that if it turns out that one of them has to move to another centre, it should be him. He has the motorbike for transport; it's easier for him to go further afield.

'It's not just that,' Maria told him. 'I've been with Blue Group for three years, I don't think I could just up and leave them for another centre.'

Dezzie understood.

He was happy letting Maria set the date, the sooner the better he said, but he wasn't bothered. Whatever she wanted was fine by him. Maria favoured a spring wedding. They would try for permission to have the ceremony at Culzean on the cliff top. Failing that, they'd have it on the beach. No-one could stop them having it there. They were of a similar mind about celebrating it: nothing expensive or showy, just a few close friends, Blue Group obviously, and family. She was dying to tell the girls, especially Anna, and see their faces, their pity turning to envy when they met her gorgeous fiancé. In some ways she was more excited about telling the KSK than about any other aspect of her wedding.

They'd each put their flats up for sale and buy a house, a proper house with a garden, a safe place for kids to play in. They planned to get a dog, a lifelong dream of Maria's, and even came up with a name: Sadie. They thought of children's names too. They argued and laughed about it all the time, but

313

they couldn't decide on anything. Dezzie said not to worry, that they'll know when the babies come along what to call them. And before they left the cliff top they made love, seriously and without protection, in the gathering dusk. All the way home in the car Dezzie kept saying that she'd made the right decision, that she wouldn't regret it, that she'd made him the happiest man in the world.

She's had time to get used to the idea now. She's accepted that she has as much right as any girl to have her dreams come true.

The final week of rehearsal zoomed past in a haze of last-minute costume fittings and scenery painting. Apart from Magic Marshall's heightened security with his rabbits, the dress rehearsal went very well. As she spent virtually every waking hour in the church making preparations for the show, Maria saw very little of her fiancé. Dezzie – wisely, Maria thinks – stayed well out of the way and let her get on with things. He kept himself occupied watching football most evenings at Brian's house.

Bert reluctantly agreed that the centre would cover the cost of taxis for Blue Group to and from the church on the night of the show, so long as they shared. Maria and Dezzie discussed possible routes and arranged to pick everyone up in two taxis. Dezzie will first leave his bike at the church and then go by taxi to pick up Fiona, Martin and Jane. She will pick up Brian.

And now, at last, tonight's the night. Maria reluctantly removes her engagement ring and puts it on the gold chain she wears around her neck. She keeps the chain under her jumper, out of sight and close to her heart. Blue Group is so jumpy and nervous that she doesn't want to risk any further upsets, tonight's their night.

When Maria arrives at Brian's house it's his mum who brings him out to the taxi. Normally quite a friendly woman, Brian's mum draws Maria filthy glances as she roughly stuffs her son's chair into the taxi.

'He's got my heart roasted, so he has,' she says to Maria, and then sharply to Brian, 'I'll be telling your father the minute he comes in, don't think I won't. I'm warning you, boy!'

Maria doesn't know what she means and Brian smiles when she asks him.

'It's. A. Secret. You. Don't. Know,' says Brian.

It might be a secret but Maria knows, or at least thinks she does. It must be to do with the Hanson T-shirt trick the boys are going to play on Mike, but when she asks him he refuses to answer. She knows it's pointless to ask again. She won't get any sense out of him. Brian is in one of his warped teenage moods, and he's best left to himself when he's like this. No doubt he's nervous, but so is she.

The church hall looks like the Albert Hall. It's amazing, unrecognizable. It's clean and tidy, swept late last night by Aldo and Bob of wood shavings and silk threads. The school has been emptied of chairs. They've been transported here and laid out in tidy rows, packing as many in as the hall can take.

Pastor McKenzie has proved himself invaluable. Good things can apparently come from wild unfounded allegations. The pastor, always one to put a positive spin on things, thought that Maria's hastily assembled Truth and Justice meeting went so well that they should form a health and safety committee. This has admittedly gone some way towards building bridges between Alice and Maria. She has apologized to Alice repeatedly but it wasn't until Ray had a word that Alice relented and spoke to Maria.

With the approval of the committee and the help of the local fire-safety officer, the pastor has drawn up a fire-evacuation plan. The building has been designated a no-smoking area for the duration of the show, and even Ray and Alice have agreed to it. McKenzie has ordered his nominated fire exits to be well lit, clear of impediments and open throughout the show. Alice was miffed, saying that those who had been unable to get tickets might be able to sneak in, but the pastor, usually open to compromise, would brook no argument. Especially with so many wheelchair users in the building, safety must take priority over a few people sneaking in, he said.

The hall has a feeling of order and safety to it, and it looks lovely. The stage curtains have been washed and mended and now roll along the runners as smooth and quick as a dancer. The snooker table no longer squats in the middle of the floor. Ray has made a wooden cover as a lid for it, and it now serves as the coffee bar at the back of the hall. Margaret Wallace, one of the Kitchen Belles, had a fantastic idea for decorating the stage.

A poster went up in the café a week ago requesting the loan of pot plants, after which almost everyone coming in came with their arms filled with greenery and their name stuck on the side of their plant. People, mostly those who are not otherwise involved in the show, are desperate for their plant to be included, and those who had no plant to begin with went to the trouble of buying one. Everybody wants to be in show business. The lip of the stage is covered three deep in shiny green vegetation, which gives the place an air of class. But Maria has not seen the classiest yet.

The director, the stage manager and the compère for the evening are one and the same person, Marianne Bowman. Marianne has lost all traces of her pearl-strung glasses and tweed suit. Her make-up and jewellery are perfectly understated. Her dress, a pale blue full-length Grace Kelly number, highlights her girlish figure. She looks good enough to eat, which is confusing to the senses because unfortunately, as usual, she reeks of Giorgio perfume. People in the audience ten rows back will go home tainted with the smell. Apart from this one small foible, Marianne has so much style and grace that she could be a presenter for the Eurovision Song Contest.

Advance ticket sales have been tremendous. They could have sold every seat in the house three times over. Other than to check tickets and sell programmes, Pastor McKenzie and his Victory Singers have very little to do.

The various committee rooms have been pressed into service as makeshift dressing rooms and Marianne has thoughtfully allocated Blue Group exclusive use of the one nearest the stage. By way of a welcome Alice has hung a big gold cardboard star on the door. The others haven't arrived yet.

Apart from chaperoning Blue Group, Maria has been pressed into service as an understudy scene-shifter, and has been instructed by Marianne to dress in black. She's already wearing her black trousers and has brought a black polo jumper to change into. It is whilst she's yanking it over her head and trying to disentangle her hair that Brian catches sight of the ring on the chain.

'Who. Is. The. Lucky. Man,' he asks.

Maria smiles, giving nothing away.

'Are. You. In. Love.'

Again she smiles, this time as confirmation.

'Me. Too.'

Now they're both smiling.

'Who's the lucky woman?' Maria teases.

'Man,' Brian corrects.

'Oh,' says Maria, raising an eyebrow, 'you're a dark horse, aren't you?'

Really she's quite shocked that Brian has a love life at all, never mind the fact that he appears to be saying he's gay. But Maria is so delighted for him that she can't resist giving him a hug. Like her, he deserves to be happy and in love. Life is wonderful.

She's glad the others aren't here yet. She almost never sees Brian on his own these days. Without this time alone together, he might not have told her. With all the time she's had to spend on the show, her relationship with Brian has drifted without her noticing.

'Well, go on then, who is it?'

Brian repeats the words.

'It's. A. Secret. You. Don't. Know.'

Ah, thinks Maria, so that was the big secret. 'OK, you don't have to tell me if you don't . . .'

'Dezzie,' says the Dynavox.

Maria laughs.

'Dezzie?' Maria says, still laughing.

Brian is smiling.

'You're in love with Dezzie?'

Brian has such a beautiful smile.

'Oh Brian, sweetheart.'

She moves to hug him again, this time a slow tender hug. Poor Brian. He has a crush on Dezzie. It's understandable, but heartbreakingly sad. How awful it must be to want someone without any chance of there ever being a relationship. They mustn't let Brian find out about their engagement while he feels like this; it'll break his poor heart.

'You're only young, Brian. I'm sure there are a lot of nice guys out there. And one of them will be right for you.'

'Young. But. Not. Daft.'

'Sorry Brian, I didn't mean anything other than . . .'

'We. Are. In. Love.'

Maria doesn't know what to say. She hates to shatter his dreams, but for his own sake and for Dezzie's professional reputation, Brian must grasp the difference between reality and wishful thinking.

'No, Brian, that's not true. You might think now that you're in love with Dezzie, but you won't always think like that.'

'We. Are. In. Love. We. Make. Love. Ergo. Dezzie. Loves. Me.'

'Did Dezzie tell you that he loves you?'

Brian smiles.

'No he didn't, Brian.'

'Yes.'

'No he didn't, Brian!'

'Dezzie. Touched. Me. Made. Me. Come.'

Maria's legs collapse under her and she falls on the floor. When she looks up Brian is smiling, proud of the shocking effect his words have had on her.

Chapter 32

Maria rushes out of the dressing room and runs to the toilet. She throws up, retching until her belly is empty. She's left Brian alone, which is dangerous. If he's sick, and the chances are he will be, he could choke. She can't go back in there. She can't face him. She hates Brian but even as she hates him she knows this is not his fault.

He's nineteen, old enough to go to the pub, old enough to have sex with whomever he chooses. But not really. He's not like other nineteen-year-olds, he hasn't snogged at school discos, he hasn't had the normal shy fumblings, the tentative experiments. His physical disabilities are such that he can't even find out about his own body. No wonder he's fallen in love with the first person to have touched him. Maria feels sick again.

She shakes her head until she's dizzy, her damp hair clinging to the sides of the toilet bowl. But no matter how much she denies it, she knows it must be true. She even knows why it must be true.

Dezzie is too nice, that's his problem. She's seen it time and time again in the way he puts himself out to do everything he can for people. It's what she loves about him. He's not a bad person. He only wants to help; he's so desperate to give what he can to help others that he doesn't see the line. And not being able to see it, he has irrevocably crossed it. Really he's not a bad person, but a flawed one.

Eventually Maria finds the strength to move to the hand basin. As she splashes water she catches sight of her slack face in the mirror and nods an acknowledgement. Yes. She was right. A bona fide proposal was too good to be true because Dezzie, sweet stupid fucking Dezzie, is too good to be true. What is she to do?

She knows what she *should* do. She should report it without delay to her line manager. But then what would happen? Dezzie's feet wouldn't touch the ground, that's for certain. Brian's family might want to involve the police and Dezzie would end up with a criminal record as a sex offender. Tarred for ever as a dirty pervert.

Would any of this benefit Brian? Probably not. Considering how Brian's dad Phil responded to the threat from the flasher, he'd go absolutely mental. His parents would probably keep Brian on an even tighter leash and he'd never find love, and certainly not gay love, his father would not tolerate it. If Dezzie went he'd lose his football buddy, his pal to take him to the pub, his best mate. Dezzie has been so good for Brian. Up until now.

And what would Maria lose?

The door opens and three of the choirgirls burst in, giggling and shoving each other to get to the mirror. Maria has to get back to the dressing room. Her duty lies with Brian.

321

On the way she has to dodge Ray and Alice, who stand smoking at an open fire exit.

'That's your ten-minute call, everybody,' Marianne calls along the corridor, clipboard in hand.

Why did Brian have to tell her? He seemed to take an evil delight in doing so. Up until the moment he spewed that poison Maria was happy. She was excited about the biggest night and highest point of her career. She was engaged to be married to a wonderful man.

She can't face anyone now. There is no excitement left in her for the show. She has to decide what action she must take, but first she has to get through the rest of the evening. There's nothing she can do about it right now, anyway. And she owes it to the rest of them to get through tonight. The show must go on.

They're all there in the dressing room: Fiona, Martin, Jane, Brian – and Dezzie. She can't look at him. Her stomach turns when she thinks of him with Brian. He doesn't seem to notice; perhaps he thinks she's nervous about the show. Fiona has arrived wearing her costume, the velvet dress Maria bought her. Martin and Jane make huge efforts to reassure Fiona that she looks lovely, while Maria busies herself brushing Fiona's hair. This close to the stage they are able to hear the hubbub of the audience, and the hush that descends when Mr Spencer takes up his baton. Orchestre Octogéne open, not with their classical repertoire but with a medley of rousing Scottish classics: 'A Hundred Pipers an' Aw an' Aw' seguing into 'Scotland the Brave'.

There's a peremptory knock at the dressing-room door and Marianne enters.

'Ladies and gentlemen, I'm pleased to inform you that we have a full house tonight!'

Blue Group are delighted by this news. A frisson builds in the dressing room that cannot touch Maria.

Marianne sticks her head out into the corridor.

'Beginners please! Hexton Hot Steppers, that means you, come on girls. Quietly!'

She turns her attention back to Blue Group. Though she's dressed like a movie star, her manner is as brisk as ever. Like a general before a battle she moves among her troops, reassuring and motivating them.

'I just came in to tell you that they're a lovely audience, everybody out there is rooting for us.' She cocks an ear and a finger and says, 'Listen to that!'

Unused to the conventions of theatre, the audience are singing along with 'Flower of Scotland', complete with harmonies. They are raising the roof and this is only the overture. Everybody wants to be in show business. The whole of Hexton want to be involved in Maria's show. She should be savouring this immense achievement. Instead she feels sick.

'I'm so very proud of you all,' says Marianne, 'and I know you're going to do your best and make it a great show. Break a leg, everybody!'

Luckily Blue Group already know what, in theatrical terms, this expression actually means.

'Break your legs Miss Bowman!' they all call, including Dezzie, as she leaves.

Maria can't take this any longer. She has to speak to him.

'Jane, look after everything here for a minute please, will you? Everybody, run through your lines again with Jane please. And Jane, come and tell me if there is a problem, I'll just be outside. But only come out if there's a problem, OK?'

'OK.'

'Dezzie, can I have a word with you please?'

Once they are outside Dezzie tries to pull her into his arms and kiss her. Maria shrugs him off violently.

'I know.'

Dezzie's laughing.

'You know what, you horny little strumpet?'

'Dezzie, I know about what you did to Brian, he told me.'

'I didn't do anything.'

'Really?'

Thank God. Once again she's jumped in with both feet first, exactly as she did with Ray. Nothing happened. Brian has made the whole thing up. Thank God. Maria's life is still intact.

'Well, I didn't do anything he didn't want me to do.'

Oh no it isn't.

'And what did he want you to do? To touch him? Did you touch him, Dezzie?'

Although he doesn't answer, she can see by his face that he did. All hope of saving this situation is gone.

'Don't you know what you've done? Brian told me you made love to him. He says he's in love with you.'

Dezzie laughs.

'Don't be ridiculous. He couldn't do it himself and he asked me to help him out, that's all. I swear to you.'

'Ridiculous? You think this is ridiculous, do you? You think it's a joke, a bit of a laugh? You are a paid member of staff. You were trusted to look after a vulnerable young man and you exploited that trust, Dezzie, that's what you've done. That's how people will see it. You had no right to do what you did.'

'Hey, hey, now don't be like that. OK I was stupid, I

admit it. But I never meant any harm, Maria, you have to believe me. Brian asked me and I couldn't . . . I found it hard to say no.'

Maria nods. Everything that Dezzie is saying confirms the way she feels it must have happened. But it happened. It definitely happened.

'I swear it's the first time. It'll never happen again . . .'

'It's not the first time, Dezzie,' says Maria sadly. 'This is all my fault. I saw you cross the line a few times; I should have known when you took them to the pub, but I let it go. I let you carry on encouraging the boys' rebelliousness and disrespectful behaviour. This isn't the first time you've bent the rules. But don't you see, Dezzie? That's what the rules are for. To protect people. To protect Brian. And to protect you from your own well-meaning dangerous stupidity.'

'Maria, you're not going to report it, are you? I mean, it doesn't change things between us, does it? You still love me, don't you?'

With tears in her eyes Maria whispers, 'I really wish I didn't.'

The stagehands, Bob and Gerry, have come to collect Blue Group. Maria and Dezzie are forced to leave their discussion and go back into the dressing room. Blue Group are on next after the Hot Steppers, and are to be brought to wait quietly in the wings. After a few minutes' discussion it is agreed that it is probably better to leave Brian's chair here in the dressing room, safely out of the way of the excitable dancers. The girls are like a herd of young tap-shoed buffalo. There will be tears and broken shin bones if they rush offstage and straight into a wheelchair.

Once the others leave the dressing room, an uneasy

silence is palpable amongst what Maria thinks of bitterly as this sad fucked-up *ménage à trois*. Fiona only increases the tension by returning to the room to get her lucky key ring. She leaves and is back a few minutes later to give Maria a last-minute hug and tell her she loves her. This brings tears to Maria's eyes again.

'Look. Out. She's. Got. A.'

Brian punches his machine and waits, his finger hovering over the touch screen, staring hard at Dezzie all the while.

'Gun.'

'Look. Out. She's. Got. A.'

'Gun.'

'Look. Out. She's. Got. A.'

'Brian stop it,' snaps Maria.

If this is a coded message to Dezzie, it's too late.

Dezzie says nothing, but he will not return Brian's gaze. He stares at Maria. Maria cannot look at either of them. This would be funny if it weren't so tragic. The dancers have taken the stage and the noise from here is a low rumble like a volcano about to explode.

The door opens again and Maria assumes it's Fiona back with another insecurity. But it is not. Brian's dad and his brother burst through the door and make a lunge at Dezzie. Dezzie is fast on his feet but not fast enough.

'Scumbag!' Phil spits in Dezzie's face.

His twin brother Billy has grabbed Dezzie by the hair and pulled his head back. Phil throws fierce punches and kicks at Dezzie's unprotected face and body.

Maria and Brian have become invisible. Phil and Billy do not look at or speak to them. The brothers only have eyes for Dezzie. Phil is piledriving punch after punch into Dezzie's body. Even Billy seems shocked by such ferociousness and releases his hold on Dezzie.

To a thunderous soundtrack of fifty feet tapping out 'Lullaby of Broadway', while Phil gets his breath back Dezzie sees his chance, pulls himself to his feet and runs out along the corridor. Billy tries to restrain his brother.

'Leave it Phil!'

But his efforts are in vain. Phil wriggles free and sprints down the corridor in pursuit of Dezzie. Billy follows him, leaving Maria screaming and Brian being sick.

Without ever being aware of it, Maria makes a subtle and complicated judgement call. She knows consciously and otherwise that she must not leave Brian; that to run out on him while he's being sick is dangerous and negligent. But a co-worker's life is under threat. A co-worker, her fiancé, the man she is in love with. Yes, it's unprofessional, a disciplinary committee might infer. It's punishable, but understandable and ultimately forgivable.

Chapter 33

So, in a split-second decision, Maria runs out and leaves Brian. She bolts along the corridor and straight into Ray. She hasn't the breath to explain, but thank God he seems to understand what's happened, he must have seen them. He runs towards the back staircase to the bell tower.

'Up here!'

Ray takes the rickety wooden stairs two at a time and she tries to keep up with him. Maria hears other chests heave and feet clump on the stairs above: Dezzie, running for his life, Phil, wanting to take Dezzie's life, Billy, trying to control his brother. She hears Ray's and her own heavy breathing and feet clumping, trying to prevent Dezzie's murder. Or witness it.

When they reach the top Dezzie is already at the very edge of the unprotected part of the platform. He has nowhere else to go. His options are limited: be beaten to death or fall among the mossy gravestones below. His eyes are wide with terror. Billy stands between Dezzie and Phil, trying to hold off Phil.

Phil is struggling fiercely against his brother. The

twins are of similar height and build, and, apparently, similar strength. It is a contest of motivation. Does Phil want to kill Dezzie more than Billy wants to stop him?

'What's going on?' asks Ray. He says this neither aggressively nor passively, he just asks the question.

'Fuck off, none of your business mate,' says Phil, still wrestling with his brother.

'Aye, it's my business. It's my church.'

Phil stops wrestling Billy and turns menacingly towards Ray.

'I'm telling you pal. I'll . . .'

Astoundingly, rather than try to calm things down, Ray aggravates the situation by launching a punch at Phil's face. He then retreats back to the doorway onto the stairs.

'Come ahead then!' says Ray, gesticulating.

He's wearing an expression of utmost contempt, and this momentarily lures Phil towards him. Billy does nothing to restrain him. Phil moves towards the doorway and Ray makes a lunge and throws his arms around him, locking Phil's arms by his side. Phil is now disabled and Ray tries to lever him out to the stairs.

'C'mon mate, let's take this downstairs,' says Ray, 'we don't need to end up flying off the roof.'

'Did it give you a thrill, putting your hands in my boy's pants?'

Dezzie, who until now has silently cowered, seems to feel that the immediate threat has been contained and attempts to defend himself against the accusations.

'I didn't want to do it, honest to God! Brian begged me to!'

This has the effect of freshly enraging Phil.

'I'm going to fucking kill you!' he screams. His face is purple with straining.

'But he pleaded with me, he put me on the spot. I didn't want to do it, I'm straight, there's my girlfriend.'

'It's true, Mr McEndrick. I am his girlfriend. Dezzie's straight, honestly, he's completely straight.'

'And my boy's a fucking cripple! He's a wee boy in a wheelchair that can't do anything to stop you!'

But Dezzie continues to argue.

'He's not a cripple; he's a person. He makes his own choices. You can't expect him just to sit in his chair and never experience life. Believe me, I would never do anything to hurt Brian. I care about him.'

In a heavy exhaled sigh the fight leaves Phil's body as he slumps forward, still entwined in Ray's arms. Ray loosens his grip but keeps hold of him. Their bodies remain close. The two men, against the starry night sky, could be mistaken for lovers. It strikes Maria that the only time most men willingly make physical contact is when they're trying to hurt each other.

Dezzie has moved from the edge and stands, by necessity, close to Phil, close to everyone, on the crowded platform. But although Phil has appeared to give in, it has only been a ruse.

He breaks free of Ray and charges at Dezzie, bringing them both dangerously close to the edge. With the force of the onslaught Dezzie loses his footing and is lying sprawled on the wooden platform, where Phil kicks him hard in the groin. Dezzie puts up no resistance.

Billy and Ray obviously consider it too dangerous to try to restrain Phil now. He's too close to the edge. He might take them with him. Dezzie covers his face with his hands and curls protectively into a tight ball.

The orchestra are playing down in the church, something Mozart, 'Haffner' it says in the programme, while Phil kicks and kicks at Dezzie's head and hands. Dezzie doesn't even cry out.

'Stop it Phil, you're going to kill him!' shouts Billy.

But it is unlikely that Phil even hears him.

'You're supposed to care,' Phil screeches hysterically at the pile lying on the floor. 'That's what you get fucking paid for! That's how you earn your money, pretending to care about the cripples.'

Phil punctuates nearly every syllable with another vicious kick.

'Phil, get a grip mate,' says Ray calmly.

'Just fuck off, all of you!' Phil screams.

'No can do. You see, we're witnesses. And what are you going to do? Give us a kicking as well? Shove us off the edge?'

'He's right Phil, leave it, c'mon.'

'Triple murder?' Ray continues. 'I don't think so. I don't think you're really like that, Phil. Understandably you've got a bit carried away, haven't you? But you've not really thought this through.'

Phil has stopped kicking but apparently only to get his breath back. However, the bait Ray has set has caught him and he engages with the argument.

'He's a fucking . . . He's made my boy a poof.'

'Och, away you go!' says Ray somewhat cavalierly. 'Get your boy a woman, a working girl with a nice arse and a good heart. That'll maybe sort him out, and if it doesn't, well, your boy's going to be whatever he's going to be. Kicking the shit out of this guy isn't going to change anything.'

'Please, Phil,' pleads Billy.

Billy is crying, hard loud sobs.

This works. Phil moves towards his brother to comfort him. Now that Phil has moved closer Ray puts himself protectively between Phil and Dezzie, but it seems it's all over. Phil and Billy are now in a tight hug, both of them streaming with tears.

'Go on now,' says Ray decisively. 'Down the stairs, out the back door and away, eh?'

'This isn't finished,' says Phil. 'D'you hear me?' he says to Dezzie. 'I know where you live and I'll be back for you. This isn't finished.'

But Phil allows himself to be led, his arms around his brother, down the stairs.

Even though the two brothers have left, Ray still won't let Maria go to Dezzie. He moves forward cautiously and hauls Dezzie by his shirt away from the edge. He pulls at him gingerly, as though scared of actually touching him. Now Maria can go to him. She helps him sit up. He has cuts over his eyes and his face is already starting to swell.

'Are you OK?' asks Ray, staring hard into Dezzie's eyes.

Too shocked to speak, Dezzie nods.

'How many fingers am I holding up?'

Dezzie tries to speak but his voice is thick with phlegm.

'Three,' he says, 'three fingers.'

'I don't think you're concussed but you'd better get it checked out, somewhere as far away from Hexton as possible.'

'Ray, look at him! He's in no fit state to go any-where.'

'Listen, Maria,' says Ray, the gentle tone now gone from his voice, 'you heard Arnie Schwarzenegger there, this isn't finished. He'll take his weepy brother home and come back to finish him off. That guy's not going to let this go.'

Ray helps Dezzie to his feet.

'You're finished here, Dezzie. For your own sake, you have to get out of Hexton. And not come back.'

As Maria helps him down the wooden staircase, she is astounded by how quickly Dezzie appears to recover. He has been chased, severely beaten and almost thrown off a rooftop, and yet he's as high as a kite. It must be adrenaline.

'Maria,' he says, holding her arms so tight it hurts, 'I know this seems like a disaster but we can get over this.'

Maria almost laughs. Talk about understatement.

'Ray's right,' says Dezzie.

He talks fast, excited, spraying little droplets of blood when he speaks. His eyes are shining and he's smiling.

'It's probably best to get out of Hexton. I'll have to resign now anyway. We can go somewhere else, make a fresh start. Leave right now. Jump on the bike and head off into the sunset. Wssssh, gone. We can go to London, London's better for us, more opportunities.'

'We?'

'We're still getting married. We're not going to let this change anything. We can start again. Please, don't leave me, Maria, please! I can't do it without you.'

In an abrupt change of mood Dezzie is weeping. His breath is coming out in forceful bursts. At this moment Maria only feels a crude pity for him. She wonders if, having felt like this, she can ever feel any differently, if she can ever go back to her simple love and respect for him.

'Look, OK, I know you've got the show. I know you can't walk out on it, I understand that, but please darling, don't do this to me. It's going to be OK, we can make it work.'

Once they reach the bottom of the stairs Dezzie grabs Maria again and pulls her into a tight hug. He still feels nice, still smells nice, these things haven't changed. He's still the same person.

'I'll phone you after the show. I'll come and pick you up. Maria, I've learned my lesson, I promise you I'll never do anything like this ever again. I promise you.'

Dezzie's eyes rove across her face repeatedly. At first she cannot look at him, she can't give him the eye contact he seems so desperately to want.

'You stood by me and I'll never forget that. Maria, you saved my life. I owe you. And I'll make this up to you; I'm going to spend the rest of my life making it up to you, you're going to have the best husband! It's OK, we can get away and we can have everything we've talked about, our house, our kids, the dog, camping holidays. You still want that, don't you? Don't you?'

And then Maria looks into his face. She meets his eye. It's Dezzie who breaks the contact.

'You want it as much as I do, Maria, you know you do. Look, don't worry about this, we're young; we can put it behind us, no bother. And one thing's for sure, I'll never let you down again, I swear.'

Maria frees herself from his grip and opens the door a crack to check that Phil is not lying in wait. The brothers are nowhere to be seen. As she closes the door Dezzie is wrapping himself around her again, searching her face again. For what?

'I have to get back, I left Brian.'

'And Sadie, remember? Our lovely dog? Maria please, we can't throw away our lives because of this. OK something bad happened, it's my fault and I was really, really, fucking unbelievably stupid but we can't let that ruin the rest of our lives, think about it.'

'Dezzie, you need to get out of here, it's not safe and I have to get back to Brian.'

'I'll phone you after the show then, Maria, and you'll come?'

'I don't know, Dezzie.'

'Please Maria, look, I'm sorry about this, I'm so sorry.'

'I know you are, Dezzie.'

'And I really mean it, that's a one-off, never again, I absolutely promise you.'

'OK.'

'I love you.'

'I need to go.'

'Maria, wait, listen to me.'

'What is it?'

'I love you.'

Maria makes no reply.

'I'll phone when the show's finished. I'll be waiting for you and I'll come and get you. Everything's going to be OK.'

Chapter 34

Back in the dressing room, Maria is relieved to discover that Brian has not died chewing his own vomit.

Ronald, who has been allocated the dressing room next door, heard the commotion and came in. He has wiped the sick from Brian's shirt with a wet cloth and washed his face and hands. He has to go now and finish getting dressed, he explains to Maria, and she nods.

'The stagehands came to get him but he wasn't well,' says Ronald in a whisper.

Brian is slumped lower in his chair than usual. His arms, for once, seem relaxed, defeated. He has given up trying to control them. Ronald has combed Brian's hair flat into an unfamiliar schoolboy side parting, and now his face seems old and tired. He reminds Maria of an unwatered seedling, a shrivelled child.

'Brian, it's OK,' she tells him once Ronald has left, 'nothing happened. Your dad didn't hurt Dezzie. Ray talked him out of it. Honestly, Dezzie is fine.'

'Where. Is. He.'

'He's gone. He had to, he had no choice. Your dad was making threats.'

'Where.'

'I don't know Brian, honestly I don't.'

'So. I. Have. Lost. Him,' says Brian's machine as fresh tears stain his clean face.

'So have I,' says Maria and joins him crying.

She knows it's indiscreet to tell Brian this. She's not even sure if it's true.

'You. Can. Get. A. Lover. Or. A. Job. Or. A. Fucking. Sandwich. Anytime. You. Want.'

This only makes Maria cry harder. She's no longer crying only for herself.

'I. Have. A. Power. In. Me. Stronger. Than. Fear. And. Rage. More. Terrible. Than. Palsy.'

Maria doesn't get it. Is Brian trying to make a joke?

'It. Will. Propel. Me. From. This. Chair.'

Maria stops mid-sniffle and tries to understand what he means.

'And. I. Will. Kill. Him.'

'Brian, I know you're angry but . . .'

'Death. Is. My. Only. Weapon.'

Brian has stopped crying, concentrating hard on getting the words out of his Dynavox. The automated voice does not lessen the melodrama of the curse, it only makes it more sinister.

'Stop it, come on now. Just listen to yourself.'

'My. Father's. Death. Or. Mine.'

Maria will not tolerate this kind of talk. She has to come down hard.

'Oh for God's sake get a grip, will you? You've been watching too much children's TV. You sound like Masters of the Universe or something. It's not helping.'

The idea of Brian's tiny frame bounding from his chair and murdering his dad is ridiculous, and so pathetic it makes Maria want to cry again. But his own death . . . She knows he can do that, she's seen it before. Some clients, enraged at their impotence, employ the only power they have: the power to die. They don't do anything, they just give up, and eventually they fade away. Maria has never seen Brian so floppy.

'Brian, don't talk like that, you're going to university next year. You're going to get your own flat. You're going to have friends and lovers and a career just like plenty of other disabled people. That's the power you have, not some superhero vengeance mission, that's really negative and stupid.'

'Get. Rich. Yes.'

'See? Being rich would be the sweetest way you could ever get back at your dad. He'll never be rich.'

'And. Take. Out. A. Contract. On. Him.'

'Oh grow up. A minute ago you were a Master of the Universe, now you're a gangster.'

'It. Will. Propel. Me. From. This. Chair. It. Will. Propel. Me. From. This. Chair. It. Will. Propel. Me.'

'Yeah, OK. I think I've got the message.'

Maria knows she's being harsh but she's exhausted, and Brian's fury is more than she can cope with.

There is a polite knock on the door. Maria still has to sort this out with Brian, but for the moment she's glad of a distraction.

'Come in.'

It's Marianne.

'Maria, where have you been? We could have done with you for the scenery changes.'

'Long story, tell you later.'

'What's going on with your lot? They were supposed to be on after the Hot Steppers. I had to put the Golden Belles on, two dance groups back to back, but they were the only ones ready.'

'I'm really sorry, Marianne, Brian wasn't feeling well.'

'OK, is he well enough now? Are you well enough now, Brian? We're only left with singer after singer; all my careful programming has been shot to hell.'

'Not. Going. On.'

'You're not going on?'

'Yes he is.'

'Stage fright, is it? Don't worry, Brian; you're not the only one. Magic Marshall was refusing to come out of his dressing room. You've missed all the excitement, Maria. Apparently during the interval somebody punched your boss.'

'My boss, you mean Mike?'

'Yes, the bloke in the T-shirt. Is he gay?'

Maria looks to Brian, but even this won't make him smile.

'Oh, it's been fun and games,' says Marianne. 'Listen, I'd better press on. I'll send the rest of them back here. There's no point in them hanging about backstage if you're not going to go on, Brian, they're only taking up space.'

'No, Marianne, he'll go on. Give me a minute with him.'

'OK.'

And she is gone.

'You have to do it,' says Maria quietly.

Brian shakes his head.

'Stop being so bloody selfish! What about Martin and Jane, don't you care about them? They've worked solidly for a month on this. For Christ's sake, Brian, you'll propel yourself from your chair for revenge but you won't fulfil your duty to your friends.'

'The. Power. Of. Christ. Propels. Me.'

'Yeah, funny. You're good with words. No good with promises though, are you?'

'I. Am. Not. Going. On.'

'Who is it you're taking revenge on? Blue Group? What for? Or is it yourself? D'you want to sit here and wallow in self-loathing? You're the guy who wants to be a normal adult, to experience all of life, well, the big news is: you've arrived, this is it. It's full of pain and disappointment. And opportunity and duty. Get busy living or get busy dying, it's your call, Brian.'

Moments later the rest of Blue Group file back into the dressing room. In their disappointment they don't even notice Dezzie's absence. They are dejected but at the same time concerned for Brian.

'Are you OK?' asks Nurse Jane, stroking his hair.

Martin pats Brian's shoulder and says nothing, no recriminations, although he must be gutted.

'Are you scared?' asks Fiona without malice.

Brian pulls his head back and drops it in a slow nod.

'So am I,' says Fiona. 'I'm not doing it.'

'Oh c'mon Fiona,' says Maria, 'don't you start! Martin and Jane don't have an act without Brian, but there's no reason for you not to go on.'

'You. Are. Going. To. Sing.'

'No I'm not. I'm not going to be the only one!'

This causes a storm of protest.

'But you have to!'

'You. Can. Do. It.'

'You're the best out of all of us.'

'I'm not doing it by myself.'

'You. Don't. Need. Us.'

'You can't make me!' shouts Fiona, becoming upset.

'It's OK, Fiona,' says Maria gently and tells the rest of them, 'Fiona doesn't have to do it if she doesn't want to.'

'See?' says Fiona, 'so I'm not. They'll laugh at me. They'll call me a daftie.'

'OK, Fiona.'

Maria looks at Brian and he's furiously jabbing at his touch screen.

'OK. If. You. Want. To. Define. Yourself. By. Their. Terms.'

'You're a fine one to talk,' says Maria, doing nothing to disguise the bitterness of her tone.

'Can. You. Lot. Not. Do. Anything. For. Yourselves.'

Brian has asked a question but nobody answers, they all look to Maria.

'Why. Do. I. Always. Have. To. Take. Responsibility. For. You.'

Maria can feel her and everyone else's hackles rise, but she holds up her hand to stay their protests.

'Fiona. Is. Going. On.'

'I'm not . . .' begins Fiona, but Maria stops her.

'All. The. Dafties. Are. Going. On.'

Again they all look to Maria for confirmation and she smiles.

'Bring. On. The. Dafties.'

'Jane,' says Maria quickly before Brian has a chance to change his mind, 'you run through the lines again, I'll go and tell Marianne.'

'Right,' says Marianne, consulting her clipboard. 'I've managed to juggle things around a bit and, so long as you don't mind going on after Ronald – admittedly a pretty hard act to follow – we'll still have time for your sketch and then your song, Fiona. In fact, you'll be the last act on before the grand finale. Top of the bill!'

Bob and Gerry come back once again to take Blue Group, all of them this time, to wait in the wings.

Fiona insists on more hugging all round before they leave Maria alone in the dressing room. She would like to go backstage with them, but she's promised to go out front to 'laugh it up'. They're nervous that the audience will be too confused to laugh at dafties acting daft.

As she has a few minutes alone she sits down and closes her eyes, takes three deep breaths and quickly pops herself down to the shimmering river.

They're all there to meet her, arms reaching, smiling sweetly – except the little yellow bird, who has no arms but extends his tiny wings. Nelson and Madonna embrace her; she relaxes and soaks up their love.

'You weren't to know,' says Madonna softly.

'It is never wrong to love and trust,' Nelson concurs.

'I can't be without him, it'll kill me.'

They both smile.

'It won't.'

'I don't know if I can forgive him.'

'You can.'

'I don't know what I should do. It's hard to decide.'

Nelson and Madonna are still smiling.

'Yes,' they say, 'it's hard.'

A few moments later Maria emerges from the meditation. She's in the most positive frame of mind she can be, ready for whatever awaits her.

She stands at the side of the stage where she'll get a good view. It will be a few minutes until Blue Group are on. Ronald is just finishing his last number, 'Express Yourself', and, as predicted, it's going down very well with the crowd. They're hooting and clapping and it's not clear if the Hextors know or care whether Ronald is a woman or a man.

As the wolf whistles fade and the lights come back

342

up, against the painted backdrop of a shop there are now two men, one of whom is in a wheelchair. The shop is an off-licence. The shelves are stacked from floor to ceiling with one product and one product only, the cheap but potent tonic wine Buckfast. Outsize neon-bright orange and green cards, cut into clumsy star shapes, display information:

We have in stock an excellent selection of fine wines.

Buy One Get One Free – offer applies only to employed persons.

Please do not ask for credit as a punch in the mouth often offends.

For your throat's sake drink Buckfast!

Warning: Shoplifters will be severely pummelled.

Milk tokens accepted here.

Please note this register holds minimum cash as everyone in Hexton is rooked.

Please respect our neighbours and smash your Buckie bottles in another street.

Wife giving you a hard time? Drink Buckie!

Titters break out here and there as the audience read the notices. They are pointing them out to each other and laughing. Maria breathes a sigh of relief. At least they get these jokes, and this sets them up to expect comedy. Backstage, Bob and Gerry will be pleased; they designed and painted the set with Ray.

Martin in his brown overall carries a Moët & Chandon box and heaves it onto the counter. He rips it open and produces a bottle: of Buckfast. He looks at the bottle and rechecks the box, then brings out another bottle: Buckfast again. He shrugs acceptance

343

and the audience cheer. Thank God. They're off to a flying start.

'How. Long. Is. It,' says Brian's machine.

Maria laughs loudly, a lone voice in the packed hall. It's not the audience's fault. They're not used to hearing a talking machine. There is an uncomfortable silence until Martin speaks.

'How long is what?' he says, with his hands protectively across his crotch.

Maria laughs again. The audience laugh. Not spontaneously, but politely, in recognition that a joke has been made. Encouraged by this, Martin now proceeds to look down the inside of his trousers. This gets a slightly stronger laugh. Then he looks at the audience. His expression is not a happy one; he has obviously not liked what he's seen down there. They laugh again. Martin follows this up with some more traditional stage business, grimaces and jerky movements, and they laugh more. Maria can hear relief in the laughter now, the audience have tuned in to the willy jokes.

As the sketch progresses, they catch on quicker each time Brian sets one up. As Brian and Martin's confidence increases, the timing gets sharper and the pauses get longer. By the time Jane delivers her rabidly hysterical *Pulp Fiction* line, the actors are forced to stop for a few moments until the applause dies down. Maria is laughing, not because she's supposed to but because they're so funny. Blue Group can't hear her anyway, she's being drowned out by two hundred other people laughing. They leave the stage triumphant.

And now it is Fiona's turn.

There are a few pregnant moments while she stands alone, waiting for the orchestra to find her sheet music. She looks so vulnerable and brave. She's beautiful. Her green velvet dress is catching and reflecting the stage lights and her rich dark hair falls around her face in soft curls.

'*You promised me, and you said a lie to me,*' she sings, pitch perfect. She sings 'Donal Og', the old Irish ballad she has rehearsed so thoroughly, as though it were a prayer. Fiona is a diva; lost in her song she's oblivious to the audience and the thirty-piece orchestra that swells and swoons as it follows her voice.

'*I gave a whistle and three hundred cries to you,*
and I found nothing there . . .'

Maria has heard her sing this at least three times a day, every day, for the last month. She knows the words better than Fiona does, but until now she didn't feel the loneliness and grief and longing.

'*You promised me a thing that was hard for you . . .*'

With each verse she feels it stronger.

'*You promised me a thing that is not possible . . .*'

She expected so much of him. Dezzie was her religion. She should have known it couldn't be true.

'*You have taken the east from me; you have*
taken the west from me;
you have taken what is before me and what
is behind me;
you have taken the moon, you have taken the
sun from me;

345

and my fear is great that you have taken God from me!'

Fiona finishes her song and receives the applause with a modesty and dignity that Maria didn't know she possessed. She is also generous: in her moment of triumph she claps and stretches her hand out to indicate the orchestra, sharing the glory with them.

The audience are clapping and whistling. Fiona is smiling graciously, majestic and effulgent. Her talent shines from her, every inch the star, a hundred times more gifted and graceful than the synthetic celebs she worships in the magazines. The night is a runaway success. Blue Group have been the icing on the cake; they have topped the bill and stolen the show.

But it's drawing to a close. Suddenly it's the finale. The orchestra begins playing 'Nessun Dorma'. The choirgirls file onstage from each side, followed by the primary school kids. They stand on benches or stand or sit or kneel, raked rows of young heads like a tidy field of cabbages, only just visible to the parents who squint to pick them out.

The Hot Steppers can be heard before they're seen, beating the floor with their metal-clad feet as though it owed them money. Blue Group come on, Jane pushing Brian's chair, Martin holding Brian's arm out victoriously, Fiona elegant and modest. Two lines of Golden Belles in their Moulin Rouge costumes high-kick their way onstage from opposite sides in a pincer movement. They earn a laugh from the audience because dangling at each end of the silk and feathers line is an under-rehearsed man. Ray and Aldo cling on, kicking when they should be knee-bending and hopping ignominiously. This only highlights the smooth professionalism of the Belles. Ronald leads on the solo artistes who, except for Magic Marshall, try to outdo each other in the applause they receive.

The audience are on their feet and clapping feverishly. Mums and dads gush proud tears. Light pulses in the darkness as cameras and phones flicker and flash.

Martin, unable to restrain himself, begins to sing along with 'Nessun Dorma'. He doesn't know the words but at this stage his exuberance far outweighs his professionalism.

'Nah nah nah nah nah nah nah nah.'

The jubilant audience need no encouragement to join in. They don't know the words either, but ever since this song became a football anthem everyone is acquainted with the tune. In the absence of a libretto, well-punctuated *nah nah nah*s suffice very nicely. The orchestra must play louder to match the passion of the congregation as the church sings with one voice. Everybody's here, except of course Dezzie.

When 'Nessun Dorma' ends Marianne walks to the front of the crowded stage and gives a formal vote of thanks. Still struggling with her dilemma, Maria isn't paying attention. Suddenly Pastor McKenzie is at her side.

'Come on, Maria,' he says, 'everyone's waiting for you.'

Dazed, Maria lets herself be led onto the stage. Here she receives from Blue Group an enormous bouquet accompanied by hugs and wet kisses.

'As I've said,' says Marianne, 'without the stubborn efforts of Miss Maria Whyte there would have been no show.'

From here onstage the applause sounds different, a

frightening crashing noise, a noise that demands everything of Maria, but what else has she to give?

'Tonight you've heard how, under the auspices of the show, a café and youth club have been established. Well, I am very pleased to tell you that, thanks to the incredible generosity of Mr Ray Emmanuel, Mrs Alice O'Connor, the ladies of Autumn House and other members of the community, the café and youth club will continue to run. Of course, all are welcome, "come one come all" as it says outside, but we are particularly keen for volunteers – male and female – to get involved in the new five-a-side football group.'

Maria's breathing has just about returned to normal. Thank God Marianne didn't expect her to make a speech.

'Of course, given the tremendous success of tonight's show, we are hoping that Maria will consider running it as an annual event. Maria,' says Marianne, putting her on the spot, 'what do you think? Will you produce an annual community show for Hexton?'

Under this kind of interrogation Maria can only nod blindly. She's not lying, of course she'll consider it, but she has one or two more pressing matters to consider at the moment.

'Ladies and gentlemen, please join me in ratifying our support for an annual event.'

The audience are happy to ratify. Ratify all you like, Maria thinks, all the while nodding and smiling, I'm not making any promises, I don't know where I'll be a year from now.

'Ladies and gentlemen, please feel free to stay behind and join us for refreshments served by the ladies from Autumn House. I hope you enjoyed our show as much as we enjoyed performing for you, and it only remains for me to say thank you very much for your support, safe home and we hope to see you here again next year.'

The orchestra, for the final time, plays a brief reprise while the curtains close. Marianne is shouting instructions for people to leave the stage in an orderly fashion. Blue Group are given priority and everyone stands aside to let them pass. The Hot Steppers are impatiently pawing the floor. Everyone is pushing forward, keen to get front of house and receive their own bouquets and plaudits. All of Blue Group quickly make their excuses and go out front to mingle.

'Can Brian come with me?' asks Martin.

Maria nods, too tired to argue. It's not until they've gone that she realizes she hasn't had a chance to tell them how great they were.

The Golden Belles are exiting and Alice is barking out instructions.

'Right girls, show's over, get your tutus off and your aprons on, there's customers waiting to be served!'

Maria is still holding her bouquet. Like a bride jilted at the altar she stands alone on the empty stage, expectant and yet hopeless. She goes back to the dressing room and dumps the flowers in six inches of water in the sink. Outside there is an excited hubbub of performers in the hall, congratulating each other as they pass. Perhaps another quick meditation, but Nelson and Madonna have deserted her. Bastards.

Now when it's important, when she *really* needs them, they've melted away. They'll be back tomorrow, no doubt. Whether she's in a cheap B. & B. with Dezzie en route to London or alone weeping in her flat, they'll be back to tell her she's made the right decision.

Maria knows, she's always known, that Nelson and

349

Madonna aren't reliable. The only person she can completely rely on is herself. Not that she's ungrateful. In the same way that praying to Jesus helps the pastor and his flock, Nelson and Madonna have helped her. But she knows, she's always known, that in every challenge she faced pulling the show together, it was she alone had to see it through. And now, when she has this important life-changing decision confronting her, she, alone, has to make it.

No point in sitting here doing nothing, might as well get changed and get organized. As she pulls her jumper over her head she remembers her engagement ring dangling around her neck. She takes it off and looks at it. It's so beautiful. Dezzie paid an awful lot of money for this ring, much more than he can afford. What the hell is she going to do? Crying might not be a practical solution, but at the moment it's all she can do.

The dressing-room door flies open.

'Oh sorry, I didn't know you were still here, Maria.'

It's Alice. Maria tries to hide the ring and the fact that she's crying, but as she's facing the mirror Alice has a pretty good view.

'Are you OK, love?'

'Yes, yes, I'm fine. Just a bit of post-show anticlimax, I think.'

This is a stupid thing to say, because Alice obviously doesn't have a clue what she's talking about and now she'll have to explain herself further. But Alice doesn't seem to be listening.

'To be honest,' she says in a conspiratorial whisper, 'I'm in here for a quick smoke, d'you mind?'

'No, no, go ahead.'

'Cheers love,' says Alice as she takes her cigarette

350

purse from her apron. 'Bliddy Ray, he's become a born-again non-smoker. Nobody's allowed a fag now that he's given up.'

'Has Ray stopped?'

'Aye, pain in the arse. He says we've to set a good example. There's no smoking in the building any more, that's it finished. Bliddy pain in the arse.'

Alice takes a deep draw of her cigarette and blows out a long stream of smoke.

'Post-show anticlimax, eh? Never mind love, when you've been in showbiz as long as I have you get used to it.'

The door opens again. This time it's Ray.

'I bloody knew it! I could smell the smoke. I knew you'd be hiding somewhere having a fly one!'

'Oh, dry your eyes, I've smoked it now anyway.'

'Aye well, it'll be your last. This is a non-smoking building as you very well know, Alice O'Connor. And anyway, they're all queuing up out there for coffee.'

'I'm going, I'm going! See what I mean?' Alice says to Maria. 'After the feathers and sequins you always have to go back to old clothes and porridge, life's like that. But we get through it, don't we? Nothing else for it.'

Alice smiles, tucks her fags back in her apron and is gone.

'Old clothes and porridge, eh?' says Ray. 'She's full of it, isn't she?'

'Mmmm.'

'But I suppose she's right. That's it all over. It's going to be helluva quiet around here.'

'Mmmm,' says Maria again, it's all she can trust herself to say.

'Are you OK, Maria?'

'Yeah, fine.'

She had hoped that she might get the dressing room to herself to do a bit of thinking.

'Sorry, you need some time on your own, don't you?'

Maria purses her lips and nods, managing not to look at him.

'Yeah.'

'Sorry.'

Ray begins to leave and then turns back.

'I know you've got things to think about, and I don't know what to say to help, I'm not very good at this kind of thing, but, it's just . . . Well, I think you're great. And if you need someone to talk to, I'm here, OK?'

'OK Ray, thanks,' she says quietly as he leaves.

She takes a big breath in and holds it, steeling herself against what she has to do now. Old clothes and porridge. She can do that.

Dezzie's right. About one thing at least. This isn't the end of the world. The show's been a steep learning curve, but the most important thing she's learned is that her life is bursting at the seams with love and commitment. She believed she was missing out. All these years she's been making it hard for herself, when really it's quite straightforward. But all is not lost. Dezzie's right, she's young, there's plenty of time for what she wants.

With one last look at the engagement ring she puts it down on the shelf in front of her. She does it slowly, watching herself in the mirror, a witness. She has a final check round the dressing room to make sure she hasn't forgotten anything, but there's no hurry. The show's over. Now all she has to do is get Blue Group organized and see them safely home.

THE END